Life on the Edge

by
Jennifer Comeaux

To my sister Melissa and my friends Sylvianne and Debbie,
for being my most faithful readers
and reading every single draft of this story.
You gave me an audience and the inspiration to continue writing.

To my parents
for always supporting me and giving me the opportunity to succeed.

To my critique partners
who gave me invaluable advice on improving my writing.

A special thank you to Clare
for challenging me and helping me work through all my ideas.

And to my friend Kate
for your encouragement and your belief in this story.

CHAPTER ONE

June, 2000

BAM!

MY ELBOW WHACKED CHRIS'S FOREHEAD FOR the fourth time during practice. He grunted and caught me before I hit the ice. Though I'd skated over half of my nineteen years, I'd never had so many collisions. Of course, until a year ago, I'd never skated with a partner.

I cringed and touched Chris's sweaty brow. "I'm so sorry."

"It's okay." He raked his hand through his thick dark hair. "A little head trauma never hurt anyone."

I laughed wearily and arched my neck, stretching the sore muscles. The cold air wasn't helping loosen them. Looking up, my eyes honed in on the red, white, and blue banner above the rink:

Emily Butler and Christopher Grayden—2000 National Silver Medalists

Only four months had passed since Chris and I placed second at our first national championship, but it seemed like a lifetime. The triple twist, the high-flying element we needed to learn before next season, continued to elude me. *If we don't master this move, we'll never compete with the top teams in the world.*

I grasped Chris's hand. "Let's try it again."

We took matching determined strokes across the ice, and the burst of wind cooled my face and loosened damp tendrils from my long ponytail. With a quick motion, Chris squeezed my hips and launched me into the air. I wound myself tight and spun but fell into Chris's waiting arms before finishing three revolutions. A sigh heaved my shoulders.

Sergei glided toward us around the other practicing skaters. Our coach was often mistaken for one of us because of his youth. He nodded and regarded us with his deep blue eyes. "The rotation is getting faster. Focus on what you did right today. I see a lot of improvement."

I relaxed into a smile. Before I'd started working with Sergei, I'd heard many horror stories about Russian coaches. Sergei demanded discipline and maximum effort, but his energy stayed positive, and he provided constant encouragement.

Chris and I left the ice and sat on the short set of wooden bleachers. My ankles thanked me as I untied my skate laces and gave them space to breathe.

"I guess it's an improvement I didn't give you another black eye," I said.

Chris poked his swollen freckled cheek. "I kinda like my shiner. Makes me look tough." He grinned, displaying his dimples.

"You're going to need more than that to make you look tough," I teased as I walked away.

Inside the locker room, the musty scent of sweat and metal contrasted with the cool freshness of the ice. After stowing my skates in my locker and slipping on a pair of sneakers, I pulled a fitted T-shirt over my leotard and winced as I bumped the fresh bruises on my arms. If people only knew how much pain went into chasing the Olympic dream.

I needed to talk to Sergei before his next lesson, and I found him in the rink's upstairs lounge, which overlooked the ice. He was holding a cup of coffee and talking to a couple of the skating moms. As usual, they sat captivated, totally engrossed in his words, and I couldn't blame them. When I'd met Sergei, I stammered through our introduction, spellbound by his captivating eyes and gleaming smile. His personable manner had quickly put me at ease, though, and I'd gotten past staring at his good looks. Important, obviously, if I wanted to get any work done on the ice.

As Sergei spoke to the moms, I remembered I had to phone my own mother. She expected a daily call once I'd moved from Boston to Cape Cod a year ago. I lingered near the water cooler and read the announcements stapled to the bulletin board until Sergei finished his conversation and moved toward the stairs.

"Sergei, do you have a minute?"

"Sure." He glanced at his sport watch. "I have about ten. What's up?"

"I was thinking of doing some coaching in the afternoons like I used to in Boston. Just a few kids, but I wanted to see what you thought." I toyed with my silver cross and chain. "If it might be too much to take on right now."

He took a long sip of coffee and gave me a pensive look. "I might have a better idea. Walk with me."

I followed him down the narrow steps to the rink, and he set his paper cup on the boards. Skaters swooshed past us, creating a chilly breeze.

"Would you be interested in helping me with one of my novice teams?" Sergei asked. "Teaching them the pair elements would reinforce everything you've learned."

I bobbed my head with vigor at his show of confidence. "That sounds like a great idea."

He spread his hands apart. "Don't I always have all the answers?"

"Yes, Oh Great and All-Knowing Coach." I performed a playful bow.

"I've never had an assistant before. Maybe you should call me Mister Petrov when we work together." He lifted his cup to his mouth, a hint of a smile on his lips.

"You're joking, right?"

His eyes widened with innocence. "Why would I be joking?"

"You're only six years older than me." I laughed and started for the weight room, and Sergei chuckled behind me. "I'm not calling you Mister."

WITHIN A WEEK, I began assisting Sergei with his newest and youngest team of twelve-year-old Courtney and fourteen-year-old Mark. They were struggling with their double loop throw jump, so I acted as Sergei's partner to demonstrate the technique. The kids stood next to the boards while Sergei's strong hands grasped my hips and vaulted me across the ice. A double felt light and easy compared to the triples I normally did.

Courtney and Mark studied us attentively and tried the throw on their own. Attempt after attempt, Courtney failed to land on a clean edge. Her pink cheeks deepened to crimson as she huffed with frustration.

"It's alright." Sergei patted her shoulder. "Mark, she needs a little more height. Make sure you've got your weight balanced on the takeoff."

"Courtney, also try pulling in tighter and quicker." I brought my arms sharply against my chest.

Our students worked on the element each afternoon, some days having more success than others, but Sergei never lost patience. Watching him handle Courtney and Mark's roller coaster of emotions with gentle authority gave me a new level of respect for him. He knew just how to reassure the kids and light up their eyes with understanding.

After Courtney and Mark's sessions, I often stopped at the Starbucks near the rink on my way home. I learned Sergei was a frequent patron, too, and every time we ran into each other, our conversations grew longer.

One afternoon, we finally gravitated to one of the tiny tables and had been sitting there over half an hour. Sergei had gone to the counter for a refill, and when he rejoined me, he caught me softly singing Sting's "Fields of Gold" along with the piped-in radio.

"Are you a Sting fan?" he asked, stirring a packet of sugar into his black coffee.

"Huge." I sipped my latte. "Are you?"

"I have all his CDs. 'Fields of Gold' is one of my favorite songs."

I leaned forward and rested my elbows on the small table. "Did you know he's having a concert up in Mansfield next weekend? None of my friends want to go. They said his music is for old people." I frowned.

Sergei laughed. "Yeah, I don't know anyone interested in going either."

"I wonder if there are tickets left. Maybe we could go together."

He stared at me over his cup, and I shifted backward in my seat. I hoped he didn't think I was suggesting anything like a date. The U.S. Figure Skating Federation wouldn't approve of a coach and student dating.

I hastily added, "You know, since no one else wants to go… and we don't know when he'll have another show here."

Sergei nodded and his mouth gradually opened into a smile. "Yeah, we should go. The last concert I went to was about five years ago, right after I moved to Virginia from

Moscow. It was Dave Matthews Band. I hadn't heard of them, but some people at the rink invited me."

"Ahh, I love them. I've never seen them live."

"They were great. Turned me into a big fan." He tapped his fingers on his cup. "But what I remember most about that night was the taxi ride home. I didn't have a car, and I lived *way* outside the city. The taxi driver didn't speak good English and neither did I at the time. I fell asleep, and when he woke me up, I had no idea where we were. He'd misunderstood me and taken me to a town twenty miles from where I lived."

I burst into laughter. "Oh, no!"

"When he finally got me home, I didn't have enough cash to pay the ridiculous fare, and we got in an argument about whose fault it was he took me to the wrong place." He chuckled and shook his head. "I gave him all the money I had and left him outside my apartment, cursing me out."

Giggles echoed in my throat. "That's crazy. Well, the good news is we can drive ourselves to Mansfield. Speaking of which, I should get home and check on the tickets." I snagged my car keys from my purse. "If I find some, I'll go ahead and order them."

"Let me know later how much I owe you."

"Don't worry, I won't curse you out if you don't pay me right away." I smiled, and Sergei laughed.

With my keys in one hand and my coffee in the other, I stood and aimed for the door. "I'll call you when I get them!"

Typical summertime traffic slowed my drive home. I loved the beauty of the Cape during summer with the hydrangeas in bloom and the deep orange sunsets, but I missed the peacefulness of winter on the island. After crawling bumper to bumper on Route Six from South Dennis to Hyannis, I finally arrived at my parents' vacation townhouse, which had become my year-round home.

In the sun-splashed living room, my roommate, Aubrey, was hunched over one of her ice dance costumes, needle and thread in hand.

"What happened to your dress?" I dropped down beside her on the beige chenille couch.

She pushed a few stray blond hairs out of her eyes and squinted at the pink fabric. "Some stones fell off last time I wore it."

I picked up my laptop from the coffee table and drummed my fingers while it booted up. With a few clicks, I landed on Ticketmaster.com.

Aubrey glanced at the screen. "What are you buying tickets for?"

"Sting's concert in Mansfield. Turns out Sergei is as big a fan as I am."

Her perfectly-shaped eyebrows curved upward. "You're going on a road trip with Sergei?"

"Mansfield is an hour away. I don't call that a road trip."

She straightened the short skirt of the costume and examined the shimmering silver stones around the hem. "You two seem pretty chummy these days," she said with a sidelong glance.

I shrugged. "We like to talk when we get coffee. No big deal."

"It's a big deal when you start going out at night together. Coaches aren't supposed to be that friendly with their students. Especially not young, hot coaches."

My face warmed, and I focused on the computer screen. "We work together and have a few common interests. It's nothing more."

"I'm just trying to look out for you, Em. You need to be careful."

My fingers paused on the keyboard. Aubrey was the same age as me, but her dating history could fill a book three times the size of mine. She'd been breaking hearts since I'd met her at thirteen. Our gap in boyfriend experience sometimes led her to treat me like a little sister.

"Sergei and I have a professional relationship. You don't need to worry."

She didn't look convinced, but she didn't press the issue. I turned back to the computer and concentrated on selecting two seats for the concert, ignoring the tiny voice in my head that echoed Aubrey's warning.

A RUMBLE OF THUNDER rolled in the distance, and both Sergei and I looked skyward. Fast moving clouds hid the moon. A roof covered half the amphitheater but not our seats in the farthest reaches of the venue. Sting had finished his first set, and I was regretting not bringing my rain slicker.

Sergei rose from the long bench. "Do you want a soda or anything?"

"I'll take a bottle of water." I reached into my jeans pocket for the cash I'd stashed.

He waved away the money. "I've got it."

I smiled as I watched his long legs take him down the packed aisle. I hadn't been on a date in so long that I'd forgotten how nice it was having a guy do the little things like fight the crowd for concessions and... *Wait a second.* I shook my head. *This isn't a date, remember?* Just because Sergei opened his car door for me and wiped the dirt off my seat at the amphitheater didn't mean our outing was anything more than friendly. *He was being polite.*

The smell of popcorn wafted past me as people returned from the concession stand and climbed into our row. Sergei came back with two bottles of water and handed me one.

"This is definitely the best concert I've been to," he said.

"I saw U2 a few years ago in Boston, and they blew me away." I paused, and Sergei raised an eyebrow. "But so far, this is even better."

A lone raindrop plopped on my nose, and my eyes

drifted to the sky again. "I think we're about to get drenched."

A few more drops fell, and Sergei said, "If it gets too bad, we can leave if you want."

"No way. I don't wanna miss any of the show. Unless you're afraid you're going to melt?" I bit my bottom lip to stifle a smile.

He laughed. "No, I can handle it."

The drops soon increased to a steady drizzle and pelted us on and off through the rest of the show. I sang along to every song while the rain coated my lips. Next to me, Sergei patted his leg in time to the beat of each tune, and every now and then, his arm bumped mine. His skin felt warm despite being wet, and with each touch my arm tingled.

By the time Sting finished his second encore, my navy T-shirt clung to me and my hair was soaked, but I was too awed by the music to care. I peeked at Sergei, and his short golden brown hair had darkened from the rain, making his blue eyes stand out even more. We moved with the thick crowd to the parking lot and had just hopped into Sergei's SUV when the drizzle became a downpour.

"We got out of there right in time," I said.

"You mean you wouldn't want to sit outside in this? What, afraid you would melt, Emily?"

I laughed. "Oh, I could've handled it."

The windshield wipers slapped back and forth, drowning out the classic rock on the radio. Sergei turned on the heater and drove slowly until we reached the interstate and pointed south to the Cape.

"I'm so glad we came," he said. "He sounded amazing live."

I combed my fingers through my hair, unknotting the long, damp waves. "I know. I'd see him again in a heartbeat."

"Next time he comes, we'll have to get tickets early so we can be closer to the stage." He shot me a smile. "And out of the rain."

"Definitely." I returned his smile.

A shiver sped down my spine at the thought of spending another evening with Sergei. I didn't know if I was still on a high from the concert, but being in the dark car with him was heightening all my senses. I'd always thought he was attractive, but only now did I notice how his smile softened the sharp angles of his face, how sexy my name sounded in his Russian accent, how his T-shirt hugged his lean yet muscular chest.

I gulped and set my eyes on the highway in front of us. *You need to put those thoughts out of your mind right now.*

CHAPTER TWO

"SLICE THE DOUGH THINNER, EM-I-LY." I mimicked Grandma's heavy Italian accent and gestured wildly with my hands. "Spa-*ghetti*, not fett-u-c*cine*!"

Sergei stopped drinking mid-sip and coughed, his coffee rattling in his throat. His shoulders shook with laughter, and he pounded a fist to his chest, his breathing steadying with each thump.

"You don't look Italian at all," he said, still chuckling at my imitation of my mother and late grandmother teaching me how to make spaghetti from scratch.

"Because I have blond hair and blue eyes?" I smiled and tugged on one of my dark blond locks. "You've seen my dad. I got all his features and none of my mom's. Got my athletic genes from him, too. My mom is ridiculously uncoordinated."

"Remind me to thank him for that," Sergei said.

He pushed his chair away from the table, and my heart clouded over, as it did every day when we'd emptied our cups. Our coffee shop chats were the highlight of my days. The lush greenery of summer had faded into autumn, but my thoughts about Sergei had grown even more vibrant. We'd discovered our shared love for literature—classics for him, contemporary for me—and our obsession with Italian food.

We stepped outside, and I squinted from the late afternoon sun. Sergei slipped his aviator shades over his nose. "Do you have any exciting plans this weekend?"

"Aubrey and I are cooking and having a few friends over tomorrow night. Or rather, *I'm* cooking and Aubrey is cleaning the kitchen. That's our standard arrangement."

"Are you making Italian?"

"I am. My grandmother's spinach lasagna recipe."

"From scratch?" he asked with a teasing smile.

"Of course."

The tip of his tongue moistened his lips. "Sounds delicious."

The opening was too perfect. Since the concert, Sergei and I hadn't seen each other outside the rink and the coffee shop, and my sensible side told me to keep it that way. But my swirling emotions overpowered my usual sensibility.

"Why don't you come over tomorrow night and find out?" My invite came out in a rush. "You know everyone who'll be there—Chris, Marley, Trevor."

An immediate grin appeared. "I can't pass up homemade pasta."

"We'll see you at eight then."

He jangled his keys and walked backward toward his SUV. "So, should I expect master chef level cooking?"

I gave him my best I-mean-business face. "Oh, prepare to be blown away."

"You know I'm not easy to please."

"And you know not to doubt me." I smiled and opened the door of my sedan.

He laughed. "Very true. I'll see you tomorrow."

I didn't stop grinning the entire drive home. Knowing Aubrey was going to give me a hard time about inviting Sergei, I planned to keep that information to myself until tomorrow night, leaving her little time to lecture me.

WITH ONE FINAL TWIRL in front of my bedroom mirror, I deemed my outfit complete. I'd tried on six different ones for dinner before deciding on a soft pink scoop-necked blouse and a white flouncy skirt. From my closet, I retrieved the four-inch espadrille sandals that gave me the height I always craved. As a skater, being petite had its advantages, but off the ice I wore heels every chance I got.

I jogged down the four flights of stairs from my room to the kitchen and opened the oven to check on the lasagna. The room filled with the aroma of bubbling mozzarella cheese. The doorbell rang, and my stomach jumped with anticipation. I looked toward the stairs. Aubrey was still getting ready, and I hadn't told her about our extra guest yet.

Fluffing my hair over my shoulders, I shut off the oven and bounded up the steps to the foyer. I unlocked the door, and the sight of Chris across the threshold settled my stomach.

He handed me two of the four large bottles of soda in his arms. "What's up, Short Stuff?"

We went down to the kitchen, where Chris hopped onto one of the bar stools along the counter. My partner cleaned up well. His casual polo and jeans perfectly fit his athletic build. People asked why Chris and I didn't date, but from day one of our partnership we'd had a sibling vibe. Since I was an only child, I enjoyed the feeling of having a slightly older brother.

Aubrey sailed in behind us, fumbling with the chunky jade green necklace around her neck. "Em, can you clasp this for me? Hey, Chris."

She held up her long flaxen hair while I connected the tiny metal hooks. "This goes great with your eyes."

"Thanks. I got it when Marley and I went shopping yesterday."

Chris fiddled with the oversized oven mitt on the counter. "Marley's coming tonight, right?"

Aubrey eyed him with interest. "Yeah," she said and piled five plates next to the stove.

"Um, we need one more plate." I shifted from one wedge heel to the other. "I invited Sergei."

She stopped in the middle of gathering silverware. "You invited Sergei?"

"Sergei's cool," Chris said. "He's not a jerk like your coach."

The doorbell chimed, and Chris leapt from the stool and up the stairs before I could react. Aubrey clamped her hand around my elbow.

"Em, what are you doing?" she asked in a hushed voice. "You already spend too much time with Sergei. And what is he think—"

"Shhhh! He's a friend, and this dinner is for friends, right?"

Aubrey's mouth opened, but Chris, Marley, and Trevor burst in with loud talking. Marley was an ice dancer and Trevor a pairs skater in Sergei's camp.

Trevor deposited two bags of ice onto the counter while Marley gave me a hug. The sweet, flowery smell of her perfume matched her disposition.

The bell rang again, and I scooted past Aubrey and Marley. Sergei stood on my doorstep, holding a white pastry box. I'd fantasized about that moment so many times, except my fantasy didn't include any other dinner guests.

"Come on in. You didn't have to bring anything."

"Just something to go with that mind-blowing meal you've made." He flashed a smile, and my face heated several degrees.

I took the box from him and peeked under the lid. "Mmmm, brownies. Can't ever go wrong with chocolate."

We joined the group in the kitchen, and Sergei exchanged

handshakes with Chris and Trevor.

"Hey, Sergei!" Marley said.

Aubrey shook her head at me and pulled the salad I'd tossed out of the refrigerator. I shoved the oven mitt over my hand and took the lasagna from the oven.

"We're going to eat upstairs on the terrace," Aubrey announced.

Everyone poured drinks and reached for plates, and Sergei moved next to me as I cut into the lasagna.

I gave him a wide smile. "You ready to be amazed?"

"EM, YOU WANT MORE soda?" Trevor asked as he stood.

I passed him my empty plastic cup. "Yes, please."

We had long finished dinner, but everyone remained around the big patio table, talking and listening to the stereo Aubrey had set up. Sergei had eaten two helpings of lasagna, and his compliments made me giddy. I couldn't stop staring at him. His oxford shirt matched his eyes, and its opened top button revealed a glimpse of smooth, tanned skin.

Whenever my gaze roamed to Sergei across the table, I found him looking back at me. Sometimes his lips curled into a smile; other times, he quickly averted his eyes. Our evening-long tango of stares had my head spinning. Thankfully, Chris was too busy ogling Marley to notice us, and Aubrey and Trevor were engaged in their usual snappy banter.

Trevor returned with my drink and nudged Aubrey's arm. "Have you been playing *Death Race*?" Despite her girly-girl appearance, Aubrey was a fierce video game competitor.

"Last time I played was the night I kicked your butt."

"Ouch!" Chris bumped Trevor's broad shoulder. "You gonna take that, man?"

Trevor pointed at Aubrey. "It's time for a rematch. You game?"

Aubrey jumped up. "You. Me. Downstairs."

"Marley, we can show 'em how it's done," Chris said.

"I need to get going. I have to drive to Providence tomorrow morning for my sister's birthday."

Chris's face sagged, and I made a mental note to harass him later about his apparent new crush.

"Tell her happy birthday for me," I said, walking Marley to the door.

Chris, Aubrey, and Trevor disappeared into the house, and Marley waved her dainty fingers. "See you Monday!"

Sergei had gotten up with everyone, and he stood next to me in front of the sliding glass door. I put one hand on my hip.

"Don't tell me you're leaving, too?"

"What, you don't want to join in the fun downstairs?" His tongue poked inside his cheek, suppressing a grin.

I dropped onto one of the wrought iron chairs. "They could be down there for *hours*. You have no idea how serious they get when they play."

Sergei stuck his hands in his jean pockets and took two hesitant steps toward the table. "I don't want to overstay my welco—"

"Trust me, you're not," I interrupted. "I'd love the company."

He smiled and sat across from me. "I didn't realize it's after midnight. I guess time really does fly when you're having fun."

"We do these little dinner parties a lot. Consider yourself with a standing invitation."

"I appreciate that. There are a few people at the rink I do things with but no one I consider a close friend." Sergei looked me straight in the eyes. "I think I talk to you more than anyone else."

My heart fluttered like a leaf in the crisp night breeze. "I'm glad we get along so well. It definitely makes working together more pleasant."

"No, it wouldn't be much fun if I couldn't stand you." He winked and sipped from his bottle of water.

Dim light from a couple of lanterns shone on the table, while deep shadows hid the rest of the terrace. We'd never been alone quite like this, and my pulse quickened with each passing second.

"I have to tell you again… that was the best lasagna I've ever had," Sergei said.

"Wait till you try my pesto pasta. I'll make that next time."

He angled forward, and the lantern illuminated his intrigued smile. "What other hidden talents do you have?"

I tilted my head to the side and ran a finger along the rim of my cup. "I can't give away all my secrets."

A few wisps of hair blew across my face, tickling my cheek. The terrace usually served as my serene oasis; the bay breeze had a way of washing away the stress of training. But tonight the place had a new feel. The air crackled with energy.

The CD changer shuffled to "Sparks" by Coldplay, and I sighed. "I *love* this song."

"You and Chris should skate to this for your show program," Sergei said.

"How is it you and I always agree on music?"

He held out his hand, palm upward. "We both have excellent taste."

I giggled. "Of course. And while we're being modest, we both have great ears for skate-able music."

"Bring the CD to the rink next week, and we can start working on the program."

"Chris already nixed this song. He wants to do hard rock, and I want something slow and beautiful."

"You make every program you skate look beautiful."

Sergei's eyes lingered on mine, mesmerizing me with their shine. Goosebumps covered my arms. The music played on, and the crickets continued chirping as if the awkward pause didn't exist.

Sergei looked at the stereo and cleared his throat. "So, what other songs have you talked about?"

I rubbed my forearms and took a sip of soda before giving him my ideas. While debating each song, we drew up choreography using empty water bottles as skaters and the tabletop as ice. I rolled with laughter as Sergei tried to balance one bottle on top of the other, imitating an overhead lift.

Somehow we got to talking about pop music in Russia and then our lives growing up in such different places. The night deepened, but we didn't move from our seats.

"Do you miss home?" I asked.

"I miss my family, but the Cape feels like home now. It's quite different from Moscow, but I love it."

"It's amazing how well you speak English, living in the States only five years. Before we met, I was afraid I wasn't going to be able to understand a word you said."

"I should've talked to you in Russian just to scare you." He grinned. "But I wanted to make a good impression."

"You made a great impression."

After I spoke, I realized how gushy I sounded, but Sergei didn't seem to mind. He was wearing that little smile again—the one I'd caught him giving me throughout dinner.

The wind picked up, rustling the trees and sending my empty cup skittering over the table. Sergei snatched it and noticed the time on his watch.

"Oh, wow, it's two thirty. I'm sorry, I didn't mean to stay this late."

"No worries. I can sleep till noon tomorrow."

He rose from his chair, stretching his arms. "Do you think they all killed each other downstairs?"

"My guess is they played so hard they passed out at some point. That's been known to happen."

I got up and smoothed my skirt. I'd kicked off my sandals hours ago, and the weathered wood of the patio was cool under my bare feet.

Sergei took a step toward me. "Thanks again for the great meal. And the even better company."

"You're very welcome. I'm so glad you came."

I stood on tippy-toes to give him a quick hug, but Sergei's strong arms held me against him, enveloping my small frame. His body exuded warmth. I closed my eyes and breathed in the woody scent of his cologne. We'd shared plenty of hugs at competitions, but this felt so different, like we belonged nowhere else but in this embrace.

After what seemed like both an eternity and a split second, Sergei pulled away, his hands brushing down my back. He glanced downward and gestured to the door.

"I can let myself out."

My head bobbed weakly. "Okay. I'll see you Monday."

"See you." He held my gaze a moment longer than necessary. Then he was gone.

I stood paralyzed, listening to the blood pulse in my ears. My heart beat so fast I thought it might pound out of my chest. I couldn't have imagined the electricity I'd felt in Sergei's arms. It was too real. And I had no idea how I could ever forget it.

CHAPTER THREE

Daylight hadn't yet appeared when I pulled into the rink's parking lot on Monday, fingers tapping nervously on the wheel. I'd woken before my alarm and gotten an early start, even earlier than the ridiculous hour I usually began my day. All Sunday, I'd relived every look and smile Sergei and I had shared on my terrace. I wasn't sure what to expect from him this morning. Awkwardness? Normalcy? I hoped for the latter.

Inside the rink, two pairs of novice ice dance teams occupied the ice, while two moms on the bleachers yawned. Aubrey and Marley's coach, Viktor, barked at the skaters over the jazzy tune playing on the sound system. I made a sharp left for the locker room and startled Sergei as he came out of the gym in a sleeveless T-shirt and shorts.

"You're very early." He blotted his face with a towel.

I slapped my hands together, using exuberance to hide my anxiety. "I'm ready to work."

"Don't you need a partner to do that?" He smiled and wiped his arms, toweling the tight curve of his biceps.

Seems like same old Sergei.

"I guess I didn't give Chris the memo," I said with a little laugh.

"I had to run five extra miles on the treadmill to work off that great dinner you made." He patted his stomach. "It was worth it, though."

Every smile he gave me melted another morsel of my nervousness. He threw his towel across his shoulder. "I need to take a shower. See, I'm usually done with all this by the time you get here."

A flicker of heat stirred inside me as I pictured the hot water running over his muscles and down his chest. My hand flew to my cheek. "Um, carry on then. Pretend you never saw me."

Sergei strolled toward the locker room, and I nibbled on my lip. He didn't seem fazed by our night of flirting and our lingering hug. As much as I didn't want any awkwardness, I couldn't deny my tinge of disappointment. Had I imagined the spark between us?

"HEADS!" CHRIS YELLED BEHIND us as we blazed across the ice, setting up for the triple twist. Two dancers scattered, and Chris vaulted me into the air. Holding my arms tight to my body, I spun two and a half times, but gravity pulled me down before I completed the "triple" part of the element. Chris caught me sideways, and we struggled to keep our balance.

"How many have we done?" He asked once we disentangled.

"Nine. And we've only done six clean."

"One more." Sergei skated past us. "You need seven out of ten." He moved over to help Trevor and his partner, Leigh, but called out over his shoulder, "Must be fully rotated."

I swiped the perspiration from my forehead with the back of my hand and repositioned the bobby pins holding up my loose bun. At the start of practice, Sergei had informed us we needed to perform seventy percent of our triple twists cleanly every day that week. Otherwise, he would allow us to do only a double in our programs at Skate America, our first international competition of the season. Doubles meant lower scores—not what we wanted in our debut.

"We got this," Chris said. "No problem."

My partner never lacked confidence. He could miss a jump five times in a row and stand up smiling. I, on the other hand, overanalyzed every mistake I made.

We sped into the takeoff, and I twisted myself into three revolutions. On the free fall down, Chris took hold of my waist, and my right skate found the ice with a smooth run out.

Chris let out a whoop and held up seven fingers as he skated over to Sergei.

"Success!"

Sergei smiled. "Keep it up the next four days."

After a water break, we started working on sections of our long program, set to Massenet's "Meditation." Sergei had envisioned romance when he'd choreographed the program, aiming to strengthen the emotional connection between Chris and me on the ice. Our relationship was so far from romantic, though, we had to do our best acting jobs to achieve Sergei's vision.

Sergei watched us practice our star lift and then asked us to repeat it. Above Chris's head, I sailed in a vertical split position, his hand on my hip and my hand on the back of his shoulder.

"More stretch, Em," Sergei called. "Chris, smoother on the dismount."

I pointed my toes, not easy to do in skates, and extended my free arm as far as I could. Chris set me down, and we transitioned into the next movement, where he touched my face and we looked into each other's eyes. We held the pose a few seconds before Sergei sprinted over.

"You're not feeling it. You have to maintain the emotion

throughout the program and especially in these moments between the elements. Chris, as soon as Em comes down from the lift, you need to lock your eyes on hers and pull her close. Em, you have to look at him like he's your whole world. I'll put on the music and show you."

He glided to the ice door and popped our CD into the sound system queue. Trevor and Leigh were almost finished with a section of their short program, so Chris and I idled near the boards to wait.

Sergei pushed up the sleeves of his fleece jacket. "I'll run through it with Em so you can see what I'm looking for."

I followed Sergei through the mine field of skaters jumping, falling, and dancing to the music in their heads. He grasped my hand, and we did long, powerful crossovers in tandem, building up speed for the lift. Since Sergei had been a Junior World Champion with his former partner Elena, he owned all the skills to demonstrate his teaching points.

With one arm he lifted me, and we flew across the rink. A brisk wind cooled my skin. On the dismount, my right blade carved into the ice, and Sergei swept me up to his side. His fingers stroked my cheek, while his eyes stroked my heart. The sparkling blue pools held an intensity I'd never seen before.

My breaths came out in shallow puffs. The dreamy notes of "Meditation" floated around us as we glided together, bonded by our unblinking gazes. I didn't know if I was looking at Sergei as if he was my whole world, but he certainly was making me feel like I was his entire universe.

We skidded to a stop near Chris, kicking up a light spray of ice. Sergei's eyes broke from mine as he backed away and rubbed the nape of his neck. I grabbed my water bottle from the boards and gulped down the liquid. I'd lost all the moisture in my mouth.

"That's, uh… that's how it should look," Sergei said, still avoiding eye contact with me.

Chris stared at us and waited a second to speak. "Sure, I

can do that."

He and I skated to the opposite end of the rink and came around in the lift. Chris copied Sergei's movements, but my body didn't sing like it had under Sergei's touch. I looked up at Chris with the most convincing adoration I could muster.

Sergei clapped and finally threw a glance in my direction. "That was better."

We finished our lesson with back-to-back run-throughs of our short and long programs, and Sergei met us at the ice door on our way out.

"Let's talk a minute."

Chris and I sat on the first row of bleachers while Sergei stood with his hands in his jacket pockets.

"Last year you made people notice you with your athletic ability. No other teams are doing side-by-side triple Lutzes or the triple Lutz throw. You have that advantage over everyone else. And you're getting closer on the twist every day. Once you have that down, the technical content in your programs will be unmatched.

"This season you need to show the judges you have the full package. You both have a great feel for the music and know how to present to the audience. Now you have to work on relating to each other. Have you heard the phrase 'Two shall skate as one'?"

We nodded, and Sergei continued, "That's what I need from you every second of every program."

We nodded again with more gusto, and Sergei told us, "Good job today," before leaving to prepare for his next lesson. I was going to make a comment to Chris, but his attention had shifted to the ice, where Marley and her partner Zach were practicing the Westminster Waltz compulsory dance. Marley's balletic arms highlighted the nuances of the regal music, while Zach stood tall with strong ballroom posture.

I went ahead to the locker room to change and then to the

gym for two hours of off-ice conditioning. The cramped room included a couple of exercise bikes, two treadmills, and an area with weights and mats for strength and balance training. My legs were already pumping the bike pedals when Chris settled onto the bicycle next to mine.

"So, I have an idea how we can be more connected when we skate. You should pretend I'm Marley." I gave him a toothy grin.

He pedaled faster. "I don't know what you're talking about."

"You were hanging on everything she said at my house the other night."

His rosy cheeks deepened in color, possibly from the workout, but more likely from my teasing.

"She's a nice girl," he mumbled over the whirr of the spinning cycles.

"I could put in a good word for you."

He jerked his head to face me. "No, don't say anything to her."

"I don't get you. You're Mr. Confidence on the ice, but you're scared to ask a girl out?"

"I'm not scared. She just broke up with her boyfriend back home. I don't wanna be the rebound guy."

I tapped his arm. "You want to be her serious guy."

"Why don't we get back to the original subject . . . this whole emotional connection thing. You could pretend I'm Sergei." He stuck out his tongue.

My legs stopped moving. "Why would you say that?"

"It's obvious you worship the ground he walks on. You were all googly-eyed when you were skating with him earlier."

"I don't worship him. I was doing what he told us to do." I resumed cycling with a fury.

"Hey, I'm not judging. All the girls swoon over him." He touched the back of his hand to his forehead and laughed.

"Some of the guys, too."

I snickered, but on the inside alarm bells rang. My feelings for Sergei had shown on the ice—a dangerous development. Whatever spark existed between us needed to be doused because we couldn't act on it. The federation would never approve, and Sergei's position as our coach could be in jeopardy. If Chris and I were going to be the first American pair to win Olympic gold, I must stay focused on skating.

Starting today, I had to stop hanging out with Sergei at Starbucks. If I just saw him at the rink, then my feelings would eventually fade. Wouldn't they?

INSTEAD OF GOING TO the coffee shop that afternoon, I decided to take a walk from my house to Main Street to window shop in the galleries and gift stores. Strolling past the harbor, I inhaled the nippy autumn air. The summer crowds were gone, so there were no lines of people waiting to dine at the waterfront restaurants. The Martha's Vineyard and Nantucket ferry docks were also quiet.

I walked through the little park along the harbor and passed Sergei's apartment building. My parents had recommended the place when his old apartment had been sold a few months back. I noticed his black SUV in the parking lot, which meant he hadn't gone to Starbucks either. A weight heavier than I wanted to admit settled on my chest. Maybe Sergei was avoiding me, too.

On Main Street, many store windows featured Halloween displays of oversized jack-o-lanterns and tangled cobwebs. I wandered from shop to shop, making note of some items I thought Mom and Dad might like for Christmas. With my busy competition and training schedule coming up, it was never too early to think about the holidays.

I stopped in front of a gift shop and peered through the

window at a display of handmade jewelry. Further into the store, a familiar blue sweater caught my eye. Sergei was standing beside a shelf of silk scarves, examining one with a black and white striped design.

Who is he buying a scarf for?

I watched him refold the scarf and pick up another one. Curiosity encouraged me to go inside, but I'd be violating my new rule of not socializing with him. While I played an internal tug-of-war, Sergei spotted me.

A smile spread across his face as he lifted one hand in a wave. I stuck my hand up in reply, and he motioned for me to join him. I couldn't walk away now.

Inside the store, the strong cinnamon potpourri scent choked me. I moved through aisles of wind chimes and crystal figurines and met Sergei next to the scarves.

"I'm glad you're here," he said. "I need a woman's opinion."

"Oh?"

"I'm looking for a birthday present for my mother, and I could use some ideas."

I tried not to smile too big when he said 'mother.' "What do you usually get her?"

"I usually send flowers, but it's her fiftieth birthday, so I wanted to get something special."

"Hmm…" I touched my finger to my chin. "Does she like jewelry?"

"She doesn't wear much. She has pretty simple taste."

I scanned the cluttered shelves around us. "What about something Cape Cod-inspired? Something that will give her a piece of your life here?"

"She does love all the photos I've sent her."

"How about a framed print?" I led him over to the rows of colorful prints. "They have some beautiful ones of different scenic spots on the island. My mom bought two here for our living room."

We shuffled through the selection, and I gaped at one in particular. "This is gorgeous." I stared at the portrait of the quaint rain-slicked city street shining from the gaslight lamps. "It's Beacon Hill, one of my favorite areas in Boston. I would love to have this hanging over my desk at home."

"You should get it."

"No, I don't need to spend this much." I returned the print to the bin. "By the way, thank you again for talking to Courtney and Mark's moms and making me one of their official coaches. The money helps a lot. My parents spend so much on my skating that I don't like to ask them for anything extra."

"You earned it. You're doing a great job with them. I think Courtney, especially, is learning a lot from you."

"Thanks." I smiled. "I've learned a lot from them and from working with you."

Sergei's eyes regarded me with deep thought. He looked like he was going to say something, but instead he pulled the next print from the bin. "This one is nice."

A blue sky filled with white wispy clouds hovered above a lighthouse surrounded by marshy grass and the sunlit ocean. I imagined Sergei and I picnicking along the water, snuggling on a red and white checked blanket as seagulls serenaded us with their soft cries.

"Em?" Sergei's voice broke me from my daydream. "Do you like it?"

"Yeah. It's the perfect Cape Cod scenery."

He smiled and started for the checkout desk. "Thanks for your help. I owe you a latte."

When he was out of sight, I banged my forehead against the nearest shelf. Putting Sergei out of my mind was going to be much more difficult than I'd thought.

CHAPTER FOUR

I SHRUGGED ON MY BLUE TEAM USA jacket and rolled my small bag through the concourse of Colorado Springs' World Arena. The souvenir stands were bustling to life with stacks of Skate America programs, T-shirts, and hoodies. Ducking into the section of seats facing center ice, I carried my bag down the steps and approached my parents.

"Hi, sweetie!" Mom's exuberant greeting could likely be heard ten rows away, even with the noisy hum of the Zamboni. She hugged me, and I smiled at Dad over her shoulder. His kind, blue-gray eyes shone behind his wire-rimmed glasses.

"You looked great at practice," Mom said. "I was so worried we weren't going to make it in time when our connecting flight from Denver took off a little late and then the cabbie from the airport drove like an old lady…"

I slid past her and kissed my father on the cheek. "Hey, Dad."

His quiet hug showed his and Mom's differing personalities. Both were professors at Boston University, but the similarities ended there. My mom spoke first, usually emotionally, and thought later, while my dad personified "easy-going" and viewed the world logically. They'd balanced each other for twenty-five years.

"Aubrey and Nick's group is practicing after the ice cut," I said, sitting in the empty purple seat beside Mom's. "I want to stay and watch."

"That's fine," she said. "We can do lunch after."

I jiggled my knees up and down. "I'm not sure how much I'll be able to eat, thinking about tonight."

Dad reached across Mom and squeezed my hand. "Try not to get too worked up. It's the first event of the season."

"But this is a really important season. We're only sixteen months away from the Olympics. We have to show we can compete with the top teams. Starting now."

"The Canadians were sharp at practice," Mom said.

I'd watched a few minutes of Madeline Hyatt and Damien Wakefield's session before ours, and the Canadian champions hadn't missed an element. As World silver medalists, they were the heavy favorite in the competition.

"How did Claire and Brandon do?"

"Brandon was having trouble with the triple toe." Mom smoothed one stray lock of her short, chestnut-colored hair. "I still think you and Chris had them beat at Nationals. Brandon fell in the free skate! The judges held them up on reputation and didn't want a new team to win."

I massaged my right temple, the one nearest to Mom. "Let's not rehash that again." Anyone who knew my mother knew where I'd gotten my competitiveness.

"I'm just saying, the judges better be fair here. If you skate clean, you should be rewarded."

My stomach clenched. I had a bad habit of focusing on the possible results instead of my performance, and listening to Mom's tirade wasn't helping my mindset.

I felt a tug on my ponytail, and a voice behind me said, "Hey, stranger."

Spinning around, I found Drew Henry, National men's bronze medalist, grinning at me. He had one of those faces that always seemed to be smiling.

"Hey, how are you?" I stood and hugged him then turned to Mom and Dad. "I don't think you met Drew at Nationals?"

The three of them exchanged handshakes, and Drew poked my arm. "So, what have you been up to lately? You've been slacking on email."

"Sorry, it's been crazy, getting ready for the season and everything."

"We'll have to catch up this weekend." He brushed his shaggy brown hair out of his eyes and leaned toward me. "And I can school you some more on the dance floor at the closing party."

I laughed. "I think you have a short memory. At Nationals, *I* was the one teaching *you* the moves."

Drew stepped into the aisle and pointed at me. "You keep thinking that, Butler. But you'll see who the real master is." He waved to my parents. "It was nice meeting you."

Mom's big brown eyes widened as she watched Drew bound up the concrete steps. "He seemed very friendly . . . especially towards you."

"We're just friends, Mom. We've kept in touch through email."

"Doesn't he live in California?"

"Yes."

"Hmm." Mom's brow wrinkled before she shifted her gaze to the ice.

And people wonder why my dating life is practically nonexistent. I'd been constantly reminded that boys would serve as a troublesome distraction. *But what happens when the distraction is someone I can't escape?*

"WOULD THE FOLLOWING SKATERS please take the ice for the warm-up. From the United States, Emily Butler and Christopher Grayden. From Russia—"

Chris and I took off across the ice, and I tuned out the public address announcer. The six minute warm-up didn't give us much time to practice our short program elements, so every second required concentration.

Having met Sergei's triple twist challenge at practice, we ramped up speed for the element. Chris tossed me up, and I wound myself into a tight coil, but without enough air I couldn't finish the third rotation. I came down with my back to Chris instead of facing him, and he stumbled to keep his footing as he locked his arms around me.

"Get the bad one out of the way now, right?" he said.

I attempted a laugh to cover up my concern, but the sound came out like a wheeze. Dodging the traffic of the other three couples, we completed the side-by-side triple jumps and rushed into practicing the throw triple lutz. My mind was two elements back on the twist, and I landed the jump on two scratchy blades instead of one smooth edge.

Chris placed his hand on the small of my back, and I wiggled my arms and legs, as if I could shake out the anxiety. We motored by Sergei, who was leaning forward with his palms pressed against the boards. I recognized it as his I'm-not-pleased-with-what-I'm-seeing stance.

With less than a minute remaining, we transitioned into easy stroking around the ice. Our red and black costumes sparkled like gemstones under the bright lights of the arena. Chris held my hand and hummed along to the blaring pop tune, immune as always to any worry. I fidgeted with my halter neckline and played "Capriccio Espagnol," our program music, in my head.

Time expired, and we followed Sergei backstage to await our turn to skate. On cue, the muscles in my legs twitched more violently, and my stomach did a gymnastics routine.

I paced the narrow, gray corridor while Chris relaxed in a folding metal chair. The click-clack of my plastic skate guards on the cement floor echoed off the stone walls. Sergei watched me walk in circles before putting his arm around me. At the touch of his hand on my bare shoulder, my insides went from doing back flips to slowly melting like the last snow of winter.

"Em, remember what we've talked about. Your body knows what to do. Relax into it, let it feel the energy of the music."

The clarity in his eyes spoke of confidence, but the six minutes I'd just spent on the ice didn't weren't making me very sure of myself.

"Imagine the perfect program," he said. "Keep that picture in your mind through each step."

I couldn't but help think about worst-case scenarios, though. "But if we miss the twist…"

"Don't think about missing it. Think about nailing it. But if you make a mistake, remember to move past it and focus on what's ahead."

He spoke so calmly and with such assurance. Before I'd moved to the Cape, my career had stalled at the junior ladies level because of my competition anxiety. I could do the difficult jumps with ease in practice, but when I stepped on the ice to compete, my entire body would tense and my mind would fill with doubt. Sergei had worked with me on freeing my mind of negativity and visualizing a flawless program.

Those techniques didn't eliminate all the jitters, however. My nerves, plus the nearness of Sergei, sent my pulse on a sprint.

An event volunteer signaled us, so Chris and I marched through the tunnel and waited near the ice door for Claire and Brandon to finish their program. The moment they exited, we claimed the ice and circled the rink while the scores were read.

Moments before our introduction, we stopped in front of Sergei to take final sips of water. He smoothed the jacket of his dark blue suit and fed us a string of reminders.

"You're trained and ready for this."

"Take one element at a time."

"Have fun out there."

Before I left him, he gave me a smile and one final nugget of encouragement. "You're stronger than you've ever been."

I returned his smile and nodded, inhaling and exhaling a measured breath.

The audience treated us to a warm ovation but silenced as Chris froze in his starting pose. Taking deep breaths, I skated around him and tapped my toepick into the ice, positioning myself next to him. He gave me a subtle nod, his comforting sign of reassurance I'd come to rely on.

The powerful beats of the Spanish-flavored music guided us through our sharp opening movements. Approaching our first element, the triple twist, I thought, *Quick and tight. Quick and tight.*

I soared above Chris's head and spun three times, but I couldn't pull my arms out fast enough. My elbow crashed into Chris's shoulder, and I slid down his silky shirt. He grasped my waist and held onto me to keep us upright. Muted applause recognized our valiant attempt.

Chris must've seen a dazed look in my eyes because he squeezed my hand extra hard. Reminding myself to stay positive, I looked ahead to the side-by-side triple Lutzes and envisioned the perfect jump. I stabbed my right toepick into the ice and went straight up into three rotations. Chris matched me, and our blades reconnected with the ice on the same beat. That time, the response from the crowd came at a much higher decibel.

The tension in my muscles eased a bit as we moved into our circular footwork, and I let myself settle into the music. But when the throw Lutz loomed, my body tightened and I saw the image of my botched landing during the warm-up.

Positive thoughts, Em. See the perfect jump.

I flushed the warm-up from my head and pictured Chris throwing me across the ice into three revolutions, followed by a clean run-out on one foot. I thought of it again and again as he pressed his hands against my hips and sprang me into the air. My body responded instinctively, spinning the way I did countless times in practice and landing upright, one blade on the ice.

Yes!

Chris grinned at me, and we sailed into our overhead lift. A boost of energy flowed down my limbs, carrying me through our final elements and to the end of the program.

I hugged Chris and exhaled, but the mistake on the twist soon came back to me, diminishing my smile of relief. As we took our bows, stuffed animals flew from the stands and landed near our feet. Tiny sweeper girls in pink dresses scooped up the gifts. I picked up a multi-colored stuffed snake and twisted it in frustration as I skated to the kiss and cry, the sitting area to wait for the scores.

Sergei greeted us with quick hugs. "Very good start."

I continued to squeeze the furry snake between my fingers. "I should've had the twist. I opened up too soon."

"You did great." Chris swung his arm around me as we sat on the small bench. "You got the full rotation."

"Thanks for helping me keep my head on straight before," I said to Sergei.

"I just gave you a few reminders. You've come a long way."

The announcer's deep voice droned the scores—5.5, 5.4, 5.5... Out of 6.0, those were good marks, but I still wanted a do-over on the twist.

At the end of the evening, we were in fourth place behind the Canadians, a Russian team, and our American rivals, Claire and Brandon. Once we finished our media obligations, we shared a few minutes with our parents and then sought out empty seats for the Original Dance competition.

Aubrey and Nick were one of the first couples to skate. Chris whistled at our friends, and through my cupped hands I cried, "Go Aubrey and Nick!"

With her blond hair curled and slinky black dress showing off her trim figure, Aubrey was the picture of beauty, and Nick's dark good looks made him the perfect match. His black tie and tails completed the sophisticated image for their foxtrot program.

I clutched the arms of my seat and tapped my heels as Nick led Aubrey through the dance. They floated around the rink, their intricate hand-holds not hurting their speed. I watched their blades closely, and my eyes didn't see any missteps. Chris and I jumped up as soon as the program ended.

While we waited for the scores, Chris asked, "How bad do you think they'll get screwed this time?"

My mouth curled downward. "They'd better get some five-twos or five-threes."

"They won't. The judges won't give them the marks they deserve because they're young and they have to 'wait their turn.'" Chris made air quotes.

Since ice dance included no jumps, the judges could be more subjective with their scores. I often asked Aubrey if the system frustrated her, and she said she couldn't worry about things out of her control. That was a lesson I was still trying to learn.

A line of 4.9's and 5.0's lit up the scoreboard.

"Pfft" was my response.

Later at the hotel, I was showered and in my pajamas by the time Aubrey returned from the arena. Snug under two blankets, I looked up from my paperback and started to say, "Great jo—" but Aubrey's moist eyes and quivering chin halted me.

"Are you okay?"

"Yeah." She sniffled and dropped her rolling bag on the

carpet with a thud. "Just Viktor being Viktor."

I slipped my bookmark between the last pages I'd read. "What did he say? You guys did so well."

"He said I didn't give enough energy to the program."

"What? The crowd loved you. He doesn't know what he's talking about."

She hunted through the pile of clothes on the dresser and yanked out an extra-large T-shirt. "Well, he thinks he's right. As always."

Aubrey's teary voice had become bitter. I threw aside the blankets to give her a hug, but she stalked to the bathroom in a rush.

Her frequent Viktor rants made me thank God for Sergei's patience and encouragement… and a few of his other qualities. Ones I shouldn't be thinking about.

THE FOLLOWING NIGHT AT the free skate, Chris and I took the ice last, not knowing how our competitors had fared. In my ivory dress, trimmed with glittering crystals, I felt beautiful and strong, ready to make our lyrical program come alive.

The next four and a half minutes didn't feel like a long program. Every stroke, every jump was light and free, as if I had wings carrying me. Even the triple twist was the cleanest we'd ever done.

Throughout the program, Chris showered me with the loving looks Sergei had asked for, and I returned them with equal conviction. When the music ended, the entire arena stood and so did all the hairs on the back of my neck. Chris pumped his fist and wrapped me in a tight embrace.

With my ears buzzing from the cheers, I swiveled to face the kiss and cry. Sergei's smile gleamed brighter than my costume. As Chris and I approached him, he banged our skate guards together in celebration. I hopped off the ice and threw my arms around his neck.

"Absolutely beautiful," he said.

Sergei went to kiss my cheek as I turned to speak, and his lips grazed the corner of my mouth. My already pounding heart staggered against my chest. The moment had been like tasting one crumb of the most delicious dessert imaginable and then having it taken away.

Tension crept into Sergei's arms, and he made a hasty move to hug Chris. I snatched a tissue from the box behind the boards to blot the beads of perspiration from my face.

In the kiss and cry, Sergei pointed to the slow-motion replay of our lifts and spins and noted some corrections to make. Meanwhile, the delay for the scores dragged. Had we moved up into medal position? Finally, the marks appeared— 5.7's and 5.8's for technical merit, and 5.7's for presentation. The placements showed unanimous second place ordinals from the judges.

I slapped my hands over my mouth, and Chris smothered me in another hug. The audience cheered until we rose and thanked them with enthusiastic waves. As we walked backstage, Sergei beckoned us aside.

"I felt the connection between you tonight. We can build on this for your next competition. You performed very well, but the great thing is, in Paris you can be even better."

The smile on both my face and Chris's stretched wider. "Definitely," I said, and Chris concurred.

I'd switched to pairs because I thought skating with a partner would calm my nerves. Chris's steady presence indeed helped me, but I hadn't expected Sergei's impact on my skating. He'd tapped into a confidence I didn't know I was capable of.

The medal ceremony began minutes later, and I spotted my parents in the front row. Dad aimed his camera at us while Mom whooped and shouted, "Yeah, Emily and Chris!" Chris and I stepped onto the second tier of the podium and congratulated the Canadians, Hyatt and Wakefield, winners of the gold. The Russian team who'd won bronze skated out last and occupied the third tier.

An International Skating Federation official presented our awards. I fingered the red, white, and blue ribbon, admiring the dangling silver medal. Behind me, Chris pinched my waist.

"First international medal," he said.

I smiled and tilted my head to look at him. "First of many."

"THAT WAS A FABULOUS dinner," Mom said as she got up from the big round table.

Chris's parents echoed her sentiment. We'd spent the past two hours celebrating the successful weekend. Our table near the rear of the hotel restaurant had kept our noise from bothering the other dining skaters—some also celebrating, some looking grim after disappointing skates.

Mom's cell phone rang with the tune of "Fur Elise," and she checked the tiny screen. "It's your Aunt Deb." She answered her younger sister's call while Chris's parents bid us goodnight.

"What time are you going to the closing party?" Chris asked me.

"Aubrey's meeting me in the lobby in a few minutes."

"I'm gonna run upstairs. I'll see you there."

Dad and I smiled at each other as Mom continued to chat with Aunt Debbie. If the two of them went an entire day without calling or seeing each other, it would be national news.

"Mom, can you ask Aunt Deb something for me?"

Mom raised one finger. "Hang on a sec. What is it, sweetie?"

"Can you ask her if I can use her summer house next weekend? A few of us are doing a clinic for the Martha's Vineyard skating club, and I figured we could stay overnight instead of hurrying to catch the ferry home."

"We have a fundraiser at church next Saturday night, so she and Uncle Joe won't be using it," Mom said and then spoke into the phone, "Em's going to the Vineyard next weekend. She asked about staying at the house." She nodded at me. "She said of course, anytime."

When Mom finally ended her call, we weaved through the restaurant and came upon Sergei sitting with two other men, an American judge and Claire and Brandon's coach. They each had a glass of wine and an open menu in front of them.

Sergei stood and shook Dad's hand. "Hi, Jim, Laura." He bent to peck Mom's cheek. "I hope you had a good dinner?"

"It was wonderful. A nice way to end the weekend." Mom circled her arm around my waist. "Sergei, you know I wasn't thrilled about Emily doing pairs, but I can't argue with these results. Whatever you're doing, keep doing it."

He's doing more than you know, like making me crazy.

"I'm glad you gave me a chance to work with Em. I think she was born to skate pairs."

He smiled at me, and I remembered the brush of his mouth next to mine. The memory of that brief sensation was enough to make me shiver. *Yep, definitely crazy.*

A waiter walked up to the table, so we started for the door. "We'll leave you to your dinner," Dad said. "I recommend the chicken marsala."

In the lobby, Aubrey and another dancer were lounging on a plush couch, comparing their cell phones. Both of them wore jeans, a cute top, and heels, our standard outfit for skating event parties.

Dad kissed the top of my head. "Have fun."

"Goodnight, girls," Mom called as she and Dad headed to

the elevators.

We rode the escalator up to the hotel ballroom, site of the festivities. With the lights dimmed and a DJ spinning high-energy music, the room had the feel of a real dance club.

Drew motioned for us to join his group dancing among the throng of skaters. During our first song on the dance floor, two French guys next to us crept closer and closer. Aubrey had the cute one's attention, and they zeroed in on each other. The other guy persisted on invading my space, and I continued to slink away. The Frenchman had given me a creepy vibe when I'd met him at the arena. His limited English prevented him from saying much, but his awkward stares made me uncomfortable.

Aubrey yelled in my ear, "Why don't you dance with Vincent?"

"He's weird. I talked to him yesterday in the lounge."

She laughed. "Aw, come on, give him a chance."

I shook my head vehemently and snuck over to Drew, pulling him in front of me as a shield.

"Save me!"

He let out a deep laugh. "What are you doing?"

"I can't shake Vincent. You have to dance with me."

He glanced behind me and laughed harder. "Your boy's got some pretty good moves. You sure you don't wanna go back over there?" His hazel eyes glinted with mischief as he pushed me toward Vincent.

I resisted, gripping his shoulders. "No!"

"Okay, you can use me. But you better bring it 'cause you know I don't mess around out here."

I put my hand in his face. "Please. You're going to have to keep up with *me*."

He seized my wrist and moved my hand away. "You need to stop talking and start dancing, Butler."

Not wasting any time, I busted out my best dance moves. Drew challenged me, shaking his lanky frame in time with the pulsating beat. Pretty soon, we were dancing very close together, and his grin had gone from friendly to flirty.

"I think Vincent's going to be in Paris with us," he said. "I'll gladly offer up my services again if you need me."

I smiled. "I hope he's gotten the hint. I'm *so* excited about the trip. You said you've been there before?"

"A few times. In addition to bodyguard services, I also act as a tour guide, if you're interested." He flashed an expectant grin.

This is what you need. Some fun, uncomplicated flirting.

"That would be great."

We danced together most of the night, stopping only for soda breaks and to watch Chris's retro dance moves that had everyone cracking up. Drew and I were still laughing when we left the ballroom with Chris, Nick, Aubrey, and her new French friend.

"You guys wanna hang out downstairs for a while?" Chris asked as he did a few hip hop steps on the way to the lobby, sending us into more laughter. We passed the hotel bar, and I saw Sergei and his dinner companions had moved over from the restaurant.

My smile faded, recognizing yet another reminder of how Sergei was out of reach. He was where he belonged, networking over drinks with officials, and I was where I belonged, being silly with my fellow skaters.

The dividing line between our roles was too defined to cross.

CHAPTER FIVE

NO MATTER HOW MANY TIMES I visited Martha's Vineyard, I never tired of the scene in the Vineyard Haven harbor. The midday sun bathed the charming, historic homes lining the water, while the salty breeze flared the American flags flying in the marina.

Next to me along the ferry rail, Sergei focused his small digital camera and snapped every inch of the landscape. A chilly whistle of wind blew strands loose from my ponytail, and I pushed them behind my ears and smiled at Sergei.

"I can't believe you've lived on the Cape over two years and you haven't been to the Vineyard or Nantucket."

On the other side of me, Chris held onto the brim of his Orioles baseball cap. "And you live across the street from the ferry dock."

"I guess I've been busy," Sergei said.

Marley, Aubrey, and Trevor returned from the snack bar with bottles of water for all of us. When the Vineyard's skating club had asked our club for volunteers to teach a basic skills clinic, we'd signed up quickly. Working with kids on the ice brought the potential for lots of fun.

"I love this place." Marley moved next to Chris for a clear view of the harbor. "It's like a perfect postcard."

"Hey, I was thinking we could all go to the cliffs tomorrow morning to see the sunrise," I said.

"What are the cliffs?" Sergei asked.

"On the far end of the island, there are these cliffs that look like they were sculpted with different colors of clay, and at sunrise the colors are the brightest. I try to go out there every time I visit."

Aubrey threaded her fingers through her wind-swept hair. "I think I'll sleep in this time."

"I'll go," Marley said. "It sounds amazing."

Chris barely let Marley finish before he replied, "Count me in."

"Sunday's my day to sleep," Trevor said. "I'll pass."

Sergei leaned back against the rail and smiled. "What's another day of waking up early? Count me in, too."

A swell of excitement rolled through me, and I faced the water, trying to shake off the sensation. I'd failed miserably in distancing myself from Sergei. After skipping two afternoons at the coffee shop, I'd slipped back into the routine, unable to fight temptation.

The ferry horn blasted, so we made our way to our parked vehicles on the lower deck—girls in my car and guys in Sergei's. Once we docked, Sergei followed me down tree-lined Edgartown Road to the island's ice arena across from the high school.

Inside the rink, a cluster of children, ranging in age from toddlers to tweens, were lacing up skates and filling the air with chatter and laughter. The six of us put on our skates while the club's director corralled the kids and organized them into small groups on the ice. Chris was assigned the tween girls, who blushed and giggled when he introduced himself. I skated over to my group of six and seven-year-olds and clapped my hands.

"Who's ready to have some fun?"

Hands shot up and squeaky voices cried out with enthusiasm. For the next two hours, I taught the kids easy stroking and spinning. Near the end of the session, Sergei's group started to blend into mine, so he and I teamed up to hold their attention.

"What does it feel like when you do a lift?" one of my girls asked.

I opened my arms wide. "It feels like flying."

Sergei crouched to the girl's level. "Do you want to try it?"

She couldn't nod her tiny head fast enough.

Sergei explained to her what they were going to do while she stared wide-eyed at him. A minute later, he flipped her up above his shoulder. She squealed with laughter as Sergei held her up and skated circles around our groups.

A throng of little girls jostled to be next in line. Sergei gave each one of them a trip around the ice, making sure no one was left out. After the last ride, he chuckled as he flexed his neck and shoulders.

"I can skip weight-lifting this week."

I smiled. "I think you gave them the thrill of their lives."

Once we herded everyone off the ice, the director guided us to two long tables for an autograph session. We signed skates, sweatshirts, scraps of paper—anything and everything the kids slid along the table.

Setting off from the rink, we traveled west toward Chilmark on the narrow two-lane road, where we got glimpses of cranberry bogs and lonesome summer cottages. In West Tisbury, I pulled off the road to Alley's General Store, an island landmark.

The old-fashioned country store offered everything an islander might need—groceries, hardware supplies, toys, gifts, even a post office. We loaded our baskets with freshly-made sandwiches, chips, and soda for dinner, and fruit, cereal, and milk for breakfast.

When we arrived at Aunt Debbie and Uncle Joe's, I led everyone to the kitchen to unload the groceries. It amazed me how I always smelled my aunt's honeysuckle perfume in the house, even if she hadn't been there for weeks.

Through the wall of windows facing the back patio, the last rays of sunlight beamed on us as we emptied our paper sacks onto the granite countertop. The open kitchen flowed to the bright living room, where Sergei drifted to the tall bookshelves packed with well-worn novels.

I walked up beside him. "If you think that's a lot of books, you should see my uncle's library in their house in Boston."

Sergei scanned the spines. "I see some Russian authors here."

"Borrow anything you'd like."

A framed photo on the edge of the bookcase grabbed Sergei's eye. He pointed to the small girl on the left of the picture. "Is this you?"

I laughed at the image—my three cousins and I riding the antique carousel in Oak Bluffs. I was seven years old, and in true Eighties' fashion, wearing a big pink bow in my hair and a colorful air brushed T-shirt with the words "Skater Girl."

"Did the obnoxious, tacky shirt give it away?"

"Yes, but also the fact you still have the same smile." He grinned, and I touched my mouth as I dipped my head.

"Em," Aubrey called from the staircase. "Are you and I bunking in the master bedroom?"

"Um . . . yeah. Mar, you can have the guest room. Chris, you and Trev can share the room with the twin beds." I turned to Sergei. "You can take my cousin Trey's room. Just look for the Red Sox shrine."

After stowing our overnight bags and cleaning up, we gathered around the rustic oak table in the kitchen and devoured our dinner. When we later trickled into the living room, Chris spied the stack of board games on the bookshelf and sorted through the boxes.

"I haven't played this in years." He held up *Pictionary*.

"I love that game," Aubrey said. "Let's play."

I opened the gray box and set the miniature hourglass on the coffee table. "Two teams of three?"

Trevor flopped onto one of the two green-striped couches. "I don't wanna be on yours or Aubrey's team."

"That's not very nice," I said.

"You get way too intense. I don't wanna get yelled at every time I make a wrong guess."

Aubrey planted her hands on her hips. "We don't yell."

Chris snorted. "Have you forgotten the last time we played spades? Em had a meltdown when I put down the wrong card."

"Well, if you can't take the heat, we don't want you on our team." I stuck out my tongue at him.

"I'll be on your team." Sergei sat next to me on the couch. "I can handle the pressure."

"Have you played this game before?"

"I have. And I only know how to win."

I matched his confident grin. "Then you'll fit right in with us."

Standing behind Sergei, Aubrey furrowed her brow. I ignored her and went to the foyer closet for the big sketch pad I remembered using with my family during summer game nights.

Each team claimed a sofa, drawing the battle lines. In a physical game, we would've been horribly mismatched. Chris and Trevor, built like typical jocks, both stood almost six feet. Even with diminutive Marley on their side, they would've had a distinct advantage. But brawn wasn't needed in the game; only brains and the ability to draw.

With a strong start, my team took a big lead, but our opponent made a furious comeback. Chris and Trevor's chest bumping and fist pumping had my blood pressure rising. Sergei saw the scowl on my face and patted my denim-clad knee.

"Game's not over yet."

His hand lingered on my leg and I gulped. The sounds of Marley's tinkly laughter and the marker squeaking against the paper faded into the background. Sergei's touch lasted a fleeting moment but long enough to shorten my breath.

I regained focus as Chris and Trevor hopped up, shouting out guesses for Marley's sketch.

"Horse!"

"Dog!"

"Dead dog?"

Time ran out, and Marley drooped onto the sofa. Chris apologized for not guessing *Bambi* and offered to refill her soda. *He's got it so bad.* I squirmed in my seat. *And you know how that feels.*

A few successful turns later, my team landed on the last spot on the game board. One more correct answer and we'd win. Sergei passed me the pile of game cards, and I read the item I needed to draw—*Romeo and Juliet*. Tragic love story... hopefully, not an omen.

With the sands in the hourglass falling rapidly, I hurried to draw the balcony scene. My eyes flashed back and forth to my teammates as I sketched stick figures. Neither Sergei nor Aubrey was having any luck interpreting my rushed artwork. Thinking quickly, I drew a big heart above Romeo's head and locked my eyes on Sergei.

He stood and shouted, *"Romeo and Juliet!"*

"Yes!" I threw my arms in the air and jumped a foot off the shiny wood floor.

Aubrey joined me in a victory jig. After I finished dancing, Sergei put his hands up toward me for a double high-five. I slapped them, and he clasped my fingers.

"Told you we had it." He smiled broadly.

He touched my hands every day during our lessons but not like this. With our fingers intertwined, I felt an intimacy and the undeniable electricity between us. Afraid Sergei could feel my palms sweating, I slid my hands out of his grasp and laughed.

"I don't know how you figured out my scribble scratch."

"That was a fine balcony you drew. Shakespeare would be proud."

Aubrey observed us with a watchful eye. I left Sergei and helped Marley pick up the mess of crumpled paper on the floor. As the group headed for the stairs, I reminded Sergei, Chris, and Marley to set their alarms for pre-dawn. Aubrey and I retreated to the spacious master bedroom, and I programmed five o'clock into the clock radio.

Tying her hair up in a knot, Aubrey said, "The flirting would've been cute if Sergei wasn't your coach."

I threw back the heavy beige comforter and avoided her stare. "We weren't flirting."

"It may have been subtle, but it was definitely flirting." She came around to my side of the king-sized bed. "Em, you can't encourage him. You don't know what kind of game he's playing."

"He's not playing any game. Can't we have fun together without it being an issue?" I stormed into the bathroom and shut the door. *Why does this situation have to be so complicated?*

CLASSICAL MUSIC WOKE ME from my deep sleep. Aubrey made a noise next to me and pulled the comforter over her head. Shutting off the alarm and crawling out of bed, I fumbled in the dark for my jeans and long-sleeved T-shirt. After quickly dressing and making myself presentable, I tiptoed into the hallway. Marley's door was closed, so I knocked softly and opened it. She was buried under the covers, her long brunette tresses fanned across the pillow. I gave her shoulder a gentle shake as I spoke her name.

Her eyes opened just enough for me to see a sliver of brown. "I'll go next time, Em."

"Oh, come on, you've still got time to get dressed."

"I'm sorry, I need sleep," she mumbled.

"Okay. Next time."

I closed the door and pulled a tube of ChapStick from my pocket. As I applied the balm to my lips, Chris emerged from the room across the hall.

"Where's Marley?"

"She wants to sleep."

"Then I'm going back to bed."

He disappeared before I could comment. My stomach danced with anxiety of both the good and bad kind. Now it was just Sergei and me.

I walked downstairs, blinking my contact lenses into place. Sergei entered from the kitchen, and if I wasn't fully awake before, I certainly was now. His black, long-sleeved knit shirt clung to all the right places, and his slightly faded jeans did the same. Even his sleepy eyes had an alluring quality. *How can he look so good at the crack of dawn?*

"Morning." He snapped me out of my thoughts.

"Morning. Marley and Chris bailed, so it's just us."

I couldn't be sure, but I thought his eyes perked up.

He tugged his fleece jacket over his head. "I guess we'd better get going."

"Yeah, I didn't wake up this early just to miss it."

I grabbed my purse and keys from the coffee table, and we walked across the yard to my car. Not surprisingly, no other vehicles traveled the dark, twisting highway to the cliffs. I rolled down the windows to let in the crisp morning air.

After turning onto a small side road, I drove a short distance uphill and parked. Only pale light from the awakening sky lit the area. I popped open the trunk to retrieve the jacket I thought was in there and soon discovered wasn't. The air I'd found refreshing during the drive was now downright chilly. I shivered, and Sergei slipped off his fleece, handing it to me.

"Here, take my jacket."

"Then you'll be cold," I protested.

He smiled. "I'll survive."

As I passed the soft fleece over my head, the jacket enveloped me with Sergei's body heat. It was like experiencing our hug on my terrace all over again. The garment swallowed my petite frame but somehow felt as if it fit perfectly.

I guided us through the brush until we reached a familiar patch of grass and sand high on a bluff.

"Here's the spot." I sat down on the cool grass. Straight ahead, the dark outline of the cliffs rose above Vineyard Sound.

Sergei sat beside me, stretching out his long legs. I was keenly aware of every move he made. Squinting at my watch in the darkness, I said, "It shouldn't be too long from now."

I'd never realized how quiet the area was. Waves swishing onto the beach below provided the only sound. My usual trips to the cliffs included various members of my family cracking jokes over their thermoses of coffee and turning the outing into a party.

This was no family party.

Sergei pressed a button on his camera, and it came alive with a beep. "I forgot to take a picture of all of us with the kids yesterday."

"They were so much fun." I tucked one leg under me. "I loved being back at that rink. I used to train there whenever I came here for vacation."

"Training while on vacation—that's dedication."

"It usually wasn't hard-core training. I just hate being off the ice for more than a day. It's like I need that rush . . . that feeling of gliding and total freedom."

"I know exactly what you mean. It's how I knew I had to coach. I have to be on the ice every day or I feel lost."

"Yes!" I shifted slightly to face Sergei. "People ask me how I can stand to be in a cold rink most of the day, but they don't understand it's home to me and there's nowhere else I'd rather be."

Sergei observed me with the tiniest hint of a smile. One lonely bird chirped in the distance as a faint glow of light peeked over the eastern horizon.

"That's why you're so good," he said. "You have that passion that can't be taught."

The way 'passion' rolled off his tongue gave me goose bumps. I didn't stop to think before I said, "You have it, too."

Sergei's camera beeped and shut off, pulling his eyes from me. He turned it on and stared at the sky. "Looks like the sun's starting to come up."

I plucked a blade of grass and twisted it around my finger, wishing I could wind it around my heart and squeeze out the maddening feelings. Turning my attention to the sky, I watched the streaks of orange become brighter, reflecting in the water and illuminating the rocky cliffs. With each new beam of light, the touches of red, orange, and yellow in the clay grew more visible.

Sergei concentrated on shooting picture after picture of the scenery. We remained silent until Sergei put his camera down and shook his head.

"I've never seen anything like this."

"It's pretty amazing, isn't it?"

He peered at the small LCD screen on the back of his camera and scrolled through the photos. "These came out great. Look at this one."

He angled the camera, and I scooted closer to him. Reaching over his arm, I pointed to the cliffs on the screen. "The clay is so red there."

"It's really beautiful." He looked up at me.

The sun continued its spectacular rise, but our eyes didn't move from one another. In the dawning light, I saw the longing in Sergei's gaze. No one had ever looked at me that way. I was as still as the morning around me, but inside my heart raced.

Sergei's eyes flickered down to my mouth and then met mine again. Slowly, the narrow space between us disappeared. Sergei bent his head, and our lips brushed, seeking each other tentatively. I wanted more, needed more.

Sergei answered, sealing his mouth to mine with a soft intensity. Every nerve ending in my body hummed. I parted my lips, tasting the minty sweetness of Sergei's warm breath.

Kissing him was more intoxicating than I could've dreamed. I never wanted this feeling to end. Never wanted—

Sergei broke away, his breathing ragged. "We can't... I shouldn't have..."

My head reeled, and I stared at Sergei, unable to speak. He pushed his hand through his hair, tousling the short brown locks.

"Em, we can't do this." He rose to his feet.

The exhilaration I'd felt moments before was quickly replaced by a heavy awareness. It sat on my chest, threatening to smother me. Taking a deep breath, I stood up but couldn't bring myself to face Sergei. I looked toward the cliffs, their colorful beauty now a haze.

"I know," I croaked.

"I'm so sorry. I really screwed up," he said, his voice weighed down with regret.

My throat tightened, and I swallowed hard. "It wasn't just you."

He stayed quiet and motionless for a few moments before turning toward the road. "We should go."

I kept my head down until we reached the car, and I glued my eyes to the highway. Sergei and I didn't speak a word the entire drive. I went swiftly ahead of him into the house, and halfway up the stairs realized I was still wearing his jacket. I jerked it over my head, freeing myself from his scent, and draped it over the banister.

I crept through the dark bedroom and slipped into the bathroom, closing the door as quietly as I could. The tears I'd been holding in escaped my eyes, and I sank onto the floor beside the tub. Burying my face against my knees, I cried harder than I ever had.

CHAPTER SIX

A TENTATIVE KNOCK TAPPED ON THE bathroom door, and I lifted my head. Surrounded by darkness, I couldn't see my reflection in the mirror but imagined I must've been a tear-stained, sniveling mess.

"Em? Are you in there?" Aubrey asked.

On my knees, I slid over to the door and let Aubrey in. She flipped on the light and gaped at me.

"What happened?" She dropped beside me onto the tile floor.

I wiped my face with the back of my trembling hand and gave a hoarse reply, "We kissed."

"Who kissed?" Her bleary eyes sprang alert. "You and Sergei?"

I responded with a numb nod.

"Where were Chris and Marley?"

"They didn't go," I whispered.

We sat in silence as Aubrey's mouth hung open but no sound came out. Finally, she rubbed my shoulder and said, "Tell me what happened."

My chest heaved from a weighty breath. "The sunrise

was so beautiful. We were talking, and then everything just… stopped, and we were kissing, and it felt so right. But then…" The lump in my throat strangled me, and I had to swallow before continuing. "Then he pushed me away."

"What did he say?" There was an edge to the concern in her voice.

"He said he was sorry and we can't do this. Which I know, but…" I squeezed my eyes shut to halt the tears, but they refused to be stopped.

"I'm so sorry, Em." Aubrey slipped her arm around me. "Sergei shouldn't have let it get this far. He shouldn't have gotten this close to you."

"I'm to blame, too. I just couldn't stay away from him." I sniffed. "I knew I was falling deeper and deeper, but I couldn't help it."

"He's the coach, though. He needs to set the example."

Hugging my knees to my chest, I closed my eyes, their lashes further dampening my face. Aubrey tightened her hold around my shoulders.

"I think it might be good this happened," she said. "Now, hopefully Sergei's realized he needs to back off."

I shook my head. "It's not good. Before, at least I didn't know what I was missing. Now that I've kissed him, I know how amazing it feels."

"You'll get past this, Em. It's hard right now, but I promise it'll get better."

"If I didn't have to see Sergei every day, I might believe that."

"Do you think he's going to try to talk to you about this?"

"I hope not." I drew my hair back and dried my face again. "I know all the reasons the kiss was a mistake. I really don't feel like hearing him say it."

Aubrey understood and helped me avoid Sergei the rest of the morning. I skipped breakfast and merely exchanged glances with him as we left the house. On the ferry, Aubrey and I stayed in my car to nap during the forty-five minute ride, but I couldn't sleep. I could still taste Sergei's mouth and feel its gentle pressure on mine. I'd been kissed only a few times in my life and never with the level of emotion I'd felt from Sergei. Our connection hadn't been just between our lips but somewhere much deeper.

I fidgeted and tried to think of anything except Sergei—the triple loop throw I'd struggled with at practice the past week, the spaghetti dish I needed to make for potluck dinner at church, the pile of laundry waiting at home. But my mind always found its way back to the cliffs. Back to the moment when everything changed.

THE COMFORTING SMELL OF fresh ice welcomed me to the rink Monday morning. The smooth, clean surface beckoned me, but I had to get loose first. Chris waved as he jogged out of the locker room and around the rink.

After depositing my bag near the bleachers, I followed Chris's path and set off on an easy run. My eyes zipped around the room, stopping when they fell on the object of my search. Sergei stood at the foot of the stairs, talking to Viktor. An all too familiar tightness wrenched my throat. I jogged back and forth on the far side of the rink, dodging any possible confrontation.

An hour later, Chris and I stood on the ice, warmed up and ready for our lesson. Sergei glided before us, and I fiddled with the cap on my water bottle. Normally, I liked the fact he came out on the ice to teach, but today I wanted the boards and one hundred extra feet between us.

"I want to go step by step through the loop," he said. "Something was off last week."

Chris took my hand, and I set my bottle on the boards. Sergei watched as we executed a single rotation of the throw.

"Chris, I think you're gripping Em's waist too high."

He skated over to show us, but instead of taking charge in his standard manner, he hesitated and rubbed the back of his neck before approaching me. Luckily, Chris had bent to tighten his skate lace and missed the awkward moment.

Standing behind me, Sergei put his hands on my hips. All my muscles tensed up, fighting the emotions which needed to be released. *Pull yourself together. You have to push through this.*

Sergei took in a deep breath as his long fingers flexed against my leotard. I exhaled with him and commanded myself, *Focus on the jump, Em. Focus on the jump.*

We went through the motion of the takeoff a few times, Sergei assisting me into the air. With each repetition, I did feel more secure. Chris made sure he was comfortable with the change, and he and I performed a couple of doubles before attempting triples. My rotation was exactly vertical, and I landed all our attempts with ease.

For the rest of the session, we worked on sections of our long program. Every time Sergei touched me, I forced myself to concentrate on the task at hand and to see him as a faceless being, simply a voice of instruction.

Chris and I took a break after the hour-long lesson, and he observed me with knitted brows.

"You're quiet today."

"Huh? Oh... I'm just tired."

"Wild night at the church dinner?"

I broke into a smile, my first of the day. "You know how rowdy we Catholics can get."

He laughed and reached for my hand. "Ready for some double run-throughs?"

Throwing my energy into running our programs helped distract my mind, but gloom returned when the time came for Courtney and Mark's session. In the midst of lacing my skates, I saw a shadow approach from the side of the bleachers. I looked up to find Sergei, his hands stuffed in his jacket pockets. His darting eyes and the tight set of his mouth told me he'd rather be doing anything other than speaking to me.

He sat next to me and surveyed the smattering of parents at the other end of the bleachers. With his eyes trained on the cement floor, he said in a quiet voice, "I want to apologize again for yesterday."

I resumed tying my laces, pulling the strings with extra tautness. "You don't have to."

"I do. I stepped over the line, and I want you to know it won't happen again."

He sounded so composed, so unemotional, so opposite from how he'd been at the cliffs. I had an awful feeling we would never talk that openly and easily again.

"The kids are ready," I said and walked briskly to the ice.

Since I was working with Courtney on her double axel and Sergei was helping Mark with footwork, we didn't have to speak much to each other. I left the rink exhausted, worn out from reining in my emotions all day.

As I curved onto the main highway and passed Starbucks, I thought of Sergei and me sipping our coffee and passionately debating one of the novels he'd loaned me. Tears stung my eyes. There would be no more afternoons like those. Not only had my heart been broken, but I'd also lost a friend.

CHAPTER SEVEN

THE TOP OF THE EIFFEL TOWER appeared in the distance, and I squashed my nose to the taxi window. Chris slid across the narrow backseat and leaned over me to get a look.

"It doesn't look as big as I expected," he said.

Sergei twisted around in the passenger seat. "It's pretty impressive up close."

I sat back and marveled at the ornate stone buildings flashing by as we zipped through late afternoon Paris traffic. Each structure looked like it held a captivating story.

The change of scenery was a welcome relief. The past few weeks had been emotionally draining. Every morning I woke up hoping my feelings for Sergei would've somehow diminished overnight. But when I walked into the rink and saw his face, I couldn't escape the tug on my heart.

The taxi dropped us at the Novotel, the official hotel for our second Grand Prix of Figure Skating event. As we checked in, Drew entered the sleek lobby from the elevator and jogged around a pair of white chairs that appeared too pristine to sit on.

"*Bonjour*, Mademoiselle Emily," he said in an exaggerated

French accent as he wrapped his wiry arms around me.

I laughed, and over Drew's shoulder, I noticed Sergei flick his head in our direction. The desk clerk handed me a room key as Drew and Chris slapped hands.

"What are you guys doing later?" Drew asked.

"Crashing," Chris said. "I couldn't sleep at all on the plane."

Sergei gathered his luggage, and I watched him roll his suitcase across the lobby until Drew got my attention. "Butler, you up for some sight-seeing tonight?"

"Yeah, that sounds fun. What'd you have in mind?"

"Why don't we go see the light show at the Eiffel Tower? We could do dinner and then head over." He raised his eyebrows. "Meet here about six?"

"Works for me."

"Awesome." A smile glowed in his hazel eyes. "See you then."

ON THE WAY DOWNSTAIRS to meet Drew, I slipped my coat over my gray sweater dress and used the elevator mirror to position my red knit cap into place, adjusting and readjusting the hair underneath.

Stop fussing. It's just dinner… or is it?

Drew had emailed and called me quite a few times since Skate America, expressing his excitement about hanging out in Paris. After the way we'd danced at the closing party, I wasn't sure of his expectations. *Stop analyzing everything and have fun.*

I exited the elevator and scanned the lobby for Drew. He wasn't there, but Sergei was seated near the entrance, talking to Ron, a grizzly veteran pairs coach. I stood near the large windows facing the street and played with my cell phone. Meanwhile, Sergei wrapped up his conversation and strolled toward me.

"Waiting for someone?"

"Drew." I dropped the phone into my purse. "We're going to dinner."

"Where's Chris?"

I shrugged. "Probably in his room."

"He's not going with you?" Sergei rubbed his chin as he examined me.

"No. Is that a problem?"

He paused and folded his arms, looking unaffected by the chill in my question. "No, just asking."

Drew walked up and greeted Sergei. "Hey, how's it going?"

Sergei's eyes remained on me a moment. "Good."

"Ready to go?" Drew asked me.

"Yep, I'm starving." I wound my scarf around my neck and said a quick goodbye to Sergei. Since the morning at the cliffs, many of our conversations followed that pattern—brief exchanges with an undercurrent of tension. Gone were the days of our easy banter.

Drew and I took a taxi to the restaurant he'd recommended, and the eatery looked just as I'd envisioned a Parisian café would—tiny round tables bunched together, wrought iron chandeliers, and wine flowing among all the patrons. The smell of freshly baked bread warmed the entire room.

Drew smiled as I removed my cap and fluffed my hair.

"You look very pretty tonight." He took off his coat and stammered, "Not that you don't always look nice."

My face flushed, so I concentrated on putting the linen napkin in my lap. "Thanks." I snuck a peek at Drew's outfit before he sat down. His white oxford shirt hung loosely over his slender physique, and his black pants needed a bit more ironing, but he'd made an admirable effort.

The waiter placed menus in front of us, and I stared at the jumble of foreign words. All I recognized were *pain* for bread and *fromage* for cheese.

I peered over my menu. "I hope you know French because I took Spanish in high school."

"*Oui, oui*. I aced four years of French."

"Oh, good. I didn't want to end up eating liver or cow tongue."

"How do you know I won't tell you something is chicken when it's actually cow tongue?" His eyebrows danced as he flashed a mischievous smile.

"You do that, and this night will be over real quick." I laughed and pointed to the door.

"Then let's stick to something simple. The crepes here are really good."

Good didn't begin to describe the light and flavorful pancake. With asparagus wrapped inside and a creamy cheese sauce ladled on top, the crepe excited all my taste buds.

"I'm lucky I have a fast metabolism." I licked my fork. "Otherwise, all this cheese probably wouldn't be a good idea."

"One crepe can't hurt. After all, how often do you get to eat real French *fromage*?" Drew brought out the accent again.

I giggled and took a sip of water. One thing I could count on with Drew was laughter. Every time I talked to him, he made stories that weren't meant to be funny sound hilarious.

The antique clock on the far wall caught my eye, and I noted the time. "We need to go soon to make the light show."

When the bill arrived, Drew fought with me to let him pay for my dinner. Before I could protest any longer, he gave the waiter a stack of Euros.

"Thank you." I buttoned my coat. "This place was amazing."

He smiled and handed me my hat. "I thought you'd like it."

We walked a few blocks to the Eiffel Tower to wait for the show at the top of the hour. Our breath formed small white clouds as we talked. I stared up at the landmark, speechless at its size. While standing at the base of the monument, Drew put his arm around me, and I slowly relaxed against him.

"Chris is going to regret he didn't come, especially when I tell him about the food."

"I'm kinda glad he didn't," Drew said with a shy crook to his grin.

I pretended to be fascinated with the fringe of my scarf until a burst of dazzling light took over the Tower and I gasped. The brilliance of the glow resembled a million fireworks being shot into the sky. The couple next to me shared a kiss, and my heart twitched.

I wanted the arm around me to be Sergei's.

It can't happen, I reminded myself. *Move on.*

Drew and I lingered near the Tower after the show, taking in the sights and playing a game of guessing where the tourists were from.

"It's too bad we don't have more time to see the city," Drew said. "But I guess we wouldn't be here if we didn't have to skate."

"I wish I could go to Notre Dame Cathedral and light a few candles for a medal. Chris and I have to finish at least third to qualify for the Grand Prix Final."

"You guys will get it for sure. I'll be happy if I finish top six."

"You'll do great." I touched his elbow. "You skated really well at Skate America."

I envied the fact he wasn't performing with the burden of expectations. Since our silver medal at Skate America, I'd felt growing pressure to stand on the podium in Paris. The federation, the judges, the media—they all had a close eye on us. If Chris and I qualified for the prestigious Final, we'd compete against the top five teams in the world.

Now occupied with thoughts of the competition, I desired the warmth of my hotel room. "I'm starting to lose feeling in my face. Why don't we find a cab?"

At the hotel, I rocked back and forth on the heels of my boots as we waited for the elevator. I didn't know what Drew had in mind for a goodnight parting. The doors shut, enclosing us in the confined space, and I decided to take charge.

"Thank you again for dinner." I hugged him, resting my chin on the shoulder of his wool coat. "This was a lot of fun."

He held me close, letting his cheek brush against my hair. "I had an awesome time, too."

The elevator chimed for my floor, and I extracted myself from Drew's embrace, scooting into the doorway. He looked disappointed I'd distanced myself so quickly.

"Have a good night," I said.

He shuffled forward and held the door. "I'll be around the arena tomorrow after practice, so I'll probably see you there."

And I did see him, quite often the next few days. He watched all my practices, cheered Chris and me to a third place finish in the short program, and ate dinner with us at the hotel every night. His sense of humor kept me entertained and took my mind off worrying about the free skate.

The World Champions, Russians Oksana Leonova and Denis Romanov, were the leaders going into the long program. During the six-minute warm-up, I was setting up for the triple Lutz, and the pair barreled through my path, cutting me off. I braked and spun around, shaving a layer off the ice. Chris skated over from the opposite end of the rink, where he'd been practicing his spin.

"You okay?"

"Yeah." I smoothed the short skirt of my ivory dress. "That's the second time they've been on my tail. Guess they think we should all clear out of the way for them."

We finished the warm-up with a couple of clean throw jumps and then followed our competitors backstage. My right eye watered from the dryness of my contact lens, so I hurried to the locker room for some drops. Oksana was standing in front of one of the full-length mirrors, squirting hair spray over her flaming red bun. Her hair was pulled so tight I didn't think any strands had a chance of escaping.

I stood beside her to use the adjacent mirror, and she tilted her chin upward. Her heavily mascara-ed eyes sized me up as her mouth puckered with distaste.

"You have Russian coach, you think you skate like Russian?" she asked in her thick accent.

I held the bottle of eye drops aloft, contemplating whether to ignore her. My competitive fire wouldn't let me.

"We skate like Americans," I said to her reflection in the mirror.

"American good single skater, not good pair skater. Pair skating more than jump and spin."

I forced my lips together, clamping in the snarky response I wanted to give. It'd been a long time since someone had tried to intimidate me in the locker room. Not since I was a junior skater and some snotty girls had teased me about choking in competitions.

Squeezing two drops into my eye, I blinked until I had clear vision and then gave Oksana a hard glare. "We'll see."

Her criticism bounced through my mind as Chris and I began our program. Extra adrenaline pumped through my veins, and I attacked our opening jumps with a surge of power. Too much power. I over-rotated the jump, throwing myself off balance and stumbling through the landing.

Settle down.

I fell into step with Chris, and our forward crossovers tracked in unison. When I'd learned the fundamentals of pairs skating, tracking had been one of the first lessons, and my blades had collided with Chris's quite a few times. Now, our skates moved together like two halves of a whole.

We conquered the next minute of the program and cruised into our side-by-side flying sit spins. I started spinning, and in the blur around me, I saw Chris standing still. He'd missed the whole element. When I straightened up and put my hand in his, he muttered, "Rut."

After we finished with no other errors, Chris stared at the spot on the ice where his spin should've been centered. He pasted a smile on his face as we bowed and waved to the audience.

"Freaking rut in the ice," he told Sergei when we joined him in the kiss and cry.

Sergei patted him on the back and gave me a one-arm hug, the same as he'd given me after the short program. It was so fast our bodies hardly touched. *I guess that's how it's going to be from now on.*

Our scores put us in third place, but the current fourth place team still had to skate. With our mistakes, the Germans could easily bump us off the podium if they skated clean. I paced along the corridor backstage with my hands on hips, shaking my head at the stupid blunder on the Lutz.

Chris sat in front of the TV monitor, watching the German pair, while Sergei came up beside me.

"Em, don't beat yourself up."

I stopped and exhaled a long breath. "I had too much energy."

"I'd rather you have too much energy than not enough."

A smile played on his lips, and my posture relaxed. Through the babble of skaters, coaches, and volunteers milling backstage, Chris's excited voice burst forth.

"We got third!"

He picked me up in a bear hug, and I squealed with delight. As soon as he set me down, another pair of hands grabbed my waist from behind. I twirled, and Drew pulled me into an embrace.

"Congratulations!"

"Same to you! I'm sorry I didn't get to see you after you skated. I had to go back to the hotel to do my makeup and stuff."

"Yeah, fourth place was better than I expected, so I'm super happy."

I turned around and Sergei and Chris were shaking hands, but Sergei didn't make any move to congratulate me. He just gave me a smile and bobbed his head.

"Good fight tonight," he said to both of us. "Great effort."

The Germans' coach tapped Sergei on the shoulder and shook his hand. They started talking, and Drew slid closer to me.

"Celebration dinner later?" He looked back and forth from me to Chris.

I nodded. "Definitely."

Oksana wove around us and shot me a disdainful look, as if I wasn't fit to polish her skates. She had no idea she was giving me more motivation. The World Champs had captured another gold medal to add to their stuffed trophy case, but I believed the tide was going to shift soon. It was time for the Russian dominance in pairs to end.

AS WAS ALWAYS THE case with Chris and Drew at the dinner table, we spent the meal laughing as much as eating, and by the end of the night my sides ached. We walked back to the hotel from the nearby café, and Drew stopped me before we reached the double glass doors.

"Can we hang here for a minute?"

Chris took the hint and bid us goodnight. A group of Canadian skaters piled out the entrance and strolled down the sidewalk, their chatter trailing behind them in the frosty air.

I stuck my hands in my coat pockets and gave Drew a tentative smile. We hadn't been alone since our date. Without Chris around, Drew might act more than just friendly. I chewed on my lip as he stepped closer to me.

He's nice, cute, and fun. Give him a chance.

"It looks a little crowded in there." Drew jerked his thumb toward the hotel.

The large windows revealed a mixture of skaters and fans jumbled around the art deco furniture. Flashbulbs popped continuously as the athletes posed for photos.

I laughed as a pack of teenage girls swarmed around my partner. "Chris just got mobbed."

"I bet you guys are going to get that a lot at Nationals with it being in Boston."

"That week's going to be nuts. My mom said she'll try to keep my family under control. I've got some crazy distant cousins, and they're all going to be there."

Drew shifted his weight on the soles of his sneakers. "I'm glad it's less than two months away. I'll need my Emily fix." I dipped my head, and he inched toward me. "It's been great hanging out this week."

I looked up at him, and the brightness in his eyes made me smile. "You're sweet, you know that?"

"Sweet enough for a goodnight kiss?" His eyebrows lifted as he grinned.

My over-analytical brain was about to take over, but I squashed all thoughts and leaned into Drew, looping my arms around his neck. As I closed my eyes, a flash of Sergei's face appeared, and I pressed my lips to Drew's, wanting to feel the fireworks I'd experienced at the cliffs. But they never came. Only a nice comforting sensation settled over me.

Our lips broke apart, and I nestled my face against Drew's collar. A few yards away, two figures darkened the doorway of the hotel. Ron stepped onto the sidewalk first, lighting a cigarette, and Sergei followed, his eyes trained on Drew and me. From his penetrating gaze, I suspected he'd seen the kiss.

But why should it matter?

CHAPTER EIGHT

"I'M DREAMING OF A DRY CHRISTMAS," I said to Chris, mimicking the classic holiday tune playing over the bookstore's loud speaker. We'd had nothing but rain and sleet for a week, and the gloomy weather wasn't helping me get into the holiday spirit.

"Maybe it'll actually snow soon," Chris said, always the optimist.

"With the luck I'm having this week, there'll probably be a blizzard right over my house."

Chris laughed as he picked up a coffee table book about ballparks and flipped through the glossy pages. "Overreacting much?"

"Shall I recap the list of my disasters? Sunday, my oven breaks in the middle of baking fifty cookies for the Christmas party. Monday, I slice both thumbs with my blades, and yesterday, I drop my groceries in a huge puddle." I ticked off each calamity on my fingers. "Drew asked if I'd walked under a ladder or broken a mirror."

"You been talking to Drew a lot?"

I ran my fingers along the cover of another baseball-themed book. "Kinda." I may not have felt sparks with Drew in Paris, but he was so easy to talk to and joke with.

"Hey, guys!"

Marley stood at the end of our aisle. Chris shut the book, putting his full attention on her, and a bright smile burst onto his face. "Hey."

She beamed back at him, and I suddenly felt like an outsider.

"Are you Christmas shopping?" she asked.

"Yeah, we're looking for a present for Sergei," Chris said.

"That's sweet. Zach and I aren't getting Viktor anything. I wouldn't even know what he likes."

"I don't think Aubrey and Nick are getting him anything either," I said.

Marley shifted the stack of three hardbacks in her arms and checked her watch. "Eek! I need to get to ballroom lessons. Have fun shopping!" Her warm brown eyes stayed on Chris as she backed out of the aisle.

When she was gone, I pinched Chris's arm. "When are you ever going to ask that girl out?"

"When I'm ready," he mumbled and rubbed the sleeve of his thin sweater. "But I'm not sure if she wants to go out with me."

"Are you blind?" I waved my hand in front of his eyes. "Don't you see how smiley she is around you lately? I swear, guys can be so dense sometimes."

"Why do you want me to ask her out so bad?"

"Because if two people like each other and nothing's stopping them from being together, then they should go for it." The insistence in my voice came from a very deep source of frustration, one that had nothing to do with Chris.

"Alright, alright, chill out." He rested one arm on the shelf and stared at the display of sports books. "Maybe I'll ask her to a movie this weekend."

"Yes!" I clapped my hands.

The shoppers near us gave me curious looks, and Chris covered my hands with his, snuffing my applause. "Let's look for Sergei's gift." He led me toward the fiction aisles. "Doesn't he read old books?"

"You mean classics?" I asked with a dry laugh. "Yes, he does."

Problem was, I didn't know which particular books he'd read lately. He used to share all his literary finds with me, but that was when our conversations consisted of more than five sentences. *Oh, well. It's not my problem if we buy him something he already has.*

We passed the entertainment section, and I noticed a gold-colored book jacket with Sting's picture and the title *Lyrics.* I picked up the book and thumbed through its pages. Chris discovered I'd stopped, and he backtracked to me.

"What's that?"

"It looks like it has the lyrics to all of Sting's and The Police's songs plus the stories behind them."

I couldn't deny my rush of excitement from finding this perfect gift. Sergei would love it. And he might think of me whenever he read it. *Ugh, every time I try to make myself not care, I get sucked back in.*

Chris got distracted by a book on grunge rock, so I read the page in front of me with the song "Fragile." I remembered when Sting had sung the ballad at the concert. It was after the rain began. The scene played like a movie in my head—Sting's rich voice carrying through the humid air, while Sergei sat so close to me I could smell his cologne and see the rain drops tracing a path down his cheekbone and along his strong jaw.

My breath stuck in my throat and I closed the book.

"You wanna get that for Sergei?" Chris asked.

"Huh?" I blinked at him. "Oh. Yeah, let's get it."

THE NEXT DAY, I hounded Chris before and after practice about asking Marley out. "One more day until the weekend. Better get a move on."

He gave me a look that said "Back off."

After finishing my weight training, I went out to the rink and sat on the bleachers to watch one of Sergei's junior teams practice. They were working on speed and power, and Sergei was racing around the ice, making the pair keep pace with him. His long, lean body moved with superb ease over his blades.

Courtney climbed up to my row with her skates in hand, and I gave my young student a smile.

"What's up, chickadee?"

"I'm ready to do two clean run-throughs today," she said with determination.

"Now, that's the kind of attitude I love."

She took off her sneakers and set her eyes on the ice. "Sergei is such an awesome skater. I wonder why he quit so young."

"I don't know. He never talks about it. He and Elena had just won Junior Worlds when they retired. No one seems to know why."

"You've never asked him?"

"No, I figured it must be a sore subject because he never mentions it."

Since I'd met Sergei, I'd been curious about his skating career and why he'd quit when he was eighteen. But the few times Chris or I had brought up his partnership with Elena, Sergei had quickly diverted the conversation. I assumed the split hadn't been amicable.

Through the blue double doors from the lobby, Aubrey waltzed in, carrying a large crystal vase of flowers. She approached us with a big smile.

"Em, these were delivered to the office for you."

"They're so pretty!" Courtney cried.

I hopped down and took the card from the bouquet as Aubrey set the vase on the bleachers. Bending over, I sniffed the sunflowers, and the scent of summer filled my nose, taking me away from the dreary winter and into my mom's garden.

I slipped the tiny card out of its envelope and read the note to myself.

Thought you might need some sunshine—Drew.

Aubrey read over my shoulder and said, "He's a doll."

"Who's a doll?" Courtney asked as she pulled on her skates.

"Drew Henry," Aubrey said.

"Ooh, he's cute."

I fingered one of the smooth sunflower petals, and my heart warmed at Drew's thoughtfulness. The only flowers I'd ever received were from my family at competitions.

"I need to call him," I said and brought the vase into the locker room.

Drew didn't answer, so I left a message. "Hey, I got your flowers, and they're so beautiful. They've definitely brightened my day... my whole week. Thank you *so* much. I'll talk to you soon."

After Courtney and Mark's session, I stored my skates in the locker room, put on my down jacket, and picked up the flowers to bring home. Sergei was walking out of the rink ahead of me, and he held the door. I thanked him as we strode out into the frigid evening.

He glanced up at the sky. "Looks like the rain has finally stopped."

"It's about time," I said. Was he intentionally not commenting on the huge floral arrangement in my hands?

Sergei walked toward his car, and I took a step toward mine, gazing at the bouquet. My feet flew out from under me, and I landed hard on my bottom while the vase crashed to the ground, spraying glass and flowers across the slush-covered pavement.

"Em!" Sergei cried, hurrying over and crouching next to me. "Are you okay?"

My tailbone throbbed, similar to when I'd first practiced triple jumps and spent more time on my butt than in the air.

"Yeah, I'll just be a little sore tomorrow."

"Let me help you up." Sergei held my arm, and I stood gingerly. As soon as I was upright, he released me from his grasp.

I stared at the broken vase and scattered flowers lying in half-frozen puddles. My little bit of sunshine was now a wet, dirty mess.

"They're all ruined," I lamented.

"Don't worry about the stupid flowers." His voice rose with intensity. "You could've really been hurt."

"They're not stupid!"

I bent down to try to salvage the bouquet. When I reached for one of the stems, Sergei squatted next to me and touched my hand.

"Em, there's glass everywhere," he said softly. "Let me pick them up."

He pulled his hand away, and I stood back as he retrieved every single flower, deftly avoiding the shards of glass. Meanwhile, the rink manager came out, saw the potential hazard, and went to get a broom.

"We can wrap them in some paper towels," I said.

Sergei followed me inside and through the swinging door to the snack bar. The café was full of noisy teenagers sipping on sodas and sharing baskets of french fries.

I grabbed a handful of napkins from the counter as Sergei laid the flowers on an empty table. Bundling the stems together, I folded three layers of paper around them.

"What's the occasion… for the flowers?" he asked.

"I've just had a bad week."

"Anything I can do to help?"

We looked up from the table at the same time. Sergei's

eyes showed genuine concern, and I lost myself in their sea of blue.

You can take me in your arms and never let go.

I lowered my eyes and tightened the napkins around the flowers. "It's just been one of those weeks when everything goes wrong. Drew thought I needed a little pick-me-up."

Sergei's jaw clenched and he didn't say anything further as we made our second attempt to leave for the day.

"Thanks for helping with the flowers," I said.

"Sure. Watch your step from now on, okay?" He gave me the same concerned look as earlier.

I walked head down to my car, watching for any slick patches. As I placed the flowers on the floor mat of my backseat, I thought how fitting it was I'd turned Drew's gift into yet another disaster. But there'd been one thin silver lining—seeing how worried Sergei was when I fell.

Of course he cares. You're his student.

And nothing more.

CHAPTER NINE

"I STILL CAN'T BELIEVE YOU HAVE to skate on Christmas. Today is the Lord's birthday," Mom said as she loaded dirty plates into the dishwasher.

"Nationals is only a few weeks away." I handed her the grill pan from the stove. "And I got to spend Christmas Eve and this morning with you and Dad. Sergei made sure we had time with our families."

I wiped the tile-covered island with a dishrag and watched Mom scrub the pan in the sink. We'd just finished our customary Christmas breakfast of pancakes and baked pancetta. Being home in Brookline and partaking in my family's holiday traditions was exactly what I needed before the Nationals frenzy began.

"When are Chris's parents going back to Baltimore?" Mom asked.

"Tonight. Dr. Grayden's on duty at the hospital tomorrow."

Dad came down the stairs, pulling an old knit cap over his thinning gray hair. Slipping into the mud room off the kitchen, he grabbed his jacket and gloves.

"I'm going out to scrape the ice off Em's car."

I planted a kiss on his cheek. "Thanks, Dad."

He went out the back door, sending a blast of cold air into the warm, cozy room. I perched on the stool next to the island, my favorite spot in the kitchen.

"Did I tell you Chris and Marley went out on a date? Well, actually, three dates now. They've become inseparable."

Mom twisted her neck to look at me. "What do you think about that?"

"I think it's great. He's been crushing on her so long, I'm glad they're finally going out. They're really cute together."

"You're not worried Chris will get distracted?"

"Chris? Distracted? This is the guy who can tell jokes five minutes before he competes and then nail every element. He's incapable of being distracted."

"He really is the best partner you could ask for."

I picked up the dishrag and folded it into a neat square. "Believe me, I thank God every day he chose to skate with me when he could've found a more experienced partner."

Mom shut off the sink and dried her hands on her yellow apron, one I'd given her a few years ago. It was embroidered with the message *Don't Mess With the Cook*. I'd thought it was fitting since my mother was not someone to mess with in general.

She stood beside the island and patted my hand. "I have to say, even though I was upset you didn't take the scholarship to Boston University and you postponed college, I think you made the right decision switching to pairs. There's a glow about you now when you compete."

I smiled. "That's because I'm not scared to death anymore. Having Chris out there with me is so comforting. And you know the coaches I had growing up were great technically but not so much with the psychological stuff. Sergei's helped me tons with my confidence."

"He definitely has the magic touch with you."

I stifled a snort. *He's touched something for sure.*

"We should've invited Sergei to dinner at Aunt Deb's last night," Mom continued. "It must be hard for him, not seeing his family at the holidays."

No doubt he would've declined that invitation faster than Mom could deliver it.

"I heard him say he was having dinner with another coach and his family."

"Still, it's a shame he doesn't have someone to spend the holidays with. He's such a nice, good-looking guy. I'm surprised women aren't lining up to date him, but I guess he's pretty engrossed in his job."

The thought of Sergei with a woman made my breakfast rise to my throat. I jumped down from the stool and poured myself a fresh glass of apple juice to wash away the sour taste.

Once Dad finished defrosting my car, I got on the road to the Cape. As I drove, I thought about the next time I'd travel that highway—the trip to Nationals in Boston in three weeks.

With our strong showing in the Grand Prix series, Chris and I were the favorites to win. The championship was a title we needed to cement ourselves as contenders for a medal at the World Championships in March. And a medal at Worlds would make us one of the top teams going into next season. The Olympic season. Every competition was a building block for the potentially life-changing event. Sergei always reminded us not to look ahead, but I knew how crucial winning Nationals was to the big picture.

A blaring car horn startled me from my thoughts, and I realized I'd started drifting into the next lane. I gripped the steering wheel harder and jerked it to the right, my leather gloves squeaking against it. Easing my push on the accelerator, I exhaled and shook my head. *Can't win anything if you don't make it to practice alive.*

MY BLADE HIT THE ice, carving a deep groove, and I reached for Chris's hand. He lifted me into the air, and I suppressed another laugh at the Santa hat he'd worn to practice.

Aubrey and Nick whizzed past us, concentrating on their midline footwork sequence. Moving in the opposite direction were Marley and Zach, executing circular steps. Those two couples were the only company we had on the ice.

We struck our ending pose, and Chris exclaimed, "Perfect run-through! Merry Christmas, Sergei!"

Sergei applauded and skated over to us. "Not quite perfect. There were a couple of little things, but it was very good."

"Can't you humor us for once?" Chris asked. "It *is* Christmas."

Even Sergei couldn't keep a straight face looking at Chris. He cleared his throat, trying to regain composure. "I do appreciate you both coming in and cutting short your day with your families. You did a great job today. We'll pick it up bright and early tomorrow morning."

"Before we go, we have something for you," I said. "Can you meet us in the lounge in a few minutes?"

Chris and I changed out of our skates in the locker room and headed upstairs. The lounge was void of the usual crowd of skating moms peering through the glass with critical eyes at their kids on the ice. Sergei stood alone beside the water cooler.

"You didn't have to get me anything," he said.

"We wanted to solidify our position as your favorite students." Chris's face locked into a grin.

With a bounce in my step, I handed Sergei the present. He smiled as he tore the shiny red and gold wrapping paper. Flipping through the pages of the book, his smile stretched wider.

"This is so cool. I didn't know Sting had made a book like this. Thank you." I tried to contain my goofy grin of excitement as he continued, "Em, I'll have to let you borrow it when I'm done. I know you'll enjoy it, too."

He smiled at me and another little piece of my heart crumbled. I hadn't received many of those smiles lately.

Chris balled together the shredded wrapping paper from the counter and swished it into the trash can with a basketball toss. "I'm gonna wait downstairs for Marley." He gave me a hug. "Merry Christmas. Same to you, Sergei."

Sergei waved as Chris walked to the stairs. "Enjoy the rest of the holiday."

The room was silent except for the hum of the vending machines. Sergei opened the book again.

"I'm really looking forward to reading this. I'm guessing you picked it out?"

"When I saw it on the shelf, I knew I had to get it."

He slowly closed the cover. "I, um, I have something for you, too, since you've been such a big help with Courtney and Mark."

"Oh." Blood rushed to my cheeks, and a smile formed on my lips. "You didn't have to. I was just doing my job."

"A really great job," Sergei insisted. "The present's in the staff office if you want to wait here."

My pulse thumped faster with anticipation each second Sergei was gone. When he returned, he held a large square gift covered in silver paper.

"Merry Christmas."

The present was heavier than I expected. I set it on the nearest table and ripped away the thin wrapping, uncovering an unmarked cardboard box.

"Hmm, mysterious," I said and opened one end of the box.

Sliding my fingers inside, I gripped what felt like a frame and pulled it out. Before me was the print of Beacon Hill I'd admired in the gift shop on Main Street when I'd helped Sergei shop for his mother.

My mouth hung open as I stared at the picture. I raised my eyes to Sergei. "You remembered."

He didn't answer right away. His eyes darted from me to the print and back to me. "You seemed to really like it."

"I know, but that was months ago, and we looked at a lot of prints that day."

"I was hoping you hadn't bought it already." He continued to sidestep my amazement.

"No, I still have the spot above my desk for it." I gazed at the enchanting scene of a rainy evening on Beacon Hill. "Thank you so much. It's a very thoughtful gift."

He gave me a little nod. "You're welcome."

Under ordinary circumstances, a hug would be appropriate, but I couldn't be responsible for what I might do if I got that close to Sergei. I slid the picture into its box and discarded the gift wrap.

"Did you have a good Christmas Eve?" I asked.

"Yeah, Will's wife cooked a great dinner. It's still a little strange for me, celebrating now instead of after the New Year."

"Oh, right, because Christmas is in January in Russia. Well, you could celebrate twice, have double the fun," I said with a smile.

Sergei laughed, and I wondered if maybe there was some holiday magic happening, allowing us to chat comfortably once again.

"How was your time with your family?"

"It was great. Aunt Deb and Uncle Joe cooked an Italian feast last night." Sergei's eyes widened as I spoke. "There were five different pasta dishes and homemade cannoli. You would've loved—" I stopped myself and then finished quietly, "Loved it."

Sergei took a noticeable swallow. "It sounds great."

I picked up my present and held the box with both arms. "Thanks again for the picture. I'm going to hang it up as soon as I get home."

"I'm headed out, too," he said, turning toward the stairs.

He trailed behind me on the steps, and I went in the direction of the locker room to get my purse. Marley and Chris were standing next to the boards, laughing and touching each other's hands in the fun-new-relationship kind of way I'd seen others do. Little cartoon hearts practically floated above their heads.

I smiled at their giddiness, but a pang of envy snuck up on me. If only things could be that easy for Sergei and me.

CHAPTER TEN

Aubrey breezed into our Boston hotel room and tugged on the hem of my black fitted blazer. "Look at you, Miss Professional Coach."

Laughing, I smoothed the mauve silk blouse under my jacket. "Tonight's a big night. Courtney and Mark could be my first medal-winning students."

"They're doing awesome for their first Nationals," Aubrey said, turning on the TV. "I'll be there with the whole gang cheering for them."

I sat on the bed and pulled on my tall leather boots. "How was your practice?"

"It was good. There were about five fans watching."

"There'll be a lot more by the end of the week." I rose and checked my black skirt for lint. "I'm going down to Court's room to do her hair and makeup."

"Tell her good luck for me."

Grabbing my coat and purse, I headed toward the door. "Will do!"

Courtney's parents had gone downstairs to the lobby, giving Courtney and me privacy. As we'd done before the short program the prior night, we spread the cosmetic products around the bathroom sink, and I positioned my young student in front of the mirror. Courtney was going through the gawky phase most twelve-year-olds experience, and I wanted her to feel pretty and confident when she and Mark took the ice.

She was unusually quiet as I applied light pink blush to her fair cheeks.

"Talk to me, girlie," I said.

Her blond head dipped. "I'm really scared I'm gonna mess up, and if we drop out of fourth place, we won't win a medal."

She's like a mini-me.

"I'll tell you what Sergei always says to me. Let your body take over, and it'll stop your mind from getting in the way."

"You make it sound so easy."

I placed a reassuring hand on her shoulder. "You're gonna do great. Think about all the clean run-throughs you've done at home. You can do this program in your sleep."

She stared in the mirror, and I watched her green eyes narrow with resolve. When she faced me, they enlarged with gratitude. "I'm so glad Sergei asked you to work with us. He's cool and all, but it's great having you to talk to."

I hugged her, careful not to mess up her makeup. "Anytime you need me, I'm here."

She smiled, revealing the clear plastic braces covering her teeth. As I brushed a light coat of mascara onto her lashes, she asked, "You're gonna keep working with us next season, right? I know it'll be busy for you with the Olympics."

"As long as Sergei thinks it's okay, I'm definitely planning on it."

"He will. You guys make a great team."

I paused between brush strokes. "You think so, huh?"

"Yeah. You know, how sometimes he'll come up with an

idea for a move, and you'll start showing us before he even finishes talking… like you can read his mind."

Oh, how I'd love to read his mind. Or maybe not. In our situation, ignorance might indeed be bliss.

Courtney continued babbling, "You should coach together full-time after you win the Olympics."

I laughed. "You sound pretty confident Chris and I will win."

"Aren't you always telling me to have more confidence?"

I set down the mascara and picked up a tube of lipstick. "Yes, I am. Point well taken. Now, I need you to be quiet for a minute while I put on your lipstick."

After one last check of Courtney's makeup, I rolled her long, curly hair into a neat bun and spritzed it with hair spray. Squeezing her shoulders, I gave her a broad smile.

"Let's go have some fun."

The novice-level events were being held at Matthews Arena on the campus of Northeastern University, a smaller venue than the twenty thousand-seat Fleet Center, where Chris and I would compete later in the week. When it was time for Courtney and Mark to skate, Sergei and I took our positions next to the ice. I felt very official standing by the boards with him, and I could picture myself down the road doing it full-time and loving it.

As Courtney and Mark began their program, I slid my sweaty palms back and forth along the smooth paper-covered barrier. The kids set up for the side-by-side double axels, and I inhaled a short breath. They completed the jumps, but Courtney spun out of the landing, wearing a look of panic. I patted the boards and tapped the heels of my boots. *Come on, keep it together, Court.*

The *Sleeping Beauty* ballet music built to a high, and Mark propelled Courtney across the ice for the throw double loop. I didn't breathe as she twirled in the air. She came down on one foot and opened her arms out wide, a smile as big as I'd ever seen on her face. I clutched Sergei's forearm and squealed but kept my eyes glued to the ice.

With each executed element, I pumped my free hand into a fist, while Sergei slapped the boards. As our students hit their final pose, I screamed and turned to Sergei, tears clouding my vision. I realized I was still squeezing the sleeve of his suit jacket and quickly let go.

"Sorry," I said, laughing and crying at the same time.

"It's okay." He smiled and put his arm around me. "It's hard not to get excited."

We must've looked like beaming parents as we waited for the kids in the kiss and cry. Courtney jumped into my arms before I could hand over her skate guards.

I embraced her and sniffed back tears. "I'm so proud of you."

I hugged Mark next and told him the same thing. He and Courtney chattered with excitement as we listened to the scores and then went backstage to wait for the results. We huddled around the monitor, watching the final two couples perform.

I clasped my hands together and held them under my chin, hoping to see Courtney and Mark's names no lower than fourth place, the pewter medal position. Sergei stood beside me, rubbing his knuckles.

A blank blue screen filled the monitor, and a second later, the standings popped up.

"Fourth place!" Courtney screeched.

I added to her screeching and smothered the kids in hugs. When I faced Sergei, he draped his arms around my shoulders.

"I can't thank you enough for your help."

"You're welcome."

I put my hands on his waist, and he shuffled backward. Courtney shook my arm as she jumped up and down, and I grinned at her, moving past the awkwardness with Sergei. I'd become a pro at that.

At the medal ceremony, Sergei and I stood in the kiss and cry, snapping photos. "Look how adorable they are," I said as Courtney and Mark accepted their enormous bouquets of flowers.

Sergei laughed. "They might sleep with their medals tonight."

I lowered my camera and gazed at the podium. "I don't think I've ever been prouder of anyone in my life."

"Now you know how I feel when you and Chris skate."

Our eyes met, and I felt the unmistakable connection between us. As quickly as the moment arrived, it vanished when the winning team's coach came over with congratulations.

THE FOLLOWING EVENING, COURTNEY and Mark's mothers treated Sergei and me to a celebratory dinner with the kids. My suggestion of Panificio, an Italian bistro on Beacon Hill, was a hit with everyone in our party. As Courtney and Mark finished their pizzas and the rest of us cleaned our plates of pasta, Courtney's mom Karen said she would call two taxis for the return trip to the Sheraton Back Bay.

Sergei dabbed his mouth with his linen napkin. "Actually, I have something I want to talk to Emily about." He focused his eyes on me. "Can you stay for a cup of coffee? We can get a cab back after."

I sat up a little straighter. "Sure."

By the time Courtney, Mark, and their mothers left, my heart was hammering from the suspense. I specified decaf for my coffee because I couldn't afford to lose any sleep the night before my competition. Plus, I was already hyped up enough, being in the romantic setting with Sergei. The small room was softly lit, allowing us to see out the wall of windows onto Charles Street, where tiny white lights twinkled in the trees.

Only one other couple occupied a table near the door, so it felt as if we had the whole place to ourselves.

Across the candlelit table, Sergei's blue eyes reminded me of two sparkling sapphires. He nudged up the sleeves of his gray sweater and took a sip of water.

"I wanted to talk to you about Courtney and Mark, and how I'd like to handle next season. I want to make a big change."

I stiffened. Did he not want me to be part of the team anymore?

He continued, "I don't want you—"

"Are you thinking I shouldn't work with them next season?" My words rushed out. "Because I can manage my time and the pressure of the Olympics—"

"Em, slow down." Sergei placed his palm on the table, and his face spread into a smile. "That's not what I was thinking."

"Oh. Sorry." I gave him a sheepish look.

"I was going to say . . ." He paused. "I don't want you to just help with the choreography next season. I'd like you to create their entire short program, if you're interested."

"Yes!" I grinned. "Definitely, I would love that."

"You have great ideas, and you work really well with the kids. Courtney's improved so much as a performer, and it's because of you."

The waitress set down two steaming mugs of coffee, and Sergei passed me two packets of Sweet & Low, just like old times. I smiled to myself. Every time I smelled brewing coffee or heard the whirr of a cappuccino machine, I still thought of Sergei.

"Thanks. I love coaching them. Courtney's become like the little sister I always wanted."

Sergei blew on his coffee, making a low whistle. "I always wanted a brother."

"Classic only child wishes." I smiled. "I'm lucky, though,

that I have a bunch of cousins I'm close to."

"Will they be part of your cheering section tomorrow night?"

"Oh, yeah. And there'll be some relatives there I haven't seen in ages. I think everyone I'm remotely related to who lives within a hundred miles is coming." I scratched my thumbnail along the handle of my mug. "No pressure or anything."

"It can be tough, skating at home. But as long as you stay focused on the program and forget who's watching, you'll do fine."

"I just feel like there are so many expectations, and I don't want to disappoint everyone." I lifted my coffee, and the steam floated toward me, warming my nose. "I don't just want to skate well. I want to have two amazing skates."

Sergei put down his cup. "Em, you can't let yourself think about blowing everyone away with amazing performances. You have to trust your training and let it happen."

"I know, but sometimes it's hard to block out all the outside voices."

"Well, I'll remind you over and over again tomorrow."

"Maybe you should call me every half hour," I joked.

"I was thinking every fifteen minutes." He grinned and laid his arm across the back of the chair next to him.

I laughed and soaked in the positive energy between us. As I sipped my coffee, I watched Sergei rest his hand on the table next to his mug. What would happen if I reached out and put my hand on his? Let my fingertips caress the smooth skin, the soft brush of hair just below his watch. Would the earth stop turning?

I didn't have a chance to find out because Sergei picked up his cup. He asked me more about the family I was expecting at the short program, and we chatted until both our mugs were empty.

Sergei pulled his phone from the pocket of his black

leather jacket to call a taxi, but I didn't want the nice evening to end so quickly. "Why don't we take the T back to the hotel? We can walk to the Arlington station from here."

"It's pretty cold out. You sure you want to walk?"

"We can cut through the Public Garden. It's not too far."

The sidewalks were slick in some spots from the earlier snowfall, so I strolled carefully in my heeled boots. As Sergei and I waited at the traffic light on the corner of Charles and Beacon Streets, the Starbucks behind us hummed with activity, full of people getting their coffee fix. When the light changed to green, we crossed over Beacon and entered the Public Garden.

Snow covered all the trees and statues, giving the park an even more serene feel than usual. A beautiful oasis from the busy streets surrounding it, the Garden was one of my favorite spots in the city. On summer days, the space was alive with tourists riding the Swan Boats in the lagoon and children feeding the ducks. Tonight, stillness reigned in the frozen landscape.

"Aunt Deb and Uncle Joe live about a block from here. They don't have a backyard, so my cousins and I used to play here all the time. We'd have bike races around the lagoon, and Trey would always beat me." I frowned.

"Did you cry when you didn't win?" Sergei teased.

I jutted out my chin but tried not to laugh. "I'm not *that* sore of a loser."

He smiled. "No, you're just incredibly interested in winning."

"You should be grateful for my competitiveness."

"Oh, I am." Sergei stopped walking and softened his voice. "I'm very, very grateful."

We stood as still as the large statue of George Washington in front of us. When we both started to speak at the same time, we laughed as we talked over each other.

"You go ahead," Sergei said.

I toyed with my gloves, contemplating if I should keep my thoughts to myself. After all, I shouldn't have such feelings, and I wondered every day if they would ever go away. But standing there with Sergei, I couldn't let the moment pass.

"I was going to say I've missed this." I peeked up at Sergei. "Talking to you like this."

He stuck his hands in his pockets and stayed silent as his eyes studied me. I could've kicked myself for opening my mouth and getting mushy.

He finally said quietly, "I wish things—"

My phone rang, cutting him off. I internally cursed it and hoped if I let it ring, Sergei would carry on.

"Do you want to get that?" he asked.

"No, it's okay," I said as the ringing stopped. "What were you saying?"

No sooner were the words out of my mouth than the phone rang again. I wanted to throw it into the nearest tree.

"You should probably get it," Sergei said.

I took the phone out of my purse and saw Drew's name on the screen. Guilt rolled in my stomach. He'd been scheduled to arrive in town that evening, and we'd made plans to meet after dinner. Once Sergei had asked me to have coffee, the whole world had disappeared, and I'd forgotten I needed to be somewhere.

"Hey, Drew. Did you have a good flight?"

Sergei wandered away from me and toward the statue where I couldn't see his face.

"Yeah, we were right on time," Drew said. "I was just wondering where you were because I saw Courtney at the hotel and figured you must be done with dinner."

"Sergei wanted to talk to me. We're on our way back now."

"Cool. I'll meet you in the lobby."

"Okay, see you soon."

I hung up the phone and went over to where Sergei stood. He cleared his throat. "We should get going."

The warmth between us had disappeared. He started walking, so I assumed our previous conversation was over. Meaningless chit-chat was all he offered as we rode the train to Copley Station. When we arrived at the hotel, he couldn't get away fast enough.

"Have a good night," he said over his shoulder and vanished into the elevator.

Drew greeted me with a hug and tried to kiss me, but I turned my head so his mouth hit my cheek. His face dropped, and I knew I had to say something before I hurt him any further.

"Why don't we go sit over there?" I pointed to a sofa outside the shuttered lobby coffee shop.

He followed me to the couch. Concern creased around his eyes. "Did I do something?"

"No, not at all. I just don't think I can get involved with anyone right now. I mean, I'm East Coast, you're West Coast .. . I think it's best if we keep things chill." He was quiet, so I added, "I'm so sorry to dump this on you here. I should've said something before."

"So, you just wanna be friends." Disappointment was evident in both his voice and his eyes.

"I hope that's okay? I still want to hang out this week, especially at the party. You're the best dance partner out of everyone here." I tapped his arm.

Thankfully, I got a little smile out of him. "Don't you forget it."

"Does that mean we're good?" I looked at him anxiously.

"I'm not gonna lie... I wanted more, but I understand why you don't wanna start something when I live across the country."

Another twinge of guilt hit me for not being completely honest, but I pushed it down. "I'm so glad you're not mad. I was scared you were going to tell me to get lost."

"You can't get rid of me that easily," he said with a crooked grin.

I needed to wake up early for practice the next morning, so we kept the rest of our visit brief. As I prepared for bed, I thought about the scene in the Garden earlier and scrubbed my face extra hard in frustration, wondering what Sergei was going to say when he'd been interrupted.

Somehow, I had to put aside the turmoil in my heart and focus on performing the next day. Unlike my emotions, skating was a part of my life I could actually control.

CHAPTER ELEVEN

Only a few empty seats remained when Chris and I boarded the bus to the Fleet Center for our short program. Filled with skaters, coaches, and spectators, the large charter bus pulled away from the hotel, escorted by two Boston Police motorcycles to guide us through rush hour traffic.

Knowing I didn't like to chat before competitions, Chris turned to Trevor across the aisle. The two of them joked and laughed like they were on their way to a party instead of the biggest event of the year. I would kill to be that loose.

My ears picked up on the conversation between two fans sitting in front of us. The two women didn't appear to be acquainted but brought together by the lack of available seats.

"Have you been to Nationals before?" the older lady asked.

"This is my first," the younger one replied. "It's so wild, riding on the bus with the skaters!"

I smiled, thinking how crazy it was that people were excited to be on the same vehicle as me. I'd signed hundreds of autographs and posed for countless photos at our practices in Boston but still didn't think of myself as a celebrity. Celebrities were skaters like Kristi Yamaguchi and Brian Boitano.

Soon, you could be a champion like them.

I shivered and stared out the window at the brownstones on Beacon Street, trying to channel my thoughts on the clean run-through we'd done at practice that morning. Every time I'd envision myself completing an element, the police sirens would wail and spike my adrenaline further.

The bus rolled up to the arena, and I shot to my feet before we even parked.

Trevor laughed. "Ready to go, Em?"

Was I ready? I was physically prepared, for certain. But was I mentally ready to live up to everyone's expectations? To my own?

Those questions plagued me for the next hour. Hovering around us backstage, Sergei reminded us, "Trust your training. Trust your body." But the nagging thoughts wouldn't leave me alone. Before I put on my skates, I jogged up and down the hallway, clearing my head of the buzz that had followed us all week.

America's next great pair. Best technical skills in the world. A team that can finally challenge the Russians. All statements I'd heard during our interviews and from the fans. If we mucked up the short program, I'd go back to being known as the girl who choked under pressure.

Chris and I took the ice for our introduction, and the massiveness of the arena struck me. We'd practiced there earlier in the week, but full to capacity with screaming fans, the building suddenly appeared ten times bigger. The Celtics and Bruins banners hanging from the rafters seemed miles away.

I closed my eyes and concentrated on breathing. In. Out. In. Out.

Dear God, please help me through this.

The announcer's voice boomed, and my eyes popped open.

"She represents the Skating Club of Boston, while he comes to us from the Lighthouse Figure Skating Club in Dennis, Massachusetts. Please give a warm welcome to Emily Butler and Christopher Grayden."

The audience erupted, their vigor rattling through me. I settled next to Chris to begin, and he whispered, "We got this."

Our music filled the air, and my body reacted with a jolt of movement. We'd trained this program almost every day for eight months. The choreography was practically a reflex now. But the upcoming triple twist required more than reflexes. I needed a strength and power I didn't feel in my legs at the moment.

Gritting my teeth and saying another prayer, I flew straight up and muscled three rotations. I descended into Chris's waiting hands, and the crowd responded with thundering applause. A spark of confidence spread from my fingers to my toes.

With each completed element, I gained strength. After we nailed the jumps, we put more of our energy into the choreography, and the audience was with us every step, clapping along to the Spanish suite. Chris pressed me up into our overhead lift, and the wind blew across my smile, drying my lips. The crowd "oohed and aahed" as we covered three-quarters of the rink. Upon the clean set down, the cheers rang louder and didn't lower while we whirled into our final move, the pair spin.

Right on the highest note of the music we spun to a stop, and a shower of applause and gifts rained down on us. My body relaxed with a deep exhale as Chris hugged me.

One shrill cheer stood out from the rest, and I spotted my sixteen-year-old cousin Bri running down the aisle. She flung a pink garment onto the ice, so I skated over and retrieved it, giving her a wave as I headed for the kiss and cry. I unrolled the bundle and discovered a pink Red Sox jersey bearing number five for my favorite player, Nomar Garciaparra.

Chris laughed but then complained, "No Orioles jersey for me?"

I giggled. "Not in *Bahston*."

Sergei met us with a satisfied smile. "Best short this season."

I basked in the glow of his praise, unable to stop grinning. We filed onto the bench in the kiss and cry, and I slipped the jersey over my costume. With a wave to the TV camera, I pointed at the front of my shirt. "Thank you, Boston!"

Sergei offered us a couple of tissues, and I patted my face. The bright television lights positioned on us were making me sweat even more. On the monitor, the first of numerous 5.8's flashed, and Chris let out a quiet, "Yes." The scores reflected Sergei's assessment of our program—5.8's for technical merit and 5.9's for presentation, the highest we'd received all season.

Our names showed at the top of the leaderboard, and Chris and I high-fived. On my other side, Sergei squeezed his arm around my shoulders.

"You took a big step forward tonight," he told us. "Let's keep the momentum going."

I gazed up at the Jumbotron and our names in first place. In forty-eight hours, we could be national champions.

The gold medal was so close I could feel it hanging around my neck.

AFTER LUNCH THE NEXT afternoon, Aubrey, Marley, and I walked to the mall connected to our hotel. My friends were competing in the free dance that night, and they needed a distraction to keep from stressing.

We came upon a kiosk selling stuffed animals, and Marley picked up a teddy bear with a red heart sewn on its chest.

"I should get this for Chris for tomorrow night."

Aubrey shook her head. "You two are so sickeningly sweet."

"What do you have against romance?" Marley asked.

"It's too much effort. It's easier to date casually and not make commitments," Aubrey said, moving around the cart.

I petted the bear's velvety fur. "It's adorable. Chris will love it. I think he has something special for you tonight."

Marley smiled, breaking into the moony look she wore whenever we talked about my partner. "How are things with you and Drew? Has he sent you any more flowers?"

Aubrey rejoined us as I said, "I told him we should just be friends. You know, since he lives in L.A. and all."

"Oh." Marley's smile deflated. "That's too bad. From what Chris said, it sounded like he was pretty into you."

She went to the cashier, and I wandered to the adjacent kiosk, which was selling Russian nesting dolls. Aubrey followed me and stood at my elbow as I examined a doll bearing a picture of an angel.

"Is distance the only reason you blew off Drew?"

"I can't handle more than friendship right now." I kept my eyes on the figurine.

Aubrey lowered her voice. "I was wondering if maybe you still have a thing for Sergei."

I carefully returned the doll to the display. "He and I can't happen, so . . ."

"That's not answering the question."

"It doesn't matter how I feel," I said and walked briskly over to Marley.

Aubrey caught up with me, and the three of us started in the direction of the Sheraton. Viktor came toward us from the opposite side of the walkway and pointed a dark glare at Marley and Aubrey.

"You should be resting at the hotel."

They both froze and viewed him with unblinking stares.

One command from Viktor's heavy Russian tone had that kind of power. In his mid-thirties, he wasn't a bad-looking guy—jet black hair neatly slicked back, deep set eyes, and a firm build. But he always seemed to be appraising everything and everyone around him.

"We're on our way back," Aubrey said quietly.

Viktor continued to glare at her. "Don't forget, you're wearing your hair down tonight."

"Yes. I know." Aubrey sounded like a robot.

"Marley, remind Zach to bring the red tie, not the black one," he said.

"I will," she said in the same obedient manner as Aubrey.

Viktor left us without any further words, and we moved along in silence. The man was known for his networking prowess with judges and officials, but he sure didn't waste any conversation on his students.

WATCHING AUBREY AND MARLEY skate their best and win the silver and pewter medals gave me an extra boost of inspiration for the free skate. As Chris and I stood alongside the boards in the moments before our program, Sergei zoned our attention to him and empowered me even further.

"You have the courage and the ability to do this."

I connected with the belief in his eyes and grasped Chris's hand with purpose. My anxiousness was rooted more in anticipation than fear. I wanted to show everyone we were indeed the next great champions.

Chris and I were the last skaters of the night, so the crowd's energy had built to a frenzied level. Above the cheers, I could barely hear our names announced. Skating to center ice, we faced one another and each placed one knee on the smooth, cold surface. I didn't even feel the burn of the ice as I focused on Chris's warm hands around mine.

The romantic strains of "Meditation" began, and the violin notes flowed through me. Using the ballet lessons we took as part of our off-ice training, we stretched every muscle down to our fingertips and created elegant lines to express the feeling of the music.

The calming tempo of the classical piece allowed me to relax and let my muscle memory take over. When I did my jumps, I felt like I was floating on air. After each key element, Chris gave me a slight nod, and I sensed my smile growing bigger with every tip of his head.

As we advanced further into the program, we gained speed rather than lost it. Going into our second throw jump, the triple loop, the audience was a blur as we raced past the boards. Chris seized my hips, and I set my right blade on its back outside edge, ready to push off.

He assisted me up into the air, and I knew as soon my feet left the ice that he'd thrown me with too much force. I was leaning, and the ground was coming fast.

You are not going down!

My blade hit the ice with a thud, and I pitched forward at the waist, trying to control the momentum and avoid putting my other foot down. With all of my strength, I held my arms out for balance and kept myself upright on one leg to nail the clean landing.

Chris looked too stunned to nod this time. I squeezed his hand, and he broke into a smile as we accelerated into the closing seconds of the program. When the four and a half minutes were over, my exhausted body told me I'd poured every ounce of my heart and soul into the performance.

The audience had stood before the music ended, and I couldn't hold back the tears as Chris embraced me.

"Thank you so much." I wished there were stronger words to tell him how much I appreciated him as my partner and my friend.

He squeezed my shoulders. "You saved me on the loop."

I grinned. "You've saved *me* lots of times."

As we bowed, Marley ran down to the boards and tossed the teddy bear. Chris snatched it from the ice and blew Marley a kiss.

Tears blurred my contact lenses as I glided toward the ice door, so I couldn't see Sergei clearly. When I finally saw his face, I started crying harder. His cheeks were flushed with elation, and his smile couldn't be any bigger. He opened his arms, and I pressed my face against his chest, my tears dampening his paisley tie.

"Wow," he said in awe.

I wanted to thank him, too, but between catching my breath from the program and choking on sobs, I couldn't speak. Sergei embraced Chris and continued to slap him on the back as we stepped into the kiss and cry.

People in the crowd chanted, "Six! Six!" I laughed and soaked in every moment of the experience. The deafening cheers, the look of amazement on Chris's face, Sergei's proud smile—everything seemed surreal. I'd had the performance of my life when I'd needed it most, and doing it in my hometown made it even more unbelievable.

When the technical scores appeared on the Jumbotron, all I heard were screams of glee. 5.9's covered the board. The presentation scores followed, and except for two 5.9's, every other judge had given us 6.0. I put my hands over my mouth and began crying all over again. Not once in twelve years of skating had I seen the mark of perfection under my name.

Chris's eyes expanded, and he threw his arms around me. "No way!"

My whole body shook from the excitement. We stood to wave to the audience, and I placed my hand over my heart to thank them for their support.

Our competitors showered us with congratulations as we made our way backstage. Claire and Brandon, the two-time defending champs who'd finished second, were very gracious in offering us compliments and hugs.

Sergei trailed close behind us. He stopped us outside the locker rooms and paused, appearing to gather his thoughts.

"What you did out there… don't ever forget how that felt."

"It felt darn good," Chris said with a laugh.

A couple of Chris's former training mates from Baltimore stole him away, leaving Sergei and me smiling at each other.

He brought me into a tight hug. "I'm so proud of you, Em."

"Bet you never thought you'd see this day when you first started working with me. I could hardly stay upright in the lifts."

"I always knew you had it in you."

His hot breath teased my ear, stirring the feelings I'd locked away when I was on the ice. With my arms wrapped around his strong shoulders, my mouth so close to his neck, I fought to push those feelings down again. I put all my energy into expressing gratitude, the one emotion I was allowed to convey to him.

"Thank you for believing in me," I whispered.

He closed his arm harder around my waist, and my breath suspended. His voice dropped low with emotion. "You were on fire tonight."

I bit down on my lip. *Sergei, you're killing me.*

He held onto me another moment before stepping back. "The medal ceremony will be starting soon."

I hurried into the locker room and grabbed my makeup case. With an unsteady hand, I cleared my face of all traces of tears. A few minutes later, I reconnected with Chris, and we waited next to the ice to be introduced as the gold medalists.

When we took our place on the top step of the podium, I bobbed up and down, unable to contain my enthusiasm.

Chris laughed. "This is so awesome."

I skimmed over the stands for my family, and Bri got my

attention, waving her arms in the front row. My parents, aunts, uncles, and other cousins stood beside her, half of them with cameras aimed at me. Mom dabbed at her eyes with a tissue, and I willed myself not to cry again.

The president of the U.S. Figure Skating Federation presented us with our medals and silver championship platters, while event sponsors handed us flowers and champion pins. Chris chuckled as my tiny arms overflowed with the loot.

After we posed for the official photographs, we were instructed to take a victory lap. Chris and I led the way, stopping when we reached our parents. I gave Mom my bouquet, and she and Dad embraced me at the same time.

Mom touched my cheek and smiled through her tears. "You were so beautiful, sweetie."

"Absolutely wonderful," Dad said.

Once I'd spent a few moments with the rest of my family, I skated along the boards to the spot where my friends stood. Chris was already there, taking pictures with Marley. Aubrey started the train of hugs as I went down the line from friend to friend. Drew was at the end of the line, and he reached out to hug me.

"You rocked it out."

"Thanks! You're gonna rock it out tomorrow. I can feel it."

"Maybe some of your good mojo will rub off on me."

I laughed. "Take as much as you need."

Over an hour later, I arrived at the hotel, finished with the media obligations at the arena. Mom and Dad greeted me in the lobby as I unwound my scarf and unzipped my jacket.

"Everyone's in the restaurant," Mom said. "Chris's parents, Aubrey's family, Marley's family. We put a bunch of tables together. Where's Chris?"

"He stopped outside to talk to one of his old coaches. Have you seen Sergei? He must've left the arena when we were in the press conference."

"He passed through here a little while ago." Mom waved her hand. "I invited him to come celebrate, but he said he was tired."

My heart sank, and I looked toward the elevators as if Sergei might change his mind. But that was wishful thinking. Every time I sensed us becoming closer again, he pulled away.

CHAPTER TWELVE

When I woke up the next morning, the first thing that popped into my head was *National Champs*. I couldn't stop myself from smiling as I climbed out of bed to retrieve the newspaper. Opening the hotel room door, I squealed at the front page.

Under the *Boston Globe* masthead was a picture of Chris and me performing a lift during our free skate. The headline read, "Golden Homecoming." I squeaked again.

Aubrey rolled over in her bed and asked groggily, "What is it?"

"Look!" I switched on the nightstand lamp and displayed the newspaper.

"That's really cool," she said with as much enthusiasm as she could muster after just waking up.

After I read all the skating articles, I got dressed to go down to the coffee shop. The elevator doors opened on my floor, and Sergei looked up, his eyes brightening. I had a feeling he saw the same reaction from me.

"Did you get any sleep last night?" he asked.

"I did. Once my head hit the pillow, my body finally gave out from all the stress."

"I didn't get much of a chance to talk to you at the arena. Was that the amazing skate you were looking for?" He gave me a little smile, just enough to tease my heartstrings.

"Yeah, it was pretty amazing. Hey, did you see the paper this morning? We made the front page!"

Sergei's smile widened. "You'd better get used to it."

The elevator reached the lobby, and we both started toward Starbucks.

"I'm treating myself to a large frozen cappuccino with extra whipped cream," I said.

"Wow, don't get too crazy," he teased as we approached the counter.

I laughed. "I'm saving the crazy for the closing party tonight. I plan on dancing till I drop."

Sergei folded his arms, putting up the invisible barrier again. "Don't wear yourself out. You have to skate in the Exhibition tomorrow."

What did I say? "I know," I replied curtly. "I have plenty of energy to spare."

We gave the barista our orders and waited quietly for our names to be called. When Sergei received his coffee, he gave me a polite goodbye and headed to the lobby. I poked a straw into my drink and shook my head.

One step forward, five steps back.

AUBREY AND I HAD brought half our wardrobes to Boston, and we spread every item of clothing across our beds. I spent a ridiculous amount of time trying to decide what shirt to wear with my jeans to the party. Settling on a teal blue, textured silk halter top, I slipped it on and gave my hair one last brush over my shoulders before we left our room.

Trevor had become the annual host of the "pre-party," and he had a well-stocked bar in his room. Bottles of beer, liquor, juice, and soda covered every inch of the desk. Deciding to try a cocktail, I asked Drew to mix a screwdriver for me.

I toasted his beer bottle with my plastic cup. "To your bronze medal and a standing ovation!"

"And to the champion!"

Marley squeezed next to us, tugging Chris's hand behind her. "What are we toasting?"

"Our awesomeness." Drew lifted his bottle again.

We all tapped our drinks together and took long gulps. The vodka burned a searing line from my throat down to my stomach. I coughed and set the cup on the desk. That was enough alcohol for me.

People kept coming in until we had hardly any space to stand. Once the room became too crowded, we made our way downstairs to the official party. Music blared through the double doors of the ballroom. Aubrey, Drew, and I danced inside, and our feet didn't stop moving for the next hour.

A song ended, and Drew made a timeout signal. "Restroom break."

"I'll take a walk to the lobby with you." I fanned myself.

I limped behind Drew as we went out to the escalator. "My heels are killing me," I explained.

"Hop on, I'll give you a ride." Drew grinned and motioned to his back.

I jumped on piggyback style and let out a loud peal of laughter as he galloped through the near-empty lobby. Outside the restrooms, I slid off his back, still laughing. When I spun around and faced the hotel bar, I saw Sergei sitting with three other coaches. He was wearing the blue sweater I always thought made him look especially hot.

I pivoted on my heel. *Forget about him. Tonight is about having fun.*

Waiting for Drew, I rested against the back of an overstuffed couch and was about to slip off my shoes when a voice startled me.

"What are you doing with him?"

Sergei came around the sofa and stood in front of me. He was holding a drink, and the glassiness in his eyes told me he'd already had a few more.

"Excuse me?" I sputtered.

He leaned closer, and I got a pungent whiff of whatever liquor he was drinking. "Why are you wasting your time with him?" he asked with more persistence.

My blood pressure surged upward. "That's none of your business."

"Everything you do is my business."

I gaped at him, having never seen him so aggressive. "I think you've had too much to drink."

Drew came out of the men's room, and I joined him in stride, fleeing Sergei's intense stare. I didn't realize my hands were trembling until I went to tuck my hair behind my ears.

What was that? Had Sergei suddenly become dictatorial or was there another reason for his questions? Either way, his method of asking had been unnerving.

Despite the pain in my pinched toes, I resumed dancing with my friends. My body moved to the beat of the music, but the movements felt involuntary. Sergei's behavior had my mind whirling.

After we exhausted ourselves on the dance floor, Trevor announced his room would also be the site of the after-party. On the way there, I thought again about what Sergei had said to me, and my pulse heightened. *Why did he act so controlling?*

"I have to run to my room for a minute," I told Drew. "I'll be back."

I returned to the elevator and punched the button for Sergei's floor but couldn't quite remember the room number he'd given Chris and me. *Was it 1214? Or 1204?*

Hoping I was going to the right place, I strode toward 1214 and rapped my knuckles on the door.

Sergei opened it, and I marched past him into the room, which reeked of coffee. "What is your problem?" I spat out. He followed me while I kept talking. "You have no right to question who I hang out with—"

"I know. I was out of line." The glass-like sheen had lifted from his eyes.

"That's right, you were out of line." I crossed my arms over my chest. "What is your issue with Drew anyway?"

Sergei stood with his hands on his hips. "I don't see why you'd want to get involved with someone who lives so far away."

"I'm not involved with him. We're just good friends."

"He doesn't want to be just your friend."

"No, he doesn't, but he knows it's what I want."

"Then what was that kiss I saw in Paris?"

My mouth opened, but no words came out. I wasn't going to offer any explanations without knowing why I was being interrogated.

"Why do you care?"

Sergei's eyes darted across my face, but they didn't give me any hint of his thoughts. He shifted his gaze over my shoulder. "Your personal life affects your skating life."

I looked down at the carpet and nodded slowly. "Of course. You're concerned because you're my coach. What other reason could there be, right?"

I glanced up at Sergei. His lips parted, and I took a small step, anticipating a response. But he didn't offer one as he avoided my stare and shuffled toward the desk.

Shaking my head, I hurried to leave, thinking how stupid I was for expecting some grand revelation.

"Em, wait," Sergei said, but I opened the door anyway.

He came up behind me and shut it. "I said wait!"

With my hand on the knob, I spun around, and my face nearly brushed Sergei's left arm. He stood there, looking at me as if he had something to say but couldn't get it out.

"I'm waiting," I said, my voice barely audible.

Sergei dipped his head and relaxed his arm but still didn't speak. I'd had enough of the torture, so I twisted the handle.

"Don't go." He grasped my hand.

All the blood in my body rushed to that hand, where Sergei laced his fingers through mine. He inched forward, leaving only a millimeter of space between us. I feared I would cease breathing any second.

"Em, I can't..." He paused and swallowed hard, the silence excruciating. My heart sent deep, vibrating beats to my core.

"I can't stop thinking about you." His eyes captured mine. "And I don't want to."

A thousand volts of electricity shot down my spine. If I hadn't been wedged between Sergei and the door, I might've fallen over. I wanted to throw my arms around him, but fear of being rejected again paralyzed me.

"What are you going to do about that?" I whispered.

He seemed to move even closer to me, if that was possible. "What do you want me to do?"

I knew exactly what I wanted, what I desired every time Sergei walked into a room and I felt the magnetic pull.

I kissed him. Hard.

He pressed me against the door, his hands on my face and in my hair. I locked my arms around him, digging my nails into his sweater. His muscles were hard and tight.

All the months of dancing around each other, holding in the feelings we shouldn't feel—through each deep and searching kiss, we released those frustrations. As the pace of our kisses slowed, I became more aware of Sergei's tender touch. His fingertips grazed the nape of my neck, tickling my skin like a feather and sending goose bumps all over my body. I sighed against his lips. I'd waited so long for him to touch me like that.

Sergei wrapped me in an embrace and buried his face in my hair. Laying my head on his chest, I closed my eyes and listened to his heart racing. I didn't want to leave his arms, that spot, that moment.

We remained still for a few minutes until Sergei pulled back just enough to face me. He brushed strands of hair from my cheek.

"I guess we have a situation here."

CHAPTER THIRTEEN

I SEARCHED SERGEI'S EYES, HOPING I wouldn't see the regret they held the first time we kissed. "Is that what we are—a situation?"

He touched his forehead to mine and combed his fingers through my hair. "I wasn't expecting this to happen."

"I'm really glad it happened." I tightened my arms around him, afraid he could slip away at any moment.

"Emily." He sighed, his voice thick with emotion.

He'd spoken my name thousands of times, but the way he said it now made me weak in the knees. The silkiness of his hands in my hair was also making me light-headed. I leaned into him, but he stepped backward and unraveled my arms from around his neck.

Holding onto my hands, he said, "This isn't going to be easy."

Red flashing alarms went off in my head. I'd been down this painful road before, and I couldn't travel it again.

"Please don't push me away," I half-pleaded and half-demanded.

"I'm not. I'm just thinking out loud… about where we go

from here." He stared at the backs of my hands, where he traced tiny circles with his thumbs. "We can't be seen together."

Since the moment I'd kissed Sergei, I'd tried to shut out reality and pretend our situation wasn't a complicated one. But now I was in a free fall from the clouds, back to Earth, where I competed in a sport with more unwritten rules than I could count.

I took a little walk past Sergei, needing space to process his statement. "What would happen if we were?"

He joined me in front of the dresser. "Your commitment and my credibility would be questioned," he said softly. "We need all the support we can get from the federation, and they wouldn't approve of this."

"Then it doesn't sound like we're going anywhere from here." I looked away, trying to hide the frustration brewing in my heart.

"No, you're wrong. I don't know how, but there has to be a way we can make this work." He slid his hands around my waist and drew me to him. "Because I have to be with you."

The passion blazing in his eyes sent a thrill of both excitement and fear through me. What I felt was more powerful than anything I'd ever experienced in my life.

Sergei kissed me, his lips stroking mine with a slow caress. I brought my hand up to his cheek, touching the prickly stubble. So many times I'd wanted to do that, to feel the warmth of his skin.

"Maybe I can make us private dinners at my house." I smiled. "I have a very large recipe box."

"You also have a roommate."

"I can trust Aubrey. She won't tell anyone." *But she probably will yell at me and list a thousand reasons why this is a bad idea.* I pushed that thought aside and curled my fingers along the back of Sergei's neck and into his hair.

He cradled my face in his hands, and I shivered from the

softness of his touch. "We have to be very careful, Em."

My mind raced. Everything between us had changed so quickly. "What made you finally tell me how you feel?"

"I couldn't pretend anymore that I don't care. I missed you so much." He trailed his thumb along my jaw. "And seeing you with Drew—"

"Drew! Oh no! I told him I'd only be gone a minute. He's probably wondering what happened to me."

"Does that mean you have to go?" Sergei nudged me closer to him.

With a reluctant nod, I slipped out of his embrace, and we crept toward the door. Before opening it, I said, "I know we have a lot of things to figure out, but—"

Sergei pressed his mouth to mine, silencing me with a long kiss that made me dizzy. When we parted, I had no idea what I'd been saying.

"Sorry, I couldn't stop myself." Sergei's lips brushed mine as he spoke.

"Not a problem," I whispered, still catching my breath.

Sergei opened the door and glanced both ways down the hallway. I scooted around him, but before I made it through the doorway, he grabbed my hand and gave it a squeeze. I resisted the urge to seek another kiss, instead smiling and mouthing, "Bye."

On the ride down to Trevor's room, I used my fingers as a comb, smoothing my hair where Sergei's hands had been tangled. My face grew hot just thinking about his touch.

Did that really happen? Are we together now? Like a couple?

I had no idea how I was going to walk into the party and act like everything was normal.

Drew greeted me at the door with a beer in hand. "Are you okay? You look a little frazzled."

"I'm just tired." *And so begin the lies.* "I'm going back to my room, but I wanted to tell you thanks for a fun night." I gave him a hug.

"Yeah, it was great. I wish we could hang out more often."

Surrounded by so many people crowded together and talking loudly, I felt smothered and still overwhelmed from what had happened in Sergei's room. "I'm gonna talk to Aubrey for a sec."

I snaked through the throng standing around the bed and found Aubrey sitting on Zach's lap. They were laughing as they thumb wrestled and tickled each other with their free hands. I raised an eyebrow, and Aubrey saw me staring at her.

"Where'd you disappear to?" she asked.

"Can you take a walk with me?"

"What's going on?"

"I just need to talk to you."

She stood up and flipped her blond hair over her shoulder. "I'll be back," she told Zach.

When we reached the hall, I gave her a sidelong glance. "What's up with you two?"

"Marley asked me the same thing. We're having fun. Not everything has to be a big romance."

I held up my hands in surrender. "Okay."

In the darkness of our room, I groped for the lamp switch. Aubrey sat on my bed and curled her legs under her, while I kicked off my heels and sat beside her.

"What I'm going to tell you has to stay between us. Absolutely no one can know."

Concern narrowed her green eyes. "You're scaring me a little."

"It's nothing bad." I hesitated and ran my palm over the silky flowered comforter. "I went to see Sergei because he said something to me about Drew earlier, and when I was in his room..." I paused and smiled a little. "He told me he wants to be with me."

Aubrey's face froze with her mouth slightly ajar. "What do you mean, he wants to be with you?"

"I think, in a relationship."

"A relationship?" She looked at me like I'd committed career suicide. "Are you serious? If the fed finds out, they will *flip out.*"

"I know, but if we're careful…"

"This isn't like you, Em. You don't do crazy, impulsive things like this. I thought you would've gotten over your crush—"

"It's not a crush." I slid off the bed and wandered to the desk. Turning around, I took a deep breath and hugged my arms. "I think I'm in love with him."

It felt liberating to admit what had been hiding in my heart for so long. But Aubrey's look of pity squashed my moment of relief.

"Did you tell Sergei that?"

"No." I shook my head vigorously.

"Good." Aubrey swung her legs over the side of the bed and stared across the room, seemingly at nothing in particular. "Why would he do something this risky? He has to know all the things that could go wrong."

"We tried to stay away from each other, but we can't help how we feel."

"Can you really trust him, Em? What if…" She softened her voice. "What if he's just looking for sex?"

I planted my feet in a firm stance. "He's not like that. And I *can* trust him."

"I just don't want you to get hurt. If things go bad between you, think how hard it'll be to train with him. There's a reason why the fed doesn't want coaches and students getting involved."

I relaxed my posture and rested against the desk. "I'm willing to take that chance."

"This is so cra—"

A loud knock on the door interrupted her. I marched through the room and answered it revealing Chris, Marley, and Zach, all bundled up in jackets.

"It's snowing like crazy outside," Chris said. "We're going downstairs to check it out."

"We're kinda in the middle of something," Aubrey called from the bed.

I went over to the tiny closet for my jacket and boots. "Actually, I could use some fresh air."

Aubrey grabbed her coat, and as she passed me, she whispered, "We're gonna talk more about this."

Outside, the snow blew sideways, swirling around us and piling up on the sidewalk. I pulled my knit hat further down over my ears.

Zach picked up a handful of ice and slung it at Chris, smacking him in the chest.

"Dude!" Chris yelled.

He rolled a large ball of snow, while Zach took off running down the street. As Chris dashed after him, their howls broke the silence of the quiet night.

"Boys," Marley said, shaking her head.

Tiny snowflakes stuck to my face, and I closed my eyes, imagining they were kisses from Sergei. Tonight had been magical, no matter what Aubrey said. As I gazed up at the hotel, I wondered if Sergei was thinking about me. What if he changed his mind about us once the light of morning came?

CHAPTER FOURTEEN

BY MORNING, A FOOT OF SNOW had fallen over Boston. I stared out my hotel room window at the city blanketed in white. The bright sunshine made everything look clean and calm in the wake of the previous night's storm.

As champions, Chris and I had to skate in the Exhibition featuring the medalists from all the events, so I gathered my bag and my costume and headed downstairs to the bus, glad Aubrey had already left. She'd peppered me with concerns and questions into the wee hours. Questions I couldn't answer because I had no idea where Sergei and I stood. Our time together in his room had been a whirlwind of confessions and kisses, and I wasn't sure what any of it meant for the immediate future.

Coaches often didn't attend the show, so I wasn't counting on seeing Sergei at the arena. If I did see him, I didn't know what I'd even say.

The gold medalists wouldn't skate until the end of the Exhibition, so I sat in the lounge backstage at the Fleet Center and watched the show on the monitor, keeping one eye on the door. With no sign of Sergei, I donned my royal blue dress and prepared to take the ice.

The arena lights were down for the event, adding to the "show" atmosphere, and the crowd erupted as soon as Chris and I stepped into the spotlight. When the announcer introduced us as national champions, chill bumps sprang up on my arms. It was the first time I'd heard the title spoken with our names.

We'd chosen "Blue Dress" by Depeche Mode for our program, and a new confidence ruled my expression of the romantic movements. Skating as champions had lit an extra spark under me; I sensed it in Chris, too, as we flew across the rink.

We left the ice to a standing ovation, and as we put on our skate guards, Sergei came out of the shadows in the tunnel. My heart rate, which had started to simmer down from the performance, shot back up.

"Nice program," Sergei said.

"Did you see the size of the twist?" Chris walked toward the bin of bottled water down the hall. "And under spotlights!"

I fidgeted with the straps of my dress and watched Sergei's expression. He smiled at Chris's comment but grew serious when he angled toward me.

"Do you know somewhere we can talk privately later? Away from the hotel."

"Um..." I thought quickly. "We could go to the Public Garden. I doubt anyone will be out there."

"Why don't we meet at the T station at seven?"

The next three hours felt like a week. I showed up at the underground platform ten minutes early and smiled at the sight of Sergei studying the large system map on the wall. He spotted me, and his lips twitched upward.

"The show today was great," he said.

"Yeah. Everybody had a lot of fun."

Small talk seemed so ridiculous, but we couldn't have a

heart-to-heart in the station. Sitting beside Sergei on the train, I rambled about ideas for Courtney and Mark's new short program. If I kept talking, I wouldn't think about how I wanted to reach over and touch him, feel his arms around me again.

Mounds of ice coated every bench in the Garden, so we strolled along the shoveled path. We were almost to the footbridge over the frozen lagoon before Sergei stopped and spoke.

"Last night I said some things I never thought I'd admit to you."

"Do you regret saying them?" I asked in a low voice.

He stared at me for a long, aching moment. "No. But I understand if you're having second thoughts."

A number of doubts had crossed my mind after my talk with Aubrey, but hearing Sergei's certainty and seeing it in his eyes, I didn't hesitate to answer, "I want this. I want to be with you, too."

He glanced around us and then wrapped me in his arms. I pressed my face to his jacket's soft leather, inhaling the richness of its scent mixed with Sergei's spicy cologne, a dizzying combination.

Sergei stepped back, and the frigid night air replaced his cozy embrace. "It's not going to be easy. We have to keep this quiet or we could face some serious backlash."

"I told Aubrey last night, and she threw every possible bad scenario at me."

"And you're still here with me."

"I can't turn back now. Not after knowing how you feel."

Sergei's eyes danced over the area again, and he took my hand, guiding me out of the moonlight and under a canopy of snow-covered trees. He kissed me, and I opened my mouth to him, taking the kiss from soft to passionate. The temperature was below freezing, but all I could feel was the heat between us. We broke apart, and our ragged breaths crystallized in the air between us.

"I wish I could do this right," Sergei said. "Take you to dinner, touch you without looking over my shoulder…"

"We'll find a way to make it work. Like I said, I'll cook for you anytime." I smiled and tapped his chest.

"I have very fond memories of the last meal I had at your house."

"Ah, yes, the dinner party." I nodded. "That was a great night."

"I knew I was in trouble because you were all I thought about the next day." He gave my cheek a light touch.

A movement of color on the footbridge caught my eye, and I saw a couple hand-in-hand, cuddling together. Sergei followed my gaze.

"I guess we should head back," I said.

No one else was on our green line train car, and I wished we had to travel farther than two stops. Sergei held my gloved hand, and I snuggled against his shoulder.

"So, what's the first recipe I get to taste?" He grinned.

"I was thinking… there might be something we can actually go out and do together next weekend. I was going to bribe Aubrey to go with me to the symphony since she doesn't like classical music, but why don't you come with me?"

Sergei's grin disappeared, replaced by tight lips. "I don't know, Em."

"I don't think it'll look questionable. If we see anyone we know, we can say we're there to check out music for Court and Mark." I widened my eyes and stared into Sergei's. "Doesn't it sound fun?"

"You're not playing fair, looking at me like that."

"Is that a yes?"

He paused and scratched his chin. "We'll have to act very professional."

"Do you think you can restrain yourself around me?"

A slow smile spread over his lips, and he brought his

mouth close to mine. "I've had months of practice."

THE FOLLOWING SATURDAY EVENING, Aubrey popped into my room as I zipped up my little black dress. Since she'd been in bed with the flu all week, we hadn't discussed my date much. She leaned against the door frame and crossed her arms.

"It's so weird you're going out with your coach. What do you think Chris would say if he knew? Are you gonna tell him?"

Fumbling with the clasp of my necklace, I fastened the silver chain around my neck and straightened the tiny cross pendant. "I've been thinking about telling him after Worlds, when the season's over."

"What about your parents?"

I moved in front of the mirror, arranging my loose curls over my shoulders and avoiding Aubrey's concerned gaze. Every time I thought about deceiving my parents, a sharper twinge of guilt hit me.

"I've never hid something this big from them before. My dad, I could probably reason with, but my mom… well, you know how that conversation would go."

"Does that mean you're not gonna tell them? How long do you think you can keep it a secret?"

"Can you let up on the questions? I'm already nervous enough about tonight."

"Why are you nervous? It's not like you don't know Sergei."

I dropped a tube of pink lip gloss into my small black clutch purse and snapped it shut. "I know, but everything's different now."

All evening, my stomach had been turning similar to when I rode the spinning teacups at Disney World as a child. I'd had to force down a few bites of the grilled chicken I'd made for dinner. When Sergei and I had hung out as friends, I always felt comfortable, but I had a different role to play now. I hadn't been on many dates, and I didn't know what types of serious relationships Sergei had in the past.

Later, when the doorbell rang, I examined myself in the mirror once more before grabbing my coat and purse and heading downstairs. As I neared the foyer, I heard Aubrey open the door, and her voice carried up the stairwell.

"If you hurt Em, you're going to wish you never knew me."

My heels hit the bottom step. "Aubrey!"

"Sorry, I had to say it." She started down the stairs to the kitchen. "Don't bring her home too late!"

I rolled my eyes. "Please excuse her."

"She's not afraid to speak her mind." Sergei laughed and reached out to help me with my coat. "By the way, you look amazing."

His familiar smile eased my anxiety, but the admiring glow in his eyes set off a new kind of tingling in my stomach. I smiled back and fingered his burgundy tie.

"Thanks. You don't look so bad yourself."

When we arrived at the Hyannis Performing Arts Center, the doors of the theater weren't open yet. I made sure to leave an appropriate amount of space between Sergei and me as we waited in the lobby. Opening my program booklet, I began reading the summary biography of composer Sergei Rachmaninov's life.

"Em!" a voice behind me exclaimed.

I immediately recognized the squeaky greeting and turned to find Courtney and her parents coming toward us. Courtney looked back and forth from Sergei to me with a huge smile on her face.

I stepped even farther away from Sergei. "Are you guys Rachmaninov fans, too?"

"We try to make all the concerts. Have you heard the

symphony play before? They're excellent," Courtney's dad Tom said.

"This is my first time. Sergei and I are thinking about using tonight's pieces for program music next year, so we wanted to hear them live."

"Music for me and Mark or you and Chris?" Courtney asked as she removed her red pea coat.

"Well, you'll have to let us know how you like them," Sergei said.

I studied the parents' faces, looking for any sign of surprise or confusion. Nothing seemed amiss with them. Tom, the bespectacled, mild-mannered accountant, wore the same unaffected expression as always, while Karen had on her usual caring and friendly smile, one that reminded me of my kindergarten teacher. Courtney, however, still stared at Sergei and me with a goofy grin.

"The next concert is New World Symphony in a few weeks. You should check that one out, too," Tom said.

I glanced at Sergei. "I think we're going to be in Japan then. We have Four Continents in Salt Lake City and then Grand Prix Final in Tokyo. I don't know who came up with this crazy schedule of back-to-back events on different continents."

"It'll be a good test for you and Chris. If you can survive this, you can survive anything." Sergei sounded like he did every day at the rink, spouting his coach-speak. *Nicely done.*

People began to file into the theater, so we followed the crowd and said goodbye to Courtney and her parents.

"I don't think they suspected anything," Sergei said after he showed the usher our tickets.

"No, I think we're good. I didn't expect to be tested so soon, though."

"It won't always have to be this way," he said softly.

"I know," I replied with a little smile.

After the musicians finished tuning their instruments, the

room darkened, and the dramatic opening notes of Piano Concerto No. 2 filled the theater. The extreme highs and lows of the music reminded me of the emotional journey I'd experienced lately. I hoped my journey would end the same as the concerto—on a high note.

During intermission, I ran into Courtney on my way out of the ladies' room. The tiny girl stood out in the line of women touching up their makeup along the row of mirrors.

"What did you think of the piece?" I asked.

"I'd love to skate to it next year! You can choreograph our short to it."

"I'm glad you're excited about it. I'll talk it over with Sergei."

Courtney played with the ends of her long, golden locks as we walked through the lobby. "So, are you and Sergei on a date?"

I was sure all the color had drained from my face. "What? Why would you think that?"

She shrugged. "I just think you'd make an awesome couple."

I fought the urge to smile and focused on giving an appropriate response. "He's my coach, Court."

"Yeah, but you work together as coaches, too, and he's not that much older than you."

Listen to the twelve-year-old rationalizing it. Maybe I should ask her to talk to my parents.

"I think you're too young to be matchmaking, my dear." I put my arm around her and tried to ignore the guilty feeling I was becoming all too familiar with.

The lights blinked, signaling the end of intermission. I sent Courtney on her way and hurried to my seat.

"I saw Court, and she asked if you and I are on a date."

"What?" Sergei's eyes doubled in size.

"I don't think it was anything we did. More what she wants to see."

"She wants to see us together?"

I said in Sergei's ear, "She said we'd make an awesome couple."

He grinned. "I always knew she was a smart kid."

The orchestra launched into *Rhapsody on a Theme of Paganini*, my favorite classical composition. The intricate work of the pianist gave me chills; every note struck a chord in my heart. Sitting next to Sergei in the darkness with the romantic music surrounding us, I wished I could feel his hand in mine. I reminded myself of his words—*"It won't always have to be this way."*

As the musicians took their bows, I blinked back the tears in my eyes. "I can't believe how amazing they sounded. It was so beautiful."

Sergei just smiled at me as we filed out of the theater and reached his car. When we were seated inside, he said, "You were a little choked up in there."

I laughed and looked down at my lap. "Music makes me emotional sometimes."

"That explains why you have such a great connection with the music when you skate." He squeezed my knee, warming me all over. "Do you want to hang out somewhere for a while?" He asked as he started the car.

"Sure. I don't know if we can go to my house, though. Aubrey was going to a movie with Trevor and Zach, and they might end up there after."

"We can go to my place."

The butterflies from earlier in the evening returned. I trusted Sergei, but being alone with a guy in his apartment was uncharted territory for me. I wasn't ready to say goodnight, though.

The first thing I noticed about Sergei's apartment was how tidy it was. At Chris's and Trevor's , empty pizza boxes and cans of soda littered the coffee table, and the floor in front of the TV was a mess of wires and video games. Here, not a single item was out of place.

I took off my coat and draped it over the back of the sofa. Sergei set his keys on the bar between the living room and the kitchen and asked, "Would you like something to drink?"

"I'll just have some water."

I stood aimlessly in the middle of the living room and looked around me. The space featured the basic items—a couch of nondescript color, a narrow coffee table with a short stack of paperbacks on it, and a wooden entertainment cabinet housing a small television and a stereo. Twin floor lamps that bookended the couch cast a dim glow of light.

The only photo sat on the bar—a framed picture of Sergei, Chris, and me at the 2000 National Championships, posing with our silver medals. As I wandered away from the kitchen, Sergei brought me a glass of water and took off his suit jacket.

"You don't have any pictures of your family," I said.

He laid his jacket next to my coat and went over to the stereo. "My father hates posing for pictures. I think my parents' wedding photo is the only one I've seen of him."

"He wouldn't survive in my family. Someone's always got their camera out, usually my dad or Aunt Deb. And they like to capture every moment, whether it's important or embarrassing."

"My mother had one of those old cameras that you plug the flash bulb into." Sergei chuckled as he inserted a CD into the disc player. "She used to sew my costumes when I was a kid and then make me pose in them."

"Oh, I have to see those pictures!"

Soft classical music streamed through the speakers, and Sergei led me to the sofa. "They are locked deep in a closet in Moscow."

He loosened the knot on his tie and slipped his arm behind me. I put my glass on the coffee table and settled against him, sighing as his fingertips caressed my shoulder. Being with Sergei felt so natural, so right. I didn't know why

I'd been nervous.

"I guess we're not going to have much time together when we're on the road in a few weeks," I lamented.

Sergei ran his fingers through my hair, one soothing stroke after another. "We can have room service dinners or watch a movie."

"That sounds really nice. Spending time with you will help take my mind off the stress of the events."

"I know something else that can help take your mind off it."

I tilted my head up to him, and he covered my lips with his. He was right; I forgot everything except how I could kiss him every day for the rest of my life and never grow tired of it.

I thought I heard the CD player shuffle through a few different pieces, so we must've been kissing quite a long time. Sergei's hands roamed over my dress, quickening my breath and making me feel more alive than I'd ever felt. So many new sensations stirred inside me.

When his touch fell to my knee and edged upward, I tightened and pulled back with a breathless, "It's getting pretty late."

"Did Aubrey give you a curfew?"

I laughed. "No, I just... I should probably get home."

He smiled and kissed my forehead. "Okay."

After a long goodnight embrace on my doorstep, I watched Sergei drive out of the parking lot. I didn't know if he realized how little relationship experience I had. At some point, I was going to have to tell him how far I was willing to go. Or rather, not go. And I hoped he would understand.

CHAPTER FIFTEEN

"FIRST PLACE AFTER THE SHORT!" I squealed as I hurried into Sergei's hotel room.

We'd been in Salt Lake City for the Four Continents competition for three days and had managed to sneak alone-time twice already. With Aubrey as my roommate and Chris occupied with Marley, I didn't have to worry about making up reasons for my disappearances.

Sergei took my face in his hands and kissed me deeply. After giving me a long hug, he said, "There were a couple of things I forgot to mention to you and Chris earlier about your footwork and—"

I placed my finger over his lips. "Why don't we agree—no lessons during our personal time?"

He smiled and tipped his head. "Agreed."

"I'll be happy to listen to your thoughts tomorrow morning at practice. Until then..." I reached up and gave him a feathery kiss.

"Dinner's here if you're hungry. Or we could keep doing this." He nuzzled my neck.

I giggled. "That would be very nice, but I am kinda

starving."

Sergei kept his arms around me as we went over to the small round table by the window. Two covered room service dishes awaited us. I removed the silver dome from my grilled chicken salad and poured a light stream of oil and vinegar over the greens.

"It's pretty cool seeing all the Olympic ads everywhere." I speared a cherry tomato with my fork. "Just think, one year from now we could be back here, getting ready for the Opening Ceremony."

"Why don't we focus on one competition at a time?" Sergei said before taking a drink of water.

"I know, I know. Can't help dreaming a little bit, though."

"We'll get there." Under the table, Sergei rubbed his leg against mine. Even through the denim, his touch sent a spark through me.

Neither of us said much as we enjoyed our dinner, but the periods of silence were comfortable. Sergei's smile across the table spoke more than words could say.

I emptied my glass of water and set it on the room service tray. "Chris and I found out tonight *Blades on Ice* is doing their next cover article on us."

"That's great. You guys are doing exactly what I'd hoped. You're making people excited about American pairs skating."

"From all the phone calls you've been getting from prospective students, that might be true."

"I'm not going to take on too many new ones next season. My schedule's pretty full already."

"Did you ever think you'd have to turn students away this soon in your career?"

"No way. When I started the program on the Cape, I thought it would take a few years to have some competitive teams. Then you showed up one day, and as soon as I saw you skate..." He smiled, and the memory swam in his eyes. "I knew I had the start of something special. I just had to find you a great partner."

"What would've happened if none of my tryouts worked out? Hey, maybe you could've come out of retirement and skated with me." I bumped his knee under the table.

Sergei's face tightened, and he concentrated on rearranging the fork and knife on his plate. "I'm much better at coaching."

"You must've been pretty good to be a world champ." I used a light tone, hoping to encourage him to open up.

"That was a long time ago." He cleared his throat. "Do you want to come over for dinner again tomorrow night?"

His quick change of subject nibbled at my curiosity even more, but I didn't push. "I should be able to sneak away. Maybe we'll be celebrating our first international title." I clasped my hands together.

Sergei covered my hands with one of his. "Think about the program, Em, not the result."

We eventually moved from the table to the big chair in the corner of the room. Sergei stretched his legs across the ottoman, and I settled onto his lap, snuggling against his chest. He flipped on the TV and scrolled through the movie listings with the remote control.

"Any preferences?" he asked. "Comedy? Drama?"

"Comedy," I replied quickly. The darkness on Sergei's face when I'd mentioned his skating career had been enough seriousness for the evening. I cuddled deeper into Sergei's embrace but couldn't forget that stark change in his eyes. Would he ever share his story?

DESPITE THE HIGH STAKES going into the free skate, my muscles didn't contain as much nervous tension as expected. With the Canadian champions, Hyatt and Wakefield, skipping the event, Claire and Brandon stood as our main competition, and our scores had outpaced theirs by quite a bit at Nationals.

In a few strokes across the ice, Chris and I generated a gust of speed in preparation for the triple twist. My toepick stabbed into the ice, and Chris tossed me up. I pulled my arms against my body to rotate, but something didn't feel right. *Tighter, tighter!*

I couldn't adjust in time and came down too early. A glimpse of Chris's startled face flashed before me. He lost his balance as he tried to catch me, and we landed in a tangled heap on the ice, drawing a loud gasp from the audience.

Cold wetness seeped into my stockings before I scrambled to my feet. Chris wiped his hands on his pants, and our quick crossovers caught us up with the music. The side-by-side Lutzes were ahead, but the disaster on the twist replayed in my mind. I tripped on the landing of the Lutz, arms flailing to stop from falling again. *Gold is surely gone now.*

I stumbled on the next three jumps as I rushed through my technique, hurrying toward the end. *When is this program going to be over?* Chris's reassuring nods and hand squeezes didn't register with me. The music entered my ears, but all I could hear was the audience's gasps resonating in my head.

Frozen in our ending pose, heat spread over my face and down the back of my neck. *What have I done?* Saying sorry couldn't make up for mentally checking out of the program, but I apologized to Chris anyway.

He put his arm around me. "Flush it. That's all you can do."

In the kiss and cry, I steered my eyes away from Sergei. Chris clamped his hand around my shoulder, but Sergei didn't say or do anything. His stillness chilled me more than the ice on which I'd fallen.

As expected, the technical scores weren't good, and the presentation marks were the lowest we'd received all year. With one team left to skate, we sat in fourth place, off the podium for the first time that season.

I took long strides ahead of Chris and Sergei backstage, my skate guards clacking on the concrete. Before I could reach the locker room, Sergei called my name and ushered Chris and me away from the media and other skaters. Filling my chest with air, I slowly let it out and looked at him.

I was sorry I did.

He glared at me, his eyes a dark and stormy ocean about to drown me with his anger and disappointment.

"I don't ever want to see you give up like that again. The lack of effort you gave was inexcusable. You fall, you fight through it." Sergei turned to Chris. "I saw you fighting and pushing through. Emily apparently forgot how to compete tonight." He shot his scowl at me again.

Every word hit me like a bullet, and all of my frustration and humiliation threatened to burst out in the form of tears. *Don't you dare cry.*

Sergei towered over me, hands on hips. "What were you thinking about after you fell?"

I couldn't decide if I should lie because he wasn't going to like the truth. Figuring the situation couldn't get much worse, I went with honesty.

"There goes our chance at gold."

He rubbed his hand over his mouth. "How many times do I have to remind you that thinking about the results will get you nowhere?"

"I know," I croaked.

"Do you? I don't think you do. Maybe I need to repeat it a thousand more times because you obviously haven't been listening."

I fixed my eyes on the diamond pattern on his pale green tie. My chin began to tremble, so I gritted my teeth. Chris stepped closer to me and placed his hand on my back.

Sergei continued, "If you want to be the best in the world, you can't afford to slack off one second of a program. Nothing will ever be handed to you, so you'd better work harder and give your absolute best effort every time you step on the ice." He stopped to take a breath. "And you'd better show a lot more heart in Japan."

The pools of water in my eyes prepared to spill at any moment. "Got it."

Sergei marched toward the monitor to watch Claire and Brandon skate, and Chris touched my arm. "Are you okay?"

"Yeah, I just need a few minutes."

Inside the locker room, I dashed into one of the metal stalls and rooted with the flimsy lock until it latched. A cry escaped my lips, echoing off the tiled walls, so I covered my mouth with my hands. Tears poured from my eyes and trickled between my fingers.

Sergei was right, but listening to him berate me had stung my heart. The same voice that expressed affection to me every day had scolded me as if I was a disobedient child.

After a few minutes of body-shaking sobs, I repaired my splotchy makeup and met Chris in the corridor. He informed me Claire and Brandon had won, and we'd dropped to fifth place. An ABC reporter requested a television interview, so we pulled out our best media phrases.

"I just didn't have my legs under me today," I said.

"We'll learn from this and won't make the same mistakes at the Grand Prix Final," Chris stated.

Chris took the lead and answered most of the questions from the print journalists, deflecting the attention from me. I thanked him and sighed with relief when we finally escaped the media and boarded the bus to the hotel.

Sergei looked up at me from his spot near the front, but I continued down the aisle. Chris followed me to the back of the bus and shared my seat.

"I'm so sorry about tonight," I said.

"You don't have to apologize."

"I let you down," I said, leaning my head against the seat.

"I let everyone down."

He tapped my thigh. "It's happened to all of us. Don't be so hard on yourself, and try not to take what Sergei said personally."

I squirmed and faced the window. Sergei seemed to have no issue compartmentalizing his feelings. How was he going to react the next time we were alone together? Would he act like nothing had happened tonight or would his anger spill over into our relationship?

In the hotel elevator, I positioned myself on the far wall from Sergei and let a group of people fill the space between us. The doors opened on my floor, and Sergei trailed behind my rolling bag.

I peered at him. "This isn't your floor."

"I want to talk to you." His tone sounded much less severe than earlier. "Em, you're one of the most competitive people I've ever known, but you have to channel that in the right direction. I know how badly you want to win, but you're not going to get there unless you put your focus on being the best skater you can be."

"I know, and I'm trying my hardest to do that."

"Well, you didn't try very hard tonight. You gave nothing to the program, and you're too good to be pulling that crap. The judges remember—"

The elevator chimed, and a pair of Chinese ice dancers stepped out. The dainty girls paid no attention to Sergei and me as they chatted and meandered down the hall.

Sergei waited for silence. "The judges remember that kind of stuff."

"I don't know what you want me to say." I shrugged in frustration. "I'm sorry I screwed up."

"I don't want you to say anything. I want you to show me from now on you understand what I'm telling you." His volume level rose with each word.

"I understand what you're telling me, but I don't get why

you're still so mad." My voice grew louder, too.

"You know the one thing I won't tolerate is lack of effort. You could fall five times, but as long as you put your whole heart into it, I'm not going to be angry. You go out there and go through the motions, which is what I saw you doing, then we have a problem."

I kicked a nonexistent piece of dirt from my bag. "I had a bad night, okay? I'm human."

"That's not acceptable. There are no excuses for giving up."

I gave him an unwavering stare. "You can be sure it won't happen again."

"It better not."

Our eyes stayed locked on each other, neither of us uttering a word. Normally, a lingering look between us inspired a breathtaking kiss. But this look spoke of determination not desire.

"Is that all?" I asked.

Sergei's shoulders relaxed and his jaw unclenched. "I have to do my job, Em." He dropped his voice. "I don't think we should have dinner tonight."

I narrowed my eyes. "Are you punishing me?"

"You think I would..." He gaped at me and shook his head. "I just think we could use some space."

So, he's too agitated to be in the same room with me. Well, if he's going to lecture me again, I don't want to be alone with him either.

I gripped the handle of my bag tighter, straining my knuckles. "That's probably a good idea."

ON THE WAY TO lunch the next day, I checked my cell phone for the tenth time and frowned as I shoved it in my purse.

"Why don't you just call him?" Aubrey suggested.

"Because I'm afraid of what he might say."

We strolled up to the hotel restaurant and waited at the door for the hostess. My eyes swept the room but didn't find Sergei.

"Do you think he's having second thoughts about getting involved?" Aubrey asked.

The hostess greeted us and led us to a booth. I pulled the phone from my purse and set it on the table.

"I don't know what he's thinking, but I have a bad feeling."

A thick row of plants sat on the divider between our booth and the adjacent one, and a deep voice carried through it. "The veal with the roasted potatoes."

"That's Viktor," Aubrey whispered. "Watch what you say."

A female followed with her order, and I scrunched my eyebrows. "Who's that?"

We listened longer and determined the woman was Sylvia, another ice dance coach. After giving our orders to the waitress, the sound of my name jerked my head toward the greenery.

"What?" Aubrey asked but I shushed her and scooted closer to the divider.

"I couldn't believe how they skated," Sylvia said. "I've never seen Emily look so off."

I closed my eyes and pressed my fingers to my forehead. My meltdown was probably a hot topic among many.

"Sergei obviously didn't have them ready," Viktor said. "His lack of experience is showing. He's getting all the credit for Emily and Chris's success, but they had the technical goods before they came to him. He's had more luck than anything."

I gawked at Aubrey. "Did you hear him? He acts like Sergei hasn't taught us anything."

"I don't know," Sylvia rebutted. "Emily used to be a head case, and she's skated much better under Sergei."

"She looked like a head case yesterday," Viktor commented.

That wasn't Sergei's fault.

I slid back to the open end of the booth. "I don't wanna hear any more."

"You know how Viktor is," Aubrey said. "He finds fault with everyone."

I propped my elbows on the table and held my head in my hands. Besides embarrassing myself with my pitiful performance, I'd made Sergei look bad. What a fine showing I'd made as a newly crowned national champion.

My phone sang its melodic tone, and I snatched it from the table. Sergei's name stared at me from the screen. I gulped and answered, "Hey."

"Are you busy?"

"I'm at lunch, but I'll be done soon." I doubted I could eat much.

"Can you come by then?"

"Sure."

Aubrey mouthed, "Sergei?" and I nodded as I hung up the phone.

The sandwich I ordered sat half-uneaten when Aubrey and I left the restaurant later. We parted ways in the elevator, and I crossed and uncrossed my arms while waiting for Sergei to open his door.

He didn't greet me with a hug or a kiss, the first bad sign. The second came when I stood near the window and he stayed near the door, leaving what felt like a mile between us.

"I've been thinking about this," he said. "And if we're going to make these two very different relationships work, we're going to have to find a way to separate them as best we can. I think when we're at competitions we should keep things strictly professional, so all our focus can be in one place—me as the coach and you as the skater."

"That sounds reasonable, but it's not like we can flip a

switch and turn off our feelings when we're here."

"I know it's not that easy, but I have to concentrate one hundred percent on being your coach when you're competing. If we sneak around and see each other, I think the situation will be more complicated."

Through the large window I viewed the appropriately gray afternoon before turning back to Sergei. "If I hadn't messed up yesterday, we wouldn't be having this conversation."

Sergei crossed the room, shortening the distance between us. "Probably not, but it would've come up at some point. If I have to be tough with you, I need to do it without worrying if I'm hurting your feelings. That's the way it has to be if I'm going to do my job the best way I know how."

"You didn't seem too worried when you were lecturing me."

"I'm not going to apologize for what I said because you needed to hear it. Maybe you think my expectations are too high, but when I see talent like yours..." He paused and wet his lips. "You're so good, Em. The way you move across the ice... you have this incredible, graceful power. Sometimes when I'm watching you, I get so mesmerized I forget I'm your coach."

A ray of warmth broke through the gloomy fog around us. It touched my heart and sent a tingle down my spine. My voice stuck in my throat. "Really?"

"That's why I was so frustrated with you yesterday. It killed me to see you skate with so little life. I want you to understand how much better than that you are."

I responded with a steady nod. "I do. I don't ever want to disappoint you or Chris or myself like that again. And since I won't let it happen again, I don't see why we can't still spend time together."

"The stress of competition could come between us, and the last thing I want is to fight with you." He came closer to me but kept his arms at his sides. An invisible force field existed around me.

"I don't want that either." I chewed on my lip. "So, I guess I should go, then, since I shouldn't be here."

I started forward, but Sergei blocked my path. "It's not that I don't want you here. My feelings haven't changed," he said softly. "I just think we need this separation."

He moved aside, and I trudged to the door. Sergei followed me and scanned the hall, while I lingered inside the room, waiting for a show of affection that never came. Sergei's sad eyes watching me leave was the last image I saw before I walked away.

CHAPTER SIXTEEN

I TAPPED MY FOOT AND CHECKED the clock behind the hotel registration desk. Chris was never late, and he knew how anxious I was for our first Grand Prix Final practice. Had he set his alarm wrong? We'd both synched our watches with Tokyo time when we'd arrived the previous day. I paced the length of the narrow lobby and dialed Chris on my cell phone.

"I was getting ready to call you," he said, his voice tight and raspy. "I'm burning up. I hope I don't have the flu."

"Oh no." I dropped into the nearest chair. "I knew you weren't feeling great last night, but I thought it was just a cold."

"I feel like someone's sitting on my chest."

"You sound terrible. Have you called Dr. Parker?" Our team doctor took care of all our aches and pains, from a case of the sniffles to broken limbs.

"He's on his way. I already talked to Sergei."

"Let me know what the doctor says. And call me if you need anything."

I slunk down in the chair and blew out a long breath. We had two days until the short program. Would that be enough time for Chris to regain strength? The Grand Prix Final's unique format, requiring two long programs in addition to the short, could be problematic for someone not in top condition.

I went upstairs and soon received Chris's diagnosis—a respiratory infection that required antibiotics and rest. With Chris quarantined to his room and Sergei keeping his distance from me, I spent the next few days hanging out with some of my American teammates, singles skaters I knew casually from other competitions.

Our group explored the city, and I put my new digital camera, a birthday gift from my parents, to good use. Tokyo's skyscrapers and bright electronic signs reminded me of Times Square in New York City. After touring downtown, we left the bustling streets and visited a Japanese landscape garden, where we enjoyed a peaceful walk among the koi ponds and meticulously manicured trees.

I met Chris for practice the morning of our short program, and he scrolled through the pictures on my camera with a frown.

"My first trip to Asia, and I spend it in my room." His voice still resembled a heavy chain smoker's, but his fever had broken.

"Maybe we can do some sight-seeing after our last event," I said.

Chris coughed into his bicep, and his chest rattled like a clap of thunder.

"I should wear one of those surgical masks," I joked.

We took the ice, and I smiled with each crossover, relishing the sting of the cold breeze on my skin. The two-day break had put extra spring in my legs. I flexed my knees and generated speed with the slightest push. Chris kept pace with my movements as we warmed up, and Sergei gave us instructions for our program run-through.

"Skip the jumps and the throw, but do everything else full out. Chris, you feel good?"

He inhaled and nodded. "I'm good."

The music operator cued up our piece, and we performed the choreography as if we were being judged. Chris held me with his usual strong grip in the lift, but during our final element, the death spiral, his labored breathing struck my ears. He must've held in the coughs for two and a half minutes because the moment the music ended, he succumbed to a long spell.

We drifted toward the boards, and I patted the back of his black T-shirt. "Are you okay?"

He began wheezing and couldn't answer me. As he bent over and put his hands on his knees, I shot Sergei a look of panic. He'd already signaled the medical staff, who quickly scooted onto the ice in their sneakers. Two paramedics held Chris's arms and guided him to the exit while he continued to breathe in shallow gasps. I followed them to the boards and wrung my hands as they disappeared backstage.

"Stay loose," Sergei said. "I'll check on him."

I stroked around and practiced the triple Lutz and triple toe loop, but my legs weren't as steady as earlier. Being alone on the ice with two other pairs unnerved me. Especially since one of the other pairs was Oksana and Denis, who always reeled off their big elements right in front of me. I missed Chris's calming presence and the comfort of his hand around mine.

Sergei returned rinkside, and I raced over to him as fast as my skates could take me.

"He's breathing normally now," he said. "They gave him oxygen, and Dr. Parker is monitoring him."

I hopped through the ice door and covered my blades with their guards. "Will he be okay?"

"Doc's going to check him again before the competition." Sergei held my Team USA jacket open for me, and I slipped my arms inside. We walked backstage to the medical room, where Chris reclined on an exam table. A clear oxygen mask sat at his side.

He smiled between coughs. "You came to visit me."

I lightly punched his arm. "Don't ever scare me like that again."

"I was testing you to see how much you'd miss me."

"It sucked out there without you."

His grin grew wider. "That's exactly what I wanted to hear."

We went back to the hotel, and the doctor paid Chris a visit in the afternoon. He declared my partner fit to compete, so I put on my game face and prepared to skate.

The enthusiastic Japanese fans greeted us with fervor as we positioned ourselves to begin our short program. Chris's broad chest expanded and contracted, his tight black shirt stretching with the deep breath. I squinted up at the bright lights and prayed, *Please, Lord, watch over us the next two and a half minutes.*

We motored through the twist and the jumps, and I watched Chris for any sign of struggle. His eyes were set in concentration. As we sped backward into the takeoff for the throw Lutz, I heard a tiny wheeze behind me. Chris propelled me upward but with not enough air.

My blade landed on the ice, but I was tilted. A jolt of adrenaline hit me as my body anticipated the fall. I tumbled down, and my right hand slammed into the ice. A burning pain shot up my arm, causing me to gasp.

I gritted my teeth and wiggled my fingers as I stood up. Able to move them, I figured nothing was broken, so I nodded to Chris to finish the program. He gripped my hand for the death spiral, and my wrist felt like a log on a bonfire. I screamed on the inside but kept my forced smile intact through the remainder of the program.

Sergei waited at the edge of the ice door with his hand out toward me. I held my wrist close to my body, and Sergei circled his arm around my waist as we sat down in the kiss and cry.

"We'll get you to the doctor in a minute," he said.

He massaged my back, and I tried to focus on his touch rather than the ache spreading from my fingertips to my elbow. Chris started to say something but dissolved into another coughing fit.

"You okay?" I asked while Sergei handed him a bottle of water.

He sat up straighter, allowing more air into his lungs. After chugging the water, he panted. "I'm sorry about the throw."

"You don't have to be sorry. No apologies, remember?"

Coughs consumed him again, interrupting his reply. *Thank God this isn't live on TV back home.* Our families would surely freak out if they saw our current state. I'd call my parents as soon as I found out the extent of my injury.

The fall put us in fifth place out of six teams. We hustled backstage after the last score was read, and Dr. Parker gave me a quick examination. He wanted an X-ray, so I changed out of my costume, and an event volunteer offered to drive us to the hospital. Sergei ordered Chris to rest at the hotel while he accompanied the doctor and me.

The other patients in the emergency room regarded me with curiosity as I still wore my heavy makeup from the competition and my hair shone from the glittery hairspray. I sat between Dr. Parker and Sergei, listening to the babble of Japanese around us and wrinkling my nose at the pungent antiseptic odor.

After a short wait, a petite nurse brought me to a small curtained area, where a technician took images of my wrist. Dr. Parker waited outside for the attending physician, and Sergei came in when the technician left. He pulled the green curtains tighter and placed a soft kiss on my forehead.

"How's the pain?" Worry resided in his eyes.

My lips formed a tiny smile. "I'm trying not to think

about it."

He skimmed his fingertips along my swollen skin, and for a moment, the throbbing sensation disappeared, supplanted by a deep yearning to pull Sergei against me.

The curtains flew open as the two doctors entered, and Sergei backed away.

"You have a mild sprain," Dr. Parker said. "We'll get it wrapped and then talk about treatment."

"Will I be able to skate tomorrow night?"

The doctor scratched his gray-bearded chin. "We'll have to see how the swelling looks tomorrow and how you feel."

I straightened my spine and glanced at Sergei. He'd said he wanted to see "more heart." If Chris could skate through illness, then I could skate through pain. I was going to show Sergei just how much heart and desire I had.

BETWEEN ICING MY WRIST and keeping it elevated, I didn't get much sleep. I'd lucked into a single room, so I had no roommate to bother during my restless night. By morning, the swelling had decreased, but my wrist ached as if someone had twisted it with a wrench. Dr. Parker looked at it before practice, and I held my breath, waiting for his opinion.

"Test it off the ice first to see if it's strong enough for the lifts."

I exhaled and smiled. "Will do."

With my arm rewrapped in a tight bandage, Chris and I walked through our free skate backstage at the arena. Sergei hovered nearby, observing with a keen eye. Chris took my hands and swung me up into the lasso lift, the one that required the most strength. I grimaced as my right arm burned, supporting all my weight, but I maintained my upright position without wavering.

"How did it feel?" Sergei asked after we finished the

walk-through.

"It's sore, but I think it'll hold me."

"We'll do each lift once on the ice for practice." Sergei rested his hands on my shoulders. "Let me know at any point if something doesn't feel right."

We survived a shortened practice with no coughing spells or other disasters, and I retreated to my hotel room to apply more ice to my wrist. As I lay against a pile of pillows and watched the sole English station on the television, I thought how wonderful it would feel to be nestled in Sergei's arms right then. Why'd he have to insist on the separation?

My attempt to nap was unsuccessful, and I headed to the arena with a swirl of nervous energy. While Dr. Parker secured my wrist with a new dressing, I fidgeted on the exam table, anxious to show everyone the injury wouldn't keep me down… anxious to show Sergei I could thrive under adversity.

Chris and I charged onto the ice for the six-minute warm-up. He pressed me up into the lasso lift, and I balanced myself with my right hand clasped in his. My forearm wobbled, sending a wave of unease over me, but I kept my posture stiff and we completed the element.

"That was a little shaky," Chris said.

I fingered the edge of my bandage. "I just need to lock in the grip better."

We skated around the two other pairs and into our second lift, a lasso with a change of position. I went up with the support of two hands but had to let one go and rely on my injured wrist to hold myself up. This time, the wobble escalated into a forceful tremor, and my arm began to collapse.

"Down!" I alerted Chris.

I dropped and latched onto his shoulders, holding on with all my strength. He slowed his motion and steadied himself to prevent us from both ending up on the ice. My feet, quivering from the close call, found the ground, and I patted Chris's chest as a thank-you.

We skated over to the boards to regroup, and Sergei leaned forward, hands spread apart on the barrier. "Em, if your wrist is too weak—"

"It's not." I avoided his concerned gaze and inspected my flesh-colored wrap. "I think this should be tighter."

"Em, look at me."

My eyes met his, and he angled further toward me. "If you can't be completely secure in the air, it's too risky to skate. You need to listen to your body."

I set my jaw. "I can do this."

His lips pursed in response, and he pointed at Chris. "If she's loose on the first lift, even a tiny bit, I want you to stop the program. Understood?"

Chris nodded, and we finished the warm-up with easy stroking to keep our legs warm. As time expired, I rushed off the ice to find Dr. Parker, and he adjusted my bandage.

I can do this, I repeated over and over.

We were second to skate, so I didn't have much time to become anxious. Just like in the short program, our opening elements presented no problems. But the first lift was moments away, and if I wavered a centimeter, Chris had to follow Sergei's demand, and we'd be out of the competition.

I rose above Chris's head and locked my arm into an immovable pillar. The strain pulled all the way from my abdominal muscles, stretching my pain tolerance to the maximum level. I dove deep inside my mind, searching for a tranquil place to block out the discomfort. With pinpoint concentration, I remained still and balanced myself without a single twitch.

Heart and desire.

In each of the remaining two lifts, I zoned in with the same focus and achieved my desired position. The rest of the program passed in a blur as the other elements seemed easy in comparison. At the end, Chris and I shared a long hug and matching sighs of relief.

"We made it through," Chris said.

"But we still have another program to skate," I moaned.

He shook his head. "I'll think about that tomorrow."

Sergei wore a wry smile in the kiss and cry, and he squeezed me to his side. "You made your point."

"I told you I could do it."

His smile diminished, and he cinched his arm around me. "If anything had happened…"

The weight in his voice showed how worried he'd been. I faced him with my hand over my heart. "I had it all under control."

With our impressive performance, we moved up one spot to fourth place, meaning we'd compete against the third place team for the bronze medal in the "Super Final" round. In third was the top German pair, a team we'd beaten in Paris. I liked our chances… provided our bodies could hold up one more day.

IN OUR HEAD-TO-HEAD BATTLE with the Germans, they skated first, so Chris and I heard their scores as we waited on the ice for our introduction. They earned 5.6's and 5.7's, marks we could surpass with a clean performance.

All the skaters were using old programs for the final round since no one had time to create new ones. We'd retooled our *La Boheme* free skate from the prior season with some changes to the lifts and jumps, but we hadn't spent much time practicing the revamped program. Relying on muscle memory was vital, and we didn't have that luxury, adding an element of uncertainty to my usual nervousness.

Because I had to think through the program as if it was new, the lingering soreness in my wrist moved to the back of my mind. We took our time with each step of the choreography, slowly building momentum, but halfway through the performance, fatigue snuck up on me. I bent my knees, but I couldn't generate the speed I needed. My sleep-deprived body wailed.

I breathed deeper and pumped my legs harder. Beside me, Chris whispered, "Almost there," and I found an untapped source of energy which carried me to the end.

Chris gave our final pose such enthusiasm that he lost his balance and went down on one knee, almost dropping me onto the ice. We both burst into laughter and continued chuckling through our bows. Such an ending summed up all the calamities of the past week.

I collapsed into Sergei's arms, not wanting to leave their warmth and comfort, but we had to sit and listen to the marks. Chris bumped my elbow as each 5.7 and 5.8 flashed on the scoreboard. I rocked back and forth on the bench, holding in my excitement until we received confirmation. Our scores were lined up against the German team's, and we had higher numbers across the board. The bronze medal was ours.

Chris and I jumped up at the same time, and he picked me up and twirled me around. Sergei joined us for a group hug, and I sniffed back tears. We'd scratched and clawed our way through the competition, proving we belonged with the top teams in the world.

After we answered the media's questions with lots of smiles, Chris ran to the locker room to call Marley, who would be waking up for practice at home. Sergei motioned me away from the jumble of people backstage and gently closed his hands around my arms.

"The way you skated tonight—that's who you are. You have the fight and the fire to overcome anything. Always remember that."

I hugged him and then stepped back, but our eyes remained in the embrace, speaking the emotions we couldn't physically express. We soon realized we weren't looking at each other the way a coach and student would and quickly averted our gazes.

Mine landed on Chris staring at us.

He walked toward us with a hesitant gait. "I couldn't get a signal on my phone. They said we're gonna do medals in a minute anyway."

We were herded to the ice with the other medalists for the ceremony, and Chris's excited grin returned. Maybe he hadn't seen anything between Sergei and me? We were right on track with our skating as we approached the World Championships, and having Chris discover my secret could lead to a sudden and fiery derailment.

CHAPTER SEVENTEEN

ACROSS FROM THE HOTEL, THE NEON orange lights of the nightclub beamed on the dark street, and the heavy bass of techno music vibrated the sidewalk beneath our feet. I paused in front of the club and tilted my head toward Chris.

"I'm *so* tired. Tell me again why I let you talk me into going out."

He slung his arm around me. "Because we can't have a party without you."

"Shouldn't you be taking it easy? You still sound pretty hoarse."

"I'm not wasting my last night here. All I've seen of Tokyo is my hotel room and the arena."

"Well, somebody better catch me if I fall over from exhaustion on the dance floor." The door opened and a couple exited, giving me a glimpse of the hefty bouncer inside. "The age to get in here is twenty, right?"

"Yeah. We're both legal here." Chris grinned.

We entered the club, and the Sumo-wrestler-lookalike positioned at the door eyed me up but didn't ask for ID. Through the thick crowd, I searched for familiar faces, and two of our American teammates waved us over to the far end of the sleek glass bar. Above us, lights twirled on the ceiling and shone on a second floor with tables, also packed with people.

After being outside in the chilly night, the warmth of the room felt good at first, but soon the humidity sank over me like a soggy blanket. I pulled the lacy neckline of my tank top away from my skin, where tiny beads of sweat had already formed.

Chris beckoned the bartender and took care of my request for water. I set my cell phone on the bar and grabbed an empty stool, while Chris jumped onto the one next to me, swiveling in my direction.

"So, what was Sergei telling you before the medal ceremony?" he asked. "You guys looked pretty intense."

I gulped and choked on my water. "Oh... um... he just reminded me I have the ability to fight through anything. You know, since I had some problems in Salt Lake."

"I think he was too hard on you last week. It's like he expects you to be perfect all the time."

Chris doesn't suspect anything. I bent my head and let my hair fall across my face so he couldn't see me exhale with relief.

"That's because you hardly ever make mistakes." I poked his arm.

"Yeah, right." He snorted and swigged his soda. "I'm the reason you're wearing that bandage."

"No, you're not. We both messed up. And you were dealing with a lot of issues at the time, like coughing up a lung, not being able to *breathe* properly—"

He shook his head. "All excuses."

"And valid ones! You shouldn't talk about Sergei being too hard on me when you're always too hard on yourself."

Our friends waved for us to go dance with them, and Chris hopped off his stool. "You coming?"

"Not yet. I need a few more minutes of rest."

"Only a few minutes!" he said as he headed toward the mob on the dance floor. I didn't know where Chris had found his second wind, but lack of sleep from tending to my wrist had sapped my energy.

Next to me sat a group of Russian skaters speaking their language, so I didn't care that the pulsating music drowned out their voices. Oksana rose from her stool and slithered up to me in her skin-tight mini dress and stiletto heels, a cocktail in her hand.

"Nice comeback today," she said.

I lifted one eyebrow. "Thanks. We were pretty happy with how we skated."

"You were happy with bronze medal?" she asked, a snicker to her tone.

Ah, yes, there's the condescension I expected. I sipped my water and gave her a closed-mouth smile. "Happy for now. So you shouldn't get too comfortable."

Behind her, Sergei and a Russian ice dance coach appeared in the crowd. The coach went over to his team, while Sergei came toward us. The colorful lights flashed over him, streaking his golden brown hair with splashes of blue and red. My skin tingled and I straightened up. Suddenly, I felt much more energized.

Oksana moved close to Sergei and pointed her green cat-like eyes on him. Cocking her head, she uttered something in Russian, and I clenched my hand around my glass. Sergei backed away from Oksana and sat on Chris's stool.

"Thanks, but I need to talk to Emily."

I bit my lip to contain the grin, loving the fact he replied in English. Oksana sashayed back to her group, and Sergei began rolling up the sleeves of his striped button-down shirt. I found myself staring at his tanned forearms and imagining their taut muscles wrapped around my waist.

"It feels like a sauna in here," he said.

"I know. I'm sweating just sitting here." I put down my water and fanned myself with my hand. "So, did you really need to talk to me?"

"No, I just wanted to get rid of Oksana. She asked me to sit with them." He flicked his head toward the Russians and then treated me to a smile. "But I'd much rather sit here."

I couldn't contain my grin now. "I didn't expect to see you guys out."

"We finished dinner and heard everyone had come over here. I thought you were going to sleep?"

"I got peer-pressured into coming." I laughed. "You know Chris can talk me into anything."

"Well, I'm very glad he did."

Chris squeezed through the mass of bodies and yanked on my non-injured wrist. "You're not going to sit down all night."

He guided me onto the dance floor, and I pouted at Sergei over my shoulder. A couple of songs later, I escaped for hydration. Sergei was still in the same spot, now watching a replay of the competition on the TV behind the bar. I asked him to order a fresh glass of water for me, and I pulled my hair up, twisting it in a roll. A few damp tendrils stuck to the back of my neck.

Sergei passed me the water and drank in my appearance. Luckily, no one was paying attention to us as his eyes traveled the length of my body. Judging from his smile, he liked what he saw.

"Your face is red," he said.

I touched the glass to my flushed cheek. It cooled my face but not the heat I felt from Sergei's appreciative stare.

"I'm just really hot," I stammered.

Sergei's smile widened, and he took a sip of his drink. "No comment."

One of the Russian coaches called out to Sergei and asked him a question I couldn't translate. They started a long exchange, so I went upstairs to see if it was less stuffy. I found a pocket of space away from the tables and rested my elbows on the railing to watch my friends dance below.

After a few minutes, I sensed someone behind me. My pulse quickened as Sergei's woody cologne floated under my nose. Sergei mimicked my stance and stood close enough to me his forearm touched mine on the railing. The scene looked perfectly innocent, but no one could see the million sparks of electricity generated through that slight physical contact.

"Do you know how bad I want to kiss you right now?" Sergei's eyes wandered down to my mouth.

I let out an exaggerated gasp. "Wouldn't that be against your rules?"

"The competition is technically over."

"Yes, it is."

"Can you get out of here soon?"

My heart skipped a few beats, and I nodded.

"I'll leave first." He stood up straight. "Meet in my room?"

"Okay."

His lips drew into a slow smile as he walked away, leaving me to count the minutes before I could make my exit. I tapped my high heels on the wood floor, waiting for an entire song to play. When the music transitioned, I went downstairs and sought out Chris.

"Hey, I'm going back to the hotel. You stay and have fun."

"It's still early! You're bailing already?"

"I'm beat. I'll see you in the morning!"

I scurried away and couldn't get out the door and across the street to the hotel fast enough. A light rain had begun to fall, but I danced so quickly between the raindrops I stayed dry.

As I jumped into the elevator, I realized going to Sergei's room in the middle of the night might send him a message I didn't want to send. I'd always had a clear idea of when I wanted to experience my first time with a man. My ideals were very conservative, but I'd intended to adhere to them. However, Sergei had unlocked feelings within me I didn't know existed.

By the time I knocked on his door, I had more adrenaline pumping through me than I had when I competed. The door had barely shut before Sergei pulled me to him, his lips claiming mine. The hunger and passion in his kiss overwhelmed me with an aching rush. I clung to his biceps; his strong, tense muscles in my grasp.

We stumbled further into the room, and Sergei brushed my hair back, placing a tender kiss on my collarbone. Everything inside me turned to liquid. Only a week had passed since he'd last held me in his arms, but it seemed so much longer.

"I want you so much," he breathed against my parted lips.

With his body pressed to mine, I felt just how much. Both my heart and my mind raced, in direct conflict with each other. How could something I believed was wrong feel so right?

The hem of my shirt rose with Sergei's hands, and my breath hitched as his fingertips explored my back and my stomach, leaving a path of goose bumps. I was having a hard time hearing any rational thoughts in my head. Every touch set my skin on fire and awakened a new desire.

Stop thinking and let yourself go. Then the voice of reason interjected, *No, this isn't how you want this to happen.*

Sergei slipped his hands from under my blouse and laced his fingers through mine. Our mouths melded together, he eased me with his body toward the bed. The battle in my mind came to a grinding halt.

"Sergei, I'm..." I swallowed to catch my breath. "I've never..."

He brushed a soft kiss on my lips. "We can take it slow."

His tempting eyes and luscious mouth had my head spinning, but I fought to stay strong.

"I'm sorry, I can't," I whispered.

He shifted slightly backward and caressed my hair, letting his fingers follow the waves. "It's okay if you're not ready."

I sat on the bed and looked down at my lap. "You don't understand."

"Then talk to me." He dropped to his knees in front of me.

I picked up my head. "I'm not going to be ready anytime soon because I'm waiting until I'm married."

His face didn't twitch, crease, show any reaction, so I rambled, "I know it's old-fashioned and seems ridiculous to a lot of people, but it's something I feel strongly about. I should've told you this before. I just had no idea how or when..." I bent forward, setting my elbows on my thighs.

Silence remained as I gathered Sergei was digesting the information. The pitter-patter of raindrops against the window grew louder the longer the stillness stretched.

Sergei gently clutched my hands. "Em."

Our eyes met, and I marveled at how his cool blue eyes could also radiate warmth.

"I want to be with you in every way... so much," he said. "But if this is what you want, then I'll respect that."

"You're really okay with this?" I searched his face for any signs of doubt.

A tiny smile tugged at his mouth. "It's not my preference, but I can deal with it."

"Are you absolutely sure? You might feel that way right now, but if you think it's going to be an issue, I need you to tell me now before we get even deeper into this."

The smile left his face, and he studied me with a powerful stare. His hesitation clawed at my gut.

He released my hands and sat next to me on the bed. "I'm sure." He cupped my chin. "Because I am absolutely, completely in love with you."

My heart did somersaults. I wasn't expecting to hear that, and the words rang in my ears like the most beautiful melody ever played.

I palmed his firm chest and locked my lips on his. Looking into his eyes, I prepared to say what I'd longed to tell him, what I'd known since the sunrise at the cliffs.

"I love you, too."

Sergei brought me closer and kissed me, dizzying me with joy. Wrapped in his arms, I smiled up at him. "You're probably thinking 'Why'd I have to fall in love with the most chaste girl on the Cape?'"

He chuckled. "No, I'm not."

"Then tell me what you are thinking. Honestly."

"I'm thinking I'm going to be taking a lot of cold showers." He laughed again.

I cringed while laughing with him. "I'm sorry."

"Don't apologize." He kissed the tip of my nose.

"Seriously, though, I shouldn't have let you think it was going to happen. I let myself get caught up in the moment."

"It's very easy to get caught up with you." Sergei ran his hand lightly down my arm. "I should've talked to you instead of assuming you were ready."

A sharp rap on the door froze us. We gave each other startled looks.

"Who could that be?" I whispered.

We both stood as another knock came. When Sergei pointed to the bathroom, I nodded and crept toward it. Before closing the door, I noticed a trace of lipstick on the corner of Sergei's mouth. I erased the smudge with my thumb and made myself scarce.

Sergei answered the knocking, and Chris's voice carried through the crack in the bathroom door.

"Hey, sorry to bug you so late. Have you seen Emily since you left the club?"

Sergei hesitated. "No, is something wrong?"

"She forgot her phone on the bar, so I went to her room and knocked a bunch of times, and she didn't answer."

I sucked in a breath. *Oh, no.*

Sergei paused again. "She's probably in the shower. Why don't you wait and call her room in a little while?"

"Yeah, maybe so. Thanks, man. Sorry to bother you."

"No problem. Let me know if you don't find her."

Chris left, and I emerged from the bathroom. "I'd better get to my room before he calls." I leaned against the door. "I could come back afterward."

"As tempting as that sounds, I don't want anyone to see you coming back up here."

"Good point." I reached out and put my hands on Sergei's waist. "I'm still glad we decided to break the rules tonight."

He angled toward me and rested one arm on the door. With his finger, he traced a line down my breastbone, stopping where the V of my neckline came to a point.

"You're a bad influence on me," he whispered in my ear.

His chest pressed me to the door as his kiss warmed me all over. I smiled to myself. I was always going to have a fondness for hotel room doors.

I stroked his cheek, letting my hand slide down his prickly skin to his open collar. "Thank you for being patient with me."

He touched his forehead to mine. "You're worth every second of the wait."

I sauntered down the hall, reflecting on Sergei's loving response, and turned the corner to the elevators. Seeing Chris there, I jumped backward. Seconds later, the elevator chimed, and I took a cautious peek. Chris was gone. *One more month of hiding this from him. Shouldn't be too hard… right?*

CHAPTER EIGHTEEN

I blinked in surprise at the sight of the bright bouquet in Sergei's hands. He handed them to me with an equally vibrant smile, and I brought the hot pink roses close to my nose. They held the sweet smell of love and promise. I reached up and thanked Sergei with a lingering kiss.

"I'll get a vase and put them on the table for dinner."

With one week remaining before the World Championships, we had a rare opportunity for an evening alone at my house. Aubrey was out with Marley, and Chris and Trevor were playing basketball at the gym, so we looked forward to no interruptions.

Sergei followed me to the kitchen, where I rummaged through the cupboards above the sink. I retrieved a large cut-glass vase from the corner cabinet and delicately removed the flowers from the green tissue paper.

"The pizza smells amazing," Sergei said.

"Thanks, I hope it tastes as good as it smells. I haven't made one from scratch in a long time."

"I have no doubt it will be delicious." He slipped his arm

around me.

"If it isn't, you'd better tell me. Pretend we're at the rink where you have no problem criticizing me." I tapped his nose with the tip of a pink bloom.

I finished arranging the flowers and took in another whiff of their scent. "Can you grab the sparkling water and the glasses? I already brought the plates and silverware up to the terrace."

While Sergei set the patio table, I placed the vase in the center and positioned candles on either side. Their flickering light illuminated the bouquet, making the roses appear an even deeper shade of pink.

"I'll get the pizza," I said. "I put a stack of CDs on the stereo if you want to pick out a few."

"You're sure you don't need any help?"

"No, I've got it." I waved Sergei toward the CD player on the edge of the patio.

In the kitchen, I pulled the pizza from the oven and admired the crust I'd kneaded, now golden and crisp. The gooey mozzarella cheese had melted in perfection around the green peppers, black olives, spinach, and artichokes. My mouth watered, so I pulled a tiny bundle of spinach from the pizza and blew on it before taking a taste. I hummed in approval as the cheese and leafy greens combined for the ideal flavor marriage in my mouth.

As I prepared to make the last slice through the pie, a loud knock on the door halted me. My neck tensed, and I wiped my hands on a dishtowel, bunching it into a clenched ball as I climbed the steps to the foyer and opened the door.

"Surprise!" Mom cried.

All the blood rushed from my head. I gripped the doorknob tighter.

"Mom! What are you doing here?"

She walked past me, rolling a small suitcase behind her. "I don't have class tomorrow, so I thought I'd surprise you and watch you practice. It's been so long since I've done that."

I realized my mouth still hung open, so I shut it halfway. "Oh, that's… that's sweet."

She sniffed the air. "Did you make pizza? It smells wonderful."

My mind worked overtime. How could I spin the situation to make it look innocent? I wasn't ready to drop the big bomb on Mom.

"Yeah, um, I've been telling Sergei how good my pizza is, so I made one to show him. He's on the terrace. We're going to eat up there."

As soon as the words left my mouth, I realized what Mom would find if she went upstairs—the candlelit table, the bouquet of roses…

In a quick babble, I added, "But it's getting kinda chilly out, so we should probably eat down here. There's plenty enough for all of us."

"No, it's such a nice evening. We should eat outside. I don't get to enjoy this place much anymore." She smiled and patted the oak banister. "I'm going to go up and say hi to Sergei. Is Aubrey here?"

"She went out with Marley." I hoped she couldn't detect the shakiness in my tone. "I'll get the pizza and we can go up together."

On the terrace, Sergei had his back to us as he inserted a CD into the disc player. I slid the glass door shut, and he said, "I was getting ready to come look for—"

Turning and seeing Mom, he swallowed. "Hi, Laura."

U2's "With or Without You" streamed from the stereo. The love song only added more evidence of a romantic setting.

There's no way I can spin this.

Mom paused next to the door and took in the scene. Her eyes darted around the terrace before settling on Sergei. She put on a smile, one I instantly identified as insincere.

"Hello, Sergei," she said.

Normally, he would greet Mom with a kiss on the cheek, but he looked so stunned he didn't move. I stood motionless with the pizza in my hand, not sure what to say or do next. Thinking quickly, I set the pan on the table.

"Um, Mom, you need something to drink. Why don't you go down and get whatever you'd like?" I needed to talk to Sergei so we could decide how to best explain the situation.

"Why don't you come with me?" she said. "I'm not sure where you keep everything."

That was a lie, so I knew she wanted to corner me downstairs. She walked ahead of me, and I gave Sergei an apologetic frown as I trailed Mom inside.

When we reached the kitchen, I opened the refrigerator and stuck my head behind the door. "We have tea, juice—"

"Look at me, Emily."

My mother stood small in stature, but she had a powerful voice that commanded attention, and years of delivering classroom lectures had strengthened her tone. I closed the refrigerator door, my sweaty palm sliding down the handle.

"What's going on here?" she asked.

"What do you mean?" I said in a weak attempt to delay the certain anguish.

"Emily, I'm not stupid. What I saw upstairs was not dinner between a student and her coach or even dinner between friends. It had romantic date written all over it, and I want you to tell me exactly what's going on."

Drops of perspiration collected on my forehead, a result of the heat surrounding the oven. "Mom, please promise you'll hear me out before you start lecturing."

"I need to hear what you're going to say before I make any promises."

I steadied myself against the counter and blurted out in one breath, "Sergei and I are seeing each other. We know there are risks involved, but we have it under control and nothing has changed with my training."

She inhaled, her nostrils flaring. "How long has this been going on?"

"Since Nationals."

Her caramel-colored eyes darkened until they were almost black. "So, for two months you've been lying."

A lump formed in my throat. There were few things I hated more than disappointing my parents.

"I wanted to wait and tell you after the season so you could see we've been able to make it work."

"Emily, have you really thought this through? What if he breaks your heart? What will you do then? Would you be able to keep training with him? What does Chris have to say about this?"

Her questions spun around me like a tornado. I chose to answer her last one. "I haven't told him yet," I mumbled.

"Huh! Well, at least I'm not the last to know."

"The only person who knows is Aubrey. We're keeping it quiet for obvious reasons."

"So, you're sneaking around. Is that part of the appeal to you?"

"No, I wish it didn't have to be this way. I wish I could tell everyone and have a normal relationship."

She started toward the stairs. "I need to speak to Sergei about this."

"Mom, please...." I reached out a feeble hand.

"I'm paying this man to teach you, not to seduce you." She clenched her jaw. "Please tell me you're not sleeping with him."

My mouth formed a perfect O. "Mom! You know I wouldn't."

"I don't know anything anymore. You're lying and sneaking around. Who knows what else is going on here." She threw her hands up in the air.

"You're blowing this up into way too much."

"Can you blame me? I'm more than a little concerned.

You've never had a boyfriend, and suddenly, you're involved with your coach, a man who's much older than you—"

I rolled my eyes. "He's twenty-six. It's not like he's forty."

"And you just turned twenty and don't have much experience with men. I don't want to see you taken advantage of."

"He would never do anything to hurt me," I insisted.

"You can't be naïve, Emily. How much do you really know about him? What do you know about his past?"

"I know enough—" I stopped when Sergei stepped into the doorway.

Mom scowled at him. "Emily was just telling me about your relationship. I have a few questions for you."

I closed my eyes. *Oh, no.*

"I understand if you have some concerns, but I want you to know I only have the best intentions," Sergei said calmly.

"If you had the best intentions, you would've kept your hands off my daughter," she snapped.

I wanted to speak, but utter mortification prevented me from forming any coherent sentences.

Sergei moved next to me. "I had my own doubts about whether we could make this work, but we've been able to do it so far."

Mom folded her arms across her chest and gave him a pointed stare. "Is Emily the first student you've dated?"

Here comes the interrogation.

"Yes, and I didn't think I ever would. It just kind of... happened."

"What exactly 'just kind of happened?' I'd like to know how all of this started." Mom shifted her scowl back and forth from Sergei to me.

"Maybe it would be better if Sergei left, and just you and I talked," I suggested. No need to put him through the torture, too.

"No, I'm interested to hear how he thinks this is a good

idea."

I dropped my head in defeat. "Can we at least sit down? It's sweltering in here."

Mom led the way to the small den adjacent to the kitchen. She and I sat on the couch, while Sergei perched on my dad's old leather recliner.

"You said you've been dating since Nationals," Mom said. "I assume something started before then."

I snuck a glance at Sergei. "We sorta knew we had feelings for each other, but we weren't going to do anything about it."

"What made you change your mind?" Mom glared at Sergei.

He leaned forward in the chair. "All I can tell you is I love Emily, and I'll do everything I can to protect her and her career."

"How do you know your feelings won't change?" She shifted her inquiry from Sergei to me. "I could ask you the same question. This might seem new and exciting right now, but what happens if it all falls apart? Or if someone in the federation finds out? You've worked so hard to get to the Olympics, and you could find yourself in a world of trouble in the most important year of your life."

"My feelings aren't going to change," Sergei said without hesitation.

"You can't know that for certain," Mom shot back.

Sergei's eyes met mine, and I saw the depth of love in them. "I know," he reiterated.

The hairs on the back of my neck rose, and my lips parted into a smile.

"I'd like to talk to Emily alone now," Mom declared.

I jerked my head in her direction, shocked at her sudden request, but I didn't question it. "Okay, I'm gonna walk Sergei out."

"I'm sorry we weren't up front with you," Sergei said as

he stood. "I'd be happy to talk more whenever you want."

"Oh, I'm sure I'll have more questions," Mom replied in a biting tone.

Outside, next to Sergei's car, I said, "I am so sorry. I know that had to be painful."

"It's okay." He wrapped his arms around me. "It could've been worse."

"You should've heard some of the things she said before you came down. I can only imagine the earful I'm going to get when I go back inside."

"Call me later to let me know how it goes."

"I will. I'm sorry our night got ruined."

His hands massaged my back. "We'll have plenty more nights."

He kissed me, and I momentarily forgot about the evening's drama. As Sergei climbed into his car, I rolled my knotted neck and steeled myself for the second round of interrogation.

I walked into the house, and Mom came out of the guest bedroom off the foyer. Her mouth was clamped so tight the tiny wrinkles at the corners were more visible than her lips.

"You two looked pretty cozy," she said.

I stopped at the foot of the stairs. "Were you watching us through the window?"

"Can you blame me for being curious?"

I placed my hands on both sides of my face, forcing myself to stay calm. "I need to get everything we left on the terrace."

Upstairs, I shut off the stereo and picked up the pizza. Once piping hot and mouth-watering, my culinary creation was now cold and unappealing. I blew out the candles and fingered a rose petal, silently mourning my lost evening with Sergei.

Mom eyed the bouquet. "Those are pretty."

"Wow, a positive comment," I said dryly.

"Don't be smart with me."

I didn't say anything else as we cleared the table and made a couple of trips up and down the four flights of stairs. My wish that Mom would tire and forego more discussion didn't come true. She requested I join her in the living room, where she parked herself on the sofa. I slipped off my wedge heels and tucked my legs under me, trying to get as comfortable as possible. This was not going to be a brief conversation.

"I'm surprised you let Sergei leave so soon," I said.

"He had such smooth answers for everything. I figured I would get more information out of you without him here."

Would you rather he sound like a bumbling idiot? I kept that comment to myself and said, "Tell me what else you want to know."

Mom's stare bore into me. "I want to know how my smart, independent daughter has gotten herself into such a mess."

"Mom, come on."

"Sergei already has so much control over your life with your skating, and now he's controlling your personal life, too. Making you lie to everyone—"

"It was my decision not to tell you about us. He's not *controlling my life.*"

"You're so blinded by this... *love,*" she sputtered. "I don't think you can see anything clearly."

Heat spread over my scalp. I squeezed my temples and counted to ten. "Why can't you open up your mind a little bit and consider the possibility this isn't a horrible thing?"

"Because I have a bad feeling about this, Emily. I don't see this ending well for you."

"Is it that hard for you to believe Sergei could love me?"

The firm lines on her face softened, and she laid a hand on my forearm. "I'm concerned this is more infatuation than love. You work so closely together, and I know how much you look up to Sergei and admire him. I'm worried you've both blurred all the lines somehow."

I removed my arm from under her touch. Her gesture wasn't comforting; it felt patronizing.

"Please give me some credit. I'm not some naïve girl who's fallen under his spell. Our relationship took a while to develop. We were friends first."

"Maybe you should explain how this came about, then."

I launched into the story of how Sergei and I went from being friends to falling in love, telling her about all the cups of coffee we'd shared, the Sting concert, and the dinner party. Mom's eyebrows jerked up and down as I recounted the first kiss at the cliffs and the second one at Nationals. She didn't interrupt, not even once, which was almost as strange as sitting there, describing those romantic highlights to her.

Mom stayed quiet, apparently processing my long and involved explanation. When she finally spoke, she said, "That's quite a story. Makes me wonder how you've managed to skate so well with all these distractions."

"I told you none of this has affected my training, and it's the truth."

"Are you going to tell Chris about this after Worlds?"

"That's the plan. I'm hoping he won't be as negative about it as you are." I picked up one of the small red throw pillows and fluffed it as a release of frustration.

"I'm being realistic, which is something you need. You're living in a fantasy world if you think you can keep this a secret. Look at tonight. You didn't expect me to show up here. How long do you think you can hide this?"

"As long as we have to. It can't become public knowledge."

"Because you know it wouldn't be well received. And there's a reason for that—because it's not an appropriate relationship."

I threw my head back with a loud sigh. "We're not doing

anything wrong. I'm an adult, and Sergei is six measly years older than me. He's not manipulating or controlling me. Reactions like yours are the reason we have to keep this quiet. People wouldn't understand, and they'd jump to all the wrong conclusions."

Mom pursed her lips, and I could see her forming a new list of questions. I often thought my mother must've been a lawyer in a former life or perhaps an investigative journalist.

"Do you know anything about Sergei's past relationships?" she asked.

Avoiding her penetrating gaze, I focused on the seascape painting on the opposite wall. "We haven't talked much about them."

"Maybe that's because he's trying to hide something. You know, before you started working with him, I asked him why he retired from skating so soon, and all he said was he'd wanted to move on. Considering he was part of Russia's most promising young team, I doubt it was that simple."

I slapped the pillow in my lap. "I don't care what happened eight years ago." Actually, I was very curious, but I wasn't going to give Mom the satisfaction of knowing that.

She tilted her head to one side and touched my shoulder. "You're so trusting, Em. You always have been. It can be a good thing, but you have to be careful."

"I think I have pretty good instincts, and Sergei's never given me any reason not to trust him."

She retracted her hand and brushed the back of the sofa, wiping away imaginary dust particles. "Well, trustworthy or not, I don't like this situation and I'm not going to pretend to. I suppose there's nothing I can do about it, though, since I'd only be hurting you if I fired Sergei."

"Could you just give us a chance?" I pleaded. "There are so few people we can tell about our relationship. It would be really nice to have your support."

"I can't support something I think will end up causing

you pain. I hope you'll come to your senses soon and see what a mistake this is."

My throat tightened, and I rocketed up from the couch. "I can't listen to this anymore. I'm sorry you can't get past your doubts and suspicions to see that I have someone very special in my life. I hope in time you can understand."

I stalked toward the stairs and escaped to my bedroom. Flopping down on the bed, I took deep breaths. The cool breeze from the open window drifted over me, but my skin remained flushed with frustration. With the World Championships a week away, I didn't need my mother's negativity bringing me down. What I needed was her support as I prepared for the most important competition I'd ever faced.

CHAPTER NINETEEN

I STOOD AT MY HOTEL ROOM window, legs jiggling. Back and forth I glanced from the Vancouver skyline to the clock on the nightstand, willing the red digital numbers to surge forward.

Three o'clock p.m. Four hours until show time.

I wanted to skate our short program right at that moment, before my nervous energy could spiral out of control and cause me to have a panic attack at center ice. That would certainly be a memorable start to our World Championships.

Thankful Dad had called and suggested taking a walk, I scribbled a note on the Fairmont's stationery, letting Aubrey know I was going out. I set it against the pillows on her bed and grabbed my fleece jacket from the closet. As I swung open the room door, Sergei's clenched hand paused in mid-knock. We both laughed.

In Sergei's other hand, he held the book I'd given him for Christmas. He offered it to me with a smile. "I kept forgetting to let you borrow this at home, so I brought it with me."

"Thanks, I could use something relaxing to read."

Tiny creases formed on his brow. "You hanging in okay?"

I took a deep breath. "Getting a little jittery."

"Just keep thinking positive thoughts."

"I will." I leaned against the door frame and hugged the book to my chest. "Sitting around here is making me stir crazy, so Dad and I are going for a walk."

"Good. That'll help pass the time." He walked backwards down the hall. "I'll meet you and Chris downstairs at five."

I stayed in the doorway and sighed as Sergei turned his back to me. The man definitely knew how to wear a pair of jeans. Once he disappeared from sight, I brought the book over to the nightstand, excited to curl up with it in bed later.

I went down to the lobby and found Dad sitting in one of the stiff decorative chairs. He was examining a colorful tourist map of Vancouver. I pecked his cheek, and he folded the map.

"The waterfront's a few blocks away if you want to check it out," he said. "There's supposedly a great view of the mountains there."

"Sounds good. You should be able to get some great shots." I pointed to the camera bag in his lap. "Is Mom still upstairs working?"

"Yeah, she has three more essays to grade. She wants to finish them before tonight."

We headed for the revolving glass door, while Sergei came out of the skaters and coaches' hospitality room, his path crossing ours. My already jumpy stomach quivered even more.

Dad and Sergei hadn't seen each other since I'd told my father about Sergei and me. He'd expressed his concerns to me in a gentle manner, unlike Mom, but I wasn't sure what to expect from a face-to-face meeting.

"How are you, Jim?" Sergei extended his hand.

Dad didn't hesitate in accepting the handshake. "Good to see you, Sergei." He glanced at me and back at Sergei. "Why don't you join us on our walk? It'll give us a chance to talk."

"Dad . . ." I said with trepidation. An intense conversation about my relationship with Sergei was not what I needed now.

"Nothing heavy," Dad promised. "Just want to get to know Sergei better."

After witnessing Mom's snippiness, Sergei was wide-eyed at Dad's cordial behavior. "Sure, I'd be glad to."

The three of us ventured out, and between the buildings along the busy downtown corridor, I spied mountains in the distance. Our four-block walk took us straight to Burrard Inlet, its crystal blue water glistening under the afternoon sun. Behind the waterway sat North Vancouver and a stretch of mountains with a dusting of snow on its peaks.

While Dad snapped photos of a sea plane coming in for a landing, Sergei and I leaned against the concrete barrier lining the inlet. I closed my eyes and breathed in the fresh sea breeze. The gentle, salty wind reminded me of sitting on my terrace at home. I tried to summon the serenity I always felt in my favorite spot, but the looming competition kept all my muscles tight.

"Positive thoughts," Sergei said.

My lips tweaked into a smile, and I opened my eyes. "How did you know what I was thinking about?"

"It's part of my job." He winked.

Dad stood next to Sergei and asked, "Is this your first time in Vancouver?"

"It's my first time in Canada. Before I started coaching on the Cape, I didn't do much traveling to competitions. I was mostly a secondary coach, so I didn't get to attend many events."

"You coached in Chicago before the Cape, right?" Dad asked.

Sergei nodded. "And Virginia before that."

"Chicago's a fun city. I've been to a few seminars there."

"I liked it a lot, but I've realized I enjoy living in a small town more, even though I grew up in a big city."

Dad inspected his camera lens and wiped a smudge with

his sleeve. "Do you think you'll ever want to go back to Moscow?"

I suppressed a grin. Dad was a lot smoother than Mom at digging for information. What he really wanted to know was, *Are you going to go back to Russia and leave my daughter behind with a broken heart, or worse yet, take her away from us?*

Sergei shoved his hands in the pockets of his jeans. "No, I'm actually trying to talk my parents into moving to the States after my father retires in a few years. I know my mother would love it, but my father's pretty set in his ways. Neither of them speak English, so it would be a big adjustment."

Sergei's phone rang, and he pulled it from his pocket. "Speaking of my mother…"

He wandered a few steps to answer the phone, and I smiled at Dad. "His mom always calls to wish his teams luck when we compete."

"Sounds like they have a close relationship."

"They talk a lot." I turned to watch a flock of seagulls descend on the pavement. "Can you imagine if I lived that far away from Mom? She was bawling when I moved an hour from home."

"I miss having you around, too." Dad put his arm around me and kissed the top of my head.

"I really appreciate you making an effort with Sergei. I know this situation is less than ideal."

"You've always made good choices. I don't think you would've decided to pursue this relationship if you weren't absolutely certain you could handle it." Dad hugged me to his side. "All I want is for you to be happy."

I circled my arms around him. "Thanks, Dad." With a laugh, I added, "Can you make Mom feel the same way?"

He chuckled. "You know I don't have that kind of power."

After Sergei finished his call, we strolled back to the hotel, where I found the note I'd left for Aubrey now on my bed.

Under my message was Aubrey's bubbly script—*Out with Nick. Good luck tonight!!!!*

I checked the clock and began to assemble my beauty products. The process of getting ready for a competition took twice as long as fixing hair and makeup on a normal day. Every pore needed to be covered with layers of foundation and powder, every eyelash perfectly lengthened. The lipstick had to shine enough to be seen from the top row of the arena.

Chris showed up at my door as I finished corralling my hair into a tight bun. "I got tired of sitting in my room, so I thought I'd come sit in yours."

"I'll be ready in a few minutes." I plucked the bottle of hair spray from my rolling bag and returned to the bathroom.

Satisfied every lock of hair was firmly in place, I gathered my makeup case and spare hairpins and shut off the bathroom light. Chris was sitting on my bed, reading the *Lyrics* book.

His brow wrinkled. "Did Sergei loan this book to someone else before you?"

I shoved everything from my hands into my bag. "Mm… I don't think so. Why?"

"He wrote something in here."

Curiosity and concern combined to speed up my pulse. I held out my hand for the book. "Where?"

Chris passed it to me, opened to the page for the song "Desert Rose." Under the lyrics was a handwritten note—*You are my desert rose.*

After my heart stopped fluttering, reality slapped me in the face. I stared at the page, not wanting to look at Chris. *This cannot be happening. We have to skate the most important program of our lives in two hours.*

"Why would he write that?" Chris asked.

I made a snap decision to lie because this wasn't a discussion we could have in ten minutes. "I don't know, but this wasn't meant for me." I set the book on the bed and turned to my bag.

"Who's it for, then? I've never seen him with anyone or heard him talk about a girlfriend."

I zipped and unzipped the compartments of my bag with such force I was surprised they didn't break. "I don't know his personal business."

Out of the corner of my eye, I saw Chris pick up the book and flip through the pages.

"What are you doing?" I asked.

"I'm looking to see if he wrote anything else."

Oh, no, what if he wrote my name…

I shot over to the bed and tried to pull the book out of Chris's hands. "Don't worry about it. We don't have time for this."

He gawked at me and refused to loosen his grip. "What's your problem?"

"Nothing! Just forget about it. We need to go."

He took a quick look at the clock. "We still have time."

My mind scrambled with thoughts, some of which spilled out of my mouth. "If he wrote stuff, then it's private and we shouldn't be reading it. I'm going to give it back to him."

"If it's private, why'd he lend it to you?"

I returned to my bag, swallowing the bile in my throat. "I don't know. Maybe he forgot that was in there." *How many more lies can I tell?*

"There's something you're hiding. You're acting too weird."

I focused on the striped wallpaper in front of me and prayed for a phone call, a fire alarm, a miracle from above—anything to interrupt the conversation.

"I'm not acting weird," I said, but my voice betrayed me with a discernible crack.

Chris became quiet. "Has he tried to put the moves on you? Is he messing with you? That's it, isn't it? You can tell me if he's doing something—"

My stomach plummeted. I whipped around and blurted

out, "He's not doing anything I don't want him to!"

CHAPTER TWENTY

CHRIS PICKED UP HIS JAW FROM the floor and sputtered, "You're hooking up with Sergei?"

"No, not like… not like that." I forced myself to take a deep breath. "We're not *hooking up*. We're dating… seriously."

His face contorted, and he stood up, tossing the book onto the bed. "How did I not know about this?"

"I was going to tell you next week when we got home. I know it's a shock and it sounds a little weird, but it should tell you something that you haven't suspected anything. It means nothing has changed." I went over to Chris and put my hand on his arm, hoping to make him understand. He shook off my gesture and shoved past me.

"It doesn't sound a little weird. It sounds a *lot* weird." He paced up and down the small space between the two beds. "What happens if you break up?"

"We're not breaking up."

He stopped pacing to glare at me. "What, are you marrying him?" He snorted.

I had a hard time finding my voice. "I… I don't know. I mean, not right now."

He ran both hands through his thick hair, causing tufts to stand up like the mountain peaks I'd admired earlier. Any other time, I would teasingly nag him for messing up his hair before a performance. This was not a moment for jokes, however.

"I can't believe this," he said.

"We know what we're doing. Nothing has changed as far as our partnership is concerned, and that's what's important."

The melody of an incoming call on my cell phone prevented Chris from responding. The cheerful ringtone contrasted sharply with the mood in the room. Chris resumed wearing a hole in the sandy brown carpet as I dug in my bag for the phone.

"Hey, are you on your way down?" Sergei asked.

"Yeah, I'm with Chris. We'll be there in a minute."

I hung up and Chris said, "We're not finished talking about this."

"I don't blame you for being upset, but we need to put this aside for now."

He didn't move, and I feared he might refuse to leave until he'd said his piece. "Please, Chris." I tried to reach his stony eyes with a pleading look. "We have to go."

After a long pause, he picked up his bag and walked to the door.

On the bus ride to the arena, I kept a close watch on him. The only thing that could make the situation worse would be Chris confronting Sergei.

We made it to GM Place without incident and followed the long gray corridor to the bowels of the arena. The area buzzed with skaters walking through their programs, coaches mingling, and media personnel running around with tape recorders and notepads. In the distance, the familiar tune of *Swan Lake* played. The competition had already begun, but with the large number of pairs in the field, the event would span over four hours.

Chris and I split off from Sergei to stretch and warm up, and I eyed Madeline Hyatt and Damien Wakefield as they jogged past us in perfect tandem, chatting with ease. The Canadians didn't have a monstrous cloud hanging over them like we did.

"How long have you been dating?" Chris asked before I could begin my exercises.

"We can't talk about this right now." I sat on the painted concrete floor and stretched my legs.

"It's a simple question."

I held his stare, begging him to let the issue drop. He raised his eyebrows, urging me to answer. I let out a sigh and reached out to touch the toes of my sneakers.

"Two months," I said quietly.

He squatted next to me but didn't make any motion to start warming up. "Wow. I must be really blind."

"You're not blind." I touched his knee. "No one knows except Aubrey and my parents."

"What did your parents say?"

"My dad is being amazingly cool. My mom, on the other hand…"

"Is that why she showed up out of the blue at practice last week?"

"I'll tell you about it later, I promise." I stood up and extended my arms over my head. "Please let it go for now."

"Em, are you sure this is what you want?" He straightened up and peered down at me. "You're sure Sergei hasn't been putting pressure on you—"

"No! I'm with him because I want to be with him."

He gazed down the hallway, and I thought we were done with the discussion until he said, "This whole thing is weirding me out."

I set my hands on his shoulders. "Then stop talking about it. I can explain everything later. Can we please focus on getting ready?"

He complied with my request and remained quiet as we stretched and walked through our program. We left each other to dress in the locker room, and I rushed to put on my costume. If Chris met Sergei outside first, I wasn't sure he could hold his tongue.

Amidst the mob of girls dressing and primping, I hastily tugged my costume's stretchy fabric over my body. With a quick check in the mirror, I determined all of the sparkly red and black beads were still in place.

Chris and I reached Sergei at the same time. He handed us our jackets, and I zipped mine up to my chin to stay warm. We had a few minutes until we needed to lace up our skates, so we did some light stretching to keep our muscles loose.

After we put on our skates and advanced to the tunnel, Sergei reminded us of the changes we'd made to our footwork. I nodded and kept silent as usual, staying in my own little world. Chris did the same, not chatting in his normal manner, and Sergei observed him with concern.

Our group took the ice for the six-minute warm-up, and the raucous cheers for Hyatt and Wakefield reminded me we were on Canadian soil. Chris and I received the second loudest ovation as numerous American flags showed in the stands. With a perfect triple twist and clean side-by-side jumps completed, we set up to practice the throw triple Lutz.

Gliding backwards with Chris's hands on my hips, I glanced over my shoulder at the last second and saw Madeline skating toward us at full speed, her back to us. Before I could yell a warning, she crashed into Chris's side, the impact knocking her to the ice. Chris held onto my waist and stumbled but didn't go down. The audience gasped, and my heart rate burst upward. Both Chris and Damien helped Madeline to her feet as she massaged her lower back.

"I'm so sorry," Chris said.

Madeline glared at Chris but didn't reply. She and Damien skated away and did slow circular strokes around the ice, while Chris and I went over to Sergei at the boards. He offered us our bottles of water and made a motion with his hands indicating, "Settle down."

My hand trembled as I raised the bottle to my mouth. Chris always checked behind him when we practiced the throw on a crowded rink. He was known as one of the most observant skaters, constantly alerting our training mates at home and preventing crashes. His mind was clearly not on the task at hand.

We were first in the group to skate, so hand-in-hand we skated leisurely around the perimeter of the ice during the warm-up's final minute. Without looking at me, Chris said tersely, "Promise me you're not gonna quit."

I swiveled my head to face him. "What?"

He kept his focus straight ahead. "If things go bad with you and Sergei, promise me you're not going to quit."

"Are you seriously bringing this up now?" I asked in hushed tone.

"I need to know."

I gave his hand a firm squeeze. "You know I would never cut and run on you."

Still staring into the audience, he said, "I thought I knew you, but I'm not so sure now."

A sharp pang of sadness cut through my anxiety. I wanted to stop and assure him he could still trust me, but the announcer alerted us the warm-up was over. We circled back to Sergei, who studied our grim expressions intently.

He smiled and spoke calmly, "Just like any other day in practice."

Pushing off from the boards, we glided across the ice and took a few moments before we prepared to start. I set my jaw and locked my eyes on Chris's.

"Let's do this."

To the rousing notes of "Capriccio Espagnol," we sailed through the elements on autopilot, executing the technique we'd practiced for countless hours. But between the elements, Chris barely looked at me. He didn't give me the positive energy I was accustomed to receiving from him. I might as well have been skating with a stranger.

The audience applauded the technical precision, but they didn't leap to their feet. The program lacked spark. Sergei waited until we'd received our scores and retreated backstage to question Chris.

"What's going on with you?" he asked.

"Why don't you ask your girlfriend?" Chris muttered and stomped toward the waiting journalists.

Sergei stared at me, unable to speak. Under my breath, I said, "He saw the note you wrote in the book. I had to tell him."

He passed his hand over his mouth. "The media's waiting. We'll talk later."

After answering every reporter's questions, we checked the standings for the short program and saw our names in third place, once again behind the Canadians and the Russians, Oksana and Denis. Those two teams were the glass ceiling we couldn't break through.

Chris avoided me on the bus to the hotel and made a beeline for his parents in the lobby. He'd gone from asking me a million questions to snubbing me. My own parents greeted me with hugs and their thoughts on the event.

"Is Chris feeling okay?" Mom asked. "He seemed out of it."

I paused, deciding not to get into the whole story. "We just have something we need to work through."

My hesitation was all Mom needed to figure it out. "He knows, doesn't he?" When I didn't immediately answer, she huffed, "Well, you had to know he wouldn't be happy. It must've been a shock, as I know all too well."

"Mom, please don't start."

My plea went on deaf ears. "You'd better talk to him and

get this squared away before tomorrow night."

I looked over at Chris and moaned, "I don't think he wants to talk to me."

Dad slipped his arm around my shoulders. "Why don't we let Em get some rest? It's been a long day."

Aubrey was already asleep in our room, not surprising since she needed to be at practice early the next morning. After I showered and put on my pajamas, I crawled under the blankets, switched on my bedside lamp, and picked up Sergei's book. Beside the lyrics to the first song, "Next To You," was a long note. Scratching my head, I thought, *How did Chris not see this? He must've started flipping from the back.*

Sergei's note read—*I had to laugh when I started reading the book and this was the first song because all I'd been thinking about for months was how I wanted to be next to you. And here it was reminding me again.*

I smiled and ran my fingers run across Sergei's words. The little notes were a treasure since I couldn't spend time alone with him in Vancouver. I read a few more songs, but before long, my eyelids became heavy. With the book in my lap, I drifted off to sleep.

Startled awake by loud knocking, I peeked at the clock. I'd been asleep less than an hour.

Aubrey groaned and mumbled into her pillow, "Who is that?"

Since she didn't make a move to answer the door, I had to get up. Through the peephole, a frowning Chris stared back at me. I rubbed my eyes and opened the door.

Chris didn't wait for an invitation as he marched past me. "We need to talk."

CHAPTER TWENTY-ONE

JUDGING FROM CHRIS'S DISHEVELED HAIR AND wrinkled T-shirt, he'd attempted to sleep. Aubrey raised her tousled blond head from her pillow to address him.

"Some of us have to wake up at five in the morning."

"Sorry, I just need Em for a few minutes," he said.

"Can we talk tomorrow before practice?" I asked.

"No, I really want to do this now."

Aubrey grumbled and pulled the blanket over her head.

"Let's go in the hallway," Chris suggested.

"I'm not going to talk about this in the hallway where anyone can hear."

He quickly surveyed the room. "Then let's go in the bathroom."

"The *bathroom*?" I gave him a you-can't-be-serious look.

"Come on." He tugged on my hand.

Chris sat in the middle of the floor, so I slumped against the door, the hard tile meeting my bottom. The fruity scent of my shower gel lingered in the air.

Chris drummed his fingers on the edge of the bathtub. "I feel like I should've known something was going on. That whole scene at Four Continents, when Sergei got so mad at you, was that all for show? To throw me off?"

I let out a dry laugh. "No, it was very real."

"It must've been pretty awkward, having your boyfriend talk to you like that."

My hair draped around my face as I bent my head. "It wasn't fun, but we got through it."

"You should've told me about this from the beginning. If we don't have trust, we don't have anything."

I bent forward and connected with his eyes. "You can still trust me. I thought I was doing what was best for us by waiting to tell you."

"When we teamed up, you said you had the same goal as me—to be the first American pair to win Olympic gold." He shifted and stretched out one of his long legs. "But you don't seem too serious about that if you're willing to do something this risky."

I blinked and jerked backward. "How can you say that? You see me busting my butt every day. My goals haven't changed."

"Don't you realize the problems this could cause for us? If the federation finds out you're dating Sergei, they could come down hard on him. Isn't he violating some ethical code?"

"There's nothing in the rulebook that says coaches and students of legal age can't date."

"Well, even if it's not in the rulebook, they wouldn't like it. They're always preaching to us about having the right image. You think they're going to want one of their top skaters involved with her coach? This isn't Russia, where anything goes."

I was starting to wish we were in Russia or any European country, for that matter. Skaters there didn't seem to be subjected to the same level of scrutiny we were. It wasn't fair that they could have publicized affairs with no consequences, while I couldn't openly have a perfectly innocent relationship with Sergei.

"We're being very discreet," I said.

A long pause followed while Chris studied me. "You must really have it bad for him."

My face warmed, and I picked at a loose thread on my pajama pants. "We're serious about each other. We wouldn't be together if we weren't."

"You know I lost my last partner when she quit skating to follow her boyfriend to college. I don't wanna lose another one because of a guy."

"I already told you I'm not going anywhere. No matter what happens."

He continued to stare as if I were an abstract piece of art he didn't understand. "How do you deal with Sergei ordering you around at the rink? No way could I coach Marley."

I shrugged. "I guess since he was my coach first, it seems natural."

"I have to tell Marley about this. I can't keep something this big from her."

I was hesitant to let someone else in on my secret, but I didn't want to start another argument. "Make sure she knows it can't go any further."

He shook his head. "Em, I still think this is such a bad idea. When you mix work with a relationship, there are so many things that can go wrong."

"I'm going to need you to trust me when I say we have it all under control."

"Your judgment isn't something I can trust right now." He braced himself against the bathtub and rose to his feet.

I stood up next to him. "I hate this tension between us. We're the pair that never fights, remember?" I tapped his chest and gave him a hopeful smile.

He didn't react to my attempt at levity. "Well, I guess there's a first time for everything." He opened the bathroom door. "I'm sorry I wasn't on top of my game tonight.

Tomorrow I'll be ready… as long as you don't hit me with any more surprises."

He left before I could make another plea for his understanding. I climbed into bed and let exhaustion take me away to pleasant dreams, where I didn't have to feel guilty for being in love.

THE MOMENT WE'D WORKED toward all year had arrived. Chris and I stood before Sergei, our hands clasped together. The building rumbled with applause for Hyatt and Wakefield's high scores, and Sergei spoke above the noise.

"Take this energy and use it. This is your time."

The crowd became silent as Chris and I knelt on the ice. In the stillness, my pounding heart echoed in my ears. The music began, and Chris gave me one of his customary little nods. Relief spread through me. A sense of normalcy was exactly what I needed. I envisioned us on our home ice, where we'd performed clean programs time and again.

With that mindset, I executed my jumps with precision, matching Chris step for step, and he maintained eye contact with me throughout the lyrical choreography as opposed to the prior night. I fed off the confidence in his gaze, ticking off each element in my mind.

Heading into the final thirty seconds, every muscle in my legs began to burn, and I had to suck in longer breaths. My skates skimmed across the ice instead of carving deep edges. As we skated past Sergei, he leaned over the boards and clapped his hands. "Push! Push!"

I bent my knees and pressed my blades deeper into the ice. *These are the last seconds of your season. Make them count.* Each stroke heightened the pain in my legs, but I powered forward through our final lift and spin.

Chris pulled me close to him, and I broke into a wide grin

as we spun into our ending pose. I threw my arms around him, and he held me so tight I gasped.

"I can't breathe," I choked out with a laugh.

He released me and pointed toward the audience for our bows. He still hadn't cracked a smile; his face stayed motionless as if he was stunned at our perfect performance.

Chris remained silent in the Kiss & Cry, while Sergei and I dissected the minute details of the program. Our scores appeared, and I thought they were good enough for the bronze medal, but I couldn't be sure until I saw the placements. A long string of three's followed on the monitor, and the announcer confirmed, "They are in third place."

I shook Chris's shoulders. "We got a medal!"

He finally smiled before giving me a warm hug. In his embrace, I felt shared happiness, relief, and pride. All the hours of practice, all the bruises, all the aches and pains—it was all worth it in that moment.

Chris and I stood to give the crowd an appreciative wave. Sergei's strong hand touched the small of my back, and he whispered in my ear, "You inspire me."

My knees threatened to give way. I avoided looking into Sergei's eyes because I wouldn't be able to resist kissing him. Instead, I put my focus on the scoreboard and let the final standings sink in.

1. Leonova/Romanov

2. Hyatt/Wakefield

3. *Chris and me!*

We were right where we needed to be in our quest for the ultimate prize.

Sergei moved to hug Chris, but his gesture was met with a stiff response, a subtle reminder that even in our moment of triumph, problems still remained.

A COUPLE OF HOURS later, Sergei and I stood with my parents at the front of the hotel restaurant, and I poked my head into the lobby in search of Chris and his parents. Our celebratory dinner couldn't begin without them.

Mom brushed the sleeves of her wool blazer. "Sergei, this is quite an item to add to your resume'. There aren't many coaches your age with these kinds of results."

"I have some pretty talented students to thank for that." He beamed a smile of pride in my direction.

Mom slid closer to him and arched her neck to look up at him. "Don't think because Emily won a medal, you're off the hook with me. I'm still keeping an eye on you."

I rolled my eyes. "Can't we enjoy the occasion? If you don't act normal, Chris's parents are going to wonder what's up."

I watched Mom throughout dinner, afraid the wine she was drinking would loosen her lips. My shoulders finally relaxed when Chris's parents declined dessert to retire to their room. Dad used Mom's drowsiness from the wine to convince her to leave soon thereafter. Sergei, Chris and I sat in silence at the table. Chris stared at the tablecloth and fiddled with an empty packet of Sweet & Low.

"This isn't awkward," I joked.

Chris slid his chair back and jutted his chin toward me. "Can you take a walk with me?"

"Uh, sure. Are you going upstairs?" I asked Sergei.

He lifted his mug. "As soon as I finish my coffee."

"I'll call you in a little bit." I tapped his foot under the table.

Chris guided me through the hotel's side entrance and stopped on the deserted sidewalk. His face held the same grim look from our conversation the previous night.

"Em, do you know what this means?" He took his medal out of his jacket pocket. "We really have a shot next year at the Olympics."

"I know." I bobbed up and down, both to stay warm and to convey my excitement.

His expression stayed serious. The tiny freckles on his cheeks that danced when he laughed didn't move. "You need to decide if you want this more than you want him."

I froze in the middle of a downward bob. "What?"

"If you want this as bad as you say, then you should put your relationship with Sergei on hold."

I took a step back and narrowed my wide eyes. "It's not that simple. How would you feel if I asked you to stop seeing Marley?"

"My relationship with Marley isn't a ticking time bomb."

"Don't you think you're being a little dramatic?"

Sergei pushed open the glass doors. "I saw you out here as I was leaving the restaurant. Is everything okay?"

Chris faced him. "I told Em she needs to stop seeing you."

"That's not your decision to make." Sergei used his familiar authoritative tone.

"Well, it doesn't look like you're gonna step up and do the responsible thing."

Sergei moved toward him, his shoulders appearing to broaden. "If you have a problem with me, then talk to *me* about it."

Chris glowered at him. "My problem is I trusted you to put your students first, but you've got your own personal agenda."

"My agenda is to help you win an Olympic gold medal, and I've put you on a strong path to do that. That's all you need to worry about."

"So, I shouldn't be concerned that at any minute, your relationship with Em could explode in all our faces?"

The two of them had inched closer to each other, eye to eye, their bodies rigid. I stepped into their circle of testosterone.

"Chris, can't you understand—" I pleaded.

"I understand you're gonna do whatever you want. You seem to have forgotten there's another person in this partnership. Or maybe you just don't care."

I winced. "You know that's not true," I mumbled through the tears in my throat.

Sergei gave Chris a warning glare. "Stop this before you say something you regret."

Chris pressed his lips together. "Think about what I said, Em."

He stalked inside, a breeze of unsettled air behind him. I shivered and knotted my scarf tighter.

"I think in time he'll understand," Sergei said. "He won't stay angry."

"I hope so." I wanted to convince myself, but my voice revealed my doubt.

Sergei glanced down at the pavement and then up at me. "Are you considering his request?"

"No, of course not. I told him it's not that easy to walk away from someone you love."

His shoulders heaved, and he locked his eyes on mine. "I promise we'll get through this."

CHAPTER TWENTY-TWO

We didn't have much time after Worlds to bask in our success. The Olympic season loomed ahead, and the first thing we needed to do was find the right music for our new programs. Chris, Sergei, and I listened to a variety of classical pieces and movie soundtracks, only to throw most of the CDs onto the "reject" pile on Sergei's living room floor.

Chris tossed the *West Side Story* soundtrack onto the expanding stack. "I skated to that with my old partner."

I picked up a Rachmaninov CD and frowned. "*Rhapsody on a Theme of Paganini* would've been perfect if Claire and Brandon hadn't skated to it this season."

"Yeah, you don't want music that's just been used," Sergei said and inserted a disc into the stereo. "How about Beethoven?"

I reclined against the sofa while Sergei sat behind me and massaged my neck. Chris, ever observant, grimaced at the sign of affection and deepened the scowl he'd worn all evening. I shifted my attention to the quiet symphony.

"This isn't exciting me," I said.

"It's putting me to sleep," Chris added.

Sergei rose and removed the disc. "That's the end of the stack I pulled. Do you want to listen to the 'maybe' pile again?"

Chris scooted on his knees over to the entertainment cabinet and examined the bottom shelf. "What about some of these other ones?" He passed his index finger along the spines and pulled one out. "*Carmen*—overused but the judges seem to love it."

"You're not skating to that," Sergei said brusquely.

I wrinkled my eyebrows, and Chris asked, "Why not?"

Sergei turned away from us and rearranged a few CDs on top of the stereo. "Because you can do better."

He picked up his empty bottle of water from the coffee table and went into the kitchen. Chris returned *Carmen* to the shelf. "O-*kay*."

I wondered if Sergei's reaction had something to do with his skating career, but I wasn't going to ask him about it with Chris around. Chris went back to searching the shelf, and I made my way to the kitchen.

Sergei was inspecting the contents of his refrigerator. I stood behind him and wrapped my arms around his waist, kissing the back of his neck. He closed the door and faced me, and out of Chris's judgmental eyesight, I gave him the deep kiss I'd wanted to give him all night.

"Em, come listen to this one," Chris called.

I took Sergei's hand, and we sat on the sofa. "Which piece is this?" I asked.

"Grieg Piano Concerto."

We all sat with rapt attention as the piano notes transitioned between soft and powerful. The music reached a dramatic crescendo, and I pictured myself high above Chris's head, soaring across the ice. Ice emblazoned with the Olympic rings. A rush of anticipation shot through me.

The disc swirled to a stop, and Chris pointed to the stereo. "I think we've found our long program music."

"The second movement gave me goose bumps," I said.

Sergei examined the back of the CD case. "This could work really well with the right cuts. I'll send it out for editing. What about the short?"

Chris stood and stretched his arms over his head. "Can we do it another night? My ears need a break."

"Sounds like a good idea," I agreed. The sooner Chris left, the sooner I could talk to Sergei.

Chris walked to the door but stopped with his hand on the knob when I didn't move from the couch. "Are you coming, Em?"

"No, I'm going to hang out for a while."

He opened his mouth and jutted his tongue against the inside of his cheek. "Of course." He swung open the door. "Later."

I cuddled close to Sergei. "I'm hoping Marley can soften him up a little. She was actually excited about you and me when I talked to her last night."

"Someone's happy for us? We should celebrate." He smiled and curled a lock of my hair around his finger.

His inviting smile almost made me forget my questions. Almost, but not quite. "I wanted to ask you something first. You were so adamant about us not using *Carmen*." I ran my hand over his soft T-shirt. "Did you have a bad skate to it?"

Sergei's muscles tensed under my palm. He waited a moment before he replied, "I was going to skate to it, but it never happened."

"You scrapped the program?"

Another pause followed. "Something like that."

My curiosity spiked with each of his vague answers. I tried to make my tone both gentle and insistent. "You never talk about your partnership with Elena. I'd like us to be able to talk about everything."

He scratched his hand through his short hair. "It was so long ago."

"I know, but it was an important part of your life. It would mean a lot to me if you'd share it with me."

The ensuing silence seemed to stretch for hours though it was mere seconds. Sergei toyed with the CD case next to him on the sofa. He slid it back and forth across the cushion, making a slight whooshing sound.

"It was a very frustrating time. There was so much out of my control."

I rested my touch on his forearm. "How so?"

"Elena's father. He dictated everything. He was the reason we stopped skating."

"Why would he make you quit when you'd just won Junior Worlds?"

"He was very wealthy and very powerful. Elena was his only child, and he wanted certain things... certain people for her. I was good enough to be her partner, but that was it."

"And you wanted more," I guessed, my heart dipping.

Sergei hadn't looked at me since he began speaking, and he continued to stare at his lap. "She and I started seeing each other, but her father wouldn't have it because my family wasn't up to his standards. We kept seeing each other anyway. Eventually, he found out, and he sent Elena away to live with relatives and threatened me and my family if I tried to get in touch with her. He wasn't a person you'd want to cross."

"He ended her skating career just because he didn't approve of you?"

Sergei returned to fidgeting with the jewel case. "To say he was angry would be an understatement."

Even though my parents had been strict with me growing up, I couldn't imagine them treating me so harshly, destroying my dreams. "I can't believe he would do something that drastic. He sounds like a total maniac."

"Elena was terrified of him." Sergei's voice dropped. "And I couldn't do anything to help her."

Without thinking, I said quietly, "You loved her."

He finally looked in my direction and slowly shook his head. "I was so young. I don't think I really knew what love was."

"Did you ever see her again?"

He shook his head again. "I heard through friends she got married and lives in St. Petersburg."

I studied Sergei's profile as I digested all the information. He was staring straight ahead at the television, which wasn't on.

"So, that's the whole story? I guess I don't understand why it's been such a big secret. It's not like you did something wrong. Elena's dad is the one who was completely psycho."

"He didn't want people to know why our partnership ended, to know his daughter had been involved with someone from the working class," he said, not hiding his sarcasm. "He told everyone Elena was ready to quit. I wasn't going to say anything different because who knew what he was capable of doing. I don't like to talk about it because it's a time I'd rather forget."

"I'm so sorry. It sounds like a nightmare of a situation." I put my arm around him and rested my chin on his shoulder. "How come you didn't get a new partner after Elena left?"

"I lost all motivation. She was the only person I'd ever skated with."

The gloom in his voice brought a jealous twinge to my stomach. "It must've been hard to lose her. Not just as your partner, but…"

He pulled me closer to him. "You know none of that matters now. It was so many years ago. What I felt for her is long gone."

"You never had any closure, though."

"I don't need closure." He lifted my chin with his fingertips. "I found you. You're everything to me, Em."

His eyes warmed with love, and I pressed my mouth to his, hoping my kiss would show him how strongly I shared his feelings.

"Thank you for telling me everything," I said, taking his face into my hands.

He enveloped me in his arms and brushed his lips against my hair. As he held me, images of Sergei and Elena stealing kisses in secret hideaways snuck into my mind. The pictures were all too familiar. I clamped my eyes shut and buried myself deeper into Sergei's embrace.

CHAPTER TWENTY-THREE

"I HOPE THE WEATHER ISN'T AN omen for this dinner," I said as the rain pounded against the windshield of Sergei's SUV.

Sergei steered the car onto my parents' street. "At least your mom was willing to invite me over. Your dad must've done a lot of persuading."

"She'd better not bombard us with reasons why we shouldn't be dating."

Sergei pulled into the driveway and dropped one hand from the steering wheel to my knee. "No matter what she says, I'm not going anywhere."

I leaned across the console and kissed him. "Good, because neither am I."

We ran under a shared umbrella up the steps to the front porch, but we couldn't escape the wind-blown rain. I flicked drops of water from the skirt of my flowered sundress, while Sergei smoothed his khaki pants and straightened the collar of his pale blue oxford shirt. I was about to insert my key into the door when Dad opened it. The smell of sautéed vegetables wafted out onto the porch.

"Hey, sweetie. I'm glad you made it in this storm." Dad

hugged me, and I kissed his freshly shaven cheek. He extended his hand to Sergei. "It's good to see you."

Sergei pumped Dad's arm with vigor, and I smiled, knowing how much my father's support meant to him. If only my mother would stop dwelling on potential problems and see the positives Sergei brought to my life. In the weeks since Worlds, I'd focused my conversations with her on skating and minimized discussion of my relationship. I couldn't handle her constant negativity.

"Is Mom in the kitchen?" I asked.

"Yep, she's working on a new recipe," Dad said.

We crossed the foyer into the cozy kitchen. Mom flitted between the stove and the narrow island in the center of the room. A bevy of mixing bowls, steaming pans, and cooking utensils surrounded her, but she moved about them with the ease of a skilled restaurant chef.

"Hey, Mom—"

She flipped on the food processor, and the loud whirring drowned out my greeting. When she appeared satisfied with the consistency of the green mixture, she shut off the machine. "Hi, honey." After a pause, she added in a dry tone, "Sergei."

He stepped toward the island. "I really appreciate you having me over."

Mom kept her head down and spooned what looked like pesto into a small bowl. "Well, I thought it was time we got together and talked."

I groaned on the inside. Mom's idea of talking would undoubtedly be preaching to Sergei and me.

Dad patted Sergei's shoulder. "I've got the Sox game on in the den. Why don't we let these two work their magic in here?"

"As long as you don't need any help," Sergei said to Mom.

She spun the rotating spice rack and selected two bottles. "Emily and I have it covered."

Sergei squeezed my hand before following Dad into the den. I picked up the recipe card from the counter and read aloud, "Pesto-Encrusted Trout."

"One of the ladies at church made it for us at a dinner party last week, and it was fabulous," Mom said as she spread a thin layer of the sauce over the fish fillets.

"I'm surprised you're not serving gruel since Sergei's here," I muttered.

The spoon froze in Mom's hand, and the tight set of her mouth relayed her lack of amusement. "I would never serve anyone a bad meal."

I circled around her to where she'd lined up the salad ingredients. "I'll work on this while you finish the fish."

From the den, Dad's and Sergei's voices mixed in with the familiar babble of the Red Sox play-by-play announcer. A loud rumble of thunder roared over the house, and Dad said, "Good thing they're playing in New York tonight."

I took a large knife to the head of romaine lettuce, shredding it into tiny ribbons. After transferring the greens to a large glass bowl, I concentrated on the long cucumber and peeked up at Mom as I sliced and diced.

"When you said you want to talk to Sergei, I hope you meant pleasant dinner conversation."

"I'd like to know more about the man my daughter is dating." She slid the tray of fish into the oven. "Like why his skating career fell apart."

My hand jumped, and the knife missed my fingertips by a centimeter. "Please don't bring that up."

"Don't you want to know?"

"I *do* know, and it's a personal matter that's frankly none of your business." I used a tone as sharp as the blade in my hand.

Mom grabbed the wedge of parmesan cheese next to the cutting board and grated furiously over the lettuce. "Anything that affects you is of concern to me, so you can either tell me or

I'll ask Sergei about it."

I pitched a handful of cubed cucumber into the bowl. "Why can't you just let it go?"

"It must be bad if you don't want to tell me."

Knowing she wouldn't relent, I reluctantly gave her a brief summary of Sergei and Elena's situation. She regarded me with one arched eyebrow.

"Surely you see the similarities in Sergei's relationships with you and Elena."

"The only similarity I see is a parent with unreasonable objections."

"It doesn't alarm you that Elena lost everything she'd worked for because of her involvement with Sergei? Don't you see how you could end up in the same position?" She clanged the metal grater onto the counter.

My face burned with anger. I gripped the edge of the island and swallowed the words I wanted to say but knew I'd regret. I replied calmly, "Elena didn't have a choice. I do. And I choose to be with Sergei."

I fled to the den and let out a breath at the sound of Dad and Sergei's laughter. The den and the kitchen were on different planets. Sergei held out his hand, and I grasped it as I sat next to him on the couch. We watched the Sox batter the Yankees until Mom alerted us dinner was ready.

The four of us occupied only half of the large oak table in the dining room. Dad, Sergei, and I carried over our baseball chatter, and Mom said, "Sergei, it sounds like you know a lot about the game. You've become pretty Americanized. Have you applied for citizenship?"

"Yes, a couple of years ago. The process takes a while."

Mom sat back and swirled the white wine in her glass. "Why did you want to leave Russia to coach? I'm sure you could've found opportunities there."

A piece of sautéed zucchini stuck in my throat, and I gulped my water to wash it down. I sensed where this line of questioning was headed.

Sergei took a sip of wine. "I had a friend who offered me a position in Virginia, and I knew the facilities and opportunities here would be better."

"I've heard the skating programs in Russia aren't as organized as they used to be," Dad chimed in.

Before Sergei could comment, Mom inserted, "I was wondering if maybe you left because of the fallout with Elena's father."

Sergei looked at me. His eyes spelled confusion. I set down my fork and touched his thigh.

Mom took care of responding for me. "I asked Emily what happened with you and Elena. I find it a little disconcerting you seem to follow a pattern in your relationships. Have you had any girlfriends you didn't have to hide?"

Thunder clapped and lightning flashed through the two tall windows. The chandelier above the table blinked twice then plunged us into darkness. Could that be God's way of telling my mother to back off?

"Let's get some candles," Dad said.

Both his and Mom's chairs scraped over the wood floor. My eyes adjusted to the loss of light, and I saw Sergei's stone face.

"I'm sorry." I rubbed his leg. "She said she was going to ask you about Elena, so I thought I could stop her by telling her myself. I should've known she wouldn't let it rest."

"Maybe we should go. I don't feel like defending everything I've ever done." The edge in his voice reached me through the darkness.

I glanced at the windows, which were being pelted with rain. "It sounds bad outside."

My parents returned with a flashlight and two thick vanilla-scented candles. The glow warmed the room but not the chill between Mom and Sergei.

Mom tilted her chin upward. "I believe I asked a question before we were interrupted."

"Why don't we give all the questions a break?" Dad suggested as he refilled his wine glass.

"Emily needs to know if Sergei can be trusted to—"

"Mom, stop!" I threw my napkin on the table.

Sergei stood. "Jim, thank you for making me feel welcome. Laura, I don't think anything I say is going to change your mind about me, so it's probably best if I leave."

My legs trembled, but I jumped up alongside Sergei. In the shadows, Mom's face held a look of disapproval that made my skin prickle.

"Everyone take a breath." Dad held up one hand, his palm facing Sergei and me. "No one should be on the road right now. Please, let's finish dinner."

"Mom's never going to let up. Sergei doesn't deserve to be badgered like this," I cried.

Dad faced Mom, and his normally gentle blue eyes were steely. "I think we can all be civil for the rest of the evening."

Mom fingered the short strands of hair against the nape of her neck. The old clock on the wall tick-tocked each second of her deliberation.

"There's no need for anyone to leave," she clipped.

Sergei moistened his lips as if to speak, but instead he sat down. I took my seat and refolded my napkin in my lap. Silence hung over the table like a black veil.

Dad cleared his throat. "Em, are you and Chris skating in any summer competitions?"

I breathed easier at the change in subject. "We might show our short program at the Cranberry Open, but we're not sure we'll be ready by the end of August."

While Dad, Sergei, and I talked, Mom said a maximum of ten words during the remainder of dinner. The torrential rain and howling wind subsided, but the power remained off, adding to the ominous mood of the meal.

Mom cleared the dishes, and I trailed behind her and the beam of the flashlight to the kitchen. "Why can't you be like Dad and accept Sergei as part of my life?"

She set the light on the counter and piled the plates beside the sink. "I love your father dearly, but like you, he trusts people too easily."

"While you always assume the worst about everyone." I squeezed my arms across my chest. "If you're going to keep treating Sergei like a criminal on trial, don't expect to see me very often. Because if he's not welcome here, then I don't want to be here either."

"Think about what you're saying. Are you willing to put him before your family?"

I couldn't see Mom's face clearly, but I could hear the distress in her high pitch. My chest ached with a pang of regret. All I wanted was for everyone to get along, but I was driving us farther apart.

"I don't know how else to make you understand what he means to me."

She swiped at the counter with a dishrag. "I'm sorry, but I can't just blindly support this. I still have a lot of questions—"

"No! No more." I shook my head and backed toward the door. "Until you can stop with the questions and accusations, I can't deal with you."

Dad and Sergei still sat in the dining room. I touched Sergei's arm with a shaky hand. "I'm ready to go."

We bid farewell to my father, whose disappointment showed in the creases around his mouth. He said in my ear, "I'll keep talking to her."

If Dad found a way to get Mom to back down, he'd be even closer to sainthood. Mom didn't come out of the kitchen to tell us goodbye, and Sergei didn't seem interested in seeing her, so he and I slipped out the front door.

I stopped before the top step and stared at the wooden swing near the edge of the porch. Mom and I would sit on that swing every summer evening when I was young. She'd drink a glass of iced tea, while I'd slurp on a popsicle. We could talk about anything—my skating dreams, catty girls at the rink, my favorite books. I never imagined a time would come when we'd barely be speaking.

My hand went to my stomach, where my dinner sat like a rock. I leaned back against Sergei's chest and let his arms close around me. "I don't think that could've gone any worse."

He kissed the top of my head. "Look on the bright side. Your dad could hate me, too."

I laughed, but the sound was hollow. "I don't know what it's going to take for my mom to see what we have is real."

I led Sergei down the steps into the drizzling rain. The drops of water refreshed my skin and washed away some of the unpleasantness of the night. Sergei opened the passenger door, and I planted a slow, rainy kiss on his lips.

He smiled. "What was that for?"

"For keeping me sane through all this."

He placed his hands gently on my neck and repaid my kiss with a tender one of his own. The longer it lasted, the more I knew being with Sergei was the right choice.

CHAPTER TWENTY-FOUR

"Good practice, guys." I handed Courtney and Mark their skate guards.

They maneuvered around the three other novice pairs leaving the ice. As host of the Cranberry Open summer competition, our rink had been overtaken by skaters of all levels from across New England.

Sergei took Mark aside for another minute of instruction, while Courtney asked, "Em, what time do we skate tomorrow morning?"

I pulled the event schedule from my purse, and another sheet of paper slipped out and floated to the ground. Courtney picked it up and saw the flight itinerary I'd printed earlier.

"You're going on a trip?"

"To Dallas for a coaches' seminar. You know, one of those classes we have to attend to keep our certification. Sergei's going, too, so you and Mark will be on your own a couple of days next month."

"Are you and Sergei the only coaches from our rink going?" Hope twinkled in Courtney's emerald green eyes.

"I think so." I shifted my eyes to the paper in my hand.

I couldn't tell her Sergei and I had made sure of that when we'd signed up for the class. We'd had our choice of seminars, and we'd deliberately picked the one to which we could travel alone.

"That should be a lot of fun." She giggled and gave me the smile she always wore whenever she hinted Sergei and I should date—something she'd done quite a few times since she'd seen us together at the symphony.

Guilt carved a deeper hole in my gut. I longed for the day when I could tell her the truth, and I hoped she'd be so excited by the news she wouldn't be angry with me for lying to her.

I was about to check the event schedule for the time of the short program when a heavy Russian accent exclaimed Sergei's name. Looking behind me, I saw the man attached to the voice. He hugged Sergei, and the two of them exchanged a flurry of words in Russian.

"This is Evgeny Bobrov," Sergei said, appearing a bit startled. "We skated at the same club growing up."

A ripple of excitement rolled through me. I'd never met anyone who'd known Sergei when he was younger. From my quick appraisal, Evgeny appeared to be in his early thirties, and his slight stature led me to believe he'd been a singles skater. We all exchanged introductions, and I asked, "Are you coaching now, too?"

"Yes, I just move to Connecticut," he said, his English slightly broken. "I have two students competing here."

My cell phone rang, interrupting my chance to find out how well Evgeny had known Sergei in Moscow. I excused myself, and my stomach knotted when I saw the number.

"Hey, Dad."

"Hey, sweetie, I was calling to check in. I haven't heard from you in a few days."

"It's been a crazy week. Chris and I have been doing a lot of pre-season interviews, and the kids are competing this week…"

"I thought maybe you were avoiding my suggestion that you come home to visit soon."

I pinched the bridge of my nose. "I'm really busy right now."

His audible sigh carried through the phone line. "I don't know who's more stubborn—you or your mother. How much longer are you going to keep up this standoff? I thought after months of not speaking, one of you would give in."

"I can't talk to her unless she's going to be fair to Sergei. I know you've tried to reason with her, and if she won't listen to you, then she's not going to listen to me."

"If you would just come over and give it a try, you might be able to reach an understanding."

I glanced over at Sergei. His handsome face broke into a smile as he patted Courtney's head. "I'm sorry, Dad, I can't. Mom has to make the first move."

THE NEXT AFTERNOON, I made my daily stop at the coffee shop but sat alone since Sergei had business at the rink. I opened the copy of *Anna Karenina* he'd loaned me and flipped to my bookmarker. With my head buried in the novel, I didn't notice a figure approach my table until I heard, "Hello, Emily."

I popped my head up to see Evgeny next to my chair with a cup of coffee in his hand. His friendly smile plus my curiosity spurred me to an issue an invitation.

"Hi! Would you like to sit?" I pointed to the chair across from mine.

"Thank you." He sat and took a sip of his drink. "I see you skate at Worlds this year. Very beautiful. You have great talent."

"Thank you, that's nice of you to say."

"And you skate pairs only two years? Sergei must be very good coach."

"He's amazing. I wouldn't be where I am without him."

He thumped his index finger on the table. "I always knew he would become coach. He help young skaters at our club many time."

"Really? He doesn't talk much about those days." Evgeny seemed like a talkative guy, so I decided to throw him some bait. "It was so unfortunate what happened with Elena."

"You know about Elena?" He put his elbows on the table and angled forward.

"I heard what her father did."

"Yes, it was bad…" He appeared to search for the right word. "Situation… with baby."

A cold chill blanketed my skin. "Baby?" I croaked.

"Yes. You know about Elena and the baby," he said as a statement rather than a question.

The chill took hold of my hands, causing them to quiver. I gripped my warm coffee cup to try to steady them.

"I know Elena's father sent her away because he didn't want her and Sergei to be together."

"Right, but also he sent her away to have baby."

My skinny latte crept up into my throat. Surely, there was some misunderstanding. Something lost in translation. My mind overflowed with questions; the most important one escaped my lips. "Did Sergei know she was pregnant?"

"Yes, he want to marry her, so they can be family together."

A sharp pain stabbed between my ribs, as though someone had pierced my heart with a dagger and continued to grind it in deeper and deeper. I pressed my jaws together in a desperate attempt to keep my swirling emotions from my face. If I didn't get out of there soon, I feared I could no longer hold in the anguish crushing my chest.

"Yes, that was, um, very sad how things turned out." I shut my book and picked up my coffee. "I just remembered I need to run a few errands. I'll see you at the rink."

He stood up along with me. "You seem upset by what I say."

"No, I just… Sergei probably wouldn't want us talking about this, so… I'll see you."

I stumbled against two chairs and bumped into the newspaper rack as I hurried toward the door. When I reached my car, I shoved the key into the ignition and paused a minute to figure out my destination. My head was so foggy I had to close my eyes to bring some clarity. Sergei had said he was going home after he finished at the rink. If he wasn't there yet, I could wait outside.

I credited God with guiding me from South Dennis to Hyannis because my attention was not on the road. After nearly side-swiping a truck in one of the Cape's many rotaries, I shook myself and concentrated on the last stretch of highway before Sergei's apartment.

His usual parking spot sat empty. I pulled in next to it and kept the engine running. The vents blasted cold air on my face, but I still felt like I was suffocating.

He sent her away to have the baby.

Over and over, Evgeny's words pummeled my brain. I rested my arms and head on the steering wheel but jolted upright when "Every Breath You Take" came on the radio, filling the car with Sting's voice. The pain in my chest tightened. I punched the button to change the channel and jumped again at the sight of Sergei's car turning into the lot.

We climbed from our cars at the same time, and Sergei smiled. "This is a nice surprise."

"We need to talk." I marched ahead of him to the stairs.

He didn't say anything until after he unlocked his door. "What's wrong?"

I stood in the center of the living room and pivoted to face him. "Did you get Elena pregnant?"

The color drained from his face. "Who told you that?"

"Just answer the question."

The shock in his voice quickly became irritation. "Was it Evgeny?"

"Answer. The. Question," I said with short breaths.

He looked down at the carpet and rubbed his forehead before his eyes met mine once again. "Yes, but—"

The anger I'd been holding in exploded, and I threw my arms out wide. "I asked if what you told me was the whole story and you said yes. How could you look me in the eye and lie to me like that?"

"I'm sorry." He reached out a hand, but I jumped back. "I was afraid what you would think if I told you everything."

"You thought I was going to judge you?"

His Adam's apple dipped hard as he swallowed. "I know you probably already are."

I pushed an angry hand through my hair, tangling its waves. "Honestly, I haven't even been able to process it yet. I'm more disturbed by how easily you lied to me."

My phone rang in my purse, but I didn't move. Above the ringing, Sergei said, "I thought it was best if you never knew. It's a part of my life I'd rather forget."

The phone quieted, leaving uneasy silence. I folded my arms and asked the question I was afraid to hear the answer to.

"What happened to the baby?"

Sergei swallowed hard again. "Elena gave it up," he said flatly.

The slight droop to his mouth made him look sincere, but I'd been fooled before.

"Is that the truth?" Bitterness soaked my tone. "Or is there a child in Russia you've been hiding from me?"

"I don't know where the child is. I haven't spoken to Elena since the day she left Moscow, but I know people who've talked to her. She's married but doesn't have any children."

Before I could stop myself, I blurted out, "Evgeny said

you wanted to marry her."

Sergei's jaw clenched. "Sounds like he gave you all the details."

"Well, it's more than what you gave me," I spat.

He wandered in a circle in front of me. "When I found out she was pregnant, I told her we could get married. Her father obviously had other ideas."

"Why didn't she stand up to him?"

"You don't understand the kind of power he had. He knew people, people who could hurt me and my family. With the threats he made, she had no choice."

My head pounded, overwhelmed with conflicting thoughts and emotions. I hated the fact I could harbor a thought such as this, but I couldn't ignore it. "How do I know you're telling me the truth? How do I know *you* weren't the bad guy, and that's why Elena's father didn't want you with her?"

His eyes paled as hurt robbed them of their color. He moved closer to me. "You know me, Em."

"Do I?" Tears shook my voice. "I'm starting to wonder how much more you've decided I shouldn't know. Maybe my mother was right about you."

He winced as if my words had slapped him. "There's nothing else, I swear. I'll get Evgeny over here and he can tell you everything I just told you." He made a frantic gesture toward the door.

"No, I don't wanna talk to Evgeny," I choked. "And I don't wanna talk to you either."

I headed for the door, and Sergei grabbed my wrist. "Don't leave like this. I need to know you believe me."

The pain on his face jabbed at my heart, but I jerked my arm away. "I don't know what to believe anymore."

CHAPTER TWENTY-FIVE

I SLAMMED MY FRONT DOOR SHUT and collapsed onto the stairs in the foyer. Salty tears flowed down my cheeks to my lips. The sound of Sergei calling my name across his parking lot rang in my ears, his desperation echoing in my head.

Footsteps creaked on the steps behind me. "Em!" Aubrey exclaimed. "What happened?"

I rose to my feet, using the banister for support. When I turned, I saw Chris standing next to Aubrey.

"What are you doing here?" I sniffed and dried my face with my palms.

"We were gonna listen to some songs for our show program, remember? I tried calling you a little while ago."

I vaguely recalled my phone ringing at Sergei's apartment. "Oh… yeah. I can't do that right now."

They gaped at me as I took the steps two at a time to the living room. Aubrey stopped me before I rounded the flight of stairs to my bedroom.

"Did you have a fight with Sergei?"

Chris watched me intently, and I could already hear "I told you so" spilling from his mouth. I dropped into my favorite chair, seeking comfort from its soft chenille fabric and wide pillowy arms.

"He lied to me about something very important," I said barely above whisper.

Chris stood with his hands on his hips. "I knew this was going to happen."

"Could you please not lecture me?" I cried as a new batch of tears watered my eyes. My contact lenses swam loose, making Chris's agitated face appear fuzzy.

Aubrey sat on the floor in front of me. "What did he lie about?"

I brought my knees up to my chest and rested my chin on them. "When he and Elena were skating together, they were secretly dating. He told me Elena's father sent her away to keep them apart. The truth was her father sent her away because she was pregnant."

Chris's mouth fell open. "He has a kid?"

"Elena gave up the baby." I shuddered as I realized Sergei had a child somewhere out there. I'd been so focused on his lie I hadn't thought about the fact he was a father.

"Wow," Aubrey said. "I never would've guessed that's why he quit skating."

Chris perched on the edge of the sofa. "Why did he lie about it?"

"He thought I would look down on him, but I could've handled the truth." I paused and sniffled. "It would've been a lot to digest, but if he just would've been honest with me . . ." I massaged my temples, which throbbed with a sickening ache. "What do you do when someone you trust with all your heart lets you down?"

A sob caught in my throat, and I buried my face against my knees. After a moment, Aubrey's arm circled my shoulders.

"Trust is a hard thing to get back once you lose it," she said softly.

I took a few deep breaths and picked up my head. Chris was staring at the carpet and twisting his hands.

"Chris, I know what you're thinking, but I'm not going to let this affect us."

"You think it's going to be that easy?" he asked quietly.

"I didn't say it will be easy." I wiped the last teardrops from my chin and focused my hazy eyes on Chris. "But I won't disappoint you like Sergei disappointed me."

SERGEI'S PHONE CALLS WERE frequent and his messages full of distress. In some, he begged me to let him explain. In others, he left long rambles repeating the entire story. The last few, he just asked me to call him, and his voice was so sad, I almost broke down and relented. But I didn't return any of them, waiting until I saw him at the rink to deliver my own message—"I need time to think, so please give me some space."

At practice, I retreated inside myself and put pinpoint focus on working my blades over the ice. Smoothly and methodically, I etched deep tracings. Being on the ice gave me a feeling of peace, but as soon as I removed my skates, my heart filled with turmoil.

After a week of evading Sergei outside the rink, I still didn't feel ready to talk to him. I kept remembering the conversation we'd had when I thought he'd confided in me about Elena. He'd lied to me so easily. How would I ever know when he was being truthful?

Aubrey and I returned home from a late dinner on Main Street, and I spied an object on our doormat. Upon closer inspection, I discovered the object was the *Lyrics* book. A long-stemmed pink rose marked one of the pages, and red swirly lines enclosed a stanza of lyrics in which Sting expressed his sorrow and asked for forgiveness.

I held the rose close to my nose. The sweet smell briefly softened my heart but not long enough to erase the sting of betrayal. If only words could make everything better.

Aubrey read over my shoulder. "I guess Sergei's trying to break the silence."

I placed the flower between the pages and started for my car. "I'll be back."

During the short trip from my house to Sergei's apartment, I steeled myself for the pleas I knew I'd hear. I had to stay strong and not give in to emotion. As I climbed the steps to the outdoor walkway, I remembered the last time I'd been there, and I knocked forcefully on the door.

When Sergei saw me, his face brightened. He opened the door wider to let me inside, but my feet didn't move.

I stuck his peace offering over the threshold. "You can't fix this with a book."

My chilly tone stole the apparent hope from his eyes. He slowly took the book from me.

"I know. I just thought it would remind you how good we are together." His voice contained a heaviness I'd never heard before.

I tugged on the end of my long ponytail. "I told you I need space."

"Shutting me out isn't the answer. I made a terrible mistake, but don't let it ruin what we have." He stepped outside, and I backed away as far as the narrow walkway would allow. "I love you so much, Em." His words broke with emotion. "Let me make this right."

His pleading eyes reached out to me. I felt myself being pulled toward him until the deep horn of the Nantucket ferry pierced the night and shook me to my senses. I gripped the paint-chipped rail lining the walkway and watched the boat dock in the harbor across the street.

"Talking isn't going to help right now because I'm going to doubt everything you say."

"Then let's not talk." He moved behind me, the warmth of his body heating mine. His hands slipped around my waist while his lips brushed the back of my neck.

My head spun as I yielded to his touch. I wanted to believe in him, wanted to believe he would never betray my trust again. But his kisses couldn't ease my fears.

"Please stop." I untangled myself from him and hastened toward the stairs. "I need time to think."

MY FIRST STEP IN distancing myself from Sergei was changing my seat on our flight to Dallas. I opted for a dreaded middle seat near the back of the plane over sitting next to him for hours.

On the long journey, I tried to concentrate on the paperback I'd picked up at the airport, but I couldn't tear my mind from my troubles. The last few times I'd spoken to my dad, I couldn't bring myself to tell him Sergei had lied about his past. I was already upset enough without adding Dad's disappointment to the situation. And Mom would never let me hear the end of it. I had to figure out if or when I could trust Sergei again before I disclosed anything to my parents.

Our flight landed in mid-afternoon. When we'd planned the trip, we'd wanted to arrive early to sightsee and have dinner alone together at a restaurant—something we couldn't do on the Cape. Now, I wanted to be as far away from Sergei as possible.

I walked to the mall connected to our hotel and wandered aimlessly in and out of the shops. When my feet grew tired, I found a bench next to the mall's ice rink. On the ice, a group of tiny girls and boys surrounded their coach with eager smiles. They practiced the most basic spin, some doing the move with precision, others wobbling and falling on their bottoms. None of them stopped smiling, though.

I observed the kids with a touch of envy. It was hard for me to remember a time when the sport was that simple. No political judging, no thousand dollar costumes scrutinized down to the smallest sequin, no heavy expectations. As much as I loved competing, there were days when I longed to skate free of restrictions.

Noisy teenagers soon overtook the rink, so I made my way back to the hotel and the solitude of my room. Never able to sleep soundly in hotels, I awoke early the next morning and was the first person in the meeting room downstairs. I took a spot at one of the long tables and read the class agenda. The opening session would be Professional Ethics. *How appropriate.*

Fellow coaches filed in and filled the tables around me. When Sergei entered, I dropped my head and started reading through the class materials. He bypassed several empty seats and slid into the one next to me.

"Good morning." He delivered it like his typical daily greeting at the rink.

I picked up my purse to switch seats but realized I was stuck. It wouldn't look good if I moved to get away from my coach. I set my bag down in defeat.

The instructor welcomed everyone and launched into an introductory speech. My attention drifted to and from the woman at the podium. I didn't want to admit how distracted I was by the alluring scent of Sergei's cologne. Being this close to him was giving me a tingly feeling I wished I could deny.

We were asked to silently read the Code of Ethics enclosed in our binders, so I quickly pulled out the sheet of paper, eager to busy my brain. As I read through the eight rules, I highlighted number four and slid the paper in front of Sergei.

Members shall be ever mindful of the influence they exercise over their pupils and under all circumstances this trust should never be abused.

His lips pressed together. On the bottom of the page, he

wrote—*It will never happen again.*

My chest tightened, and I shifted in my chair. I slipped the sheet into my binder and listened to the instructor recap the professional standards.

The moment class ended, I jumped up. I needed to take a walk before the next session. Sergei started to say something but was interrupted by a young woman who approached our table.

"Sergei! I didn't see you when I came in."

She hugged him, and I noticed her tight grasp around his shoulders and how she ran her palm down his back as he released her.

"Leah, this is Emily." Sergei motioned to me.

She took my hand, and I sized her up. Fit and petite with long raven hair and dark eyes, she exuded confidence.

"Emily, I'm a big fan. I knew Sergei when he was starting out in Chicago, and he only dreamed of finding talented students like you."

A wave of déjà vu hit me. Didn't I have a similar conversation with Evgeny? And that didn't end so well.

"Leah coaches in Chicago," Sergei explained.

"It's nice to meet you," I said. "I have to run out for a minute, if you'll excuse me."

As I left, I heard Leah say, "We need to catch up later." I'd gotten a few feet down the hall when Sergei jogged up beside me.

I picked up my pace. "Looks like you have a friend to occupy your time now, so you don't have to bother me anymore."

He glanced behind us and said quietly, "I'm going to keep bothering you until you talk to me."

"Maybe I should have a chat with Leah. The last time I spoke to someone from your past, I learned quite a bit, and you two seem pretty friendly."

"Forget about Leah. This is about you and me."

I stopped and raised my eyes to his. "If there is still a you and me."

I ducked into the restroom and inside a stall, and my hands flew to my head. *Why did you say that? Do you really believe it might be over?* I swallowed hard, pushing down an onslaught of tears. I'd never felt so confused.

CHAPTER TWENTY-SIX

I RETURNED TO THE MEETING ROOM as the next session began. Sergei looked up at me, but I avoided eye contact. I opened my class binder and immediately saw the note written on the top of my agenda—*I know you didn't mean what you said.*

I bit my trembling lip and flipped the page. Out of the corner of my eye, I could see Sergei staring straight ahead, but I felt as though he was watching my reaction. Shielding my face with my hand, I turned to the section on skater nutrition and read along with the instructor's lecture.

Leah appeared at our table again as soon as the session ended. She skirted past me and touched Sergei's bicep. "So, how's life on Cape Cod?"

"It's great." Sergei glanced at me as I stood up and gathered my purse and binder. During our lunch break, I wanted to re-read the materials since I'd zoned out a few times during class.

"I bet it is," Leah said. "Everyone's talking about all your success. You're going to have kids lining up to work with you."

Curiosity almost made me stay to listen to their

conversation, but Leah's flirty laughter turned my stomach. I shot out of the room while she had Sergei cornered.

After nibbling on a turkey sandwich in the mall's food court, I went back to the hotel for the afternoon classes. The first thing I saw was Leah sitting comfortably in my chair next to Sergei's empty one with her binder open, ready for the lectures. Rather than make a fuss, I searched for a vacant spot. Sergei returned just as the instructor stood behind the podium, and he shot me an apologetic look. As much as I wanted to put distance between us, I couldn't deny the jealousy creeping across my skin.

I sat two rows behind Sergei and Leah and spent most of the afternoon watching the backs of their heads. Every time Leah leaned in close to Sergei to say something, my foot tapped harder against the floor. There had to be some history between them. She was way too comfortable invading his personal space. I noted Sergei stayed out of hers, keeping a polite distance.

When we were dismissed at the end of the day, Sergei caught up to me outside the elevators. Surprisingly, Leah wasn't glued to his side.

"I'm sorry about Leah. She moved her stuff while I was out."

I shrugged and made my voice sound as emotionless as possible. "It wasn't a big deal."

"A few of us are having dinner later. I'd really like you to come."

"I think I'm going to get room service. I'm not feeling very social."

"It's going to be low-key, I promise."

A gathering of coaches might be low-key for him but not for me. I'd have to be "perfect skater Emily," saying all the right things and answering questions about the upcoming Olympics, which I was leery of discussing. The closer the Games got, the more superstitious I became.

"I'd rather do my own thing. But you have fun," I said with zero enthusiasm.

The already dim light in his eyes faded even more. "Maybe we can get together after dinner then. I can come to your room —"

One of our colleagues, an older man from Detroit, called down the corridor, "Seven o'clock for dinner?"

I jumped on the elevator while Sergei answered him. The doors closed, leaving Sergei's disappointment behind.

"COME ON, COMPUTER, CONNECT." I slapped the base of my laptop and cursed the hotel's uncooperative network.

After two more unsuccessful attempts, I decided to try one of the computers available for guests downstairs. The sofas and chairs in the lobby were largely unoccupied, but the open-air bar to the right of the sitting area was hopping with after-dinner patrons. I recognized a number of coaches from the seminar, so I did a quick scan for one person in particular. It only took a few seconds for me to spot Sergei at one of the tall tables. He shared it with three other people, one of whom was Leah.

Sergei's back was to the lobby, so he couldn't see me. I chose the computer far in the corner where I'd have a view of all the action but wouldn't be noticed.

While I scrolled through my emails, I kept one eye on the bar. Leah's hand found its way to Sergei's arm more times than I could count, and her touchy-feeliness didn't extend to the other two guys at the table. If I wasn't under twenty-one, in a secret relationship, and currently not speaking to my boyfriend, I'd march into the bar and tell her to keep her claws to herself.

When Leah got up to leave, she whispered in Sergei's ear and started to walk away, but he stopped her and whispered something in return. She smiled, said a few words, and left, not seeing me in the corner. I tried to analyze her smile, but she had been too far away for me to get a good read. Was it a seductive smile? A friendly one? While I mulled it over, Sergei stood and said his own goodbyes. No more than a minute had passed since Leah had departed. A chill of uneasiness caused me to shiver.

I logged off the machine and scrambled behind a large plant so Sergei wouldn't see me. After he stepped into the elevator, I watched the numbers rise above the silver doors. I waited for them to stop on twelve, his floor, but they kept climbing. With each number, my heart sank further into a pit of fear.

The elevator finally stopped on eighteen, my floor but also Leah's. I'd seen her leaving her room when I'd gone to get ice before dinner.

The pit of fear swallowed me whole.

My clammy hand punched the Up button. The ride seemed to last an hour. I slowly turned down the hallway to my room, hoping to see Sergei at my door.

The corridor was empty.

I clutched my stomach as I passed Leah's room. Thoughts of what might be happening in there twisted my insides into knots of pain. I briefly considered knocking on the door but had no idea what I would say or do if I saw Sergei inside.

In my room, I crawled into bed fully clothed and pulled the blanket up to my chin. I felt feverish. My entire body shook, fighting off sobs of disgust, anger, and regret. *You pushed him away.*

THE SUN CAME UP in the morning, but I couldn't see it through the dark cloud surrounding me. I packed my suitcase in an exhausted daze and examined myself in the mirror. Red streaks covered my face, and matching lines filled my bloodshot eyes. I slapped powder on my cheeks and squirted eye drops over my pupils. I needed to be presentable for the trip home.

I didn't see Sergei in the lobby, so I hailed a taxi and called him as the driver sped toward the airport.

"Hey, I'm downstairs. Do you still need to checkout?" He sounded so casual, as though nothing out of the ordinary had occurred.

"I was up early, so I'm on my way to the airport."

"You didn't wait for me?" His casualness changed to frustrated hurt.

I rolled down the window and inhaled a deep breath of fresh air. The mustiness of the cab mixed with the driver's rapid acceleration was making me woozy.

"I was ready to go. I'll see you at the gate." I hung up without waiting for a response.

Once I passed through security, I strolled up and down the terminal, rolling my carry-on bag behind me. I stopped in a café for an extra-large cup of coffee, read magazines in the gift shop, and perused the newest novels on display. Anything to delay seeing Sergei.

When I finally arrived at the gate, there was no room to sit or stand. A crowd of anxious faces stared at the television on the far wall, so I crept closer to see what was drawing so much attention. Sergei leapt to his feet and navigated around piles of luggage and families camped on the floor.

"There you are. Did you hear what happened?" His wide eyes and rushed question unsettled me.

"No, I've been walking around." I looked back at the TV and saw a news reporter with a grim expression.

"A plane hit the World Trade Center."

I thought immediately of an inexperienced pilot losing control of his single engine plane. "A small one?"

"No, a jet," Sergei said gravely.

"How can that happen?" I moved toward the TV and mimicked the position of everyone around me—neck arched upward, mouth agape, eyes glued to the raw images on the screen.

As reports of a second crash surfaced, the shock and horror in the crowd intensified. Muffled cries, nervous chatter, and the persistent buzzing of cell phones dominated the area. Sergei and I didn't speak as we stood shoulder to shoulder, staring at the smoking towers on the television. When the first plane was identified as a flight out of Boston's Logan Airport, I shuddered. We had flown out of there two mornings ago.

My phone rang, and Dad didn't give me a chance to say hello. "Are you at the airport?" he asked.

"Yes, we're watching everything on TV." I couldn't tear my eyes from the screen.

"Do not get on that plane, Emily. We'll find a way to get you home."

The pictures on television seemed like a bad dream, but the fear in my father's voice made them a terrible reality.

"I don't even know if we're taking off. They haven't said anything yet."

"Well, whatever they do, you're not getting on the plane. I want you out of that airport as soon as possible." He paused and took a heavy breath. "Is Sergei there? I want to talk to him."

"Um, yeah, he's right here. Hold on." I passed the phone to Sergei. "My dad wants to talk to you."

As Dad spoke, Sergei didn't say anything except "I will" and "Yes, sir."

Sergei returned the phone to me, and Dad continued his instructions. "You're going to have to get a rental car. Call me as soon as you're on the road. I love you."

"I love you, too, Dad."

I hung up and asked Sergei, "What did he say to you?"

"He told me to make sure you get home safe."

The events of the prior night came rushing back, and I dropped my gaze to the phone. Dad had no idea he was asking a liar and a cheater to look after me. But now wasn't the time to think about what Sergei had done.

I straightened my shoulders and grabbed my suitcase. "We should hurry to the rental car office before it gets too crowded."

Everyone else in the airport had the same idea. I couldn't see where one line ended and another began. Sergei and I didn't talk during the wait, and neither did most of the people around us. We were all too dazed by what we'd seen on television to comprehend it or discuss it.

As the throng of people moved forward at a turtle's pace, I wondered how I was going to survive a cross-country drive with Sergei. Just looking at him made me want to scream. He didn't appear to harbor any guilt. How was I going to spend days locked in a car with him?

My phone rang again, and the name on my caller ID was one I hadn't seen in months. I lifted the phone to my ear. "Mom?"

"Sweetie, oh thank God, I'm so glad to hear your voice." High-pitched hysteria filled hers. "I was in class when I heard about the crashes, and I didn't know if you were already in the air. I was so scared I wouldn't be able to talk to you, and if something happened to you..."

Tears overtook her, and I clamped my hand over my mouth as I began to cry, too. I turned away from Sergei and gripped the phone tighter.

"I'm so sorry, Mom. I never should've let our stupid fight go on so long."

"No, I shouldn't have put you in that position. It wasn't fair. I'm going to try to be more understanding."

I placed my palm on my forehead, not knowing if I should laugh or cry even more at the irony of the situation. *Now* Mom was ready to accept Sergei.

My phone beeped and a red light flashed. "Mom, my battery's low. I can use Sergei's phone to call you later, okay? We're almost to the rental car desk."

"Be careful, sweetie." She sniffled. "Call me soon. I love you."

I took off my glasses to dry my eyes, and Sergei's hand touched my shoulder. I flinched. He balled his hand and stared at it until the desk clerk motioned us forward.

Armed with a large foldout map of the entire country and keys to a Ford Explorer, Sergei and I set off on our long journey home. He offered to drive first, so I settled into the smooth leather passenger seat. I used his phone to let Dad know we were on our way and left a message for Mom when she didn't answer.

The radio fed us a constant stream of updates about the terrorist attacks. Neither of us said much as we listened to the gruesome eyewitness accounts. I rested my arm on the console between the seats, but when Sergei squeezed my hand, I quickly pulled it out of his grasp.

"I can't even touch you now?" His eyes crinkled with hurt and confusion.

I hugged my chest and faced the window. "Not after last night."

"What happened last night?"

I shook my head in disbelief at his innocent act. "I saw you go to Leah's room."

"What? I didn't go anywhere near her room," he insisted.

"I saw you whispering together in the bar, and when you left, your elevator stopped on her floor."

He lowered the volume on the radio. "I stopped on *your* floor. I was going to talk to you."

I whipped my head in his direction. "Then how come I didn't see you when I went upstairs?"

"I decided when I got up there I shouldn't bother you. I figured you'd probably get madder at me."

His explanation sounded so plausible, but I couldn't forget what I'd seen in the bar. "What were you whispering about? And why was Leah all over you?"

"She wasn't all over me. How did you see us, anyway? Were you spying on me?"

"I was in the lobby checking email, and the bar was in plain view. Why don't you answer my question?"

"Are you going to believe me when I tell you?"

I noticed the speed of the car had picked up along with the tension of the conversation. The flat Texas landscape flew by outside my window.

"Just tell me."

He glanced in the rearview mirror and slowed the car. "She gave me her room number, but I told her I'm seeing someone, and that was the end of it."

"Why would she ask you up to her room unless she thought you were interested?"

"I don't know. We went out a few times in Chicago. I guess she got the wrong idea."

I peered at him sideways. "Are you sure you didn't give her the wrong idea?"

"No." He took his eyes off the interstate to look at me. "I can't believe you thought I would sleep with her."

"You left within a minute of each other and you ended up on her floor." My voice shook. "Tell me what I was supposed to think."

Anguish darkened his face. "You're supposed to know I love you and would never even consider doing something like that."

I slunk down in my seat and bowed my head to hide the tears. Everything was such a mess. So many miles lay both between us and ahead of us, and I didn't know how long it would take to travel either distance.

CHAPTER TWENTY-SEVEN

Those were the first words Sergei spoke in almost two hundred miles. After I'd accused him of cheating on me, he'd turned up the radio and gone quiet.

"A little," I replied.

We were somewhere in Arkansas. I looked at the map for the fiftieth time and sighed at how far we were from home.

Sergei exited the interstate and followed the signs to the nearest fast food drive thru. I searched for the healthiest item on the menu and was happy to have the salad as a distraction in the silent car.

The radio reports became even more devastating as the hours passed, and phone calls home revealed everyone's continued state of shock. Aubrey said the skaters at the rink were already thinking of ways to raise money for the victims' families, while Chris said prayer services were being planned across the island. Mom kept me on the line the longest, seemingly trying to make up for the time we'd lost. She described the scene on Boston University's campus—American flags were popping up in dorm windows and hundreds of students had gathered to pray on the quad.

I couldn't stop thinking about the passengers on the planes and the people trapped in the towers. What must've gone through their minds during their final moments?

I stared at the radio and shook my head. "All those people got up this morning, went to work, went to the airport, having no idea they would never see their friends and family again."

Sergei gave me a quick glance and paused a few moments before he spoke. "I can't imagine making that last phone call like some of them did. How do you say everything you need to in a minute or less?"

"Makes you realize how important it is to not wait until it's too late to say those things."

A longer pause hung between us, and Sergei snuck another look my way. "It's good you and your mother are talking again. I went through something similar with my father." He rubbed his hand slowly over the steering wheel. "After I quit skating."

"What happened?"

"He thought skating was my one chance to do something great. When Elena got pregnant, he kicked me out of the house and didn't speak to me for a long time."

"How long?"

"A couple of years. Until he found out I was moving to the States."

"A couple of *years*? Wow." I threaded my fingers through my hair, pushing it away from my forehead. "I can't imagine how tough that must've been."

"It was very hard on my mother. She blamed my father when I told her I was leaving Moscow."

"Was he the reason you left?"

Sergei shook his head. "When I got the offer from my friend to coach in Virginia, I felt it would be a fresh start. I wanted to put everything behind me."

I absorbed the new information, yet another important part of Sergei's life he hadn't shared with me. "All those months my mom and I weren't talking, you never mentioned your dad."

He shifted in his seat and kept his eyes on the road.

"Because then you would've had to tell me about the baby," I added quietly.

A few pairs of headlights zoomed past us before Sergei said, "You never would've screwed up like I did. You're perfect and—"

"I'm not perfect."

"You are to me." He turned to face me and then looked away. "I didn't want you to know the mistakes I've made, to regret getting involved with me."

"You were eighteen when you made those mistakes. You're a different person now. You want me to trust you, but you didn't trust me enough to open up to me." I kept my tone as calm as possible.

"If I could do it over again, I'd tell you everything."

I lowered my eyes to my lap. "I want to believe that."

"But you don't." He wasn't able to mask the pain in his voice.

"I don't know," I said sadly. My heart longed to put all my faith in him, but my head wouldn't get out of the way.

Silence returned to the car. Not long after we passed Nashville, Sergei started massaging his neck and squirming against his seatbelt. "We should probably stop soon for the night. I saw signs for some motels up ahead."

The lights of Cookeville approached. Sergei drove slowly down a row of motels and pulled into the Country Inn, which appeared the newest of the bunch. A handful of cars dotted the parking lot of the neat two-story building, so vacancy didn't seem to be an issue.

The young clerk welcomed us with an easy smile. He told us about the complimentary breakfast and directed us to adjacent rooms on an exterior corridor. As we unloaded our suitcases from the car, I asked Sergei if I could borrow his phone. I'd forgotten my charger at home, so mine was useless.

A strong lemon scent greeted me upon entering my room. I felt my way in the darkness to the lamp, peeled away the comforter, and collapsed on the bed, stretching out my stiff limbs. I wasn't accustomed to being so immobile.

A hot shower beckoned, so I set aside Sergei's phone to call my parents later. The steaming water loosened the knots in my back and neck. I stood under the powerful spray longer than usual, letting the warmth relax both my body and my mind.

After I put on my pajamas and combed my damp hair, I curled up on the bed and called my parents' house.

"Hey, Mom, we're at a motel in Tennessee."

"Do you have your own room?"

I let out a tired laugh. No matter how upside down the world had become, some things never changed. "Yes, Mom."

"Make sure your deadbolt is locked. You never know what kind of people are staying at those places."

I smiled and shook my head. I never thought I'd miss Mom's over protectiveness, but her safety reminder gave me a comforting feeling.

"We'll probably be home late tomorrow night. I can't wait to get back on the ice."

"Will you come to the house after you pick up your car at the airport? It's been so long since I've seen you," she whimpered.

"Definitely." I swallowed the lump in my throat. "I should get to sleep. Tomorrow's going to be another long day."

Slipping on my flip flops, I went out into the muggy night to return Sergei's phone. I knocked on his door and gulped when he answered. All he wore was a pair of gray pajama pants tied low on his waist. Even without my contacts, I could see the sculpted muscles of his shoulders and chest. My eyes drifted lower, following the light trail of hair down his flat stomach.

Sergei gave me the same once-over, his gaze lingering on my thin tank top and tiny shorts. A flush of heat spread from the nape of my neck up to my cheeks.

I handed him the phone. "Thanks for letting me use it."

"No problem. Can you take a look at the map with me?" He gestured behind him. "I think I found a shorter route."

I hesitated, but his magnetic eyes drew me inside. "Sure."

I picked up the opened map from the desk and held it close to my nose, while Sergei positioned himself next to me, accelerating my heart rate. He smelled like soap—really good-smelling soap.

He pointed to a highway on the map. "We can bypass Baltimore and Philadelphia if we take Interstate Seventy-Eight. Less traffic."

My mouth felt drier than a saltine cracker. "That's a good idea."

He cleared his throat. "Have you ever driven that way before?"

"Mmmm..." I was having trouble focusing. Lack of sleep and food plus Sergei's half-naked body hovering near me did not equal sharp thinking. "I don't think so."

His hand dropped from the map and grazed my arm. This time I didn't flinch. I couldn't move. Sergei was so close one slight shift would put my face against his bare chest.

"I know how much you want to get home." His voice, so soft and tender, wrapped around me like a loving embrace.

I made the mistake of looking up into his eyes. Their intensity hypnotized me, taking me outside of myself. The map slid from my fingers as I pressed my body to Sergei's. His breath hitched, and he took my face between his hands.

Our lips met, and I savored the initial spark. We eased into the kiss, our tongues slow dancing with each other. His fingers got lost in my hair, while my hands ran across his back. The heat of his skin on mine sent rapid impulses down to my toes.

"I'm never going to let you down again, I promise." Sergei's lips touched mine as he spoke.

In a flash, I remembered my hurt and anger when I'd found out Sergei had lied to me. The idea of going through that again terrified me.

"This… this isn't right." I stumbled over the words and my feet as I backed into the desk.

He brought me into his arms and tilted my chin upward. "Yes it is. I know you feel it."

I scooted away. "It's not enough. I'm sorry."

I bolted from the room and pulled my key from my pocket. It fell to the cement, and Sergei grabbed it.

"You're not running from me anymore." He held the card over his head, high above my reach.

"I don't know what else to say." I tugged on his shoulder, but he locked his arms around me, trapping my hands between us.

"Then I'll say what *I* need to. I should've been honest with you. I should've trusted you could handle it. But I was too afraid you wouldn't see me the same, and I couldn't risk losing you."

"So, how am I supposed to know this won't happen again? That you won't keep something from me because you think it's for the best?"

"Because I don't ever want to see that look in your eyes again. The one you had before you ran out of my apartment. You looked at me like I was a stranger, and it killed me." His chest heaved against my hands, and tears crept into my throat.

"I didn't know what to think. I was scared that everything I thought I knew about you was a lie."

"I'm so sorry." Sergei buried his face in my hair. "Please give me another chance."

A weight of emotion fell on me, weakening my knees, and I leaned into Sergei's embrace.

I felt his love in his touch, heard it in his voice, and saw it in his eyes. He hadn't given up on me when I'd pushed him away. I thought of all the people who had lost loved ones that day, who wouldn't have any second chances. They would give anything to have this opportunity. I couldn't let fear hold me back. I had to listen to my heart.

"I want you in my life forever." My gaze met Sergei's. "So no more lies. No more secrets."

His fingertips brushed a gentle path down my cheek. "No more. I promise."

He kissed me long and deep. When we stopped to take a breath, he wrapped his arms around me and held onto me as if he was afraid to let go.

"I love you so much," I whispered.

"I love you, too. More than you know." He gave me another spine-tingling kiss, and I caressed his face.

"I'm so sorry I doubted you last night."

Sergei's hands pressed against the small of my back, bringing our bodies even closer together. "You are the only woman I want to be with. Now and always."

Looking into his eyes, I knew I could trust him with my heart forever. I sank into the warmth of his chest as we shared our most passionate kiss yet.

"Why don't we continue this inside?" Sergei asked, taking my hand.

I smiled. "I don't know if I trust myself in your room right now."

"I'm that irresistible?" One side of his mouth curled up.

"Dangerously."

He tenderly touched my face. "I've missed that smile."

"Well, you're going to see a lot of it because I don't plan on being apart from you ever again."

CHAPTER TWENTY-EIGHT

I HUMMED TO MYSELF AND GAVE the cake batter one final stir before dipping my finger into the chocolate goodness. As I aimed my finger for my mouth, Sergei entered the kitchen.

"Shouldn't I get first taste since it's *my* birthday?" He slid his arm around me.

I pretended to deliberate and then broke into a smile. "Of course."

I lifted my fingertip to Sergei's lips, and he licked the dollop of chocolate. His mouth was warm and too inviting for me to resist. I reached up and kissed him, tasting the sweetness on his tongue.

Life was good. In the three months since September Eleventh, Sergei and I had become closer than ever. He'd shared with me the pain of his past mistakes, giving me a new understanding of him. I'd refrained from telling my parents the truth about Elena. Now that Sergei and I had put it behind us, I didn't see the point. Mom had agreed to be more open-minded, and I'd relished bringing Sergei home to spend time with my family.

On the ice, Chris and I had won gold medals at both our

Grand Prix events, which qualified us for our second Grand Prix Final. In four days we'd travel to Kitchener, Ontario to face the top five teams in the world.

Sergei returned my kiss with a longer one. "I wish I didn't have to go to this dinner."

"I know, but you can't let your friends think you'd rather spend your birthday home alone than go out to eat with them. They don't know you have a super hot girl back at your apartment, baking you a cake." I smiled and licked some batter from the big wooden spoon.

"I'm going to eat as fast as I can." He nuzzled my neck.

I giggled. "Is it just going to be Will, Sydney, and Jeff?" I asked, naming the three coaches at our rink who Sergei was closest to.

"And Viktor."

"Viktor? I didn't think you talked to him much."

Sergei shrugged and picked up his car keys from the counter. "Will made all the plans. I'm just showing up."

"Oh! I want to give you your present before you go." I wiped my hands on a dishtowel and hurried into the living room to retrieve the small gift bag from my purse.

Sergei took the bag and shook it next to his ear with a devilish smile. Reaching inside, he pulled out the rectangular pendant on a silver chain. He looked closely at the Russian inscription and read aloud, "Always."

"I thought it would be something to wear close to your heart that would always make you think of me," I said.

He looped the chain over his head and slipped the pendant inside his sweater. "I love it. But I don't think it's possible for me to think about you any more than I already do."

He drew me near and kissed me softly. After a reluctant parting, he threw on his leather jacket and headed out. When he opened the door, I shivered and hustled into the warm kitchen.

An hour later, the entire apartment smelled like heaven, and the cake was ready to be frosted. I spread the smooth chocolate topping over the cake and jumped when I heard keys opening the front door.

"You really did eat fast!" I laughed and came out of the kitchen to greet Sergei.

He wasn't laughing or smiling. His eyes held an eerie stillness.

"What's wrong?" I rushed toward him.

"My mother called. My father was in a car accident. He's in surgery, and it sounds bad." His voice broke. "Really bad."

"No…" I wrapped my arms around him and felt the tension in his body. "I'm so sorry."

"I don't know what to do. I want to be there, but we have the Final next week."

"You should go home. Chris and I can manage. Your mom needs you more right now."

"Viktor offered to go with you and Chris to Canada if I go to Moscow."

I wrinkled my nose against Sergei's shoulder. From what I saw at the rink and heard from Aubrey, Viktor's temperament was quite different from Sergei's. I wasn't sure his presence would be helpful to my nerves.

"One of the team leaders can help us," I suggested.

"I know, but I think it would be better for you to have a coach there." He slowly loosened his grip around me. "I should try to book a flight. I just hope by the time I get there it's not too late."

I took his face in my hands. "Don't even think that. He can pull through this."

He nodded numbly and embraced me again.

After Sergei made a reservation for an afternoon flight to Moscow and packed his small suitcase, we lay on the couch and stared at his cell phone on the coffee table. Hours had passed since he'd first heard from his mother.

I fell asleep in the comfort of Sergei's arms and didn't awaken until he jerked upright. He grabbed the phone, and I prayed for good news.

My limited Russian vocabulary didn't allow me to follow the conversation, so I watched Sergei's eyes. Encouraged by their steadiness, I held my breath as he hung up and relayed the update.

"The surgery went well, but he has severe liver damage. He's still in critical condition."

I rubbed comforting circles on his back. "That's great about the surgery. One small step at a time."

"My mother sounds exhausted. She said two of her friends have been with her at the hospital since the accident. I was worried she might be alone."

"It's hard not having any family nearby. She's going to be so happy to see you. And think how great it will be when your dad wakes up and finds you there."

He reclined onto the sofa and gently laid me down with him, my back snug against his chest. We dozed on and off the rest of the night. In the morning, Sergei called Viktor to accept his offer. Every time the phone rang, the fear in Sergei's eyes was clear. The only call from his mother let us know nothing had changed in his father's condition.

When it was time for Sergei to leave for the airport, he drove me home. We stood on my doorstep, the overhang sheltering us from the light dusting of snow.

I squeezed his hands. "I'm going to ask everyone at church to pray for your dad. You have to keep believing the best."

"I wish you were coming with me."

"You know I would if I could."

"You're going to do great this week." He gazed firmly into my eyes.

"We'll make you proud, I promise."

With great tenderness, he placed his lips against my

forehead. "You always make me proud."

I soaked in Sergei's embrace, not knowing how long I'd have to wait for the next one. Neither of us wanted to let go, but time wasn't on our side. Blinking back tears, I watched Sergei get in his car and drive away.

"WHAT IS IT SERGEI always says?" Chris asked and, in his best Russian accent, answered his own question. "Just like practice."

I smiled at his spot-on imitation, but inside my heart ached. We were minutes from our short program, and Sergei wasn't in his usual spot next to me, giving me encouragement. He was thousands of miles away at his father's bedside, waiting for him to wake up. I'd hoped by now my prayers would've been answered, but Sergei's dad remained unresponsive.

Viktor stood a few feet from us in the tunnel to the ice. A man of few words, his ever present stern jaw and critical stare spoke for themselves.

Chris and I skated onto the ice, careful to dodge the stuffed animals that had been showered upon Hyatt and Wakefield. Little girls in red velvet dresses swarmed around us, picking up the Canadians' loot.

Once the crowd settled down and we were introduced, I blocked out all thoughts except the required elements we needed to execute. As the instrumental beat of "Hotel California" blared through the arena, I tried to put pizzazz into my movements, but my mind focused on the technical elements. One by one we completed the jumps, spins, twist, death spiral, footwork, and overhead lift with no bobbles, no stumbles. Everything was crisp and clean.

Viktor clapped and nodded. "Very nice, very nice."

In the kiss and cry, I watched the replay of our perfect

side-by-side triple Lutzes and wondered if Sergei had been able to see our program. He and his mom had been at the hospital around the clock, but he'd said there was a television in the waiting room.

I waved at the TV camera aimed at us. "Sergei, we miss you."

The announcer began reading the scores, so I put my attention on the large scoreboard. The marks were high, 5.8's and 5.9's, and the placements unanimous—all number ones. I shook Chris's arm and let out a quiet squeal. He pumped his fist and gave me a tight hug. We'd never placed ahead of Hyatt and Wakefield in any phase of competition. The glass ceiling had just cracked.

We moved backstage and watched Oksana and Denis skate on the monitor. They made no mistakes, but the degree of difficulty of their jumps was less than ours. The judges didn't seem to take that into consideration, though, as they awarded the reigning World Champions with both higher technical and presentation scores.

"Crap," I muttered.

"We should've had the tech mark," Chris said.

We said all the right things to the media, but on the bus to the hotel, we both stewed quietly. We were World medalists, not the new kids on the scene anymore. I thought that would earn us more respect from the judges. Passing the Canadians for the first time was a positive step, but the Russians remained a big hurdle.

I'd just walked into my room when my cell phone rang, and I smiled when I heard Sergei's voice.

"I have some good news," he said.

I stopped in the middle of the room. "He's awake?"

"He's still pretty groggy, but he said a few words. He saw I'm here."

I looked at the ceiling and made the sign of the cross. "That's the most wonderful news ever."

"The doctor said he has a long road ahead of him because of the damage to his liver, but he's more encouraged now."

"I wish I could be there to give you a big hug." I folded one arm across my chest, imagining Sergei within my grasp.

"I wish I could've been there to give *you* a hug after the short tonight."

"You saw it?" I fidgeted with my ponytail. "What did you think?"

"I think you nailed it. There was just one thing."

"I knew there had to be something," I said with a wry smile.

"I think the performance aspect could've been a little better, but the program was close to perfect technically."

"That's something we can easily improve next time. When you get home, we'll do an inspired run-through for you."

He was quiet, and I thought he might have another critique to give.

"About getting home . . ." He paused. "I have some not so good news. I lost my passport. I don't know if it fell out of my bag at the airport or in the cab to the hospital. I just realized it today."

I sank onto the bed. "How long will it take to get a new one?"

"I've talked to some people I know with the Russian Skating Federation. They have contacts in the government that can hopefully speed up the process." He took an audible breath. "But it could be a few weeks."

"A few weeks?" A jolt of panic shot me to my feet. "Nationals is in less than a month."

"I'm going to do everything I can to make it home in time."

The resolve in Sergei's voice calmed me for a moment, but then I thought about the possibility of Nationals without him. I'd be solely responsible for Courtney and Mark, who were top contenders for the novice championship. And even though Chris and I were heavy favorites to win our second national title, the pressure and the stakes were higher this year because of the Olympics. Only the first and second place teams would earn spots on the Olympic team.

I filled my lungs with air and exhaled slowly. Worrying wouldn't help Sergei or me; I needed to step up and give him my own reassurance. "I'll make sure the kids are one hundred percent prepared."

"I know you will. I have total confidence in you."

I sat again on the bed and ran my finger along the seams of the comforter. "I can't imagine not seeing your face for weeks."

"I can't imagine not holding you in my arms for weeks. I miss you so much already."

An ocean separated us, but Sergei's raw emotion touched me as if he were standing in front of me. I took another deep breath and steadied my trembling jaw. The judges weren't going to feel sorry for me because my coach and greatest source of comfort wasn't around. I had to stay strong and secure or my Olympic dream could be lost with one slip of the blade.

CHAPTER TWENTY-NINE

CHRIS RAISED HIS GLASS OF WATER to mine. "Two programs down, one to go."

We'd followed up our successful short program with a clean long, the first of two required free skates at the Grand Prix Final. Oksana and Denis had also skated another perfect program and maintained their slim lead over us.

I sipped my water and scanned the crowded hotel restaurant. Judges and coaches mingled at the bar, while officials of the various skating federations huddled together over their dinners. The politicking and schmoozing done at competitions was no secret. It was a game that had to be played in order to survive in the sport.

Viktor walked into the room, and I quickly looked away. "I hope he doesn't see us."

"I think it's too late," Chris said.

He strode up to our table, his hands in his pockets. "Ready for tomorrow?"

"Absolutely," Chris said as I nodded.

"It's a shame Sergei can't be here. You've had a great competition so far."

I detected no sincerity in his voice. His statement sounded more like an observation than an expression of sympathy.

"Yeah, it's not the same without him here," I said.

Viktor's gray eyes regarded me closely, though I didn't think I'd said anything questionable. I bent my head and aligned my silverware on the table.

"I'll be at the bar," Viktor said. "Enjoy your dinner."

Chris waited until Viktor left to laugh. "Does that dude ever crack a smile?"

"I'd say he might if we win tomorrow, but I don't think he cares."

"Why do you say that?"

I traced a line through the condensation on my water glass. "I've heard him make comments about Sergei. Viktor doesn't give him any credit for how well we've done. I think he's jealous of Sergei's success."

"Well, he was the top dog at the rink before Sergei came along and we started winning. He's probably not his biggest fan, especially since Sergei's like ten years younger than him and already more successful."

At the bar across the room, Viktor chatted with one of the Italian judges. The elderly man spoke animatedly with his hands, while Viktor nodded and sipped his drink.

I smoothed the linen napkin in my lap. "I think Viktor jumped at the chance to be here so he could network for himself, not to do Sergei any favors."

"Let him do whatever he wants." Chris waved his hand. "As long as he doesn't mess up our routine."

I folded my arms and narrowed my gaze toward the bar. We needed Sergei here to talk us up to the judges and sing our praises. I didn't trust Viktor to promote us in any manner.

THIS PROGRAM IS SECOND nature to you now, so allow yourself to be in the moment.

Sergei's advice ran in a constant loop in my head as Chris and I strode toward the ice. We'd had a long phone conversation earlier, and Sergei had spouted all his favorite phrases of encouragement. I'd absorbed every word like a sponge.

The Russians had just finished their free skate. We'd been in the tunnel, but a few loud gasps from the audience told me the program had been far from perfect. I circled the ice, warming up my legs and freezing my mind on one thought:

Be in the moment.

Chris reached for my hand and held me in our starting pose. The music of *The Nutcracker* danced through the air, and we hit each note with flourish and polish. We'd created the program for the Final and had practiced it for one short month, but the music flowed through me as if I'd performed it thousands of times. From the second the program began to the moment it ended, I pushed every edge deeper than I ever had.

As the crowd erupted and Chris threw his arms around me, I instinctively looked toward the boards for Sergei's reaction. Viktor's unsmiling face rudely reminded me Sergei wasn't there.

We settled onto the small bench in the kiss and cry, and Chris found the camera. "Hope you saw that one, Sergei!"

A flood of emotion overcame me, and I bit my bottom lip hard to hold back the tears. Chris saw I was about to break down. He hugged me to his side, and I rested my head on his shoulder.

Chris squeezed me even tighter as our scores were read. When the announcer repeated "Six" three times, the American fans shrieked. I kept my eyes peeled to the video board, waiting for the final standings.

"Come on," I whispered.

Chris and I breathed in harmony together, deep breath in

and deep breath out. The blank blue screen on the video board taunted me until finally the rankings appeared. My gaze went to the top of the list.

Emily Butler and Christopher Grayden

"YES!" I jumped up and threw my arms in the air.

Chris leapt to his feet and picked me up all in one motion, smothering me in a hug. A roaring ovation pelted my ears, and I could barely hear Chris when he said, "One step closer to history."

The tears wouldn't be denied anymore. They poured down my face and onto Chris's cream-colored shirt. Cheers of "USA!" broke out in the crowd and American flags waved throughout the stands.

I can't believe Sergei isn't here for this.

All Viktor had to offer in the form of congratulations was a steady clap and "Great job." Chris and I headed backstage, where we were ushered to the medalists' press conference. I grabbed a couple of tissues from our team leader and wiped the moisture from my cheeks. To our right sat the second place Russians and to our left the Canadians, winners of the bronze medal. Neither team looked pleased with their results. Oksana wore the sourest expression, maintaining pursed lips while Denis answered all the questions directed to them.

Once the media finished their jobs, we waited in the corridor for the start of the medal ceremony. Viktor took a call on his cell and passed it to me.

"There's someone who wants to talk to you."

My heart pounded as I took the phone. "Hello?"

"Em, that was amazing." The pride in Sergei's voice was crystal clear.

I wandered away from Viktor. Chris followed me, and I faced the wall of the corridor. "Thanks," I croaked. "It felt really, really good."

"I can't even tell you how proud I am of you and Chris. You worked so hard for this. You went after it and didn't hold back."

I used my thumb to blot the tears from my eyes. "I kept thinking about what you said… to be in the moment."

Silence came from Sergei's end, and I covered the receiver so he couldn't hear my sniffling.

"I'm sorry I wasn't there with you," he said.

I shook my head. "There's nothing to be sorry for. You're where you need to be."

"It was so weird watching on TV. I don't ever want to do that again."

"I bet the Russian commentators weren't too excited we beat Oksana and Denis."

"They were actually very complimentary of you. And since Oksana and Denis made mistakes, they couldn't deny you were the best."

"I'm sure there'll be people who'll say we only won because they made mistakes."

Chris piped up, "They can shove it."

I smiled and pressed the phone closer to my ear. Sergei's voice crackled over the static on the line. "You won because you skated three clean programs. You earned it."

"Was your mom able to watch or did she fall back asleep like last night?"

He let out a deep laugh, a sound I missed more every day we were apart. "She stayed awake this time and was very excited you won. She can't wait to meet you. I told her you're even more beautiful in person."

Warmth spread through me, and my smile grew wider. "I can't wait to meet her, too. And your dad."

"Emily! Chris!" one of the event volunteers called. "We're doing the podium in a minute."

"I have to go. Will you still be up in about an hour?" I glanced at the clock on the wall and did a quick calculation of the current morning time in Moscow.

"Yeah, I'm too wired to go back to sleep now. I'll call you

in an hour. Go get that gold medal."

IN THE PRIVACY OF my hotel room, Sergei and I talked on the phone until he began yawning every five minutes. I told him to get some rest and let him go. Not tired myself, I flipped on the clock radio and danced around the room as I packed for the flight home the next evening.

Soon, my dancing led to hunger. Fishing through my wallet, I scrounged up enough change for a snack. I deserved a rare junk food treat after what I'd accomplished.

My T-shirt and old gym shorts appeared suitable for a short trip down the hall, so I took my money and my key and aimed for the tiny room with the ice and vending machines. I swung open the door and found Viktor in front of the ice machine. He'd changed from his suit to jeans and a sweater.

"Oh." I stopped short. "Hey."

He gave me the familiar penetrating appraisal except one corner of his mouth twitched upward. The hint of a smile didn't make me any more comfortable.

He picked up his full bucket of ice. "Can't sleep?"

"No." I dropped my coins into the vending machine. "Don't tell anyone you saw me buying potato chips at midnight."

The small size of the room didn't allow Viktor much area to reach the door. To give him more space, I stepped closer to the machine.

As he moved behind me, he put his hand on my arm. "Don't worry, it'll be our little secret."

His body brushed against mine, though he didn't need to be so close. The stench of stale cigarette smoke and musky cologne filled my nostrils, staying with me after the door shut. My stomach turned and my mind raced. Aubrey and Marley always complained about Viktor's temper and sternness but never any inappropriate behavior. *You could have misinterpreted it. Don't jump to conclusions.*

But my crawling skin was hard to ignore.

CHAPTER THIRTY

Every day that passed without Sergei's return brought more strain to my nerves and pain to my heart. His expedited Russian passport was in process but the delivery date uncertain. As a result, he spent Christmas with his parents for the first time in years.

Although I was happy for Sergei to have time with his family, I shed more than a few tears during the holidays. I'd looked forward to exchanging gifts with him in front of the fireplace on Christmas Eve and sharing our first New Year's kiss. We'd had to settle for marathon phone conversations and instant messaging on our laptops, neither of which could compare with being in each other's arms.

Less than a week into the New Year, I boarded a plane to Los Angeles for the National Championships. Our large traveling group from the Cape included Viktor and his students. I stayed as far away from him as possible during the trip, but if Sergei didn't show up in time for our event, Viktor would have to stand in for him again, which I dreaded.

I hadn't told anyone about my encounter with Viktor at the Grand Prix Final. I didn't want to start drama when I could've misread the vibes I'd felt from him. Bigger issues like making the Olympic team and helping Courtney and Mark win the novice title needed my attention.

My young students started off the championships on a high note, winning the short program in convincing fashion. On the day of their free skate, I had to pull double duty—practice with Chris at the glitzy Staples Center followed by Courtney and Mark's event at the older L.A. Sports Arena next door.

At practice, Chris set me down from our star lift, and I stumbled as I looked up at the clock on the massive Jumbotron. He stopped in the middle of the ice.

"You keep checking the time." His tone dripped with irritation. "Don't you have more than an hour to change and get over there?"

"I'm just worried. The kids seemed really nervous at the warm-up this morning."

We stroked around the ice, hand in hand, passing three other teams jumping and spinning in unison. Chris scratched his head. "Why don't we cut this practice short? You're a little out of it anyway."

"No, I'm fine," I huffed. "Let's do the Lutzes again."

I skated ahead of him, building up speed. He quickly caught up to me, and we flew down the rink. Simultaneous matching jumps followed, eliciting applause from the smattering of fans in attendance.

"See?" I said. "I'm not out—"

Before I could finish, my blade caught the boards, and I slipped sideways onto the ice. My thigh stung from the cold impact. Chris bent and offered his hands, while I wiped mine on my stretch pants.

He raised an eyebrow. "What was that you were saying?"

We left the ice with ten minutes remaining in the session, and I ran to the locker room to shower and change. Striving to look professional, I put on a rose-colored cashmere sweater and a pair of dressy black pants. In my heels, I raced next door and met Courtney and Mark stretching backstage.

Throughout their warm-up and up until they took the ice, I reminded them how prepared they were. They did lots of nodding but remained quiet. In the seconds before their introduction, I fixed my eyes on theirs. They both had a deer-in-the-headlights look and stared at me as if I had the cure for their terror. I knew exactly how they felt and wished I had a magical pearl of wisdom to share.

I held their gazes and squeezed their hands. "Have fun out there, and good things will happen."

They skated to center ice, and I glanced at the empty space beside me where Sergei should be standing. Sadness gripped me. He and I had worked with our young pair all season for this moment, and he was missing it. He was missing so much.

Courtney and Mark began the program with tentative strokes, and on the opening double axels, Mark jerked awkwardly out of the landing. I clapped and shouted, "You're okay! Keep your heads up!"

The kids didn't appear to hear me. Bobbles punctuated all their lifts and jumps, and they didn't have the attack they'd shown all year. They were trying hard, but I could see the pressure of being the frontrunners weighing them down. They finished the program a few seconds behind the music, a fitting end to a free skate riddled with mistakes.

I bowed my head and took measured breaths. I wanted to scream, not at Courtney and Mark, but at myself. They were capable of skating so much better, but I couldn't let them see my disappointment. When they reached me, my throat tightened at their devastated faces.

I engulfed them in hugs. Courtney started crying on my shoulder, and I patted her curly hair bun.

"I'm sorry, Em," she sniveled.

"It's okay. You'll learn from this and you'll be better

because of it."

The resulting low scores were no surprise nor was Courtney and Mark's drop from first to third place. I took them backstage and hugged them longer. Mark kept mumbling about the jumps he missed, while Courtney was too teary to speak. My cell rang, and I knew the caller without looking.

Mark knew, too. "Sergei probably thinks we won."

"He's going to be so disappointed," Courtney said.

I stopped the phone from chiming and put my arm around her. "I'm going to tell him how hard you guys fought today. You never gave up."

The phone rang twice more, but I ignored it so I could continue to console the kids. When they trudged toward the locker room, I answered the next call.

"Where have you been? How'd they do?" Sergei asked.

I pulled my hair back from my face and sighed. "They had a rough day. They got the bronze, though."

"What happened? They've been competing well and you said they've been having good practices."

"Nerves got to them."

"Didn't you talk to them to help them feel confident?"

His accusatory tone surprised me. I gave the chair in front of me a look of disbelief since Sergei wasn't there. "Of course I talked to them," I spat into the phone. "But I can't control what they do on the ice. You know that."

"I'm sorry. I'm just going crazy over here, not being able to help."

I sank onto the chair and watched the champions celebrate with their coach across the corridor. "It's so tough when everyone expects you to win. They felt that pressure today."

"You're feeling that pressure, too." He must've heard the rising anxiety in my voice.

"Yes." I massaged the back of my neck. "Everyone's

practically put us on the Olympic podium already. I'm trying not to think about it, but..."

"Maybe my news will help. I'm booked on a flight to L.A. on Wednesday."

I sucked in a breath. "You got your passport? You'll make it in time for the short?"

"I'll be there."

HE WASN'T THERE.

An East Coast snowstorm cancelled Sergei's connecting flight from New York. So, as Chris and I prepared to take the ice for our short program, Sergei sat in JFK Airport.

I bounced up and down and adjusted one of the straps of my shimmering blue costume. The dress was sleek and resembled the top of an evening gown I'd seen in a department store. Sergei had been rendered speechless the first time I'd worn it. His admiring gaze had given me shivers and made me feel especially beautiful.

The creepy look Viktor currently directed my way gave me shivers of the bad kind. I paced back and forth in the tunnel, cursing Mother Nature under my breath.

"I can't believe Sergei isn't here," I muttered to Chris.

He took hold of my hands and said firmly, "We can do this without him."

I didn't doubt his statement, but I missed the extra assurance I got just from looking into Sergei's eyes. I shut mine and visualized his smiling and confident face.

The arena buzzed with palpable energy when we glided onto the ice, and I knew our music would energize the crowd even more. The last thing Sergei had told me on the phone earlier was, "Just work it." I took a deep breath and shimmied my shoulders, ready to give the program all the sassiness and spunk it deserved.

Members of the audience whistled when the acoustic strains of "Hotel California" began. I put on a flirty smile and moved like liquid to the music. With the dangerous triple twist out of the way in the first thirty seconds, we set up for the side by side jumps. Chris matched my swooping crossovers down the rink. In perfect unison, we switched to the outside edges of our blades and stabbed our toepicks into the ice.

I immediately sensed a problem. My toepick had slipped, preventing me from attaining the necessary height on the jump. I landed cross-footed and lost all balance. My backside crashed to the ice, stunning me and the crowd, too, judging from the hush that fell over the building. I hadn't missed the triple Lutz in months. But I'd just missed it in one of the most critical programs of my life.

I scrambled to get back in step with Chris, and he whispered, "Fight."

We regained momentum with our star lift that covered the length of the ice. The audience cheered us on, and I received a boost of adrenaline. We couldn't afford any more mistakes in the program. One was damaging; two would be lethal.

With a clean performance the rest of the way, I believed we'd kept ourselves in the mix, but I didn't know how the teams before us had skated or how the teams after us would fare.

Chris and I quietly waited for our scores, clutching each other's hand. Inside, I cursed the ice and my toepick. What if my slip-up put us out of contention? A fraction of an inch of my blade could be the difference between achieving a lifelong dream and watching the Olympics from my couch.

I dropped my head when I saw our names in third place. Four pairs still had to skate, so we could potentially fall further in the standings. We had to stay in the top three to be within striking distance of the gold medal, and more importantly, a spot on the Olympic team.

Television reporters grabbed us for interviews as soon as we walked backstage, not giving Chris and I a moment to ourselves. When we were finally alone and discovered we'd remained in third, I hugged Chris, but he was stiff in my arms.

"You were thinking about Sergei not being here, weren't you? That's why you missed the jump?" he asked in a biting tone.

"What?" I pulled away and gaped at him. "It was a fluke thing. My toepick slipped. I wasn't thinking about anything except landing the jump."

"You've been stressing about him all week, making mistakes in practice…"

"I was ready tonight. Don't make this into something bigger than it was."

I left him and changed out of my costume. At the hotel, I searched for my parents in the lobby. Skaters clad in Team USA jackets were everywhere—perched on the posh chairs, crowding the event schedule board, and lined up in front of the coffee cart. Dad caught my eye from the edge of the room, and I rushed into his waiting arms.

He kissed the side of my head. "You did great, Em."

"The Lutz was so dumb." I sighed, exhausted from analyzing my missed jump with every member of the media.

Mom stroked my back. "You really sold the program. The crowd was totally into it."

"Sergei would've been proud," Dad said.

My face crumpled, and Dad put his arms around me.

"I miss him… so… much." I choked on the words.

"He'll be here soon," Dad said in his soothing manner that had dried many of my tears over the years.

Mom returned her hand to my back. "Why don't we get dinner? You'll feel better after you've had something to eat."

I nodded and wiped my eyes with the tissue she offered me. A few of the young skaters lounging nearby gave me looks of pity, and I bowed my head. Having a public breakdown was an appropriate way to top off the night.

"Let me take my stuff upstairs." I picked up my skate bag and the hefty sack of stuffed animals I'd received from the audience. "I'll meet you back down here."

After a long wait for the slow elevator, I climbed aboard and leaned against the far wall. As the doors were about to close, Viktor slithered inside. I straightened up and stepped further into the corner.

He came toward me with a half-smile, one that spoke of trouble more than kindness. I folded my arms across my chest and held an internal conversation with the elevator, pleading it to move faster.

"You'll do better in the free skate," he said.

I pressed my back to the wall and kept my eyes focused on the floor numbers flashing above the door. Viktor slinked nearer, his ominous presence smothering me. I felt as if the elevator was shrinking.

"You can't always be perfect," he said in a throaty voice.

He caressed my arm, and I threw out my elbow. "Don't touch me!" I glared at him.

He returned my steely gaze. "I'll bet you wouldn't say that if I was Sergei."

My stomach dropped into my shoes. *He knows something.* I quickly collected myself and raised my chin. "I'd say it to anyone who tried to grope me."

"Right." He smirked.

My floor chimed, and I dashed into the hallway, dragging my bags behind me. I glanced over my shoulder, afraid Viktor had tailed me. The hall was clear, but my heart still thumped hard in my chest.

How could Viktor know about Sergei and me? We'd been so careful, and neither of us saw Viktor much outside of the rink. My friends at the rink didn't even suspect I was involved with Sergei. I didn't know what kind of game Viktor was playing, but I had a terrible feeling in my bones Sergei and I would be the losers.

CHAPTER THIRTY-ONE

Two days after the short program, Sergei finally found a flight out of snow-covered New York City, scheduled to arrive in Los Angeles shortly before the free skate. I was standing in the locker room at Staples Center, checking my makeup in the mirror, when Sergei called my cell.

"I'm in the cab, on my way to the hotel." He sounded out of breath. "I'll pick up my credentials and leave my bag with the bellman."

I suppressed a shout of joy, aware of the girls dressing around me. Holding the phone close to my mouth, I said in a hushed voice, "How am I going to refrain from giving you the longest kiss ever when I see you?"

He laughed. "I've been asking myself the same thing. We'll have to find a way to be alone tonight."

"I have a plan," I said mysteriously. "I'll tell you about it later."

He let me go so I could start my pre-competition routine. I jogged with an extra bounce in my step, feeling more relaxed than I had in weeks. With my muscles loose, Chris and I walked through our program, not leaving any detail unattended.

After I donned my costume, I left the dressing room, bursting with anticipation. I expected to see Sergei with Chris, but there was no sign of him. The trip downtown from the airport shouldn't have taken that long, and the arena was less than a mile from the hotel. I ran back to the locker room and called him.

"Where are you?"

"Traffic on the freeway was horrible. We just got to the Biltmore."

Panic overtook my feeling of relaxation. I walked in circles around the huge Lakers logo on the carpet. "Our warm-up starts in a few minutes."

"I won't make the warm-up, but I'll be there for your skate. You guys are last, right?"

"Yes," I answered shakily.

"I'll run from the hotel to the arena if I have to. I'm not missing it."

Chris saw me twisting my hands as I rejoined him in the corridor. His eyes widened with alarm. "Don't tell me he's not going to make it."

"He's running late, but he'll be here when we skate." If I made it sound definite, then it would have to come true. I couldn't entertain the thought of Sergei not showing up in time. Not after I'd gotten my hopes up so high.

During the six minute warm-up on the ice, my nervous energy caused shaky exits on my jumps, but what rattled me more was seeing Chris over-rotate the triple toe loop and the triple Lutz. He was trying *too* hard. My rock of a partner, who normally laughed in the face of pressure, had suddenly become human.

We found a quiet spot backstage to wait for our turn to skate. Chris untied and retied his laces four times, while I stared down the long hallway, hoping to see Sergei's face any second. My knees jiggled up and down, and I patted my thighs over and over. I waited for Chris to tease me about not being able to sit still, but his own legs were shaking.

With ten minutes left until we had to report to the ice, I bent my head, folded my hands and resorted to prayer. So many bigger problems than mine needed God's help, but I had to ask. Three Our Fathers and three Hail Marys later, I looked up and inhaled sharply.

My prayers had been answered.

Sergei rushed toward us, straightening his sky blue tie, the lucky one he'd worn at all our competitions that season. I held my ground, gathering my self-control. A few officials and event volunteers stood nearby, so I had to stay cool.

Sergei didn't take his eyes off mine. With every step he took, my heart rate soared higher. He reached us and swallowed me in an embrace, one I'd craved so deeply for so long. Surrounded by his love, I felt a surge of confidence and power. I didn't want to leave his arms, but the people around us were watching our reunion.

Chris jumped up and hugged Sergei. His wide smile revealed his relief.

"So glad you could make it," he joked.

I laughed, high pitched and giddy. Chris cracking jokes was a sure sign normalcy had returned.

Sergei rested his hands on our shoulders and waited before he spoke. "I'm not going to ask you how the warm-up went because it doesn't matter. The only thing that matters is the program you're about to skate. You are strong and you are special. No one else can do the things you do. I want you to show everyone tonight why you are the best team in the world."

THAT WE DID.

Chris slung his arm around my neck as perfect score after

perfect score glowed on the scoreboard. The crowd roared, knowing they were witnessing history. No pair had ever earned so many 6.0's. We'd won our second national title with our best performance of the year.

I let my eyes sweep around the bright arena. People were still on their feet from the standing ovation they'd given us. Fans held up colorful banners printed with our names and messages like "Go for Gold" and "Always Dream." Beside me, Sergei smacked his hands together in vigorous applause. He beamed at us, his face red from excitement. I wanted to remember every detail of the moment forever, the moment we punched our ticket to the Olympics.

A television reporter tried to accost Chris and me for an interview, but Sergei intervened. "Can you give them a minute?"

Chris and I hugged, and the realization of what we'd accomplished seemed to hit us simultaneously. We both sniffled, unable to speak.

I kissed his cheek, stamping his freckles with lipstick. As I removed the mark with my thumb, I said, "Thank you for putting up with my craziness."

"You keep things interesting, that's for sure." He smiled and dried the corners of his eyes with his thumb and forefinger.

"Seriously." I squeezed his hand. "Thank you. For everything."

The next two hours were a blur of interviews, congratulatory hugs, and lots of happy tears. It was almost midnight when Chris and I arrived at the hotel with Sergei and our parents. Our joyous laughter echoed off the walls of the empty lobby.

Mom pointed to the shuttered doors of the restaurant. "Guess our celebration will have to wait until tomorrow."

I feigned a yawn. "I'm beat anyway." I couldn't put "Operation Alone Time with Sergei" into motion until the group dispersed.

The parents walked ahead, and Chris pulled me into a spontaneous hug. "We're almost there, Em. One more step."

The emotion of the earlier medal ceremony hit me again. Standing atop the podium, I'd been overwhelmed with pride and felt so blessed to share the achievement with such an amazing partner.

"Don't you dare make me cry again," I said.

"No more crying." Chris ruffled my hair. "Only celebrating allowed now. Trevor's party tomorrow night will be epic."

"Oh, yeah. After the week I've had, after the *month* I've had, I might need to have a drink. Or five." I laughed.

Sergei hung back with me as the rest of the group waited for the elevator. "So, what's the plan?"

"Ah, yes, my brilliant plan." I smiled. "My parents rented a car for the week, so I thought we could use it to drive to the beach. I got directions from the front desk for the best spot to park near the ocean."

"That sounds perfect." He lowered his voice even more. "Are we leaving now because I'm going to go crazy if I don't kiss you soon."

I licked my lips, anticipating the tingle of his on mine. "Fifteen minutes. Meet me at the silver Malibu on the third floor of the garage."

In my room, I tiptoed around to avoid waking Aubrey, asleep in advance of her competition the next day. I grabbed a light sweater, the keys to the rental car, and the map the desk clerk had given me before scurrying to the parking garage.

I wasn't in the car more than two minutes when Sergei slid into the passenger seat. He'd done a quick change from his suit into jeans and a black sweater, and did he ever look good. I wanted to leap over the gear stick and into his lap.

Sergei reached out and tucked a few strands of hair behind my ear. The silky movement of his long fingers further stirred my longing to be in his arms. I tenderly kissed his palm and let my cheek rub against its warmth. He leaned toward me across the console, but I halted him mere centimeters from my mouth.

"Let's get out of here first," I said.

"You're killing me." He pressed my hand to his chest. "My heart has literally stopped."

"I'll bring you back to life very soon." I winked and turned the key in the ignition.

The ocean side parking lot in Santa Monica was deserted, just as I'd hoped. We climbed out of the car, and the wind whipping off the ocean blew my hair across my face.

I pulled my thin cardigan tighter around me. "It's kinda cold out here."

We looked at each other over the top of the car and both had the same idea as we jumped into the back seat.

Sergei wrapped his arms around me. "This is much cozier."

"Much," I murmured, curling my fingers around his neck and winding them through his hair.

Not able to hold back any longer, our lips came together in perfect harmony. The whole world faded away except for the two of us. I was totally lost under the spell of Sergei's kiss and the tender journey of his hands all over me. How had I survived a month without his touch?

Sergei continued to shower me with kisses. He nestled me to him, and I delighted in just staring at his face and seeing my love reflected in his eyes.

"Why don't we stay here the rest of the weekend?" he whispered in my ear.

I giggled at the tickle of his breath. "That would be heavenly, but I have to be there for my friends tomorrow. Aubrey and Nick are so close to making the team."

Mentioning Aubrey brought the unpleasant thought of Viktor and his disgusting smoky smell to mind. I wrinkled my nose and pressed my face to Sergei's neck, breathing in his clean, spicy scent. I wanted to forget about Viktor but knew I had to let Sergei know my suspicions.

"I need to tell you something that happened while you were gone."

"What is it?" He stroked my cheek.

"I think Viktor might know about you and me."

Sergei's hand froze on my face. "How?"

"I don't know, but he said something…"

"What did he say?" The softness in his eyes sharpened into concern.

"He got a little too… close to me, so I told him to back off, and he said 'You wouldn't say that to Sergei.'" I shuddered at the memory of Viktor's scary knowing smile.

Sergei's body became rigid and his jaw clenched. "What do you mean, he got too close to you? Did he touch you?"

"Just my arm."

"If he touches you again, I'm going to break every one of his fingers." His eyes burned with anger, and I feared what might happen the next time he saw Viktor.

"You can't confront him. That's probably exactly what he wants, to bait you into doing something crazy."

"If he knows about us, why hasn't he exposed us already?"

"I don't know, but I got some bad vibes from him," I said.

"I never should've let him go with you to the Final."

"You had no idea he was going to act this way." I grasped his hand and intertwined our fingers.

"We only have a few weeks until the Olympics. We need to be extra careful when we're together."

"He can't mess this up for us." My voice wavered and I shook my head. "Not after everything we've gone through to get here."

Sergei locked his eyes on mine. "I'm not going to let him." His arms tensed around me, and he repeated with even more firmness, "I'm not going to let him."

CHAPTER THIRTY-TWO

I LINKED MY ARM THROUGH AUBREY'S, and we followed the signs to the smallest of the Biltmore Hotel's numerous ballrooms. We passed the Grand Salon, site of the big closing bash for all competitors, where music thumped inside. Headed in that direction were Courtney and three friends, giggling and talking in the hyper way young girls do.

"You guys look hot!" Courtney exclaimed.

Aubrey and I laughed. "Don't you love Em's gold dress?" Aubrey asked and showed me off like I was a prize on a game show display.

The halter neckline and slim-fitting skirt hugged the slight curves of my petite figure. I'd hesitated on buying the dress because of its color, but Aubrey had convinced me to be confident rather than superstitious.

"It's awesome, but you're a little overdressed for the party," Courtney said.

"We have to go to a cocktail party first." Aubrey smoothed an invisible wrinkle on her purple dress. "We'll join you after we hang out with the stuffy crowd."

One of the federation's biggest sponsors was hosting the

soiree. As Olympians, we were expected to hobnob with the upper crust of the sport. Aubrey and I had made a pact to escape after we did the required mingling.

We entered the ballroom and snaked through the party-goers, accepting congratulations and accolades along the way. Two older Hall of Fame skaters engaged us in a lengthy chat, and we listened to them relive their Olympic glory and offer words of advice for our upcoming experience at the Games. The more people congratulated me on making the team, the more the accomplishment began to sink in. My feet itched to get to the closing party and dance in jubilation with my friends.

Sergei arrived while I moved between conversations, and we simply exchanged smiles as we passed each other. I stopped at the bar and fell into a daydream, imagining us one day attending parties as a couple, freely able to share an affectionate touch or glance in front of everyone.

"Hello, Emily." Viktor shook me from my fantasy and back to unpleasant reality.

"Hello." I moved left and he copied me.

"Nice dress." His eyes shifted downward just long enough to make me want to scrub my skin. "Very… appropriate."

Down the bar, I caught Sergei watching us. He took a step forward, his knuckles white around his drink. Low at my side where Viktor couldn't see, I put up a stop sign with my hand to keep Sergei at bay.

"If you'll excuse me," I said and went on the hunt for Aubrey. I found her entertaining a couple of former champions. She gracefully bowed out of the conversation and asked, "Ready for the real party?"

Viktor eyed us from across the room. I grabbed Aubrey's elbow and steered her to the door. "Never readier."

AFTER A COUPLE OF hours of high-energy dancing at the party, my friends and I gathered in Trevor's room for more celebration. I downed multiple cocktails and found myself waltzing around the room with Aubrey, who'd enjoyed just as many drinks as I had.

"Lady Marmalade" came on the clock radio, and Aubrey boosted the volume, bounded onto the bed, and pulled me up with her. We sang loud and off-key, belting out Christina Aguilera's high notes with screechy enthusiasm. Chris and Nick sat on the edge of the bed, doubled over with laughter.

In the middle of the chorus, Aubrey gripped my arms. "We're going to the Olympics!"

She jumped up and down, and I joined her, creating a trampoline effect on the bed. The bouncing started to make me dizzy, so I let my legs crumple beneath me. I bumped into Nick and shook him.

"We're going to the Olympics!"

He signaled for a high five. "Team Cape Cod!"

I smacked his hand and fell against the pillows. As I stared at the ceiling, I thought of the person with whom I most wanted to celebrate. The blood coursed through my veins at a rapid rate and filled me with a powerful sensation. I had to see him.

I rose from the bed and almost toppled over. Halfway to the door, I realized my feet were bare.

Marley saw me searching the floor. "What are you looking for?"

"My shoes."

She crouched next to the desk and pointed to a pair of peep-toe heels. "Are those yours?"

I hugged her and she let out a tinkly laugh. "Thank you, my love."

With deliberate steps, I made my way to the elevator and two floors up to my destination. Sergei opened his door and stuck his head out into the hallway with a nervous glance.

"What are you doing here?"

I stumbled past him. "I thought it should be a tradition that I bust into your hotel room at Nationals."

The bedside lamp shed faint light on the room. An open newspaper lay on the bed, and a pillow was propped up against the headboard. Without the television on, the room was silent, a stark difference from the scene I'd just left.

I pivoted to face Sergei and lost my balance. He grabbed me before I crashed into the doors of the TV armoire.

"You are so drunk."

"I'm not that drunk. I just feel really, really good." I circled my arms around his waist.

"You're feeling good, alright."

He still had on the white dress shirt he'd worn with his suit earlier, but he'd untucked it and removed his tie. I tightened my hold around him. Through the thin material of his shirt, the heat of his body brought mine alive with passion. I needed to be even closer to him. I wished I could crawl inside him.

"No one knows I'm here. And I won't tell if you don't tell," I whispered.

He caressed my hair. "I think you should get some sleep."

"No, let me stay." I pouted. "I'll be on my best behavior."

His face relaxed into a little smile. "Somehow I doubt that."

"You won't regret it. I promise," I said, low and smoky.

I covered his lips with mine. At first, he didn't respond, but before long he returned my kiss with equal fervor. I moaned softly into his mouth and brought my hands up to his chest, where I unbuttoned his shirt.

Sergei broke from our kiss. "Em."

I continued to fumble with the buttons. "I don't wanna stop anymore," I said breathlessly.

He gently grasped my wrists. "You're drunk, and you don't know what you're saying."

"I know what I want." I reached up to kiss him.

He stepped back, still holding my wrists. "Em, we can't do this. You'd regret it, and you'd hate me for letting it happen."

I jostled my hands away from him and spoke with a shaky slur, "You say you want me, but now you're pushing me away."

"You know how I feel about you." He cradled my face, his thumbs brushing my cheeks. "Sometimes I think I might lose my mind I want you so much. But not like this."

The love in his eyes only made me desire him more. I slid my arms around him. "I just wanna be close to you."

His shoulder made an inviting pillow for my spinning head. We stood quietly as Sergei rubbed my lower back, his strong hands so tender. I couldn't ignore the heat stirring within me.

Lifting my head slowly, I touched my lips to Sergei's jaw and trailed a line of supple kisses down his neck to his chest. Resting against his smooth skin was the pendant I'd given him. I ran my fingers over it and slipped my hand inside his opened shirt.

"Em, we can't do this." Sergei's voice held much less conviction.

My palm skimmed across his chest, his heart pounding under my touch. I was dizzy with emotions I didn't know how to control. The vodka had washed out the connection between my brain and my body like a flooded road in a storm.

Sergei buried his face in my hair, whispers of my name on his lips. I lowered my caress to the tight muscles of his abdomen and felt the unmistakable response of his body. The burning flame of desire in my stomach exploded into a raging wildfire.

Without warning, Sergei pulled away and showed his back to me. "You need to go."

The sound of our heavy breathing filled the quiet room.

Sergei stood with one hand on the back of his neck, and his shoulders rose and fell with each breath. I waited, hoping he would turn around and tell me everything was okay.

Receiving no such reaction, I walked on unsteady legs to the door. I hesitated in the doorway, but with still no movement from Sergei, I continued forward.

The warmth of the hallway suffocated me. I rode the elevator down to the lobby with the goal of fresh air. A group of people streamed out of the bar, but their faces were a blur. I ducked my head and weaved toward the double glass doors of the hotel's front entrance.

The chilly night air slapped my face. I steadied myself against the stone wall and ambled down the sidewalk away from the lights of the entrance. The concrete base of a large planter looked like a good place to sit. I collapsed onto it and bent over. The spinning in my head slowed to a lazy whirl, and my senses regained some of their clarity.

A siren wailed in the distance, the only sound to hit my ears until footsteps shuffled on the pavement. A figure stopped in front of me, and I raised my head.

Viktor's eyes pierced through the darkness. "You don't look so good, Emily."

I massaged my temples and groaned, "Why are you always around?"

"I saw you in the lobby and thought you could use some help." His sinister tone told me I wouldn't like the kind of help he was offering.

"Please leave me alone." I stood up and swayed, and Viktor put his arm around me. I pushed him with my forearm, but he didn't budge. "I told you not to touch me!"

"Why is that?" He backed me against the wall. "Because you're spoken for?"

"Because I'm not interested," I said through gritted teeth.

He gave me a lecherous and intimidating glare that chilled my spine. "I'm curious. How did Sergei do it? How did he get you into his bed?"

Shivers overtook my body. I clamped my hands around my arms to stop the shaking.

"I'm not sleeping with him," I said with a quiet insistence.

"Don't try to deny it. I went to your house before the Final to talk to you about the trip, and you and Sergei were outside in each other's arms. I saw you from the street, so I turned around and left. Figured I shouldn't interrupt your little moment together," he snickered.

I swallowed hard. "I don't know what you think you saw, but you're wrong."

I tried to wiggle away from him, but he blockaded me to the wall with his arms. "I don't think I am. And if you want me to keep your secret, you need to make it worth my while." He pressed himself against me, and I stiffened with fear. "Why should Sergei have all the fun?"

"Leave me alone!" I twisted my shoulders in an attempt to wrench myself free.

Viktor started to pull me around the dark edge of the building. I struggled to release my arms, but all the twisting and turning had made me dizzy again. Terror shot through me as I realized I was losing the battle. We were about to round the corner when a voice broke through the night.

"Get off of her!"

Sergei reached us in a flash and pushed Viktor away from me. His eyes darted across my face as he put his hands on my shoulders. "Are you okay?" When I nodded, he barked at Viktor, "What are you doing?"

Viktor straightened his suit jacket and said coolly, "I was just having a chat with Emily."

"This didn't look like a chat," Sergei said.

"You've got a lot of nerve accusing me of something when you're the one sleeping with your student."

Sergei's body became one large, clenched muscle as he

moved toward Viktor. "You don't know what you're talking about."

"Hey, I don't blame you. All that time you spend together…" Viktor leered at me. "I'd be all over her, too."

Sergei reared back his fist and struck Viktor in the jaw. I gasped and covered my mouth as Viktor staggered from the blow. Sergei didn't give him a chance to recover before he slammed his back against the wall.

"Don't ever talk about her that way again," Sergei seethed, his face inches from Viktor's. "Don't look at her, don't speak to her, don't touch her. Am I clear?"

Viktor shoved Sergei's chest. "I'm sure a lot of people will be interested to know the very personal attention you're giving Emily."

I clutched Sergei's forearm, holding back another punch. "And I'm sure everyone would like to know what a creep you are and how you harassed me."

Viktor rubbed his jaw. "All I did was tried to help a girl who'd had too much to drink. You misunderstood. And if you try to start trouble, then I have my own story to tell about you and your boyfriend here."

"You don't have proof of anything," Sergei said.

"I don't need proof to get people to start asking questions."

Sergei got back into Viktor's face. "What is it you want? Why are you doing this?"

"I want to see you squirm," Viktor sneered. "You've had it too easy. The first pair you touch turns to gold. You need to sweat a little."

"You don't like me, fine. But Em and Chris don't deserve to be hurt by your pathetic jealousy. They've put in all the work to get to this point."

"I'm not jealous of you. Although, you do have a pretty nice deal going." Viktor gave me another smirk that prickled my skin. "Do you coach Emily in the bedroom, too?"

"Son of a…" Sergei lurched forward, but I threw my arms around him.

"Don't," I pleaded. As much as Viktor deserved it, beating him senseless wouldn't help the situation.

Pure evil lined Viktor's laugh. "You'd better listen to her. I'm not going to charge you with assault because there are much more interesting ways I can ruin you." He walked backwards toward the entrance. "You just won't know if or when I'm going to make my move."

I gulped and began to shiver again. Sergei's brow knotted, and he ran his hands over the goose bumps on my arms. "Are you sure you're okay?"

I nodded and laid my head on his shoulder. Everything around me was still a little hazy but clear enough to sense the trouble left in Viktor's wake.

"How did you know I was out here?" I asked.

"I called your room to make sure you got there okay, and Aubrey said she hadn't seen you. I figured you couldn't have gone far."

"I wanted to get some air, and Viktor followed me. I tried to fight him off, but everything was spinning…" A sob stuck in my throat, and I put my hands over my face.

Sergei hugged his arm around me. "Let's go around to the back entrance."

He guided me around the building and through the rear of the lobby to the elevators. In my room, Aubrey had passed out on her bed still in her dress. Sergei and I stood just inside the door, holding each other in silence.

"I'm so sorry about earlier when I told you to leave," he said. "I wasn't angry with you. I just couldn't let you stay another minute because… something was going to happen."

"You're apologizing?" I picked my head up, too fast, and blinked a few times to focus. "*I'm* the one who needs to apologize. I tell you I'm not going to sleep with you, and then I throw myself at you."

"You weren't yourself. I should've walked you back here before it got to that." He brushed my hair away from my face.

"A lot of guys wouldn't have stopped it from happening." I hugged his neck and mumbled into his collar, "So, thank you."

"If I just would've walked you to your room, then you wouldn't have seen Viktor."

"I really messed up," I cried.

"No, this isn't your fault. He was planning to get at us before tonight."

Tears dripped from my eyes. Why was this happening? We'd overcome so many obstacles and were on the brink of seeing all our dreams come true. We should be having the time of our lives, planning for the Olympics. Instead, we had to hold our breath and hope Viktor wouldn't wield his vengeful dagger.

CHAPTER THIRTY-THREE

Back home from Nationals, I practiced every day with a persistent knot in my stomach, worried what Viktor might do next. Sergei attempted to ease my anxiety, saying Viktor was all talk and trying to distract us from our Olympic preparations. After a week passed with no incident, I felt more hopeful he was right.

The weekend marked our one-year anniversary as a couple, so Sergei and I planned a night of good distraction to celebrate the occasion. I offered to make dinner at my house since Aubrey would be spending the evening with her parents. After I finished grocery shopping, I pulled into my parking lot and found Sergei's car already there. The clock on my dashboard told me he was an hour early.

Sergei opened the door as I balanced the large brown paper bag on my hip.

"Did I tell you the wrong time?" I asked.

He took the groceries from my arms and gave me a kiss. "I just couldn't wait to see you. Aubrey let me in before she left."

I grinned and placed a delicate kiss at the corner of his

mouth. "You are so sweet. Do you mind waiting for me to change before I start dinner?"

"Not at all. I can chop, slice, peel, whatever you need me to do." He peeked into the bag.

In the kitchen, I set him up with the zucchini, yellow squash, and a cutting board. He started slicing while I put the shrimp, the other ingredient for my linguine dish, in the fridge. I gave him one more kiss before I dashed upstairs.

Once I'd changed my look from afternoon-errand-running Emily into evening-date-ready Emily, I emerged from my room, straightening the cropped jacket over my silky top. A surprising cold breeze hit me, and I noticed the sliding door to the terrace was ajar. I stepped through the doorway, and my hand went to my mouth at the sight before me.

Petite candles lined the terrace railing, creating a dreamy glow on the snow-covered patio. A path of red rose petals directed me from the door to the table, where four larger candles burned the scent of lavender. Centered between the candles was the *Lyrics* book.

I smiled and picked up the book. A silver heart-shaped bookmark stood between two pages and pointed to the song "When We Dance," where red curvy brackets surrounded two particular lines.

As I read the lyrics, my head whirled, and I leaned against the table for support. I stared at the words, reading them again and again until the door shut behind me, snapping me out of my daze. I turned, and Sergei moved toward me in slow motion.

He gently pried the book from my hands and laid it on the table, his eyes not leaving mine. As he grasped my left hand in his, he placed one knee on the icy wooden floor boards.

I opened my mouth to speak, but words failed me. My short and quick breaths showed in the frosty air. Sergei gazed up at me with hope, love, and a touch of nervousness. The candlelight shimmered in his eyes like sunlight on the ocean.

Sergei squeezed my hand and took a deep breath. "When you walked into my life, I felt an immediate connection to you. I thought it meant we were destined to work together, but it was more, so much more than I ever expected. One minute you were a friend, and then the next, I couldn't stop thinking about you. I wanted to be with you every minute of every day. I wanted to know everything about you. I wanted to hold you in my arms and look into your beautiful blue eyes and tell you how you'd stolen my heart."

He paused and gripped my hand tighter. "Since we've been together, those feelings have only grown stronger. I can't imagine being with anyone but you. You have so much passion and love in your heart, and you understand me like no one ever has. I don't think there are enough words to describe how much I love you." His voice cracked, swelling my heart.

"I know we've only been dating a year, and we haven't exactly had a traditional relationship, but I don't see those as reasons to wait to take this step. I feel like I've waited all my life for this moment."

Tears spilled down my face. I covered my heart with my trembling hand as Sergei reached inside his pants pocket and brought forth a small, royal blue velvet box. Quicker than I could blink, he opened and shut it, and a sparkling solitaire diamond ring appeared between his fingers. The overwhelming love in his eyes threatened to knock me from my feet.

"Emily, will you marry me?"

Time froze. I saw myself walking into the rink, seeing Sergei's smiling face for the first time. I saw us at the Sting concert, laughing in the rain, and at the cliffs, sharing our first glorious kiss. I saw the passionate look in Sergei's eyes when he'd told me he loved me for the first time and the look of despair when he'd thought he lost me last summer. Finally, I saw us celebrating with my parents at Nationals and feeling like my family was truly complete.

Sergei looked at me expectantly. When I didn't speak, he said, "Em, you are so precious to me. Please say you'll spend the rest of your life with me."

My head swirled with images of my future, and every single one of the pictures contained one constant—Sergei. I dropped to my knees and touched his cheek. His eyes widened with greater hope.

I nodded vigorously and gasped through my tears. "Yes!"

A gleaming smile stretched across his face, and he pressed his lips to mine. Of all the kisses we'd shared, we'd never had one that contained so much unbridled joy.

"We're getting married." Sergei sounded as if he couldn't quite believe it.

I couldn't stop smiling and nodding. "We're getting married."

We gazed at each other as if we were in a trance, one of pure happiness. I reached for his other hand, forgetting he still held the ring.

"Oh! I guess I get this now." I giggled and fingered the platinum band.

"Why don't you stand up first? You must be freezing down here."

"Let's both stand up. You've been on one knee long enough." I laughed.

We rose, and I extended my left hand in Sergei's. He slipped the ring onto my finger, sending sparks through my wrist and up my arm. What the stone may have lacked in size, it made up for in brilliance. I'd never seen a diamond shine so brightly.

Sergei placed his lips on the ring. "Forever."

I wound my arms around his neck and echoed, "Forever."

Over his shoulder, I took in the romantic splendor around us. "The terrace looks amazing. When did you plan all this?"

"I've had the ring for a couple of months. I wanted to propose in this spot since it was here I first knew I had feelings for you."

"The dinner party." I smiled as I remembered some of the looks Sergei had given me that night.

A couple of raindrops landed on Sergei's nose, and he glanced up at the night sky. "I think that's our cue to take *this* party inside."

I grabbed the book and helped Sergei blow out the candles. We hurried into the house, and I didn't realize how cold I was until I met the contrasting warmth of the living room. I removed my wet leather boots and cuddled with Sergei on the sofa. We both agreed dinner could wait.

"Everything you said was so beautiful." I ran my hand down his chest and smiled at my ring glinting in the light.

"I had more planned to say in case you needed persuading." He grinned and kissed the tip of my nose. "I was going to list what I love about you."

"Aww, I wouldn't have accepted so quickly if I'd known." I winked and angled my head to one side. "Can I still hear the rest?"

He kissed my lips lightly. "I love you because you are kind." Another kiss followed on my forehead. "And exquisitely beautiful." His mouth moved to my cheek. "Mind-blowingly smart." Then to my other cheek. "Gracefully strong." His lips brushed along my jaw. "Irresistibly sexy." And a gentle kiss on my neck. "And amazingly sweet."

Under Sergei's touch, my body had more than thawed. I took off my jacket and tossed it onto the coffee table.

Sergei toyed with the strap of my camisole and kissed my bare shoulder. "Did I mention sexy?"

I was sure there must be a puddle on the floor where I had melted. Sergei locked his lips on mine and eased me back onto the fluffy throw pillows. With our arms and legs entangled, I couldn't tell where one of us ended and the other began.

"I love you so much," I whispered between kisses. "I can't wait to be your wife."

"I was thinking tomorrow could work." His smile flashed mischief.

I laughed. "I was thinking more like late summer. I need time to plan."

"You think too logically." He nuzzled my neck.

"My mom's probably going to need some time to digest the news."

"Well, your dad already knows."

"He does?" I maneuvered upright.

"While you were partying at Nationals, I was having a talk with him. I wanted his blessing before I asked you to marry me."

Love overflowed in my heart and poured out as tears. I jumped onto Sergei, pushing him back onto the sofa. My hair hung like curtains around his face. I lowered myself onto him, and my mouth hovered close to his.

"Thank you so much for doing that. It means the world to me."

"I know how important your family is to you."

I kissed him and ignored the shrill ring of the phone. The answering machine picked up, and the urgency of Mom's message pulled my attention from Sergei.

"Emily, please call me as soon as possible. I need to talk to you."

I sat up and sighed. "I guess Dad told her. I should probably deal with this now." I reached around Sergei for the cordless phone on the end table.

Mom answered on the first ring, and I started talking, "Mom, please don't get negative on me again. You've been getting along so well with Sergei, and this is the happiest day of my life."

"This isn't about your engagement, although we do need

to discuss that. I called because I received a very disturbing phone call from Viktor."

The familiar tightness returned to my stomach. "Viktor?"

Sergei's eyes darkened, and he leaned toward me. Mom spoke in a rush, "He asked me if I know you're seeing Sergei. I told him what you do is none of his business. Then he asked how much your reputation is worth to me."

"What it's worth to you?"

"He wants money to keep quiet, Emily. Did you know he'd found out about you and Sergei?"

I bent forward and rested my forehead on my clenched fist. "He made some threats at Nationals, but we thought he might just be trying to scare us. I never thought he would involve you."

Sergei touched my arm. "What did he do?"

I slanted the phone away from my mouth. "He's asking them for money."

"Your father wants to go to the police. This man is trying to blackmail us." Mom's hysteria increased with each breath.

"No, you can't go to the police." I leapt to my feet. "Then the media will get hold of it, and we'll be in the middle of a huge scandal."

"Well, we can't let Viktor do whatever he wants!"

Sergei stood and planted his feet. "We have to go to the federation and tell them about Viktor's threats."

I looked at him in disbelief. "If we do that, we have to tell them what he has on us. What if they decide to make an example of us and discipline you? What if they stop you from going to the Olympics?"

"I heard what Sergei suggested," Mom said. "And I think he's right."

Sergei took my hand. "I'm not going to give Viktor any more chances to hurt you or your family. This has to end."

His eyes blazed with determination. I put my arms around him and heard Mom calling my name through the phone.

"You're going to the federation?" she asked.

I watched Sergei for any sign of wavering. His jaw remained set, and he pressed his palm against mine. He seemed so sure this was the answer, but I feared the backlash.

"Yes. God willing, they won't turn it around on us," I said.

"Dad and I will speak to whoever we need to and tell them you've done nothing wrong."

"You'll speak on Sergei's behalf?"

She hesitated, and I prompted her, "Mom?"

"Of course. I know I had reservations about your relationship, but I've seen how much Sergei loves you and how well you've handled working together. His ability to coach shouldn't be questioned."

I exhaled. "Thank you. I have a feeling we're going to need all the help we can get."

"Now, whether I think you're ready to get married is another issue."

"Can we talk about that later? We should focus on getting through this issue first."

After Mom and I wrapped up our conversation, I dug out my U.S. Figure Skating rulebook, and Sergei and I read through the grievance filing process. He helped me draft my claim against Viktor, which detailed each incident of inappropriate behavior. My next step was to fax the letter to the head of the grievance committee.

"I have to tell Aubrey I'm doing this. I hoped it wouldn't come to this and she wouldn't get caught in the middle of my problems. But Viktor couldn't let it go," I cried and flung the rulebook across the sofa.

Sergei brought me into his arms and gently rocked me. He was still holding me when Aubrey arrived home. She jogged up the stairs to the living room, shrugging out of her coat, and noticed our solemn faces.

"What's going on?"

Sergei kissed the top of my head and stood up. "I'll get out of here so you can talk. We can send the letter in the morning."

Aubrey cast a worried glance from Sergei to me. "This sounds serious."

"I'll be back in a minute," I said.

I walked Sergei to the door and hugged him. "It started out as a wonderful night. The most wonderful night ever."

"It's still the most wonderful night of my life. No matter what happens with the federation, nothing's going to change the fact that we'll be together forever."

We shared one final sweet kiss, and I trudged upstairs. I sat next to Aubrey on the couch, but before I could speak, her eyes zeroed in on my left hand.

"Em!" She grabbed my wrist and pulled my hand up to her face. "Is this an engagement ring?"

I couldn't look at the diamond without smiling. "Yes."

"Congratulations!" She threw her arms around me. "Why did you guys look so upset? Why aren't you celebrating?"

"There's something else going on you need to know about. Something that will affect you, too. It involves Viktor."

Her smile faded. "What about him?"

"He found out about me and Sergei, and he's threatening to expose us. He came after me, physically, and now he's asking my parents for money."

"What did he do to you?" She appeared afraid to hear my answer.

"He caught me alone after the party in L.A., and he got very rough and said I needed to make it worth his while to keep my secret. I'm not sure what he would've done if Sergei hadn't shown up."

Aubrey mouth twisted and her eyes glistened, not with tears of shock but what looked like tears of understanding.

"You don't look surprised," I said.

Her chin quivered, and she shook her head slowly back and forth. "I'm not. Because it's happened to me, too."

"Aubrey," I said softly and laid my hand on her knee. "Why didn't you say anything?"

"Viktor said he would tell everyone I came on to him. I didn't want to get into a big messy scandal. I just wanted it to all go away and forget about it." Her voice was firm despite her tears.

"How bad did he hurt you? He didn't . . ." I didn't want to think about the possibilities, much less state them aloud.

"No." Her head shook with more vigor. "He groped me and tried to kiss me, but I fought him off. It happened almost two years ago. He hasn't tried anything since then, so I thought he'd learned his lesson. But I guess not."

"Would you consider filing a complaint now? The more evidence we have, the stronger our case will be to have him dismissed."

She leaned back and stared at the ceiling. I twirled my new ring in circles around my finger, waiting for her response.

"I've wanted to leave him for a while," she said. "He's so negative, and sometimes he gets so angry he scares me. But Nick and I don't want to move, and Viktor is so well-connected, we figured we'd tough it out."

"You don't have to put up with him anymore. We can make sure he doesn't get away with the things he's done."

She sat up and faced me. "You know, he's the reason I was so skeptical of your relationship with Sergei. I didn't trust Sergei. I thought he might be messing with you."

"Sergei is nothing like Viktor."

"I know. It took me some time to see it, but he's crazy about you. You guys are amazing together."

"I hope the federation can see that. I'm scared they're not going to be so understanding." I lifted my feet to the couch and hugged my knees against my chest.

"What does Viktor have to gain from ratting you out,

anyway? Is he just getting some sick pleasure from all this?"

"He thinks Sergei's had everything too easy. He wants to do whatever he can to screw us up right before the Olympics."

"Well, he's going to regret he started this." Aubrey's eyes had cleared and become sharp. "It's time he got what's coming to him."

I clutched her hand and gave it a hard squeeze. "Let's do this."

CHAPTER THIRTY-FOUR

"EXCUSE ME, I NEED A GLASS of water."

Sandpaper lined my throat. I'd spent the morning at Viktor's hearing, describing his actions to a U.S. Figure Skating panel. Now, two federation officials were in my living room, questioning me about my relationship with Sergei. A trip to my kitchen would give me a minute to recharge. The officials sat casually on my couch, but with their detailed questions, I felt as if we were in a courtroom.

I returned with a tall glass of water and settled back into my favorite chair. Across from me, David Rebman and Maria Snyder, the Director and Assistant Director of Athlete Performance, shifted their notepads on their laps.

"Emily, you said you and Sergei began spending more time together after you started assisting him with Courtney and Mark." David glanced down at his notes. "In your conversations at the coffee shop, did Sergei ever invite you to his apartment or to another private location?"

"No, never."

"Did he make any comments or suggestions that made you uncomfortable?"

"No," I stated with even more firmness.

Maria removed her slim reading glasses and gave me a pensive look. "Did you ever get the sense Sergei was pursuing you? That he offered to let you assist him in order to get closer to you?"

"No." I shook my head vehemently. "When we realized we had feelings for each other, he was the one who insisted we put distance between us. He didn't plan for anything to happen."

"But he ultimately decided to enter into a relationship with you," Maria said. "What changed?"

"We just wanted to be together. It was too hard being apart."

"Did you discuss how it could impact your work as coach and student?" David asked.

"We knew it wouldn't be easy, but we were willing to work through whatever issues we might face. And we've proven we can do that."

I touched the empty spot on my left ring finger. I hadn't been able to wear my engagement ring since the public still had no knowledge I was dating Sergei, much less marrying him. According to federation policy, the hearing and all our meetings must be kept confidential. With the Olympics kicking off in less than two weeks, discretion was especially important.

David cleared his throat. "Since you've been together, have there been any instances where Sergei has used his position of power in your personal relationship? Has he made demands of you, made you feel like you needed to comply with him in order to keep your training situation intact?"

"No, he would never do anything like that." I could hear my voice getting shaky, so I took a long drink of water. "I told you up front he's never pressured me in any way. I came into this willingly and have stayed in it willingly."

Maria leaned forward and clasped her hands. "Even as a

willing party, you could still be under Sergei's control and not realize it. I know this is very personal, but I have to ask about your physical relationship. It's important we understand all the dynamics of the situation." She softened her voice. "We need to know the level of your intimacy."

I dipped my head, my face on fire with mortification. I'd done nothing wrong and yet I had to submit to this cross-examination. I couldn't imagine the harsh questions Sergei would be asked when David and Maria met with him later.

I kept my head down and picked at the fleece blanket covering the thick arm of the chair. "We're not having sex, if that's what you're asking."

"Was that a mutual decision?"

I wanted to laugh at the surreal nature of the conversation. The most private details of my life, discussed so openly as if we were talking about the weather.

"I have very strong beliefs, which Sergei has respected because he loves me. Is that enough information for you?"

"Emily, I'm sorry we have to ask these questions, but we're only looking out for you and Sergei's other students," Maria said. "We have to be thorough and find out everything we can."

"I know you're doing your job, but Sergei is a good man, and he doesn't deserve to be put through this. He would never hurt me or any of his students."

David fiddled with the cap on his pen, making a repeated clicking noise that didn't help my agitation. "Sometimes good people make poor decisions. Sergei's judgment regarding your relationship has brought up serious questions about his credibility."

I set down my water with a clang on the glass end table. "If you speak to his students, you'll find out all you need to know about his credibility. They trust him because he respects them and genuinely cares about them. He gives his heart and soul to his job. You have to see that."

David and Maria both looked down at their papers, avoiding the desperation I knew must show in my eyes. David coughed and cleared his throat again.

"We just have a few more questions."

DESPITE THE CONFIDENTIALITY OF Viktor's hearing, everyone at the rink knew something was up. Viktor remained on staff while the panel spent a few days deliberating, but Aubrey and Nick stopped taking lessons from him. And after learning of Viktor's behavior from Aubrey, Marley and Zach also cut ties with him. The rumor mill churned among the skaters in our club, spitting out a variety of theories on why Viktor's top team would leave him on the eve of the Olympics. None of the rumors included my name, however; no one had any idea I was smack in the middle of the drama.

Aubrey and I checked our cell phones after our morning training sessions, and we both had voicemails from the chairman of the panel requesting us to call him. A ruling had been issued. Because of the expedited nature of the hearing, the chairman said he could deliver the ruling verbally as opposed to the standard written decision.

We scrambled from the locker room to look for an area of privacy. On the way to our rink manager Alex's office, we ran into Viktor in the lobby. His phone was pressed to his ear, and a furious storm raged in his eyes.

He ended the call and glared at us, nostrils flaring. Aubrey and I folded our arms and stood tall, sensing we had won.

Viktor focused his contained anger on Aubrey first. "You know I'm the best coach you could ever have. You set your career back years by doing this."

Aubrey raised her chin. "Nick and I will be fine."

Viktor swung his sneer over to me next. "You think

you've won, but I got what I wanted. I know the federation is investigating Sergei, and I have a feeling he won't be so lucky for once."

"Sergei doesn't need luck," I stated. "He has integrity, something you know nothing about."

Chris walked up to my side, joining our line of opposition. Viktor inhaled and gave me one last chilling leer before he stalked to the exit.

"I'm guessing the verdict was good?" Chris asked.

"We had messages to call for the decision, but we saw Viktor first," I said. "From his reaction, I'd say the news must be good."

Alex was out to lunch, so the three of us crammed into his cramped office and crowded around the speakerphone. The panel chairman read the official ruling—Viktor had been expelled from U.S. Figure Skating for life.

"Wow," Aubrey whispered.

After the chairman debriefed us, I hugged Aubrey and together we shared tears and sighs of relief. Aubrey's tears soon became a quiet sob.

"Are you okay?" I asked.

She nodded and wiped her eyes. "It's hitting me now how huge this is. Viktor's never going to coach again."

"We did the right thing. You're not regretting it, are you?" I peered at her.

"No, he deserved this." She sniffed and put her arms around me. "I'm so glad it's all over."

But it wasn't over for Sergei and me. My relief over the verdict was quickly dampened by the knowledge that Sergei and I still had a battle to fight.

"Now, if we could get Sergei cleared," I said.

Chris pushed aside a few papers and perched on the desk. "He hasn't heard from David or Maria?"

"No, they said they'd need a few days when they got back to Colorado to meet with some of the higher-ups and decide what to do next. They should be calling any time now."

"I thought they'd wanna talk to me since I'm around you and Sergei all the time," Chris said.

"I know, my parents wanted to talk to them, too, but they blew in and out of town so fast."

Sergei peeped through the small square window on the office door. He came inside and shut the door behind him. "Did something happen?"

"We got the call." I glanced at Aubrey, who plucked a tissue from the box on the desk. "Viktor's been expelled for life."

"Good," Sergei said adamantly. "They got it right."

Aubrey blew her nose and pitched the tissue into the trash can. "The federation better stick to their promise and handle all the questions about Viktor when we get to Salt Lake. I just want to stay out of it and skate."

"Sergei, do you think the rink will bring in a new dance coach to take Viktor's place?" Worried lines creased Chris's forehead.

"I hope so," Aubrey interjected. "I don't want to move."

"Neither does Marley," Chris said.

"I definitely think they will," Sergei said. "There are too many good teams here they won't want to lose."

Aubrey dabbed once more at her eyes with her fingers before opening the door. "I have to tell Nick the news. Em, come find me for lunch."

Chris stood to follow her, and Sergei held up his hand. "I need to talk to you and Em. I was looking for you when I saw you in here."

Sergei made sure the door was closed before he continued, "David called. They're turning everything over to the Ethics Committee, but since we're leaving for Salt Lake next week, the committee is postponing any further action until after the Olympics."

"What does further action mean?" I asked warily.

"They want to do more interviews before they decide if I should be suspended." He lowered his eyes to the concrete floor.

I sucked in a breath. "Suspended?!"

Chris returned to his spot on the desk. "I thought there weren't any specific rules against coaches and students of legal age dating."

"There aren't, but if they determine I violated the code of conduct by having a relationship with a student, then I could face suspension."

I braced myself against the tall file cabinet. "For how long?"

Sergei pressed his lips together, holding in his response for an unnerving number of seconds. "Possibly five years."

"Five years?" I exclaimed.

"That's ridiculous," Chris said.

I struggled to speak, the words catching in my throat. "I can't believe this."

Sergei brushed his hand down my arm. "We need to stay focused on preparing for the Olympics. That's the most important thing."

He was maintaining such a calm, strong façade, but I knew he had to be teeming with emotion on the inside. A five-year suspension could kill his career.

"Chris, can you give us a minute?" I asked.

"Sure." He patted Sergei's shoulder as he left.

"I don't want you to feel like you can't talk to me about this," I said softly. "You have to be worried about what could happen. Five years out of the sport…"

He met my gaze and held my shoulders. "We can't do anything about it until after the Olympics, so worrying right now is useless. We have to stay positive and put all our energy into this competition."

Resolve flowed from his strong hands, and I nodded. "Okay."

But the stakes had been raised higher. If Chris and I didn't win gold in Salt Lake, we'd have to work four more years for another chance. Four years we might be without Sergei—a scenario I couldn't bear to think about.

We have to win. We just have to.

CHAPTER THIRTY-FIVE

Our van stopped in front of the Olympic Village's massive security checkpoint, and the large sign above the guards sparked smiles on all the passengers' faces.

Welcome, Athletes of the World

Chris bumped my shoulder. "We're really here."

His big excited grin got me laughing. One of the thousands of Olympic volunteers opened the van door, and I jumped out. Snow flurries stuck to my brand new navy Team USA jacket, embroidered with the five Olympic rings.

Athletes from a variety of sports spilled out of the van and lined up behind me to enter our home for the Games. Two shaggy-haired snowboarders and a diminutive speed skater whooped it up, while Claire and Brandon hopped in line next to Chris and me. I wished Sergei could experience this with us, but the Village was housing athletes only, so coaches had to stay at a nearby hotel.

After the guards checked our luggage, two team leaders escorted us through the University of Utah campus to the dormitory-style apartment building designated for the American athletes. I smiled at the sight of the Stars and Stripes decorating every window.

Inside the lobby, decked out with more flags and "Welcome" banners, the team leaders gave us our keys and a quick rundown of the building's amenities. Claire and I located our apartment on the second floor, while Chris and Brandon moved into theirs across the hall from us. Red, white, and blue streamers draped over our doors, adding to the festively patriotic atmosphere.

Claire and I would be sharing our apartment with Aubrey and Kristin, another ice dancer. Since the other girls weren't arriving until later in the week, we had first pick of the two bedrooms. I stashed my suitcase in the one closest to the bathroom and checked out the view of the snowy mountains through the narrow window. Twin beds and a nightstand occupied most of the room, and I made a mental note to decorate Aubrey's bed with a fun "Welcome" sign before the end of the week.

Backtracking into the living room, I crossed paths with Claire and bounced toward the kitchen. "This place is so cute and cozy!"

"I know, it's a lot nicer than I expected." Claire stuck her head into the bathroom, and her voice reverberated off the tiles. "Looks like we're sharing this with the apartment next door."

"Hey, we'll be getting a taste of college life," I said.

My cell phone rang, and I retreated to my bedroom. Seeing Sergei's number, I answered with an enthusiastic, "Hi there!"

He laughed. "Sounds like you're having fun."

I walked to the window. A couple of athletes in Swiss team jackets strolled down the sidewalk below. "It's starting to feel real now." I wavered between excitement and disbelief. "I am actually at the Olympic Games."

"I want you to enjoy every minute of it."

My eyes watered as I thought of what awaited us after

the Games. Amidst the exhilaration of the past few days—arriving in Salt Lake City, being outfitted with all my Olympic gear, attending team meetings—I'd pushed the Ethics Committee to the back of my mind. I needed to keep it there.

"I can't wait until my family gets here. Mom is so excited they got tickets to the Opening Ceremony."

"Oh, you're not going to believe this. I was reading the paper today, and guess who's performing at the Ceremony?" Sergei left a dramatic pause. "Sting."

"No way!"

He chuckled. "I couldn't believe it either."

The sun broke through the clouds, and its rays shone on the frozen quad between the dorms.

"I think it's fate," I said. "Good things are starting to happen."

CHRIS POINTED HIS VIDEO camera at Aubrey and me, and we waved our small American flags and chanted, "USA! USA!" The athletes around us picked up the cheer, and it spread through the entire American delegation as we waited to enter Rice-Eccles Stadium for the Opening Ceremony.

I reached up and tugged on Chris's navy beret, part of the Team USA uniform that featured a matching wool jacket and pants.

"Hey, watch it!" He swatted my hand away.

I laughed as he repositioned the hat over his thick wavy hair. He tried to grab my beret, and I yelped and ducked behind Nick.

I'd been full of adrenaline all day. Chris and I had done an inspired run-through of our short program at morning practice, and my family had met me for lunch at the USA House, a gathering spot downtown for athletes and their guests. In addition to my parents, my aunt, uncle, and three cousins from Boston had come to be my cheering section. At lunch, we'd had a blast gawking at the famous hockey players, downhill skiers, and speed skaters in the dining room.

As the host nation, the American team would bring up the rear in the parade of athletes into the ceremony. Once we received the cue to organize for the march, I linked my arm through Aubrey's and pulled my camera from my pocket. Chris stayed close to my side and held his video camera aloft above the sea of heads.

We edged forward in the tunnel. The muffled cheers of the crowd grew louder and louder until we emerged in the open-air stadium and the cheers became a deafening roar. Flashbulbs popped like bursting stars in the stands, lighting up the night. Through the fifty thousand wildly applauding spectators, I felt the support of the entire country embracing us.

"This is so freaking cool!" Chris shouted over the noise.

"It's amazing!" I hopped up and down like a kid on Christmas morning, and Aubrey did a little skip alongside me.

I was living the dream I'd had since I was seven years old and watched the 1988 Olympics on TV. Wanting to document every second, I snapped picture after picture of my friends and surroundings before putting my camera away and swaying my flag in the air. We continued our march around the stadium, and I craned my neck up at the crowd, wondering where Sergei and my family were sitting.

We settled into our seats, and a number of musical acts, ranging from Josh Groban to the Dixie Chicks, performed. When Sting and cellist Yo-Yo Ma took the stage, my phone buzzed in my pocket.

"I thought we could listen together since we can't sit together," Sergei said.

I smiled. "At least it's not raining this time."

The first notes of Sting's haunting ballad "Fragile" were enough to make me tear up. The mood of the audience went from raucous to reflective, and the hushed silence allowed me to hear every nuance of the music.

"So beautiful," I croaked at the end of the song.

Sergei and I hung up to watch the rest of the ceremony, which culminated with the 1980 U.S. hockey team lighting the Olympic flame. The blaze glowed against the dark sky and fanned the flames of my competitive fire. I fingered my small American flag and pictured Chris and myself on the top step of the podium, hands over our hearts and singing our national anthem.

In twenty-four hours, we would take our first step toward etching our names in the history books. *Let the Games begin.*

NOT ANOTHER PERSON COULD fit into the arena for the short program. The frenzied capacity crowd drowned my ears with applause, and I trembled with anticipation. The sheet of ice in front of us hadn't expanded since the warm-up, but with the audience screaming and the announcer calling our names, the gleaming white surface seemed larger than a mammoth Arctic glacier. I tightened my death grip on Chris's hand.

"I've got you," he murmured.

I hadn't expected to be this nervous. For days I'd brimmed with confidence. Then I'd arrived at the Delta Center and my heart rate went haywire. Our program required me to be flirty with the audience, but all I could think about was avoiding another fluke mishap on the Lutz like the one at Nationals.

"Em!" Sergei called from behind the boards.

He gave me a little nod and a smile that showed more in his eyes than on his mouth. The gesture was simple, but it reminded me of his sureness in my ability. I returned his signal and glided with Chris to the middle of the rink, where we rested our blades on the Olympic rings painted on center ice.

For the first forty-five seconds of the program, I was oblivious to everything around me except Chris. Not until we completed the side-by-side Lutzes did I become aware of the crowd's support echoing off the rafters. My knees relaxed more into the ice, and I flashed the audience a confident grin when I landed the throw triple Lutz perfectly on the beat.

With each turn in our circular footwork sequence, I let more personality shine, teasing the spectators with smiles, and Chris played up his movements along with me. My shimmering blue dress sparkled along with our energy as we powered across the ice and into the death spiral to end the program. Everyone in the arena jumped to their feet.

I slapped Chris's chest with both hands and strangled him in a hug. He gripped my waist, lifting me off the ice.

"Almost there," he said close to my ear.

We parted and spread our arms wide to bow to the audience. In the section of seats to the left of center, a girl jumped into the aisle, arms raised and fists pumping. My cousin Bri. To her right, the other members of my family alternately clapped and waved, all the while yelling cheers I couldn't distinguish from the thousands of other voices. I blew them kisses and laughed as they continued to stand and scream long after everyone else sat in their seats.

Sergei's smile covered his entire face now. He held me in his arms and squeezed my curly ponytail.

"That's my girl."

"One down, one to go," I mumbled into his collar.

He hugged Chris as I climbed the three steps into the kiss and cry. Leonova and Romanov had already skated and were not surprisingly in first place. Hyatt and Wakefield sat in second. Where would the judges slot us?

The scoreboard displayed a line of 5.9's for technical merit. Chris and I both let out a quiet, "Yes," and Sergei stretched his arm across our backs. The presentation scores appeared, and whistles and a few boos rang out in the audience. 5.8's outnumbered the 5.9's, and the standings showed us in second place. I maintained a smile, but inside I burned with disappointment. We still hadn't beaten the Russians in a short program.

Sergei walked with his arms around us as we headed backstage. "Second place is as good as first," he reminded us. "Whoever wins the free skate wins it all. You're in a great position."

Chris and I changed out of our costumes, but we couldn't leave the arena until we drew our start number for the free skate in two nights. We gathered with our competitors in a small room next to the press area, and I folded my hands in prayer. Chris needed to pull number twenty, the last spot in the order, out of the bag. Skating last would give us our best chance to wow the judges and show them we were most deserving of gold.

Chris reached into the satchel, and I peeked with one eye open and one closed. The first digit didn't look like a two.

"Nineteen," the International Skating Federation official announced.

My stomach contracted. Chris slouched next to me, and I patted his thigh. Oksana drew next, and I tried a different prayer that she wouldn't pull the desired number. With my eyes closed, I heard, "Twenty."

Crap.

Sergei kept a positive tone when we gave him the news. "You don't want to skate last. This way, you'll put the pressure on them."

Chris left to meet his parents and Marley, but I lingered with Sergei backstage. He watched me fidget with the zipper on my jacket.

"Em, the only thing you can control is the way you skate." He pulled me into an embrace. "And I know you're going to skate your heart out."

His passionate assurance stoked the fire inside me. I clamped my hand on his shoulder, stopping my fingers from curling into his hair.

"I miss being with you," I whispered.

He caressed the five rings on the back of my jacket. "Soon, we'll never be apart."

CHAPTER THIRTY-SIX

THE NEXT DAY, CHRIS AND I had an afternoon practice, so my family attended Sunday morning mass with me in the Village. Afterward, I gave them a tour of where I'd been living for a week. The sun warmed my face as I pointed out the coffee shop, dining hall, arcade, and internet café. When we headed toward the dorms, Dad, Uncle Joe, and my younger cousin Trey ducked into the coffee shop to get us some hot beverages for the rest of our tour.

"This place is huge. They could've let the coaches stay here, too." Aunt Debbie touched my elbow. "You must be missing Sergei."

I smiled, happy I could talk freely with my family about Sergei. Mom shared everything with her little sister, so it didn't surprise me when she'd asked to tell Aunt Debbie about Sergei and me.

"Coaches can visit anytime, so Sergei's hung out a few times, but obviously we haven't been alone."

"Em, have you talked about wedding dates yet?" my cousin Bella asked. She'd gotten engaged on Christmas Eve, and wedding plans had become her main topic of conversation.

"We might beat you and Blake to the altar. We're thinking about late July."

"I don't know what the rush is," Mom said. "You're so young."

"I'm twenty-one. We don't want to wait until fall or winter because Sergei will be so busy with his students." With my snow boot, I toed a pile of ice next to the sidewalk. "If he's still coaching, that is."

"All this uncertainty is another reason you should wait," Mom said. "If Sergei's suspended, what's he going to do for a job?"

Her question poked my most sensitive nerve. "He'll find something," I snapped.

"I'm not trying to upset you, sweetie. I just want to make sure you're thinking about your future."

"Honestly, I shouldn't be thinking past tomorrow. Tomorrow will determine a big part of my future."

"You're gonna kick butt, Em," Bri said. "Those boring Russians don't stand a chance."

"How about we talk about something besides skating and weddings?" Aunt Debbie suggested. "Let's keep it light."

I gave her a one-arm hug, and a few wisps of her soft brown hair blew across my nose. "Thanks, Aunt Deb."

She and Mom were best friends, but they couldn't be less alike. The only time my aunt had raised her voice to me was when Bella and I were kids and we stole candy bars from the corner store.

The men came out of the coffee shop with our drinks, and I wrapped my gloved hands around the tall cup Dad handed me. "I'll show you guys my apartment next."

I walked ahead of the group. Trey and Uncle Joe were telling a story about meeting a couple of NHL players in line for coffee, but my attention wandered to Mom's concerns.

Married life would be infinitely easier if I wouldn't have

to train for the next Olympics. Sergei and I had made our dating relationship work amid the stress of competitive skating, but could we do it as a married couple? Being with each other every day and every night? And this was assuming Sergei would be coaching. There was a good chance he might not be part of the skating world anymore. What if he began to resent me as the reason for his suspension?

NO MATTER HOW HARD I tried to shut out the uncertainties of my future, my brain wouldn't cooperate. All night I wrestled with my blankets, fighting a losing battle with sleeplessness. In the morning, at our final practice before the event, I had to muscle through every jump. I was tighter than the knots I tied on my skate laces.

Claire and I spent the afternoon playing ping pong in our building's activity room. Focusing on the constant bouncing of the little ball gave me some relief from my unwanted thoughts. As soon as I started to apply my makeup for the competition, though, anxiety gripped me. I spilled half of my creamy foundation in the bathroom sink and smudged my eyeliner twice.

My insides were caught in a tornado when I met Chris downstairs. I couldn't sit still in the van to the arena, adjusting and readjusting my gloves, my earrings, and my necklace. Chris twitched with each of my movements but didn't say anything.

Backstage at the arena, television cameras stayed glued to us. They filmed us passing through security, doing our stretching exercises, and walking through our program on the floor. I thought doing my normal pre-competition routine would settle my edginess, but the hovering cameras were a constant reminder this wasn't a normal competition.

Sergei pulled us aside before we went to the locker rooms

to don our costumes. "I found a little room down the hall where we can wait after the warm-up. It'll give us some privacy."

That was welcome news. My nervous breakdown appeared imminent, and I didn't want it broadcasted live to millions of viewers around the world.

I dressed and stood in front of the long mirror. The soft pink costume had seen nothing but victory all season, but the biggest life-changing victory remained. I tugged on the stretchy fabric and the lone shoulder strap. *This dress could be on the front page of every newspaper in America in the morning.* My legs began to tremble, triggering full-on knee wobbling.

Chris and Sergei awaited me in the corridor. They were smiling and looking unexplainably business-as-usual. I flexed my knees and pulled on the hem of my dress, the pink beads scratching my sweaty palms. As I paced around Sergei, he relayed the elements we should practice in the six minute warm-up. His tone had a relaxed quality, but for once, his calmness didn't reach me.

We made our way toward the ice with the three other pairs in the final group—the Russians, the Canadians, and the Germans. Crowded behind the gate, bouncing in place to stay warm, we looked like caged bulls ready to charge forward.

The ice monitor swung open the gate, and the crowd exploded. After shedding our skate guards, Chris and I did long back crossovers around the ice. Chris seemed to be pulling me across the surface; I had no power in my legs.

Once we finished our initial warm-up, Chris launched me into the triple twist and set me down with his reliable ease. Next, we set up for the side-by-side triple Lutzes. Trying to compensate for my shaky legs, I slammed my toepick into the ice for better lift. I only succeeded in throwing off my air position, and I stumbled through the landing.

Chris reached for my hand. "We can do it again."

We repeated the jump, and again I faltered.

"Let's do the throws," I said.

Chris's eyes crinkled with concern. We circled around the rink, and on both the triple Lutz and triple loop throw jumps, I put my palm on the ice to balance myself. Chris now appeared downright worried as he glanced at me and up at the clock. With a minute left, we performed one lift and cooled down with easy strokes around the rink.

Sergei walked behind us as Chris and I marched to our "waiting room." Chris stopped him before he could enter. "Can you give us a minute?"

He closed the door and massaged my neck. "When we get out there, it's just you and me. Block everything else out. You and me, skating our program. Nothing else matters."

"My legs won't stop shaking," I said, full of panic.

"They know what to do if you let them."

He hugged me, and I tilted my head back so I wouldn't smear makeup on his mauve-colored shirt.

"I've never been this scared in my entire life." Tears rattled my voice.

He tightened his hold on me. "I'll be right there with you every step of the way. Focus on me, okay?"

I closed my eyes, visualizing us skating in a bubble—no roaring crowd, no future consequences. Just the two of us, the ice, and Grieg's Piano Concerto.

Chris opened the door, and Sergei spread his arm across my shoulders and patted Chris's back. I clung to him, hoping to absorb his composure.

"There's one thing I want you to do tonight." Sergei said. "Skate with freedom. Do you remember how you skated at the Grand Prix Final? You owned the ice. When you look back on this night, I don't want you to have any regrets. Give everything you have to each other."

He kissed the top of my head and gave Chris a half-hug, half-handshake. I kept one arm around Sergei's waist until we were told to report to the ice. His warmth had slowly soothed my trembling.

We approached the rink as Madeline and Damien finished their program. The moment the Canadians stepped behind the boards, I shot off like a rocket, needing a feel for the ice. I rounded the rink a few times, my legs strengthening with each stroke. Chris skated up to me, and I held out my hand.

He grasped it and angled his head down so I could hear him above the din. "Just you and me."

I nodded crisply, and we returned to Sergei at the boards for one last sip of water. He stood tall and sure in his tailored black suit.

"This is your night." He spoke with both assurance and affection. "Own the ice."

I squeezed my eyes shut. The raucous crowd faded into the background, and the image of the insulated bubble resurfaced. Eyes open, I followed Chris to our starting spot. My focus remained on his face and the strong bond between our clasped hands.

The music began, and I pushed off on one foot, gliding backward, smooth and controlled. We flew through the triple twist, but my chest tightened as we approached the Lutzes. Sergei's voice resonated in my head. *Own the ice.*

I put total belief in my muscle memory, and three revolutions later, my right blade hit the ice on a flowing edge. My confidence jumped ten notches, and my muscles slightly unwound.

Chris nodded as we transitioned through footwork to the setup for the throw triple Lutz. With his hands securely on my hips, he vaulted me across the ice, and again my right foot executed a perfect landing. The throw triple loop produced the same result. I squashed a burst of excitement, stopping myself from celebrating too early. Half of the program lay ahead.

Through the intricate choreography, we maintained constant speed and flow, and we had just as much momentum exiting the elements as we did entering them. Every step connected to the music, emphasizing both the high and low notes. With each passing second, my skin tingled more and more with elation.

Going into our final jumping pass, the side-by-side triple toe-double toe combination, I ordered myself, *Attack, attack, attack!* We went up in the air on the triple jumps and came down on one foot in unison. Immediately, we knocked out the easy double toes. Chris saw my wide smile and reminded me, "Steady on the lift."

He picked me up, and I let myself enjoy the feeling of being on top of the world. The breeze cooled my face as I soared with the music, just as I'd imagined when we'd chosen the concerto. On the descent, I caught a glimpse of Sergei's face, and he had tears in his eyes.

My heart ballooned, and my own eyes misted. As Chris pulled me into our pair spin, I battled my emotions, careful not to botch our last element in the program. We spun face to face, grinning at each other, tears staining my cheeks. Because of the rowdy applause, I couldn't hear our music anymore. We twirled into our ending pose, not knowing if we were on the final beat, but I didn't care. The moment was ours—the moment I dreamed of every day I laced up my skates. The moment we completed a perfect skate at the Olympic Games.

Chris scooped me up and let out a loud whoop. I couldn't speak or make any sounds as I wept with joy and relief.

He put me down and turned me to face the crowd. "Never forget this."

Slowly, we rotated in a circle, taking in the entire arena. Goose bumps sprung over my arms. Everyone was standing, and their cheers rang in my ears. I squinted through my tears at the upper deck, where my family had tickets, but it was too far away for me to find them.

When we reached the boards, Sergei threw his arms around me before I could step off the ice. He held me for a long minute as my shoulders shook with sobs.

"I'm so proud of you," he said, his voice wrought with emotion.

I took deep breaths to control my crying while Sergei and Chris shared a warm, back-slapping hug. We'd taken so long to reach the kiss and cry the scores were ready as soon as we sat down.

The crowd erupted when two 6.0's dotted our line of technical marks. Just as quickly, the audience jeered when the presentation scores included all 5.9's but no perfect marks. We'd beaten Madeline and Damien, but Oksana and Denis had room to pass us. Our program was technically more difficult, but the judges could subjectively give the Russians the edge on presentation.

The anxiety I'd overcome during our program strapped itself around my heart. With one last wave to the crowd, we retreated to our secluded room for the longest wait of our lives.

Sergei hugged each of us again. "No matter what happens, you did everything you could possibly do, and you should be proud of that."

"I have no idea how I did it." I shook my head.

"You're stronger than you know." Chris squeezed me against his side.

I blinked back a couple of tears. "I want you to know how lucky I feel having you as my partner. Thank you so much for standing by me, even when things got rough."

He embraced me and cleared his throat. "I'm pretty lucky, too."

I slid over to Sergei and basked in his beaming smile. He pulled me close to him, and my fingertips grazed his light blue tie.

"Thank you for everything you've given me," I said. "You always believed I could do this."

"You've given me so much, too." He rested his forehead

against mine. "You're my muse. I can't tell you how much you inspire me every day."

Our lips touched for just a moment before we parted. The closed door didn't block out all sound, so every so often I'd hear applause, presumably when the Russians completed an element. Each sound further frayed my nerves. When the cheering became sustained, I figured the program must be over. That meant we would know our fate in approximately three minutes.

Chris gripped my hand, and we stood staring at the solid gray door. My heart beat faster than if I'd sprinted across three football fields. Sergei stood next to me, his hands in a steeple position in front of his mouth.

The doorknob twisted, and I inhaled sharply. Jackson, one of our team leaders, opened the door halfway.

"You got silver." He gave us a closed-mouth smile. "Congratulations."

His message didn't register in my brain. It was as if he spoke a language I didn't understand.

"What was the vote?" Sergei asked.

"Five to four."

My whole body went numb.

Neither Chris nor I had moved an inch since Jackson arrived. We were two statues, but I sensed I might crumble any second.

"How did they skate?" Sergei asked.

Jackson hesitated. "They were clean."

He didn't say they were great or it was one of the most amazing skates he'd ever seen. That's what I thought it would take to beat us. Not just *clean*.

"We need a few minutes," Sergei said. "Can you keep the cameras away from here?"

Disbelief dragged me down onto the folding chair in the middle of the room. "We lost by one vote." Shock resonated in my voice. "One vote."

Chris still hadn't moved. "Our program was harder," he said, completely void of emotion.

I covered my face with my hands. "I can't believe this."

Sergei sat next to me and brought me into his arms. I sobbed again on his jacket, this time from overwhelming disappointment.

He caressed my hair. "You couldn't have skated any better tonight."

"Then why wasn't it good enough?" Chris exclaimed. He'd awakened from the shock.

"You're going to get a lot of questions from the media about the results," Sergei said. "Don't let them bait you into saying something you'll regret later."

There was a knock on the door, and the federation's media relations director stuck her head inside.

"Emily and Chris need to do a few interviews before the medal ceremony."

I dabbed at my eyes. "I have to go to the locker room for a minute."

I hastened down the corridor, accepting congratulations along the way. The enthusiasm of the messages was noticeably muted, making me think Chris was right to question the results.

After touching up my eye makeup, I met Chris and the NBC reporter. She checked her microphone before the cameraman gave her the cue.

"We're here with the new Olympic silver medalists, Emily Butler and Chris Grayden. Talk about your performance tonight. You must be pretty pleased with the way you skated."

"Absolutely," Chris said. "We gave it everything we had. It was the skate we've always dreamed of."

My throat tightened, and I grabbed Chris's hand. I had to answer the next question without breaking down.

The reporter tilted her head. "Your program included more difficulty than the gold medalists' program. Do you think the judging system needs to be reevaluated to keep up with the technical advances in the sport?"

I remembered Sergei's warning and thought before answering, "Everything's still sinking in right now. We didn't see anyone else skate, so we can't comment on their programs."

When the camera stopped rolling, we were shuttled to more anxious journalists. They posed similar questions to which we gave similar answers. Claire and Brandon were backstage, and they hugged us as we waited for the medal ceremony.

"You guys won this," Claire said.

I shrugged, on the verge of crying yet again. "It is what it is."

As the bronze medalists, Madeline and Damien were introduced first, filling the bottom step of the podium. Chris and I waited at the entrance to the ice, and an explosion of cheers greeted us when the announcer called our names. We congratulated Madeline and Damien and stepped up onto the second tier. My eyes slanted toward the top step, yearning to realize my unfulfilled dream.

Oksana and Denis skated to the podium and kissed both of my cheeks in European fashion. My face hurt from maintaining a forced smile. I wanted to scream, thinking of how my future had become very muddled.

The president of the International Skating Federation placed the silver medal around my neck, and I slipped the red ribbon under my hair and gazed at the heavy disc. Second place was an amazing accomplishment, and I should feel fortunate to have won any medal. There were so many skaters who would never get near an Olympic podium. But I couldn't let go of the disappointment and sadness. They tore at my insides as I watched the three flags ascend to the rafters.

The Russian anthem played, and I looked everywhere but at the American flag, knowing it would prompt more tears.

My eyes drifted to the scoreboard and the 2002 Olympic motto—"Light the Fire Within."

I had lit the fire within me. I'd given the best performance of my life on my sport's biggest stage. But it wasn't enough. It wasn't enough to win the ultimate prize.

CHAPTER THIRTY-SEVEN

WE WENT STRAIGHT FROM THE ARENA to the USA House and were met with a barrage of cheers and honking noisemakers. Through the crowd of people waving flags and pompoms, one face stood out, and it displayed nothing but pride—not sympathy or concern or any of the other confused looks I'd received in the past hour.

I rushed toward my father and buried my face in the familiar scratchy wool of his sweater.

"We are so, so proud of you, Em," he said.

I hadn't realized how much I needed the comfort of my father's arms. For the first time since Jackson had uttered the words, "You got silver," I felt some peace.

Mom reached out to me, and we clutched each other, unable to speak.

"Sweetie," she finally said through her sniffles. "You were wonderful. Just breathtaking."

Bri, Trey, and Bella crowded around me for hugs. Red, white, and blue boas circled Bri's and Bella's necks, accentuating their Team USA sweatshirts.

"We went crazy after you skated," Bri said.

"I've never heard my mom scream that loud before." Bella laughed.

"She told everyone around us we were related to you," Trey said. "As if they couldn't guess."

"I was excited, okay?" Aunt Debbie said. "Let's see this Olympic medal." She stretched the ribbon out and took the medal in her hand as my family gathered for a closer look.

Uncle Joe put his hefty arm around me. "That's really something, Em."

"It means so much to me you're all here," I said as my face crumpled.

Sergei had hung back, and Dad motioned him forward to our group. "Congratulations, Sergei." Dad stuck out his hand but then pulled Sergei into a hug. "You've done an amazing job with Em and Chris."

"Thank you. They are incredibly special."

Mom put her hand on Sergei's elbow. "You helped Emily achieve one of her dreams, and that makes you pretty special, too."

I bit down on my lip, suppressing more tears. Sergei swallowed hard and tipped his head. "Thank you."

Bella embraced me, and I held fast to her until Marley came over. She and I shared a few teary moments before Aubrey and Nick smothered me with hugs. I was pulled in all directions for congratulations and photos. Federation officials and employees, judges, former skaters, sponsors—I couldn't keep track of all the people I talked to and posed with, displaying my medal in each picture. Some were blunter than others, expressing their dissatisfaction with the results, which didn't help me feel any better.

The media relations director informed me Chris and I were scheduled for an appearance on the TODAY show. A van would pick us up at the Village at four in the morning. The clock neared midnight already, so we could forget about sleep.

I snagged Bella between conversations and steered her to

a quiet spot. "I'm shocked my mom isn't on a rampage about the results."

"Oh, she was. We all were, but we saw how disappointed you looked at the medal ceremony. Your dad said not to upset you more."

I managed a little smile. "Always the voice of reason."

Mom approached us, buttoning her long coat. "Em, do you want to come to the house with us for a while? I don't think any of us are getting any sleep tonight."

"That sounds good. I'll find Sergei."

I ran into Chris and invited him, his family, and Marley to join us, but they were headed to Chris's parents' hotel. Once I got Sergei away from two chatty judges, we walked at a brisk pace through the icy wind to my family's rented townhouse. As soon as we were inside, Mom put on a pot of coffee and Dad switched on the electric fireplace. Along with my coat, I took off my medal and placed it inside my purse.

"Who's hungry?" Aunt Debbie asked.

I stayed still while everyone started for the kitchen. Sergei placed a gentle hand on the small of my back. "You should eat something."

Aunt Debbie looked up from the refrigerator, where she removed large covered dishes. "We've got pasta salad, baked chicken, lasagna... we went a little crazy last night. The cooking helped calm our nerves."

"I'm not really hungry," I said.

"Have a little pasta salad," Mom urged. "You haven't eaten in hours."

I raised my eyes to Sergei's. "Can we talk first?"

Aunt Debbie paused in the middle of spooning pasta. "There's a little office at the end of the hall if you want privacy."

Sergei followed me and shut the door. I sank into his arms and laid my head on his shoulder. "I just wanted to be alone with you."

I'd held myself together through the celebration at USA House, but frustration and exhaustion were now having their way with me.

"One vote," I mumbled.

"I know that's the only thing you're thinking about, but I don't want you to forget what you did tonight, how incredible it was. I saw how nervous you were in the warm-up. To overcome that and skate like you did was amazing."

My worn out tear ducts fought against another round of weeping. "Just not amazing enough," I whispered.

"This is only the beginning for you and Chris. You can dominate the next four years."

"But what if you're suspended? I can't do it without you. I don't want to."

Sergei nudged me nearer to him. "I don't want you to give up on your dream because of me."

"You've become part of my dream. I want you there, working with us every day and having that gold medal moment with us," I said, unable to stop the persistent tears.

He wrapped me in a tight cocoon and pressed his cheek to the top of my head. "It can still happen. We don't know what the committee's going to do."

"Even if you're not suspended, four years is a long time. What if I break my leg? Or Chris gets hurt? We might get to the Olympics and mess up. We had the perfect skate tonight. What if this was our best chance?"

"I can't promise those things won't happen. All I can tell you is if you work hard, you'll put yourself in the best position possible."

I toyed with the tip of his tie, rolling it around my finger. "What about you and me? Can we manage it all... being married, training, working together with Courtney and Mark..."

"I'm never going to get tired of seeing your face, if that's what you're worried about." He smiled and cupped his hands under my chin. "We've survived the toughest year imaginable, and we're stronger than ever. Together there's nothing we can't handle."

His adoring eyes had a way of making everything seem possible. Lost in their blue depth, I slid my hands along his collar and bent his head toward mine. "Have I told you lately how much I love you?"

My lips took hold of his. One kiss opened the floodgates to many more, each with intensifying passion.

"That's what I wanted to do as soon as you stepped off the ice," Sergei said.

I smiled wryly. "Maybe it would've gotten us better presentation scores."

OVER THE NEXT TWO weeks, I soaked up every ounce of the Olympic experience. Sergei, Chris, and I took advantage of the free tickets offered by sponsors and sampled a variety of events—curling, ski jumping, biathlon, bobsled—we traveled all over the city and into the mountains. After Aubrey and Nick excitedly finished their competition in twelfth place, they got in on the fun, too.

In the Village, I met numerous athletes who were ecstatic just to participate in the Games, and at event after event, competitors who finished near the bottom of the standings rejoiced, thrilled with their Olympic accomplishment. My silver medal began to shine brighter as pride lightened the disappointment weighing on my heart.

Two nights before the Closing Ceremony, Chris and I skated to U2's "Beautiful Day" in the Champions Gala, and the uplifting lyrics stuck with me long after we returned to my apartment. My roommates went to bed, and I asked Chris to stay for a talk.

"All night, I've been thinking…" I folded my legs under

me on the sofa. "Maybe it wasn't our time to win gold. We've risen so quickly in three years together. Maybe this was God's way of telling us we need to work more for it."

Chris propped his feet up on the coffee table. "You'd think God would've helped out a good church-going girl like you. Unless my religious shortcomings outweighed your virtue."

I tapped his arm. "I'm trying to be serious."

"It's a good theory," he said. "Of course, there's the other theory that some people didn't want us ending forty years of Russian dominance."

"Are you afraid we'll run into the same problem next time? You know in four years Russia's going to have another team near the top."

"I think we've got bigger problems at the moment. What are we gonna do if Sergei gets suspended?" he asked.

"I don't know." I pulled my hair away from my face and twisted it in my hands. "I don't feel like I'm done skating, but having Sergei as our coach is a big part of the dream for me now."

Chris put his feet on the floor and sat up straighter. "I'm not ready to give up either. Even after what happened here, I still think we can win. And working with Sergei gives us the best chance."

"Remember how mad you were at Sergei when you found out we were dating?" I squeezed Chris's shoulder. "I'm so glad we got past all that."

"I know he has my back just as much as he has yours. He's proven that. The three of us... we make the ultimate team."

I nodded. "We do. And I know his other students feel the same way. I have to make sure the Ethics Committee hears that." I thumped my knuckles on the sofa cushion. "I'm going to do everything I can to convince them Sergei deserves to keep his job."

CHAPTER THIRTY-EIGHT

Once we returned to the Cape, I didn't waste any time gathering support for Sergei. The Chairman of the Ethics Committee was due in town soon to conduct interviews, so I called all of Sergei's students and their parents and asked them to gather at my house the next evening. I didn't divulge the reason for the meeting, but I expressed the importance and hoped they heeded the urgency in my voice.

Sergei stayed away from the gathering so he couldn't be accused of trying to influence anyone. I welcomed everyone into the living room, where I'd brought up chairs from the kitchen for extra seating. Curious faces watched as I took a spot next to the big picture window. Only Chris, who sat beside me, knew my agenda.

"I really appreciate you all coming on such short notice," I said.

Trevor assessed the group and asked, "Are you planning a surprise for Sergei or something?"

"I wish it was something fun like that." I scrubbed my palms on my jeans. "Unfortunately, it's a very serious situation I need your help with... that Sergei needs your help with."

Courtney, Mark, and a couple of Sergei's junior-level students swapped anxious looks. Their parents angled forward, their curiosity phasing into concern. With the room staring at me, I dove into the speech I'd practiced.

"Sergei is being accused of violating the Code of Conduct because he and I are seeing each other. We've been dating over a year, and before the Olympics we got engaged."

Courtney's eyes and mouth doubled in size. A few of the parents shot each other quick, wrinkled-brow glances, and Trevor scratched his chin. "Chris, you knew?"

"Yeah," he replied. "And I support Em and Sergei one hundred percent. Sergei shouldn't be punished for this."

"He could be suspended for five years." I paused as Courtney and Trevor's partner Leigh gasped. "The Ethics Committee is meeting next week, and the Chairman will probably call some or all of you. I asked you here so I could tell you the news first and hopefully gain your support. Sergei wanted to be here, but he didn't want to chance interfering with the process."

Leigh's mom, Brenda, stretched her arm across the back of her daughter's chair. "Do you know if Sergei's had relationships with other students before you?"

I'd expected to receive that type of question and had prepared a calm and thoughtful response. "He hasn't. I know what people think when they hear about a coach and student being involved. They think the coach may have pressured the student and it's not a sincere relationship. But Sergei has never done anything questionable. He's treated me with respect on and off the ice, and he hasn't let our relationship affect his work."

Chris jumped in. "He's been totally professional this whole time. You guys would've noticed if he'd acted differently or gave Em more attention. Obviously, he's handled everything very well."

I gave Chris a thank-you smile and scanned the faces of my fellow skaters. "We have such a good group. I've heard you all talk about how much you love working with Sergei and how much you've learned from him. If you could tell that to the Ethics Committee and help them see how important Sergei is to our careers, I think it will make a huge difference."

"I'll definitely tell them," Trevor said. "There's no way Sergei can be suspended."

"I'll be glad to talk to them, too," Courtney's mom Karen said. "I see Sergei every day at the rink. I can vouch for his professionalism."

I clasped my hands together. "Thank you, it would mean so much. Having all the parents speak on his behalf would really help his case." My eyes implored the adults sitting before me.

Slowly, a series of nods and affirmative replies spread through the group. I spent a few minutes with each person, answering questions and expressing my thanks. Brenda had the most reservations, worried Sergei's involvement with me could cause distractions at the rink. I patiently addressed her concerns and assured her Sergei was fully dedicated to his job.

Courtney and her parents waited to speak to me last. I approached them with a tentative smile, not sure if Courtney was upset I'd kept the truth from her.

"I knew you and Sergei liked each other!" she exclaimed. "When we saw you at the symphony, you were on a date, weren't you?" Excitement colored her cheeks, and I exhaled with relief.

"I'm sorry I couldn't tell you. We couldn't tell anyone because we knew it could cause problems, like what we're dealing with now."

Karen touched my arm. "I'm really happy for you. You deserve to be with someone who supports you and understands everything you're going through. Sergei is a great guy."

I reached out and returned her gesture. "Thank you, that means a lot to me. It's so nice to finally reveal our good news to everyone."

After Courtney and I shared a few hugs and the crowd cleared, Chris and Trevor helped me carry the kitchen chairs downstairs before leaving me alone with my thoughts.

Besides Sergei's students and their parents, my mother and father were going to meet with the committee chairman. Mom had come so far in her attitude toward Sergei, from questioning his character to now going to bat for him, and I was counting on Dad and her to make strong statements. I was also counting on the strength of my own testimony. I needed it to be polished yet heartfelt. I needed it to be just like my Olympic performance, except this time with a winning result.

MOM AND DAD EMERGED from the Hyannis hotel's small conference room, and I stopped pacing in the hallway to rush over to them. They'd been with Brian, the Ethics Committee Chairman, for an hour.

"How did it go?"

"I think it went well." Dad wiped his glasses on his jacket. "His questions were fair, and we told him why we support Sergei as a part of both your personal and professional lives."

Mom slipped her arm around my waist. "You should've heard me singing Sergei's praises."

"Brian said to send you in when you're ready." Dad kissed the top of my head.

I closed my arms around my parents, drawing one final touch of comfort. I was the last person the chairman was going to talk to before he would report to the committee. Over the past two days, he'd conducted all his interviews and had spoken with Sergei at length.

I entered the conference room and greeted Brian with a firm handshake. In his position as a judge, he knew me from competitions over the years. I'd always been a little intimidated by his snooty demeanor. With his beady eyes peering at me, I sat across from him in a matching swivel chair and smoothed my pencil skirt. He opened a plain manila folder on the round table between us, revealing a thin stack of typed pages.

"David and Maria did a very thorough job when they interviewed you, so I don't have any questions. I wanted to give you this opportunity to share any other information you thought the committee should know." He pointed the tape recorder on the table toward me and pressed one of the buttons. "I'll be recording your statement for them."

A mix of nervousness and adrenaline, similar to competition jitters, boosted my heart rate. I swallowed and returned Brian's unblinking stare.

"Before Sergei became my coach, my career was headed nowhere. You saw firsthand how I couldn't handle the pressure of competition. But Sergei taught me how to overcome that. He's inspired me with so much confidence and given me a sense of freedom on the ice. He found a strength in me I didn't know existed.

"I've been fortunate to not only have Sergei as my coach but also to work beside him. I see the thought and care he puts into every lesson and how the kids respond to him. He has a way of finding what makes each of his students special and teaching them to let it shine.

"His work has never been compromised by his personal life. He asks us to give our best every day, and he does the same."

My eyes drifted to the recorder and back to Brian's stoic expression. "I hope the committee will understand how important he is to so many people and allow him to continue to do what he does best—teach and inspire everyone around him."

I watched for some sign of empathy from Brian, but his face remained as blank as a sheet of ice and left me feeling just as cold. He waited a moment and asked, "Is that everything you'd like to say?"

Satisfied I'd done all I could, I nodded. "Yes."

He shut off the recorder and shut the folder. "I appreciate your time, Emily."

He stood, and I did the same while extending my hand. "Thank you for the opportunity."

Mom and Dad met me outside with hugs, and I sighed. "He didn't give any hint of what he might be thinking."

"I'm sure they'll examine all our statements carefully." Mom held me against her side.

"Brian told Sergei he's going to have a conference call with the committee this evening, and we can probably expect the ruling tonight."

"I wish we could wait with you, but we have to get back to campus for a meeting," Dad said.

"That's okay. I'll let you know when we get word."

I headed to Sergei's apartment, and he welcomed me in from the damp, chilly afternoon, giving me a tender kiss and rubbing his warm hands over mine.

"How was it?" he asked.

"He didn't ask any questions, so I just talked. If they really listen to what we all said, there shouldn't be any doubt as to the right decision." I tried to sound confident, but even though we'd done nothing wrong and had done everything in our power to prove it, nerves tightened my stomach. I took a steadying breath as Sergei wrapped his arms around me.

"It's going to be a long night," he said.

I eyed the stacks of CDs covering his coffee table. "Alphabetizing your music collection to stay busy?"

"No, I thought we could try to find Courtney and Mark's music for next season. Might help the time pass faster."

"Good idea."

I stepped out of my heels and padded over to the sofa. One by one, we went through the discs, listening to sonatas, concertos, operas, and movie soundtracks. Every time Sergei shuffled in a new CD, he peeked at his watch. We ordered takeout, but for once, Sergei didn't polish off his half of the pizza and try to steal some of mine. He grew quieter the longer the night dragged on.

I was reading aloud from my notepad, recapping the list of pieces we liked, when Sergei's cell phone rang. He lurched forward and snatched the phone from the coffee table, toppling one of the CD stacks in the process. Cases flew all over the carpet. My heart felt like it was suspended in mid-air, ready to either burst into fireworks or free fall and crash to the earth.

Sergei said hello, and after the caller spoke, he followed with, "Yes, I've been waiting anxiously."

I put my hand on his thigh and observed his face, willing a smile to appear. He listened intently, not giving me any indication of what Brian was saying.

Finally, one part of him moved. His eyes closed, and when they opened moments later, they were moist. My fingers dug into his leg.

"Thank you for addressing this so quickly." He paused and answered, "Yes. Yes, I will."

The second he hung up, I blurted, "What did he say?"

Sergei gently grasped my face. His eyes gleamed at me as the lamp light reflected off of his unshed tears.

"He said I'm cleared."

Fireworks exploded within me, and I flung myself onto Sergei's lap. "Yes!"

He held me close as I laughed and cried at the same time.

"Thank you," he said hoarsely. "You made this happen." He pressed his lips to mine, and my tears wet both our faces.

"Brian said the support I received was incredible.

Everyone's statements provided indisputable evidence of my professionalism."

"I didn't tell them what to say." I smiled and wiped my eyes.

"No, but you explained everything to them and asked them to speak for me. And I know whatever you said to Brian today also had a big impact."

I threaded my fingers through Sergei's hair. "I just told him how amazing you are and how much we all need you."

"I am so lucky to be with you," he whispered.

He kissed me again, fuller and longer, and my body hummed with a powerful sensation. I didn't think I could love Sergei more, but my heart pounded with new and even stronger feelings. Every kiss we shared spoke of the promise of our future. We stayed locked in an embrace, not wanting our celebration to end.

AFTER WE SHARED THE news at the rink the next day, Trevor threw together the party he'd wanted to give Chris and me since we'd returned from the Olympics. Sergei picked me up that night, and we headed to Trevor's bungalow three towns away in Harwich. I blasted the radio in the car, bobbing in my seat to the music. Our friends and co-workers were going to see us as a couple for the first time.

The front door to the cottage was cracked open, so we let ourselves in and shed our jackets on the overflowing coat rack next to the door. The buzz of voices and laughter streamed toward us from the den, and we followed the noise down the narrow hallway to the back of the house. A few heads turned when we walked through the low archway.

Sergei reached over and took my hand, lacing his fingers through mine. His subtle gesture overwhelmed me with a range of emotions—from feeling like I could cry tears of joy to wanting to rip off his clothes.

I squeezed his hand and looked up at him through my lashes. "Can I tell you a secret?"

"What's that?" he asked.

I leaned close to his ear. "I am so hot for you right now."

He coughed, stifling a grin. "How long do we have to stay at this party?"

I laughed, something I had done a lot the past twenty-four hours. Chris and Marley came up from behind us, plastic cups in hand.

"It's great to see you guys out," Marley said. "We can go on double dates now!"

"What makes you think I want to spend more time with this girl?" Chris made a face and poked my arm.

I jabbed him back. "I'm already stuck with him for four more years. Isn't that enough?"

Chris couldn't hold in his smile any longer, and I began laughing again. We hugged, and I kissed his cheek. Sergei and I started for the kitchen, but Courtney swooped in front of us, bouncing on the heels of her sneakers.

"You two are so cute together!" she screeched. "Look, you even match!"

We glanced at each other's outfits. Sergei wore a black long-sleeved knit shirt and jeans, while I had on a black boatneck sweater, jeans, and high-heeled boots.

"We did it just for you." I pinched her pixie face.

"We need to talk about the wedding, Em. You have to let me be a junior bridesmaid."

"Who else would I possibly ask?"

She squealed and peppered us with more wedding questions before running off to the group of young skaters huddled near the back door. Trevor hooked me up with a soda in the kitchen, and Sergei and I mingled our way through the den.

Aubrey popped up from the sofa. "Hey, Marley heard

some scoop. The new dance coaches might be a married couple from California."

"Having a female perspective could be cool," I said.

"They're Russian. Like we need more of those around." Aubrey gave Sergei a toothy smile, and he laughed.

I tilted my head up to him. "I'm pretty fond of my Russian."

He smiled and tightened his arm around my waist. "That's good to know."

Once we'd chatted with almost all the guests, Sergei rested on the arm of the couch. I scooted between his knees and wound my arms around his neck, while he settled his hands on my hips.

"This feels so good… being here with you like this," he said.

I grinned. "It's kind of a rush, isn't it?"

He brushed a kiss on my lips. "I love you."

"I love you, too."

"I was thinking." He twirled a lock of my hair around his finger. "Tomorrow night we could go to dinner and a movie, maybe drinks after."

"That sounds so ordinary." I broke into a smile. "And so amazing."

MORE BOOKS BY JENNIFER COMEAUX

Edge Series
Life on the Edge (Edge #1)
Edge of the Past (Edge #2)
Fighting for the Edge (Edge #3)

Ice Series
Crossing the Ice (Ice #1)
Losing the Ice (Ice #2)
Taking the Ice (Ice #3)

To stay up to date on Jennifer's new releases, join her mailing list:
http://eepurl.com/UZjMP

Jennifer loves to hear from readers! Visit her online at:
jennifercomeaux.blogspot.com
www.twitter.com/LadyWave4
www.facebook.com/jennifercomeauxauthor
www.instagram.com/jcomeaux4
jcomeaux4@gmail.com

Please consider taking a moment to leave a review at the applicable retailer. It is much appreciated!

ABOUT THE AUTHOR

Jennifer Comeaux is a tax accountant by day, writer by night. There aren't any ice rinks near her home in south Louisiana, but she's a diehard figure skating fan and loves to write stories of romance set in the world of competitive skating. One of her favorite pastimes is travelling to competitions, where she can experience all the glitz and drama that inspire her writing.

www.ingramcontent.com/pod-product-compliance
Lightning Source LLC
Chambersburg PA
CBHW030658120726
47905CB00001B/275